THE THREE-BODY PROBLEM

CIXIN LIU is China's leading Science Fiction writer. He has won the China Galaxy Science Fiction Award nine times, the Nebula (Xingyun) award twice, and was the first translated author to win the Hugo award. Before becoming a writer, he was a computer engineer in a power plant in Yangquan.

Translator KEN LIU's short story 'The Paper Menagerie' was the first work of fiction to sweep the Nebula, Hugo, & World Fantasy Awards. His first novel, *The Grace of Kings*, is also published by Head of Zeus.

D1341293

THE THREE-BODY PROBLEM

CIXIN LIU

TRANSLATED BY KEN LIU

HEAD of ZEUS

Originally published as 三体 in 2008 by Chongqing Publishing Group in Chongqing, China. First serialized in *Science Fiction World* (科幻世界) in 2006. First published in the United States of America in 2014 by Tom Doherty Associates LLC

First published in the UK in 2015 by Head of Zeus Ltd.

This paperback edition first published in 2016 by Head of Zeus Ltd

9 7 6 8

A CIP catalogue record for this book is available from the British Library.

Paperback ISBN 9781784971571
Ebook ISBN 9781784971540

Typeset by Adrian McLaughlin
Printedand bound in by CPI Group (UK) Ltd, Croydon, CR0 4YY

Head of Zeus Ltd
Clerkenwell House
45–47 Clerkenwell Green
London EC1R 0HT
WWW.HEADOFZEUS.COM

List of Characters

Chinese names are written with surname first.

The Ye Family

Ye Zhetai	Physicist, professor at Tsinghua University
Shao Lin	Physicist, Ye Zhetai's wife
Ye Wenjie	Astrophysicist, daughter of Ye Zhetai
Ye Wenxue	Ye Wenjie's sister, a Red Guard

Red Coast Base

Lei Zhicheng	Political commissar at Red Coast Base
Yang Weining	Chief engineer at Red Coast Base, once a student of Ye Zhetai

The Present

Yang Dong	String theorist and daughter of Ye Wenjie and Yang Weining
Ding Yi	Theoretical physicist, Yang Dong's boyfriend
Wang Miao	Nanomaterials researcher
Shi Qiang	Police detective, nicknamed Da Shi
Chang Weisi	Major-general of the People's Liberation Army

Shen Yufei	Japanese physicist and member of the Frontiers of Science
Wei Cheng	Math prodigy and recluse, Shen Yufei's husband
Pan Han	Biologist, friend/acquaintance of Shen Yufei and Wei Cheng, and member of the Frontiers of Science
Sha Ruishan	Astronomer, one of Ye Wenjie's students
Mike Evans	Scion of an oil magnate
Colonel Stanton	U.S. Marine Corps, commander of Operation Guzheng

PART I

SILENT SPRING

1

The Madness Years

China, 1967

The Red Union had been attacking the headquarters of the April Twenty-eighth Brigade for two days. Their red flags fluttered restlessly around the brigade building like flames yearning for firewood.

The Red Union commander was anxious, though not because of the defenders he faced. The more than two hundred Red Guards of the April Twenty-eighth Brigade were mere greenhorns compared with the veteran Red Guards of the Red Union, which was formed at the start of the Great Proletarian Cultural Revolution in early 1966. The Red Union had been tempered by the tumultuous experience of revolutionary tours around the country and seeing Chairman Mao in the great rallies in Tiananmen Square.

But the commander *was* afraid of the dozen or so iron stoves inside the building, filled with explosives and connected to each other by electric detonators. He couldn't see them, but he could feel their presence like iron sensing the pull of a nearby magnet. If a defender flipped the switch, revolutionaries and counter-revolutionaries alike would all die in one giant ball of fire.

And the young Red Guards of the April Twenty-eighth Brigade were indeed capable of such madness. Compared with the weathered men and women of the first generation of Red Guards, the new rebels were a pack of wolves on hot coals, crazier than crazy.

The slender figure of a beautiful young girl emerged at the top of the building, waving the giant red banner of the April Twenty-eighth Brigade. Her appearance was greeted immediately by a cacophony of gunshots. The weapons attacking her were a diverse mix: antiques such as American carbines, Czech-style machine guns, Japanese Type-38 rifles; newer weapons such as standard-issue People's Liberation Army rifles and submachine guns, stolen from the PLA after the publication of the "August Editorial"[1]; and even a few Chinese *dadao* swords and spears. Together, they formed a condensed version of modern history.

Numerous members of the April Twenty-eighth Brigade had engaged in similar displays before. They'd stand on top of the building, wave a flag, shout slogans through megaphones, and scatter flyers at the attackers below. Every time, the courageous man or woman had been able to retreat safely from the hailstorm of bullets and earn glory for their valor.

The new girl clearly thought she'd be just as lucky. She waved the battle banner as though brandishing her burning youth, trusting that the enemy would be burnt to ashes in the revolutionary flames, imagining that an ideal world would be born tomorrow from the ardor and zeal coursing through

1   *Translator's Note:* This refers to the August 1967 editorial in *Red Flag* magazine (an important source of propaganda during the Cultural Revolution), which advocated for "pulling out the handful [of counter-revolutionaries] within the army." Many read the editorial as tacitly encouraging Red Guards to attack military armories and seize weapons from the PLA, further inflaming the local civil wars waged by Red Guard factions.

4

her blood. . . . She was intoxicated by her brilliant, crimson dream until a bullet pierced her chest.

Her fifteen-year-old body was so soft that the bullet hardly slowed down as it passed through it and whistled in the air behind her. The young Red Guard tumbled down along with her flag, her light form descending even more slowly than the piece of red fabric, like a little bird unwilling to leave the sky.

The Red Union warriors shouted in joy. A few rushed to the foot of the building, tore away the battle banner of the April Twenty-eighth Brigade, and seized the slender, lifeless body. They raised their trophy overhead and flaunted it for a while before tossing it toward the top of the metal gate of the compound.

Most of the gate's metal bars, capped with sharp tips, had been pulled down at the beginning of the factional civil wars to be used as spears, but two still remained. As their sharp tips caught the girl, life seemed to return momentarily to her body.

The Red Guards backed up some distance and began to use the impaled body for target practice. For her, the dense storm of bullets was now no different from a gentle rain, as she could no longer feel anything. From time to time, her vinelike arms jerked across her body softly, as though she were flicking off drops of rain.

And then half of her young head was blown away, and only a single, beautiful eye remained to stare at the blue sky of 1967. There was no pain in that gaze, only solidified devotion and yearning.

And yet, compared to some others, she was fortunate. At least she died in the throes of passionately sacrificing herself for an ideal.

Battles like this one raged across Beijing like a multitude of CPUs working in parallel, their combined output, the Cultural Revolution. A flood of madness drowned the city and seeped into every nook and cranny.

At the edge of the city, on the exercise grounds of Tsinghua University, a mass "struggle session" attended by thousands had been going on for nearly two hours. This was a public rally intended to humiliate and break down the enemies of the revolution through verbal and physical abuse until they confessed to their crimes before the crowd.

As the revolutionaries had splintered into numerous factions, opposing forces everywhere engaged in complex maneuvers and contests. Within the university, intense conflicts erupted between the Red Guards, the Cultural Revolution Working Group, the Workers' Propaganda Team, and the Military Propaganda Team. And each faction divided into new rebel groups from time to time, each based on different backgrounds and agendas, leading to even more ruthless fighting.

But for *this* mass struggle session, the victims were the reactionary bourgeois academic authorities. These were the enemies of every faction, and they had no choice but to endure cruel attacks from every side.

Compared to other "Monsters and Demons,"[2] reactionary academic authorities were special: During the earliest struggle sessions, they had been both arrogant and stubborn. That was also the stage in which they had died in the larg-

---

2 *Translator's Note:* Originally a term from Buddhism, "Monsters and Demons" was used during the Cultural Revolution to refer to all the enemies of the revolution.

est numbers. Over a period of forty days, in Beijing alone, more than seventeen hundred victims of struggle sessions were beaten to death. Many others picked an easier path to avoid the madness: Lao She, Wu Han, Jian Bozan, Fu Lei, Zhao Jiuzhang, Yi Qun, Wen Jie, Hai Mo, and other once-respected intellectuals had all chosen to end their lives.[3]

Those who survived that initial period gradually became numb as the ruthless struggle sessions continued. The protective mental shell helped them avoid total breakdown. They often seemed to be half asleep during the sessions and would only startle awake when someone screamed in their faces to make them mechanically recite their confessions, already repeated countless times.

Then, some of them entered a third stage. The constant, unceasing struggle sessions injected vivid political images into their consciousness like mercury, until their minds, erected upon knowledge and rationality, collapsed under the assault. They began to really believe that they were guilty, to see how they had harmed the great cause of the revolution. They cried, and their repentance was far deeper and more sincere than that of those Monsters and Demons who were not intellectuals.

For the Red Guards, heaping abuse upon victims in those two latter mental stages was utterly boring. Only those Monsters and Demons who were still in the initial stage could give their overstimulated brains the thrill they craved, like the red cape of the matador. But such desirable victims had grown scarce. In Tsinghua there was probably only one

---

3 *Translator's Note*: These were some of the most famous intellectuals who committed suicide during the Cultural Revolution. Lao She: writer; Wu Han: historian; Jian Bozan: historian; Fu Lei: translator and critic; Zhao Jiuzhang: meteorologist and geophysicist; Yi Qun: writer; Wen Jie: poet; Hai Mo: screenwriter and novelist.

left. Because he was so rare, he was reserved for the very end of the struggle session.

Ye Zhetai had survived the Cultural Revolution so far, but he remained in the first mental stage. He refused to repent, to kill himself, or to become numb. When this physics professor walked onto the stage in front of the crowd, his expression clearly said: *Let the cross I bear be even heavier.*

The Red Guards did indeed have him carry a burden, but it wasn't a cross. Other victims wore tall hats made from bamboo frames, but his was welded from thick steel bars. And the plaque he wore around his neck wasn't wooden, like the others, but an iron door taken from a laboratory oven. His name was written on the door in striking black characters, and two red diagonals were drawn across them in a large X.

Twice the number of Red Guards used for other victims escorted Ye onto the stage: two men and four women. The two young men strode with confidence and purpose, the very image of mature Bolshevik youths. They were both fourth-year students[4] majoring in theoretical physics, and Ye was their professor. The women, really girls, were much younger, second-year students from the junior high school attached to the university.[5] Dressed in military uniforms and equipped with bandoliers, they exuded youthful vigor and surrounded Ye Zhetai like four green flames.

---

4 *Translator's Note:* Chinese colleges (and Tsinghua in particular) have a complicated history of shifting between four-year, five-year, and three-year systems up to the time of the Cultural Revolution. I've therefore avoided using American terms such as "freshman," "sophomore," "junior," and "senior" to translate the classes of these students.

5 *Translator's Note:* In the Chinese education system, six years in primary school are typically followed by three years in junior high school and three years in high school. During the Cultural Revolution, this twelve-year system was shortened to a nine- or ten-year system, depending on the province or municipality. In this case, the girl Red Guards are fourteen.

8

His appearance excited the crowd. The shouting of slogans, which had slackened a bit, now picked up with renewed force and drowned out everything else like a resurgent tide.

After waiting patiently for the noise to subside, one of the male Red Guards turned to the victim. "Ye Zhetai, you are an expert in mechanics. You should see how strong the great unified force you're resisting is. To remain so stubborn will lead only to your death! Today, we will continue the agenda from the last time. There's no need to waste words. Answer the following question without your typical deceit: Between the years of 1962 and 1965, did you not decide on your own to add relativity to the intro physics course?"

"Relativity is part of the fundamental theories of physics," Ye answered. "How can a basic survey course not teach it?"

"You lie!" a female Red Guard by his side shouted. "Einstein is a reactionary academic authority. He would serve any master who dangled money in front of him. He even went to the American Imperialists and helped them build the atom bomb! To develop a revolutionary science, we must overthrow the black banner of capitalism represented by the theory of relativity!"

Ye remained silent. Enduring the pain brought by the heavy iron hat and the iron plaque hanging from his neck, he had no energy to answer questions that were not worth answering. Behind him, one of his students also frowned. The girl who had spoken was the most intelligent of the four female Red Guards, and she was clearly prepared, as she had been seen memorizing the struggle session script before coming onstage.

But against someone like Ye Zhetai, a few slogans like that were insufficient. The Red Guards decided to bring out the new weapon they had prepared against their teacher. One of them waved to someone offstage. Ye's wife, physics professor Shao Lin, stood up from the crowd's front row. She walked onto the stage dressed in an ill-fitting green outfit, clearly intended to imitate the military uniform of the Red Guards. Those who knew her remembered that she had often taught class in an elegant *qipao,* and her current appearance felt forced and awkward.

"Ye Zhetai!" She was clearly unused to such theater, and though she tried to make her voice louder, the effort magnified the tremors in it. "You didn't think I would stand up and expose you, criticize you? Yes, in the past, I was fooled by you. You covered my eyes with your reactionary view of the world and science! But now I am awake and alert. With the help of the revolutionary youths, I want to stand on the side of the revolution, the side of the people!"

She turned to face the crowd. "Comrades, revolutionary youths, revolutionary faculty and staff, we must clearly understand the reactionary nature of Einstein's theory of relativity. This is most apparent in general relativity: Its static model of the universe negates the dynamic nature of matter. It is anti-dialectical! It treats the universe as limited, which is absolutely a form of reactionary idealism. . . ."

As he listened to his wife's lecture, Ye allowed himself a wry smile. *Lin, I fooled you? Indeed, in my heart you've always been a mystery. One time, I praised your genius to your father—he's lucky to have died early and escaped this catastrophe—and he shook his head, telling me that he did not think you would ever achieve much academically. What he said next turned out to be so important to the second half of my life: "Lin Lin is too smart. To work in fundamental theory, one must be stupid."*

In later years, I began to understand his words more and more. Lin, you truly are too smart. Even a few years ago, you could feel the political winds shifting in academia and prepared yourself. For example, when you taught, you changed the names of many physical laws and constants: Ohm's law you called resistance law, Maxwell's equations you called electromagnetic equations, Planck's constant you called the quantum constant. . . . You explained to your students that all scientific accomplishments resulted from the wisdom of the working masses, and those capitalist academic authorities only stole these fruits and put their names on them.

But even so, you couldn't be accepted by the revolutionary mainstream. Look at you now: You're not allowed to wear the red armband of the "revolutionary faculty and staff"; you had to come up here empty-handed, without the status to carry a Little Red Book. . . . You can't overcome the fault of being born to a prominent family in pre-revolutionary China and of having such famous scholars as parents.

But you actually have more to confess about Einstein than I do. In the winter of 1922, Einstein visited Shanghai. Because your father spoke fluent German, he was asked to accompany Einstein on his tour. You told me many times that your father went into physics because of Einstein's encouragement, and you chose physics because of your father's influence. So, in a way, Einstein can be said to have indirectly been your teacher. And you once felt so proud and lucky to have such a connection.

Later, I found out that your father had told you a white lie. He and Einstein had only one very brief conversation. The morning of November 13, 1922, he accompanied Einstein on a walk along Nanjing Road. Others who went on the

11

walk included Yu Youren, president of Shanghai University, and Cao Gubing, general manager of the newspaper Ta Kung Pao. *When they passed a maintenance site in the road bed, Einstein stopped next to a worker who was smashing stones and silently observed this boy with torn clothes and dirty face and hands. He asked your father how much the boy earned each day. After asking the boy, he told Einstein: five cents.*

This was the only time he spoke with the great scientist who changed the world. There was no discussion of physics, of relativity, only cold, harsh reality. According to your father, Einstein stood there for a long time after hearing the answer, watching the boy's mechanical movements, not even bothering to smoke his pipe as the embers went out. After your father recounted this memory to me, he sighed and said, "In China, any idea that dared to take flight would only crash back to the ground. The gravity of reality is too strong."

"Lower your head!" one of the male Red Guards shouted. This may actually have been a gesture of mercy from his former student. All victims being struggled against were supposed to lower their heads. If Ye did lower his head, the tall, heavy iron hat would fall off, and if he kept his head lowered, there would be no reason to put it back on him. But Ye refused and held his head high, supporting the heavy weight with his thin neck.

"Lower your head, you stubborn reactionary!" One of the girl Red Guards took off her belt and swung it at Ye. The copper belt buckle struck his forehead and left a clear impression that was quickly blurred by oozing blood. He swayed unsteadily for a few moments, then stood straight and firm again.

One of the male Red Guards said, "When you taught quantum mechanics, you also mixed in many reactionary ideas." Then he nodded at Shao Lin, indicating that she should continue.

Shao was happy to oblige. She had to keep on talking, otherwise her fragile mind, already hanging on only by a thin thread, would collapse completely. "Ye Zhetai, you cannot deny this charge! You have often lectured students on the reactionary Copenhagen interpretation of quantum mechanics."

"It is, after all, the explanation recognized to be most in line with experimental results." His tone, so calm and collected, surprised and frightened Shao Lin.

"This explanation posits that external observation leads to the collapse of the quantum wave function. This is another expression of reactionary idealism, and it's indeed the most brazen expression."

"Should philosophy guide experiments, or should experiments guide philosophy?" Ye's sudden counterattack shocked those leading the struggle session. For a moment they did not know what to do.

"Of course it should be the correct philosophy of Marxism that guides scientific experiments!" one of the male Red Guards finally said.

"Then that's equivalent to saying that the correct philosophy falls out of the sky. This is against the idea that the truth emerges from experience. It's counter to the principles of how Marxism seeks to understand nature."

Shao Lin and the two college student Red Guards had no answer for this. Unlike the Red Guards who were still in junior high school, they couldn't completely ignore logic.

But the four junior high girls had their own revolutionary methods that they believed were invincible. The girl who had hit Ye before took out her belt and whipped Ye again. The other three girls also took off their belts to strike at Ye. With their companion displaying such revolutionary fervor, they had to display even more, or at least the same amount. The two male Red Guards didn't interfere. If they tried to intervene now, they would be suspected of being insufficiently revolutionary.

"You also taught the big bang theory. This is the most reactionary of all scientific theories." One of the male Red Guards spoke up, trying to change the subject.

"Maybe in the future this theory will be disproven. But two great cosmological discoveries of this century—Hubble's law, and observation of the cosmic microwave background–show that the big bang theory is currently the most plausible explanation for the origin of the universe."

"Lies!" Shao Lin shouted. Then she began a long lecture about the big bang theory, remembering to splice in insightful critiques of the theory's extremely reactionary nature. But the freshness of the theory attracted the most intelligent of the four girls, who couldn't help but ask, "Time began with the singularity? So what was there before the singularity?"

"Nothing," Ye said, the way he would answer a question from any curious young person. He turned to look at the girl kindly. With his injuries and the tall iron hat, the motion was very difficult.

"No . . . nothing? That's reactionary! Completely reactionary!" the frightened girl shouted. She turned to Shao Lin, who gladly came to her aid.

"The theory leaves open a place to be filled by God." Shao nodded at the girl.

The young Red Guard, confused by these new thoughts, finally found her footing. She raised her hand, still holding

14

the belt, and pointed at Ye. "You: you're trying to say that God exists?"

"I don't know."

"What?"

"I'm saying I don't know. If by 'God' you mean some kind of superconsciousness outside the universe, I don't know if it exists or not. Science has given no evidence either way." Actually, in this nightmarish moment, Ye was leaning toward believing that God did not exist.

This extremely reactionary statement caused a commotion in the crowd. Led by one of the Red Guards on stage, another tide of slogan-shouting exploded.

"Down with reactionary academic authority Ye Zhetai!"

"Down with all reactionary academic authorities!"

"Down with all reactionary doctrines!"

Once the slogans died down, the girl shouted, "God does not exist. All religions are tools concocted by the ruling class to paralyze the spirit of the people!"

"That is a very one-sided view," Ye said calmly.

The young Red Guard, embarrassed and angry, reached the conclusion that, against this dangerous enemy, all talk was useless. She picked up her belt and rushed at Ye, and her three companions followed. Ye was tall, and the four fourteen-year-olds had to swing their belts upward to reach his head, still held high. After a few strikes, the tall iron hat, which had protected him a little, fell off. The continuing barrage of strikes by the metal buckles finally made him fall down.

The young Red Guards, encouraged by their success, became even more devoted to this glorious struggle. They were fighting for faith, for ideals. They were intoxicated by the bright light cast on them by history, proud of their own bravery. . . .

Ye's two students had finally had enough. "The chairman instructed us to 'rely on eloquence rather than violence'!" They rushed over and pulled the four semicrazed girls off Ye.

But it was already too late. The physicist lay quietly on the ground, his eyes still open as blood oozed from his head. The frenzied crowd sank into silence. The only thing that moved was a thin stream of blood. Like a red snake, it slowly meandered across the stage, reached the edge, and dripped onto a chest below. The rhythmic sound made by the blood drops was like the steps of someone walking away.

A cackling laugh broke the silence. The sound came from Shao Lin, whose mind had finally broken. The laughter frightened the attendees, who began to leave the struggle session, first in trickles, and then in a flood. The exercise grounds soon emptied, leaving only one young woman below the stage.

She was Ye Wenjie, Ye Zhetai's daughter.

As the four girls were taking her father's life, she had tried to rush onto the stage. But two old university janitors held her down and whispered into her ear that she would lose her own life if she went. The mass struggle session had turned into a scene of madness, and her appearance would only incite more violence. She had screamed and screamed, but she had been drowned out by the frenzied waves of slogans and cheers.

When it was finally quiet again, she was no longer capable of making any sound. She stared at her father's lifeless body, and the thoughts she could not voice dissolved into her blood, where they would stay with her for the rest of her life. After the crowd dispersed, she remained like a stone statue, her body and limbs in the positions they were in when the two old janitors had held her back.

After a long time, she finally let her arms down, walked slowly onto the stage, sat next to her father's body, and held one of his already-cold hands, her eyes staring emptily into the distance. When they finally came to carry away the body, she took something from her pocket and put it into her father's hand: his pipe.

Wenjie quietly left the exercise grounds, empty save for the trash left by the crowd, and headed home. When she reached the foot of the faculty housing apartment building, she heard peals of crazy laughter coming out of the second-floor window of her home. That was the woman she had once called mother.

Wenjie turned around, not caring where her feet would carry her.

Finally, she found herself at the door of Professor Ruan Wen. Throughout the four years of Wenjie's college life, Professor Ruan had been her advisor and her closest friend. During the two years after that, when Wenjie had been a graduate student in the Astrophysics Department, and through the subsequent chaos of the Cultural Revolution, Professor Ruan remained her closest confidante, other than her father.

Ruan had studied at Cambridge University, and her home had once fascinated Wenjie: refined books, paintings, and records brought back from Europe; a piano; a set of European-style pipes arranged on a delicate wooden stand, some made from Mediterranean briar, some from Turkish meerschaum. Each of them seemed suffused with the wisdom of the man who had once held the bowl in his hand or clamped the stem between his teeth, deep in thought, though Ruan had never mentioned the man's name. The pipe that had belonged to Wenjie's father had in fact been a gift from Ruan.

This elegant, warm home had once been a safe harbor for Wenjie when she needed to escape the storms of the larger world, but that was before Ruan's home had been searched and her possessions seized by the Red Guards. Like Wenjie's father, Ruan had suffered greatly during the Cultural Revolution. During her struggle sessions, the Red Guards had hung a pair of high heels around her neck and streaked her face with lipstick to show how she had lived the corrupt lifestyle of a capitalist.

Wenjie pushed open the door to Ruan's home, and she saw that the chaos left by the Red Guards had been cleaned up: The torn oil paintings had been glued back together and rehung on the walls; the toppled piano had been set upright and wiped clean, though it was broken and could no longer be played; the few books left behind had been put back neatly on the shelf. . . .

Ruan was sitting on the chair before her desk, her eyes closed. Wenjie stood next to Ruan and gently caressed her professor's forehead, face, and hands—all cold. Wenjie had noticed the empty sleeping pill bottle on the desk as soon as she came in.

She stood there for a while, silent. Then she turned and walked away. She could no longer feel grief. She was now like a Geiger counter that had been subjected to too much radiation, no longer capable of giving any reaction, noiselessly displaying a reading of zero.

But as she was about to leave Ruan's home, Wenjie turned around for a final look. She noticed that Professor Ruan had put on makeup. She was wearing a light coat of lipstick and a pair of high heels.

2

Silent Spring

Two years later, the Greater Khingan Mountains

"Tim-ber . . ."

Following the loud chant, a large Dahurian larch, thick as the columns of the Parthenon, fell with a thump, and Ye Wenjie felt the earth quake.

She picked up her ax and saw and began to clear the branches from the trunk. Every time she did this, she felt as though she were cleaning the corpse of a giant. Sometimes she even imagined the giant was her father. The feelings from that terrible night two years ago when she cleaned her father's body in the mortuary would resurface, and the splits and cracks in the larch bark seemed to turn into the old scars and new wounds covering her father.

Over one hundred thousand people from the six divisions and forty-one regiments of the Inner Mongolia Production and Construction Corps were scattered among the vast forests and grasslands. When they first left the cities and arrived at this unfamiliar wilderness, many of the corps' "educated youths"—young college students who no longer had schools to go to—had cherished a romantic wish: When the tank clusters of the Soviet Revisionist Imperialists rolled over the Sino-Mongolian border, they would arm themselves and make their own bodies the first barrier in the Republic's defense. Indeed, this expectation was one of the strategic considerations motivating the creation of the Production and Construction Corps.

But the war they craved was like a mountain at the other end of the grassland: clearly visible, but as far away as a mirage. So they had to content themselves with clearing fields, grazing animals, and chopping down trees.

Soon, the young men and women who had once expended their youthful energy on tours to the holy sites of the Chinese Revolution discovered that, compared to the huge sky and open air of Inner Mongolia, the biggest cities in China's interior were nothing more than sheep pens. Stuck in the middle of the cold, endless expanse of forests and grasslands, their burning ardor was meaningless. Even if they spilled all of their blood, it would cool faster than a pile of cow dung, and not be as useful. But burning was their fate; they were the generation meant to be consumed by fire. And so, under their chain saws, vast seas of forests turned into barren ridges and denuded hills. Under their tractors and combine harvesters, vast tracts of grasslands became grain fields, then deserts.

Ye Wenjie could only describe the deforestation that she witnessed as madness. The tall Dahurian larch, the evergreen Scots pine, the slim and straight white birch, the cloud-piercing Korean aspen, the aromatic Siberian fir, along with black birch, oak, mountain elm, *Chosenia arbutifolia*— whatever they laid eyes on, they cut down. Her company wielded hundreds of chain saws like a swarm of steel locusts, and after they passed, only stumps were left.

The fallen Dahurian larch, now bereft of branches, was ready to be taken away by tractor. Ye gently caressed the freshly exposed cross section of the felled trunk. She did this often, as though such surfaces were giant wounds, as though she could feel the tree's pain. Suddenly, she saw another hand lightly stroking the matching surface of the stump a few feet away. The tremors in that hand revealed a heart that resonated with hers. Though the hand was pale, she could tell it belonged to a man.

She looked up. It was Bai Mulin. A slender, delicate man who wore glasses, he was a reporter for the *Great Production News*, the corps' newspaper. He had arrived the day before yesterday to gather news about her company. Ye remembered reading his articles, which were written in a beautiful style, sensitive and fine, ill suited to the rough-hewn environment.

"Ma Gang, come here," Bai called to a young man a little ways off. Ma was barrel-chested and muscular, like the Dahurian larch that he had just felled. He came over, and Bai asked him, "Do you know how old this tree was?"

"You can count the rings." Ma pointed to the stump.

"I did. More than three hundred and thirty years. Do you remember how long it took you to saw through it?"

"No more than ten minutes. Let me tell you, I'm the fastest chain saw operator in the company. Whichever squad I'm with, the red flag for model workers follows me." Ma Gang's excitement was typical of most people Bai paid attention to. To be featured in the *Great Production News* would be a considerable honor.

"More than three hundred years! A dozen generations. When this tree was but a shrub, it was still the Ming Dynasty. During all these years, can you imagine how many storms it had weathered, how many events it had witnessed? But in a few minutes you cut it down. You really felt nothing?"

"What do you want me to feel?" Ma Gang gave a blank

look. "It's just a tree. The only things we don't lack around here are trees. There are plenty of other trees much older than this one."

"It's all right. Go back to work." Bai shook his head, sat down on the stump, and sighed.

Ma Gang shook his head as well, disappointed that the reporter wasn't interested in an interview. "Intellectuals always make a fuss about nothing," he muttered. As he spoke, he glanced at Ye Wenjie, apparently including her in his judgment.

The trunk was dragged away. Rocks and stumps in the ground broke the bark in more places, wounding the giant body further. In the spot where it once stood, the weight of the fallen tree being dragged left a deep channel in the layers of decomposing leaves that had accumulated over the years. Water quickly filled the ditch. The rotting leaves made the water appear crimson, like blood.

"Wenjie, come and take a rest." Bai pointed to the empty half of the stump on which he was sitting. Ye was indeed tired. She put down her tools, came over, and sat down with Bai, back to back.

After a long silence, Bai blurted out, "I can tell how you're feeling. The two of us are the only ones who feel this way."

Ye remained silent. Bai knew that she likely wouldn't answer. She was a woman of few words, and rarely conversed with anyone. Some new arrivals even mistook her for a mute.

Bai went on talking. "I visited this region a year ago. I remember arriving around noon, and my hosts told me that we'd have fish for lunch. I looked around the bark-lined hut and saw only a pot of water being boiled. No fish. Then, as soon as the water boiled, the cook went out with a rolling pin. He stood on the shore of the brook that passed before the hut, struck the water with the rolling pin a few times, and was able to drag a few big fish out of the water. . . . What a fertile place! But now, if you go look at that brook, it's just dead, muddy water in a ditch. I really don't know if the Corps is engaged in construction or destruction."

"Where did you get thoughts like that?" Ye asked softly.

She did not express agreement or disagreement, but Bai was grateful that she had spoken at all. "I just read a book, and it really moved me. Can you read English?"

Ye nodded.

Bai took a book with a blue cover from his bag. He looked around to be sure no one was watching, and handed it to her. "This was published in 1962 and was very influential in the West."

Wenjie turned around on the stump to accept the book. *Silent Spring,* she read on the cover, *by Rachel Carson.* "Where did you get this?"

"The book attracted the attention of the higher-ups. They want to distribute it to select cadres[6] for internal reference. I'm responsible for translating the part that has to do with forests."

Wenjie opened the book and was pulled in. In a brief opening chapter, the author described a quiet town silently dying from the use of pesticides. Carson's deep concern suffused the simple, plain sentences.

"I want to write to the leadership in Beijing and let them know about the irresponsible behavior of the Construction Corps," Bai said.

Ye looked up from the book. It took a while for her to process his words. She said nothing and turned her eyes back to the page.

---

6 *Translator's Note:* "Cadre," when used in the context of Chinese Communism, does not refer to a group, but to an individual official of the Party or the state.

"Keep it for now, if you want to read it. But best be careful and don't let anyone see it. You know what they think of this kind of book . . ." Bai got up, looked around carefully once again, and left.

More than four decades later, in her last moments, Ye Wenjie would recall the influence *Silent Spring* had on her life.

The book dealt only with a limited subject: the negative environmental effects of excessive pesticide use. But the perspective taken by the author shook Ye to the core. The use of pesticides had seemed to Ye just a normal, proper—or, at least, neutral—act, but Carson's book allowed Ye to see that, from Nature's perspective, their use was indistinguishable from the Cultural Revolution, and equally destructive to our world. If this was so, then how many other acts of humankind that had seemed normal or even righteous were, in reality, evil?

As she continued to mull over these thoughts, a deduction made her shudder: *Is it possible that the relationship between humanity and evil is similar to the relationship between the ocean and an iceberg floating on its surface? Both the ocean and the iceberg are made of the same material. That the iceberg seems separate is only because it is in a different form. In reality, it is but a part of the vast ocean. . . .*

It was impossible to expect a moral awakening from humankind itself, just like it was impossible to expect humans to lift off the earth by pulling up on their own hair. To achieve moral awakening required a force outside the human race.

This thought determined the entire direction of Ye's life.

Four days after receiving the book, Ye went to the company's guesthouse, where Bai was living, to return the book. Ye opened the door and saw that Bai was lying on the bed, exhausted and covered by wood shavings and mud. When Bai saw Ye, he struggled to get up.

"Did you work today?" Ye asked.

"I've been here with the company for so long. I can't just walk around all day doing nothing. Have to participate in labor. That's the spirit of the revolution, right? Oh, I worked near Radar Peak. The trees there were so dense. I sank into the rotting leaves all the way up to my knees. I'm afraid I'll get sick from the miasma."

"Radar Peak?" Ye was shocked.

"Yes. The regiment had an emergency assignment: clear out a warning zone all around the peak by cutting down trees."

Radar Peak was a mysterious place. The steep, once-nameless peak got its moniker from the large parabolic antenna dish at the top. In reality, everyone with a little common sense knew it wasn't a radar antenna: Even though its orientation changed every day, the antenna never moved in a continuous manner. As the wind blew past it, the dish emitted a howl that could be heard from far away.

People in Ye's company knew only that Radar Peak was a military base. According to the locals, when the base was built three years ago, the military mobilized a lot of people to construct a road leading to the top and to string a power line along it. Tons of supplies were transported up the mountain. But after the completion of the base, the road was destroyed, leaving behind only a difficult trail that snaked between the trees. Often helicopters could be seen landing on and lifting off the peak.

The antenna wasn't always visible. When the wind was too strong, it was retracted.

But when it was extended, many strange things occurred around the area: Animals in the forest became noisy and anxious, flocks of birds erupted from the woods, and people suffered nausea and dizziness. Also, those who lived near Radar Peak tended to lose their hair. According to the locals, these phenomena only began after the antenna was built.

There were many strange stories associated with Radar Peak. One time, when it was snowing, the antenna was extended, and the snow instantly turned to rain. Since the temperature near ground was still below freezing, the rain turned to ice on the trees. Gigantic icicles hung from the trees, and the forest turned into a crystal palace. From time to time, branches cracked under the weight of the ice, and the icicles crashed to the ground with loud thumps. Sometimes, when the antenna was extended, a clear day would turn to thunder and lightning, and strange lights would appear in the night sky.

After the arrival of the Construction Corps company, the commander told everyone right away to take care to avoid approaching the heavily guarded Radar Peak, because the patrols were allowed to shoot without warning.

Last week, two of the men had gone hunting and chased a deer to the foot of Radar Peak without realizing where they were, and the sentries stationed halfway up the peak shot at them. Luckily, the forest was so dense that the two escaped without injury, though one of the men peed in his pants. At the company meeting the next day, both men were reprimanded. Maybe it was because of this incident that the base had directed the Corps to create a warning zone in the forest around the peak. The fact that the base could issue labor assignments to the Construction Corps hinted at its political power.

Bai Mulin accepted the book from Ye and carefully hid it under his pillow. From the same place, he retrieved a few sheets of paper filled with dense writing and handed them to her. "This is a draft of my letter. Would you read it?"

"Letter?"

"Like I was telling you, I want to write to the central leadership in Beijing."

The handwriting was very sloppy, and Ye had to read it slowly. But the content was informative and tightly argued. The letter began by describing how the Taihang Mountains had turned from a historically fertile place to the barren wasteland it was today as a result of deforestation. It then described the recent, rapid rise in the Yellow River's silt content. Finally, it concluded that the Inner Mongolia Production and Construction Corps' actions would lead to severe ecological consequences. Ye noticed that Bai's style was similar to that of *Silent Spring,* precise and plain, but also poetic. Though her background was in technical subjects, she enjoyed the literary prose.

"It's beautiful," she said sincerely.

Bai nodded. "Then I'll send it." He took out a few fresh sheets of paper to make a clean copy of the draft. But his hands shook so much that he couldn't form any characters. This was a common reaction after using a chain saw for the first time. Their trembling hands couldn't even hold a rice bowl steady, let alone write legibly.

"Why don't I copy it for you?" Ye said. She took the pen from him.

"You have such pretty handwriting," Bai said as he looked at her first line of characters on the page. He poured a glass of water for Ye. His hands shook so much that he spilled some of the water. Ye moved the letter out of the way.

"You studied physics?" Bai asked.

"Astrophysics. Useless now." Ye did not even lift her head.

"You study the stars. How can that be useless? Colleges have reopened recently, but they're not taking graduate students. For highly educated and skilled individuals like you to be sent to a place like this . . ."

Ye said nothing and kept on writing. She did not want to tell Bai that for someone like her to be able to join the Construction Corps was very fortunate. She didn't want to comment on the way things were—there was nothing worthwhile to say.

The hut became quiet, filled only with the sound of pen nib scratching against paper. Ye could smell the fragrance of the sawdust on Bai's body. For the first time since the death of her father, she experienced warmth in her heart and allowed herself to relax, momentarily letting down her guard against the world.

More than an hour later, she was done copying the letter. She wrote out the address on the envelope as Bai dictated it and got up to say good-bye.

At the door, she turned around. "Let me have your jacket. I'll wash it for you." She was surprised by her own boldness.

"No! How can I do that?" Bai shook his head. "The woman warriors of the Construction Corps work just as hard as the men every day. You should get back to have some rest. Tomorrow you have to get up at six to work in the mountains. Oh, Wenjie, I'll be heading back to division headquarters the day after tomorrow. I will explain your situation to my superiors. Maybe it will help."

"Thank you. But I like it here. It's quiet." Ye looked at the dim outline of the dark woods in the moonlight.

"Are you trying to run away from something?"

"I'm leaving," Ye said in a soft voice. And she did.

Bai watched her slender figure disappear in the moonlight.

Then he lifted his gaze to the dark woods that she had been looking at a moment earlier.

In the distance, the gigantic antenna on top of Radar Peak rose once again, giving off a cold, metallic glint.

One afternoon three weeks later, Ye Wenjie was summoned back to company headquarters from the logging camp. As soon as she entered the office, she sensed the mood was wrong. The company commander and the political instructor were both present, along with a stranger with a stern expression. On the desk in front of the stranger was a black briefcase, and an envelope and a book lay next to it. The envelope was open, and the book was the copy of *Silent Spring* that she had read.

During those years, everyone had a special sensitivity for their own political situation. The sense was especially acute in Ye Wenjie. She felt the world around her closing in like a sack being drawn shut, and everything pressing in on her.

"Ye Wenjie, this is Director Zhang of the Division Political Department. He's here to investigate." Her political instructor pointed at the stranger. "We hope you will cooperate fully and tell the truth."

"Did you write this letter?" Director Zhang asked. He pulled the letter out of the envelope. Ye reached for it, but Zhang held on to the letter and showed it to her page by page until he reached the very last page, the one she was most interested in.

There was no signature except "The Revolutionary Masses."

"No, I did not write this." Ye shook her head in fright.

"But this is your handwriting."

"Yes, but I just copied it for someone else."

"Who?"

29

Normally, whenever she suffered some injustice at the company, Ye refused to protest openly. She simply endured silently, and would never consider implicating others. But this time was different. She understood very well what this meant.

"I helped a reporter from the *Great Production News*. He was here a few weeks ago. His name is—"

"Ye Wenjie!" Director Zhang's two black eyes were trained on her like the barrels of two guns. "I am warning you: Framing others will only make your problem worse. We've already clarified the situation with Comrade Bai Mulin. His only involvement was posting the letter from Hohhot under your direction. He had no idea as to the letter's contents."

"He . . . he said that?" Ye felt everything go black before her eyes.

Instead of answering, Director Zhang picked up the book. "Your letter was clearly inspired by this book." He showed the book to the company director and the political instructor. "*Silent Spring* was published in America in 1962 and has been quite influential in the capitalist world."

He then took another book out of the briefcase. The cover was white with black characters. "This is the Chinese translation. The appropriate authorities distributed it to select cadres as internal reference so that it could be criticized. As of now, the appropriate authorities have already given their clear judgment: The book is a toxic piece of reactionary propaganda. It takes the stance of pure historical idealism and espouses a doomsday theory. Under the guise of discussing environmental problems, it seeks to justify the ultimate corruption of the capitalist world. The content is extremely reactionary."

"But this book . . . it doesn't belong to me."

"Comrade Bai was appointed as a translator by the appropriate authorities. So it was perfectly legitimate for him

30

to carry it. Of course, he *is* responsible for being careless and allowing you to steal it while he was participating in Construction Corps work assignments. From this book, you obtained intellectual weapons that could be used to attack socialism."

Ye Wenjie held her tongue. She knew that she had already fallen to the bottom of the pit. Any struggle was useless.

Contrary to certain historical records that later became publicized, Bai Mulin did not intend to frame Ye Wenjie at the start. The letter he wrote to the central leadership in Beijing was likely based on a real sense of responsibility. Back then, many people wrote to the central leadership with all kinds of personal agendas. Most of these letters were never answered, but a few of the letter writers did see their political fortunes rise meteorically overnight, while others invited catastrophe. The political currents of the time were extremely complex. As a reporter, Bai believed he could read the currents and avoid dangerous sensitivities, but he was overconfident, and his letter touched a minefield that he did not know existed. After he heard about its reception, fear overwhelmed everything else. In order to protect himself, he decided to sacrifice Ye Wenjie.

Half a century later, historians would all agree that this event in 1969 was a turning point in humankind's history.

Without intending to, Bai became a key historical figure. But he never learned of this fact. Historians recorded the rest of his uneventful life with disappointment. He continued to work at *Great Production News* until 1975, when the Inner Mongolia Production and Construction Corps was disbanded. He was then sent to a city in Northeast China to work for the Science Association until the beginning of the eighties. Then he left the country for Canada, where he taught at a Chinese school in Ottawa until 1991, when he died from lung cancer. For the rest of his life, he never mentioned Ye Wenjie, and we do not know if he ever felt remorse or repented for his actions.

"Wenjie, the company has treated you extremely well." The company commander exhaled a thick cloud of smoke from his Mohe tobacco. He stared at the ground and continued. "By birth and family background, you're politically suspect. But we've always treated you as one of our own. Both the political instructor and I have spoken to you many times concerning your tendency to sequester yourself from the people, and your lack of self-motivation in seeking progress. We want to help you. But look at you! You've committed such a serious error!"

The political instructor picked up the theme. "I've always said that I thought she had a deep-rooted resentment of the Cultural Revolution."

"Have her escorted to division headquarters this afternoon, along with the evidence of her crime," Director Zhang said, his face impassive.

The three other women prisoners in the cell were taken away one by one until only Ye was left. The small pile of coal in the corner had been exhausted, and no one came to replenish it. The fire in the stove had gone out a while ago. It was so cold in the cell that Ye had to wrap herself in the blanket.

Two officials came to her before it got dark. The older one, a female cadre, was introduced by her associate as the military representative from the Intermediate People's Court.[7]

"My name is Cheng Lihua," the cadre introduced herself. She was in her forties, dressed in a military coat, and wore thick-rimmed glasses. Her face was gentle, and it was clear that she had been very beautiful when she was young. She spoke with a smile and instantly made people like her. Ye Wenjie understood that it was unusual for such a high-grade cadre to visit a prisoner about to be tried. Cautiously, she nodded at Cheng and moved to make space on her narrow cot so she could sit down.

"It's really cold in here. What happened to your stove?" Cheng gave a reprimanding look to the head of the detention center standing at the door of the cell. She turned back to Ye. "Hmm, you're very young. Even younger than I imagined."

She sat down on the cot right next to Ye and rummaged in her briefcase, still muttering. "Wenjie, you're very confused. Young people are all the same. The more books you read, the more confused you become. Eh, what can I say. . . ."

She found what she was looking for and took out a small bundle of papers. Looking at Ye, her eyes were filled with kindness and affection. "But it's not a big deal. What young person hasn't made some mistakes? I made mistakes myself. When I was a young woman, as a member of the art troupe for the Fourth Field Army, I specialized in singing Soviet songs. One time, during a political study session, I announced that China should cease to be a separate country and join the USSR as a member republic. That way, international

---

7 *Author's Note:* During that phase of the Cultural Revolution, most intermediate and higher people's courts and procuratorial organs (responsible for investigating and prosecuting crimes) were under the control of military commissions. The military representative had the final vote on judicial matters.

communism would be further strengthened. How naïve I was! But who wasn't once naïve? What's done is done. When you make a mistake, what's important is to recognize it and correct it. Then you can continue the revolution."

Cheng's words seemed to draw Ye closer to her. But after having gone through so many troubles, Ye had learned to be cautious. She did not dare to believe in this kindness, which almost resembled a luxury.

Cheng placed the stack of papers on the bed in front of Ye and handed her a pen. "Come now, sign this. Then we can have a good heart-to-heart and resolve your ideological difficulties." Her tone was like that of a mother trying to encourage her daughter to eat.

Ye stared at the stack of papers silently and motionlessly. She did not pick up the pen.

Cheng gave her a forgiving smile. "You can trust me, Wenjie. I personally guarantee that this document has nothing to do with your case. Go ahead. Sign it."

Her associate, who stood to the side, added, "Ye Wenjie, Representative Cheng is trying to help you. She's been working hard on your behalf."

Cheng waved at him to stop. "It's understandable. Poor child! You've been so frightened. There are some comrades whose political awareness is not adequately high. Some members of the Construction Corps and some of the folks from the people's court employ such simplistic methods and behave so rudely. It's completely inappropriate! All right, Wenjie, why don't you read the document? Read it carefully."

Ye picked up the document and flipped through it in the dim yellow light of the detention cell. Representative Cheng hadn't lied to her. The document really had nothing to do with her case.

It was about her father. In it was a record of her father's interactions and conversations with certain individuals. The source was Wenjie's younger sister, Wenxue. As one of the most radical Red Guards, Wenxue had always been proactive in exposing their father, and had composed numerous reports detailing his supposed sins. Some of the material she provided had ultimately led to his death.

But Ye could tell that this report didn't come from the hand of her sister. Wenxue had an intense, impatient style. When you read her reports, each line would make an explosive impact, like a string of firecrackers. But this document was composed in a cool, experienced, meticulous style. Who spoke to whom, when, where, what was discussed—every detail was recorded, down to the exact date. For someone who wasn't experienced, the contents seemed like a boring diary, but the calculating, cold purpose hidden within was very different from the childish antics of Wenxue.

Ye couldn't really understand what the document was getting at, but she could sense that it had something to do with an important national defense project. As the daughter of a physicist, Ye guessed that it was a reference to the double-bomb project[8] that had shocked the world in 1964 and 1967.

During this period of the Cultural Revolution, in order to bring down a highly positioned individual, it was necessary to gather evidence of his deficiencies in the various areas he was in charge of. But for those plotting such political machinations, the double-bomb project posed great difficulties. People in the highest levels of the government placed the project under their protection to avoid disruption by the

---

8 *Translator's Note:* This is the Chinese term for the work behind "596" and "Test No. 6," the successful tests for China's first fission and fusion nuclear bombs, respectively.

Cultural Revolution. It was difficult for those with nefarious purposes to pry into its inner workings.

Due to her father's family background, he couldn't meet the political requirements and did not work on the double-bomb project. All he had done was some peripheral theoretical work for it. But it was easier to make use of him than those who had worked at the core of the project. Ye Wenjie couldn't tell if the contents of the document were true or false, but she was sure that every character and every punctuation mark had the potential to deliver a fatal political blow. In addition to those targeted directly, countless others might have their fates altered because of this document.

At the end of the document was her sister's signature in large characters, and Ye Wenjie was supposed to sign as a witness. She noticed that three other witnesses had already signed.

"I don't know anything about these conversations," Ye said softly. She put the document back down.

"How can you not know? Many of these conversations occurred right in your home. Your sister knew them. You must, too."

"I really don't."

"But these conversations really did occur. You must have faith in us."

"I didn't say they weren't true. But I really don't know about them. So I can't sign."

"Ye Wenjie!" Cheng's associate took a step closer. But Cheng stopped him again. She shifted to sit even closer to Ye and picked up one of her cold hands.

"Wenjie, let me put all my cards on the table. Your case has a lot of prosecutorial discretion. On the one hand, we could minimize it as a case of an educated youth being fooled by a reactionary book—it's not a big deal. We don't even need to go through a judicial procedure. We'll have you attend a political class and write a few self-criticism reports, and then you can go back to the Construction Corps. On the other hand, we could also prosecute this case to its fullest extent. Wenjie, you must know that you could be declared an active counter-revolutionary.

"Now, faced with political cases like yours, all prosecutorial organs and courts would rather be too severe than too lax. This is because treating you too severely would just be a mistake in method, but treating you too laxly would be a mistake in political direction. Ultimately, however, the decision belongs to the military control commission. Of course, I'm telling you all this off the record."

Cheng's associate added, "Representative Cheng is trying to save you. Three witnesses have already signed. Your refusal to sign is pretty much meaningless. I must urge you not to be confused, Ye Wenjie."

"Right, Wenjie," Cheng continued. "It would break my heart to see an educated young person like you ruined by something like this. I really want to save you. Please cooperate. Look at me. Do you think I would hurt you?"

But Ye did not look at Representative Cheng. What she saw, instead, was her father's blood. "Representative Cheng, I have no knowledge of the events recorded in this document. I cannot sign it."

Cheng Lihua became quiet. She stared at Ye for a long while, and the cold air in the cell seemed to solidify. Then she slowly put the document back into her briefcase and stood up. Her kind expression did not disappear, but was set on her face like a plaster mask. Still appearing kind and affectionate, she walked to the corner of the cell, where there was a bucket for washing. She picked it up and poured half the water onto Ye and the other half onto her blanket, her movements never straying from a methodical calmness. Then she dropped the bucket and left the cell, pausing only to mutter, "You stubborn little bitch!"

The head of the detention center was the last to leave. He stared coldly at Ye, soaked through and dripping, shut the cell door with a bang, and locked it.

Through her wet clothes, the chill of the Inner Mongolian winter seized Ye like a giant's fist. She heard her teeth chatter, but eventually even that sound disappeared. The coldness penetrated into her bones, and the world in her eyes turned milky white. She felt that the entire universe was a huge block of ice, and she was the only spark of life within it. She was the little girl about to freeze to death, and she didn't even have a handful of matches, only illusions. . . .

The block of ice holding her gradually became transparent. In front of her she could see a tall building. At the top, a young girl waved a bright red banner. Her slender figure contrasted vividly with the breadth of the flag: It was her sister, Wenxue. Ever since her little sister had made a clean break with her reactionary academic authority family, Wenjie had heard no news about her. She had only learned recently that Wenxue had died two years ago in one of the wars between Red Guard factions.

As Ye watched, the figure waving the flag became Bai Mulin, his glasses reflecting the flames raging below the building; then it turned into Representative Cheng; then her mother, Shao Lin; then her father. The flag-bearer kept on changing, but the flag waved ceaselessly, like a perpetual pendulum, counting down the remainder of her short life.

Gradually, the flag grew blurry; everything grew blurry. The ice that filled the universe once again sealed her at its center. Only this time, the ice was black.

3

Red Coast I

Ye Wenjie heard a loud, continuous roar. She didn't know how much time had passed.

The noise came from all around her. In her vague state of consciousness, it seemed as though some gigantic machine was drilling into or sawing through the block of ice that held her. The world was still only darkness, but the noise grew more and more real. Finally, she was certain that the source of the noise was neither heaven nor hell, and she remained in the land of the living.

She realized that her eyes were still closed. With an effort, she lifted her eyelids. The first thing she saw was a light embedded deeply in the ceiling. Covered by a wire mesh that seemed designed to protect it, it emitted a dim glow. The ceiling appeared to be made of metal.

She heard a male voice softly calling her name. "You have a high fever," the man said.

"Where am I?" Wenjie's voice was so weak that she couldn't be sure it was her own.

"On a helicopter."

Ye felt weak. She fell back to sleep. As she dozed, the roar kept her company. Before long, she woke again. Now the numbness had disappeared and the pain reasserted itself: Her

39

head and the joints of her limbs ached, and the breath coming out of her mouth felt scalding hot. Her throat hurt so much that swallowing spittle felt like it was a piece of burning coal.

She turned her head and saw two men wearing the same kind of military coat that Representative Cheng had worn. But unlike her, both of these men had on the cotton cap of the PLA, a red star sewn onto the front. Their coats were unbuttoned, and she could see the red-collar insignia on their army uniforms. One of the men wore glasses.

Ye discovered that she was covered by a military coat as well. The clothes she was wearing were dry and warm.

She struggled to sit up, and to her surprise, succeeded. She looked out the porthole on the other side. Rolling clouds slowly drifted by, reflecting the dazzling sunlight. She pulled her gaze back. The narrow cabin was filled with iron trunks painted military green. From another porthole she could see flickering shadows cast by the rotors. She was indeed on a helicopter.

"You'd better lie back down," the man with the glasses said. He helped her down and covered her with the coat again.

"Ye Wenjie, did you write this paper?" The other man extended an open English journal before her eyes. The title of the paper was "The Possible Existence of Phase Boundaries Within the Solar Radiation Zone and Their Reflective Characteristics." He showed her the cover of the journal: an issue of *The Journal of Astrophysics* from 1966.

"Of course she did. Why does that even need to be confirmed?" The man wearing glasses took the journal away and then made introductions. "This is Political Commissar Lei Zhicheng of Red Coast Base. I'm Yang Weining, base chief engineer. It will be an hour before we land. You might as well get some rest."

You're Yang Weining? Ye didn't say anything, but she was stunned. She saw that he kept his expression calm, apparently not wishing to let anyone else know that they knew each other. Yang had been one of Ye Zhetai's graduate students. By the time he had obtained his degree, Wenjie was still a first-year in college.

She could clearly remember the first time Yang came to her home. He had just begun his graduate studies and needed to discuss the direction of his research with Professor Ye. Yang said that he wanted to focus on experimental and applied problems, staying away from theory.

Ye Wenjie recalled her father saying, "I'm not opposed to your idea. But we are, after all, the department of theoretical physics. Why do you want to avoid theory?"

Yang replied, "I want to devote myself to the times, to make some real-world contributions."

Her father said, "Theory is the foundation of application. Isn't discovering fundamental laws the biggest contribution to our time?"

Yang hesitated and finally revealed his real concern: "It's easy to make ideological mistakes in theory."

Her father had nothing to say to that.

Yang was very talented, with a good mathematical foundation and a quick mind. But during his brief time as a graduate student, he always kept a respectable distance from his thesis advisor. Ye Wenjie had seen Yang several times, but, perhaps due to the influence of her father, she hadn't noticed him much. As for whether he had paid much attention to her, she had no idea. After Yang got his degree, he soon ceased all contact with her father.

Again feeling weak, Ye closed her eyes. The two men left her and crouched behind a row of trunks to converse in lowered voices. But the cabin was so cramped that Ye could hear them even over the roar of the engine.

"I still think this isn't a good idea," Commissar Lei said.

"Can you find the personnel I need through normal channels?" Yang asked.

"Eh. I've done all I can. There's no one in the military with this specialization, and going outside the army raises many questions. You know very well that the security clearance needed for this project requires someone willing to join the army. But the bigger issue is the requirement in the security regulations that they be sequestered at the base for extended periods. What's to be done if they have families? Sequester them at the base too? No one would agree to that. I did find two possible candidates, but both would rather stay at the May Seventh Cadre Schools rather than come here.[9] Of course we could forcefully move them. But given the nature of this work, we can't have someone who doesn't want to be here."

"Then there's no choice but to use her."

"But it's so unconventional."

"This entire project is unconventional. If something goes wrong, I'll accept the responsibility."

"Chief Yang, do you really think you can take responsibility for this? You are a technical person, but Red Coast is not like other national defense projects. Its complexity goes far beyond the technical issues."

"You're right, but I only know how to solve the technical issues."

---

9 *Translator's Note:* The May Seventh Cadre Schools were labor camps during the Cultural Revolution where cadres and intellectuals were "re-educated."

By the time they landed, it was dusk.

Ye refused to be helped by Yang and Lei, and struggled out of the helicopter by herself. A strong gust of wind almost blew her over. The still-gyrating rotors sliced through the wind, making a loud whistling noise. The scent of the woods on the wind was familiar to her, and she was familiar to the wind. It was the wind of the Greater Khingan Mountains.

She soon heard another sound, a kind of low, forceful, bass howl that seemed to form the background of the world: the parabolic antenna dish in the wind. Only now, when she was so close to it, did she finally feel its immensity. Ye's life had made a big circle this month: She was now on top of Radar Peak.

She couldn't help but look in the direction of her Construction Corps company. But all she could see was a misty sea of trees in the twilight.

The helicopter was carrying more than just Ye. Several soldiers came over and began to unload military-green cargo trunks from the cabin. They walked by without glancing at her. As she followed Yang and Lei, Ye noticed that the top of Radar Peak was spacious. A cluster of white buildings, like delicate toy blocks, nestled under the giant antenna. The trio headed toward the base gate, flanked by two guards, and stopped in front of it.

Lei turned to her and spoke solemnly. "Ye Wenjie, the evidence of your counter-revolutionary crime is incontrovertible, and the court would have punished you as you deserve. But now you have an opportunity to redeem yourself through hard work. You can accept it or refuse it." He pointed at the antenna. "This is a defense research facility. The research conducted here needs your specialized scientific knowledge. Chief Engineer Yang can give you the details, which you should consider carefully."

He nodded at Yang and then entered the gate after the soldiers carrying the trunks.

Yang waited until the others were gone and indicated that Ye should follow him a little distance away from the gate, clearly trying to avoid the sentries listening in.

He no longer pretended that he didn't know her. "Wenjie, let me be clear. This is not some great opportunity. I learned from the military control commission at the court that although Cheng Lihua advocates sentencing you severely, the most that you'll get is ten years. Considering mitigating circumstances, you'll serve maybe six or seven years. But here"—he nodded in the direction of the base—"is a research project under the highest security classification. Given your status, if you enter the gate, it's possible—" He paused, as though wanting to let the bass howl of the antenna add to the weight of his words. "—you'll never leave for the rest of your life."

"I want to go in."

Yang was surprised by her quick answer. "Don't be hasty. Get back onto the helicopter. It will take off in three hours, and if you refuse our offer, it will take you back."

"I don't want to go back. Let's go in." Ye's voice remained soft, but there was a determination in her tone that was harder than steel. Other than the undiscovered country beyond death from which no one has ever returned, the place she wanted to be the most was this peak, separated from the rest of the world. Here, she felt a sense of security that had long eluded her.

"You should be cautious. Think through what this decision means."

"I can stay here for the rest of my life."

Yang lowered his head and said nothing. He stared into the distance, as though forcing Ye to sort through her thoughts.

44

Ye stayed silent as well. She pulled her coat tightly around herself and gazed into the distance. There, the Greater Khingan Mountains were fading into the darkening night. It was impossible to stay out here much longer in the cold.

Yang began to walk toward the gate. He moved fast, as though trying to leave Ye behind. But Ye stayed close. After they entered the gate of Red Coast Base, the two sentries shut the heavy iron doors.

A little ways on, Yang stopped and pointed at the antenna. "This is a large-scale weapons research project. If it succeeds, the result will be even more important than the atomic bomb and the hydrogen bomb."

They came to the largest building in the base, and Yang pushed the door open. Ye saw the words TRANSMISSION MAIN CONTROL ROOM over the door. Inside, warm air tinged with the smell of engine oil enveloped her. She saw that the spacious room was filled with all kinds of instruments and equipment. Signal lights and oscilloscope displays flickered together. A dozen or so operators dressed in military uniform were almost entombed by the rows of instruments, as though they were crouching inside battlefield trenches. The unceasing stream of operational orders and responses gave the whole scene a tense, confusing feel.

"It's warmer in here," Yang said. "Wait here a bit. I'll take care of your living arrangements and return for you." He pointed at a chair and desk next to the door.

Ye saw that someone was already sitting at the desk: a guard carrying a handgun.

"I'd rather wait outside," Ye said.

Yang smiled at her kindly. "From now on, you'll be a member of the base staff. Other than a few sensitive areas, you can go anywhere you want." His face suddenly looked uncomfortable as he realized another layer of meaning to his words: *You can never leave here again.*

"I prefer to wait outside," Ye insisted.

"All right." Yang glanced at the guard at the desk, who paid no attention to them. He seemed to understand Ye's concern and brought her back out of the main control room. "Stand somewhere out of the wind, and I'll be back in a few minutes. I just need to get someone to start a fire in your room—conditions at the base are a bit rough, and we have no heating system."

Ye stood next to the main control room door. The huge antenna was directly behind her and it blotted out half the sky. From here, she could clearly hear the sounds inside the main control room. Suddenly, the chaotic orders and responses ceased, and the room became completely quiet. All she could hear was the occasional low buzzing noise from some instrument.

Then a loud male voice broke the silence. "The People's Liberation Army, Second Artillery Corps,[10] Red Coast Project, one hundred and forty-seventh transmission. Authorization confirmed. Begin thirty-second countdown."

"Target Classification: A-three. Coordinates' serial number: BN20197F. Position checked and confirmed. Twenty-five seconds."

"Transmission file number: twenty-two. Additions: none. Continuations: none. Transmission file final check completed. Twenty seconds."

"Energy Unit reporting: all systems go."

"Coding Unit reporting: all systems go."

"Amplifier Unit reporting: all systems go."

---

10 *Translator's Note:* The Second Artillery Corps controls China's nuclear missiles.

"Interference Monitoring Unit reporting: within acceptable range."

"We have reached the point of no return. Fifteen seconds."

Everything became quiet again. Fifteen seconds later, as a klaxon started to blare, a red light on top of the antenna began to blink rapidly.

"Begin transmission! All units continue to monitor!"

Ye felt a light itch on her face. She knew that an enormous electric field had appeared. She lifted her face and gazed in the direction the antenna was pointing and saw a cloud in the night sky glow with a dim blue light, so dim that at first she thought it an illusion. But as the cloud drifted away, the glow disappeared. Another cloud that drifted into position began to give off the same glow.

From the main control room, she heard more shouts.

"Malfunction with Energy Unit. Magnetron number three has burnt out."

"Backup Unit is in operation: all systems go."

"Checkpoint one reached. Resuming transmission."

Ye heard a fluttering noise. Through the mist, she could see shadows lift out of the woods below the peak and spiral into the dark sky. She hadn't realized so many birds could be roused from the woods in deep winter. Then she saw a terrifying scene: One flock of birds flew into the region of air the antenna pointed at, and against the background of the faintly glowing cloud, the birds dropped out of the sky.

The process continued for about fifteen minutes. Then the red light on the antenna went out, and the itch on her skin disappeared. From the main control room, the confusing murmur of orders and responses resumed even as the loud male voice continued.

"Transmission one hundred forty-seven of Red Coast

completed. Transmission systems shutting down. Red Coast now entering monitoring state. System control is hereby transferred to the Monitoring Department. Please upload checkpoint data."

"All units should fill out transmission diaries. All unit heads should attend the post-transmission meeting in the debriefing room. We're done."

All was silent except for the howl of the wind against the antenna. Ye watched as the remaining birds in the flock gradually settled back into the forest. She stared at the antenna and thought it looked like an enormous hand stretched open toward the sky, possessing an ethereal strength. As she surveyed the night sky, she did not see any target that she thought might be serial number BN20197F. Beyond the wisps of clouds, all she could see were the stars of a cold night in 1969.

PART II

THREE BODY

4

The Frontiers of Science

Forty-plus years later

Wang Miao thought the four people who came to find him made a rather odd combination: two cops and two men in military uniforms. If the latter two were armed police, that would be somewhat understandable, but they were actually PLA officers.

As soon as Wang saw the cops, he felt annoyed. The younger one was all right—at least he was polite. But the other one, in plainclothes, immediately grated on him. He was thickset and had a face full of bulging muscles. Wearing a dirty leather jacket, smelling of cigarettes, and speaking in a loud voice, he was exactly the sort of person Wang despised. "Wang Miao?"

The way the cop addressed him by name only, so direct and impolite, made Wang uncomfortable. Adding to the insult, the man lit a cigarette as he addressed him, without even lifting his head to show his face. Before Wang could answer, the man nodded at the younger cop, who showed Wang his badge.

Having lit the cigarette, the older cop moved to enter Wang's apartment.

"Please don't smoke in my home," Wang said, blocking him.

"Oh, sorry, Professor Wang." The young police officer smiled. "This is Captain Shi Qiang." He gave Shi a pleading look.

"Fine, we can talk in the hallway," Shi said. He took a deep drag. Almost half the cigarette had turned to ashes, and he didn't blow out much smoke. He inclined his head toward the younger police officer. "You ask him, then."

"Professor Wang, we want to know if you've had any recent contacts with members of the Frontiers of Science," the young cop said.

"The Frontiers of Science is full of famous scholars, and very influential. Why can't I have contact with a legal international academic group?"

"Look at the way you talk!" Shi said. "Did we say anything about it not being legal? Did we say anything about you not being allowed to contact them?" He finally blew out the lungful of smoke that he had sucked in earlier—right in Wang's face.

"All right then. Please respect my privacy. I don't need to answer your questions."

"Your *privacy*? You're a famous academic. You have a responsibility toward the public welfare." Shi threw away the butt and took out another cigarette from a flattened pack.

"I have the right to not answer. Please leave." Wang turned around to go back inside.

"Wait!" Shi shouted. He waved at the young cop next to him. "Give him the address and phone number. You can come by in the afternoon."

"What are you really after?" Wang said, his voice now tinged with anger. The argument brought the neighbors, curious about what was happening, out into the hallway.

"Captain Shi!" The young cop pulled Shi aside and

continued speaking to him in hushed, urgent tones. Apparently, Wang wasn't the only one annoyed by his rough manners.

"Professor Wang, please don't misunderstand." One of the army officers, a major, stepped forward. "There's an important meeting this afternoon, to which several scholars and specialists are invited. The general sent us to invite you."

"I'm busy this afternoon."

"We know. The general already spoke with the head of the Nanotechnology Research Center. We can't have this meeting without you. If you can't attend, we'll have to reschedule."

Shi and the young cop said nothing. Both turned and went down the stairs. The two army officers watched them leave and seemed to sigh with relief.

"What's wrong with that guy?" the major whispered to the other officer.

"He's got quite a record. During a hostage crisis a few years ago, he acted recklessly, without concern for the lives of the hostages. In the end, a family of three all died at the hands of the criminals. Rumor has it that he's also friendly with elements of organized crime, using one gang to fight another. Last year, he used torture to obtain confessions, and permanently disabled one of the suspects. That's why he was suspended from duty. . . ."

Wang Miao suspected that he was meant to overhear the conversation between the officers. Maybe they intended to show him that they were different from that rude cop; or maybe they wanted to make him curious about their mission.

"How can a man like that be part of the Battle Command Center?" the major asked.

"The general specifically requested him. I guess he must have some special skills. In any case, his duties are quite restricted. Other than public safety matters, he's not allowed to know much."

Battle Command Center? Wang looked at the two officers, baffled.

The car they sent for Wang Miao took him to a large compound in the suburbs. Since the door had only a number and no sign, Wang deduced that this building belonged to the military, rather than the police.

Wang was surprised by the chaos as he entered the large meeting room. Around him were numerous computers in various states of disarray. They had run out of table space and put a few workstations directly on the floor, where power cords and networking wires formed a tangled mess. Instead of being installed in racks, a bunch of routers were left haphazardly on top of the servers. Printer paper was scattered everywhere. A few projector screens stood in various corners of the room, sticking out at odd angles like gypsy tents. A cloud of smoke hovered over the room. . . . Wang Miao wasn't sure if this was the Battle Command Center, but he was sure of one thing: Whatever they were dealing with was too important for them to care about keeping up appearances.

The meeting table, formed by pushing several smaller tables together, was piled with documents and odds and ends. The attendees, their clothes wrinkled, looked exhausted. Those wearing ties had all pulled them loose. It seemed as if they had been up all night.

A major general named Chang Weisi presided over the meeting, and half the attendees were military officers. After a few quick introductions, Wang found out that many of the others were police. The rest were academics like him, with a few prominent scientists specializing in basic research in the mix.

He also found four foreigners in attendance. Their identities shocked him: a United States Air Force colonel and a British Army colonel, both NATO liaisons, as well as two CIA officers, apparently acting as observers.

On the faces of everyone around the table, Wang could read one sentiment: *We've done all we can. Let's fucking get it over with, already.*

Wang Miao saw Shi Qiang sitting at the table. In contrast to his rudeness yesterday, Shi greeted Wang as "Professor." But the smirk on Shi's face annoyed Wang. He didn't want to sit next to Shi, but he had no choice, as that was the only empty seat. The already thick cloud of cigarette smoke in the room became thicker.

As documents were distributed, Shi moved closer to Wang. "Professor Wang, I understand you're researching some kind of . . . new material?"

"Nanomaterial," Wang answered.

"I've heard of it. That stuff is really strong, right? Do you think it could be used to commit crimes?" As Shi's face was still half smirking, Wang couldn't tell if he was joking.

"What do you mean?"

"Heh. I heard that a strand of that stuff could be used to lift up a truck. If criminals steal some and make it into a knife, can't they slice a car in half with one stroke?"

"There's no need to even make it into a knife. That kind of material can be made into a line as thin as one-hundredth of a hair. If you string it across a road, a passing car would be sliced into two halves like cheese—but what can't be used for criminal purposes? Even a dull knife for descaling a fish can!"

Shi pulled a document halfway out of the envelope in front of him and shoved it back in again, suddenly losing interest. "You're right. Even a fish can be used to commit a crime. I handled a murder case once. Some bitch cut off her husband's family jewels. You know what she used? A frozen tilapia she got out of the freezer! The spines along the back were like razors—"

"I'm not interested. Did you ask me to the meeting just to talk about this?"

"Fish? Nanomaterials? No, no, nothing to do with those." Shi put his mouth next to Wang's ear. "Don't be nice to them. They're prejudiced against us. All they want is to get information out of us, but never tell us anything. Look at me. I've been here for a month, and I still don't know anything, just like you."

"Comrades," General Chang said, "let's get started. Of all the combat zones around the globe, this one has become the focal point. We need to update the current situation for all the attending comrades."

The unusual term "combat zone" gave Wang pause. He also noticed that the general did not seem to want to explain in detail the background of what they were dealing with to new people like him. This supported Shi's point. Also, in General Chang's short opening remarks, he used the word "comrades" twice. Wang looked at the NATO and CIA officers sitting across from him. The general had neglected to add "gentlemen."

"They're also comrades. Anyway, that's how everyone addresses each other here," Shi whispered to Wang, pointing at the four foreigners with his cigarette.

While he was baffled by how Shi knew what he was thinking, Wang was impressed with his powers of observation.

"Da Shi, put out your cigarette. There's enough smoke here," General Chang said as he flipped through some documents. He called Shi Qiang by a nickname, "Big Shi."

Shi looked around but couldn't find an ashtray. In the end, he dropped the cigarette into a teacup. He raised his hand, and before Chang could even acknowledge him, he spoke loudly. "General, I have a request which I've made before: I want information parity."

General Chang lifted his head. "There's never been a military operation in which there was information parity. I have to apologize to all the scholars, but we cannot give you any more background."

"We are *not* the same as the eggheads," Shi said. "The police have been part of the Battle Command Center from the start. But even now, we still don't know what this is all about. You continue to push the police out. You learn from us what you need about our techniques, and then you send us away one by one."

Several other police officers in attendance whispered to Shi to shut up. It surprised Wang that Shi dared to speak in this manner to a man of Chang's rank. But Chang's response surprised him even more.

"Da Shi, it seems that you still have the same problem you had back when you were in the army. You think you can speak for the police? Because of your poor record, you had already been suspended for several months, and you were about to be expelled from the force. I asked for you because I value your experience in city policing. You should treasure this opportunity."

Shi continued to speak roughly. "So I'm working in the hope of redeeming myself by good service? I thought you told me that all my techniques were dishonest and crooked."

"But useful." Chang nodded at Shi. "All we care about is if they're useful. In a time of war, we can't afford to be too scrupulous."

"We can't be too fastidious," a CIA officer said, in perfect Modern Standard Mandarin. "We can no longer rely on conventional thinking."

The British colonel apparently also understood Chinese. He nodded. "To be, or not to be . . ." he added in English. "It's a matter of life and death."

"What is he saying?" Shi asked Wang.

"Nothing," Wang replied mechanically. The people before him seemed to be speaking out of a dream. *Time of war? Where is this war?* He twisted to look out one of the floor-length windows. Through the window he could see Beijing in the distance: Under the spring sun, cars filled the streets like a dense river; on a lawn someone was walking a dog; a few children were playing. . . .

Which is more real? The world inside or outside these walls?

General Chang said, "Recently, the enemy has intensified the pattern of attacks. The targets remain elite scientists. Please begin by taking a look at the list of names in the document."

Wang took out the first page of the document, printed in large font. The list seemed to have been generated in a hurry, containing both Chinese and English names.

"Professor Wang, as you look through these names, does anything strike you?" General Chang asked.

"I know three of the names. All of them are famous scholars working at the forefront of physics research." Wang was a little distracted. His eyes locked onto the last name on the list. In his mind, the two characters took on a different tint than the names above it. *How can her name appear here? What happened to her?*

"You know her?" Shi pointed to the name with a thick finger, stained yellow from smoking. Wang did not reply. "Ha. Don't know her. But *want* to know her?"

Now Wang Miao understood why it made sense for General Chang to have asked to have this man who was once a soldier under his command. Shi, who appeared so vulgar and careless, had eyes as sharp as knives. Maybe he wasn't a *good* cop, but he was certainly a fearsome one.

A year earlier, Wang Miao had been in charge of the nanoscale components for the "Sinotron II" high-energy particle accelerator project. One afternoon, during a brief break at the Liangxiang construction site, Wang was struck by the scene before him. As a landscape photography enthusiast, Wang often saw the sights around him as artistic compositions.

The main component of the composition was the solenoid of the superconducting magnet they were still installing. About three stories high and only half completed, the magnet loomed like a monster made of giant blocks of metal and a confusing mess of cryogenic coolant pipes. Like a junk heap from the Industrial Revolution, the structure exuded inhuman technological grimness and steel-bound barbarity.

In front of this metal monster stood the slim figure of a young woman. The composition's lighting was fantastic as well: The metal monster was buried in the shadow of a temporary construction shelter, further emphasizing its stern, rough quality. But a single ray of light from the westering sun coming through the central hole in the shelter fell right on the woman. The soft glow lit up her supple hair and highlighted her white neck above the collar of her overalls, as though a single flower was blooming in a metal ruin after a violent thunderstorm. . . .

"What are you looking at? Get back to work!"

Wang was shocked out of his reverie, but then realized that the director of the Nanotechnology Research Center wasn't talking to him, but to a young engineer who had also been staring at the woman. Having returned from art to reality, Wang saw that the young woman wasn't an ordinary worker—the chief engineer stood next to her, explaining something respectfully.

"Who is she?" Wang asked the director.

"You should know her," the director said, waving his hand around in a large circle. "The first experiment on this twenty-billion-yuan accelerator will probably be to test her superstring model. Now, seniority matters in theoretical physics, and normally, she wouldn't have been senior enough to get the first shot. But those older academics didn't dare to show up first, afraid that they might fail and lose face, so that's why she got the chance."

"What? Yang Dong is . . . a woman?"

"Indeed," the director said. "We only found out when we finally met her two days ago."

The young engineer asked, "Does she have some psychological issue? Why else wouldn't she agree to be interviewed by the media? Maybe she's like Qian Zhongshu,[11] who died without ever appearing on TV."

---

11 *Translator's Note:* Qian Zhongshu (1910–1998) was one of the most famous Chinese literary scholars of the twentieth century. Erudite, witty, and aloof, he consistently refused media appearances. One might think of him as a Chinese Thomas Pynchon.

"But at least we knew Qian's gender. I bet Yang had some unusual experiences as a child. Maybe it made her somewhat autistic." Wang's words were tinged with a hint of self-mockery. He wasn't even famous enough for the media to be interested in him, let alone to turn down interview requests.

Yang walked over with the chief engineer. As they passed, she smiled at Wang and the others, nodding lightly without saying anything. Wang remembered her limpid eyes.

That night, Wang sat in his study and admired the few landscape photographs, his works he was the most proud of, hanging on the wall. His eyes fell on a frontier scene: a desolate valley terminating in a snowcapped mountain. On the nearer end of the valley, half of a dead tree, eroded by the vicissitudes of many years, took up one-third of the picture. In his imagination, Wang placed the figure that lingered in his mind at the far end of the valley. Surprisingly, it made the entire scene come alive, as though the world in the photograph recognized that tiny figure and responded to it, as though the whole scene existed for her.

He then imagined her figure in each of his other photographs, sometimes pasting her two eyes into the empty sky over the landscapes. Those images also came alive, achieving a beauty that Wang had never imagined.

Wang had always thought that his photographs lacked some kind of soul. Now he understood that they were missing *her*.

"All the physicists on this list have committed suicide in the last two months," General Chang said.

Wang was thunderstruck. Gradually, his black-and-white landscapes faded into blankness in his mind. The photographs no longer had her figure in the foreground, and her eyes were wiped from the skies. Those worlds were all dead.

"When . . . did this happen?" Wang asked mechanically.

"The last two months," Chang repeated.

"You mean the last name, don't you?" Shi responded with satisfaction. "She was the last to commit suicide—two nights ago, overdosed on sleeping pills. She died very peacefully. No pain."

For a moment, Wang was grateful to Shi.

"Why?" Wang asked. The dead scenes in those landscape photographs continued to flicker through his mind.

General Chang replied, "The only thing we can be sure of is this: The same reason drove all of them to suicide. But it's hard to articulate. Maybe it's impossible for us nonspecialists to even understand the reason. The document contains excerpts from their suicide notes. Everyone can examine them after the meeting."

Wang flipped through the notes: All of them seemed to be long essays.

"Dr. Ding, would you please show Yang Dong's note to Professor Wang? Hers is the shortest and possibly the most representative."

The man in question, Ding Yi, had been silent until now. After another pause, he finally took out a white envelope and handed it across the table to Wang.

Shi whispered, "He was Yang's boyfriend." Wang recalled that he had seen Ding at the particle accelerator construction site in Liangxiang. He was a theoretician who had became famous for his discovery of the macroatom while studying ball lightning.[12] Wang took from the envelope a thin, irregularly

---

12 *Translator's Note:* For more on Ding Yi, see *Ball Lightning* by Cixin Liu.

shaped sheet exuding a faint fragrance—not paper, but birch bark. A single line of graceful characters was written on it:

All the evidence points to a single conclusion: Physics has never existed, and will never exist. I know what I'm doing is irresponsible. But I have no choice.

There wasn't even a signature. She was gone.

"Physics . . . does not exist?" Wang had no idea what to think.

General Chang closed the folder. "The file also contains some specific information related to the experimental results obtained after the completion of the world's three newest particle accelerators. It's very technical, and we won't be discussing it here. The first focus of our investigation is the Frontiers of Science. UNESCO designated 2005 the World Year of Physics, and that organization gradually developed out of the numerous academic conferences and exchanges that occurred among world physicists that year. Dr. Ding, since you're a theoretical physicist, can you give us more background on it?"

Ding nodded. "I have no direct connection with the Frontiers of Science, but it is famous in academia. Its core goal is a response to the following: Since the second half of the twentieth century, physics has gradually lost the concision and simplicity of its classical theories. Modern theoretical models have become more and more complex, vague, and uncertain. Experimental verification has become more difficult as well. This is a sign that the forefront of physics research seems to be hitting a wall.

"Members of the Frontiers of Science want to attempt a new way of thinking. To put it simply, they want to use the methods of science to discover the limits of science, to try to find out if there is a limit to how deeply and precisely science can know nature—a boundary beyond which science cannot go. The development of modern physics seems to suggest that such a line has been touched."

"Very good," General Chang said. "According to our investigation, most of the scholars who committed suicide had some connection with the Frontiers of Science, and some were even members. But we've found no evidence of the use of illegal psychotropic drugs or techniques akin to the psychological manipulation of religious cults. In other words, even if the Frontiers of Science influenced them, it was only through legal academic exchanges. Professor Wang, since they recently contacted you, we'd like to ask you for some information."

Shi added gruffly, "Including the names of your contacts, the times and locations of meetings, the content of your conversations, and if you exchanged letters or e-mails—"

"Shut up, Da Shi!" General Chang said.

Another police officer leaned over and whispered to Shi, "Do you think we'll forget you have a mouth if you don't use it all the time?" Shi picked up his teacup, saw the drowned cigarette butt inside, and put it back down.

Shi's questions irritated Wang again, not unlike the feeling a man has upon finding out that he has swallowed a fly with his meal. The gratitude he had felt earlier was gone without a trace. But he restrained himself and answered, "My contact with the Frontiers of Science began with Shen Yufei. She's a Japanese physicist of Chinese descent who currently works for a Japanese company here in Beijing. She once worked at a Mitsubishi lab, researching nanotech. We met at a technical conference at the beginning of this year. Through her, I met a few other physicist friends, all members of the Frontiers of Science, some Chinese, some foreign. When I talked with them, all the topics were . . . how do I put this? Very radical. They all involved the question that Dr. Ding just described: What is the limit of science?

"Initially, I didn't have much interest in these topics. I thought of them as only an idle pastime. My work is in applied research, and I don't know much about these theoretical matters. Mainly, I was interested in listening to their discussions and arguments. All of them were deep thinkers with novel points of view, and I felt that I was opening my mind through the exchanges. Gradually, I grew more interested. But all our talk was limited to pure theory and nothing else. They once invited me to join the Frontiers of Science. But if I had done so, attending the discussions would have turned into a duty. Since my time and energy were limited, I declined."

"Professor Wang," General Chang said, "we'd like you to accept the invitation and join the Frontiers of Science. This is the main reason we asked you here today. Through you, we'd like to learn more about the internal workings of the organization."

"You want me to be a mole?" Wang was uneasy.

"A mole!" Shi laughed.

Chang gave Shi a reprimanding look. He turned back to Wang. "We just want you to give us some information. We have no other way in."

Wang shook his head. "I'm sorry, General. I cannot do this."

"Professor Wang, the Frontiers of Science is made up of elite international scholars. Investigating it is an extremely complex and sensitive matter. For us, it's like walking across thin ice. Without someone from academia helping us, we cannot make any progress. This is why we're making this request. But we'll respect your wishes. If you won't agree, we understand."

"I am . . . very busy at work. I just don't have the time."

General Chang nodded. "All right, Professor Wang, we won't waste any more of your time. Thank you for coming to this meeting."

Wang waited a few more seconds before realizing that he had been dismissed.

General Chang politely accompanied Wang to the door. They could hear Shi's loud voice behind them. "It's better this way. I disagree with the plan anyway. So many bookworms have already killed themselves. If we send him, he'd be a meat dumpling thrown to the dogs."

Wang turned around and walked back to Shi. Forcing his anger down, Wang said, "The way you speak is not appropriate for a good police officer."

"Who said I'm a *good* cop?"

"We don't know why these researchers killed themselves, but you shouldn't speak of them so contemptuously. Their minds have made irreplaceable contributions to humanity."

"You're saying they're better than me?" Still seated, Shi lifted his eyes to meet Wang's. "At least I wouldn't kill myself just because someone told me some bullshit."

"You think I would?"

"I have to be concerned about your safety." That trademark smirk again.

"I think I would be much safer than you in such situations. You must know that a person's ability to discern the truth is directly proportional to his knowledge."

"I'm not sure about that. Take someone like you—"

"Be quiet, Da Shi!" General Chang said. "One more sentence and you're out of here!"

"It's okay," Wang said. "Let him speak." He turned to General Chang. "I've changed my mind. I will join the Frontiers of Science as you wish."

"Good!" Shi nodded vigorously. "Stay alert after you join. Gather intelligence whenever it's convenient. For example, glance at their computer screens, memorize e-mail or Web addresses—"

"That's enough! You misunderstand me. I don't want to be a spy. I just want to prove you're an idiot!"

"If you remain alive after you've joined them for a while, that would be the best proof. But I'm afraid for you . . ." Shi lifted his face, and the smirk turned into a wolfish grin.

"Of course I'll stay alive! But I never want to see you again."

They kept Wang out of the way while the others left so he wouldn't have to deal with Shi Qiang again. Then General Chang walked Wang all the way down the stairs and called for a car to take him back.

He said to Wang, "Don't worry about Shi Qiang. That's just his personality. He's actually a very experienced beat officer and antiterrorism expert. Twenty years ago, he was a soldier in my company."

As they approached the car, Chang added, "Professor Wang, you must have many questions."

"What did everything you talked about in there have to do with the military?"

"War has everything to do with the army."

Wang looked around in the spring sun, baffled. "But where is this war? This is probably the most peaceful period in history."

Chang gave him an inscrutable smile. "You will know more soon. Everyone will know. Professor Wang, have you ever had anything happen to you that changed your life completely? Some event where afterward the world became a totally different place for you?"

"No."

"Then your life has been fortunate. The world is full of unpredictable factors, yet you have never faced a crisis."

Wang turned over the words in his mind, still not understanding. "I think that's true of most lives."

"Then most people have lived fortunately."

"But . . . many generations have lived in this plain manner."

"All fortunate."

Wang laughed, shaking his head. "I have to confess that I'm not feeling very sharp today. Are you suggesting that—"

"Yes, the entire history of humankind has been fortunate. From the Stone Age till now, no real crisis has occurred. We've been very lucky. But if it's all luck, then it has to end one day. Let me tell you: It's ended. Prepare for the worst."

Wang wanted to ask more, but Chang shook his head and said good-bye, preventing any more questions.

After Wang got into the car, the driver asked for his address. Wang gave it and asked, "Oh, were you the one who took me here? I thought it was the same type of car."

"No, it wasn't me. I took Dr. Ding here."

Wang had a new idea. He asked the driver to take him to Ding's address instead.

5

A Game of Pool

As soon as he opened the door to Ding Yi's brand-new three-bedroom apartment, Wang smelled alcohol. Ding was lying on the sofa with the TV on, staring at the ceiling. The apartment was unfinished, with only a few pieces of furniture and little decoration, and the huge living room seemed very empty. The most eye-catching object was the pool table in the corner.

Ding didn't seem annoyed by Wang's unannounced visit. He was clearly in the mood to talk to someone.

"I bought the apartment about three months ago," Ding said. "Why did I buy it? Did I really think she was going to become interested in starting a family?" His laugh sounded drunk.

"You two . . ." Wang wanted to know the details of Yang Dong's life, but didn't know how to ask the questions.

"She was like a star, always so distant. Even the light she shone on me was always cold." Ding walked to one of the windows and looked up at the night sky.

Wang said nothing. All he wanted now was to hear her voice. But a year ago, as the sun sank in the west, when she and he had locked eyes for a moment, they had not spoken to each other. He had never heard her voice.

Ding waved his hand as though trying to flick something

away. "Professor Wang, you were right. Don't get involved with the police or the military. They're all idiots. The deaths of those physicists had nothing to do with the Frontiers of Science. I've explained it to them many times, but I can't get them to understand."

"They seem to have conducted some independent investigation."

"Yes, and the investigation's scope was global. They should already know that two of the dead never had any contact with the Frontiers of Science, including . . . Yang Dong." Ding seemed to have trouble saying her name.

"Ding Yi, you know that I am already involved. So . . . as far as why Yang made the choice that . . . she did, I'd like to know. I think you must know some of it." Wang thought he must sound very foolish as he tried hard to disguise his real intent.

"If you know more, you'll only get pulled in deeper. Right now you're just superficially involved, but with more knowledge your spirit will be drawn in as well, and then it will mean real trouble."

"I work in applied research. I'm not as sensitive as you theoreticians."

"All right, then. Do you play pool?" Ding walked to the pool table.

"I used to play a little in college."

"She and I loved to play. It reminded us of particles colliding in the accelerator." Ding picked up two balls: one black and one white. He set the black ball next to one of the pockets, and placed the white ball about ten centimeters from the black ball. "Can you pocket the black ball?"

"This close? Anyone can do it."

"Try."

Wang picked up the cue, struck the white ball lightly, and drove the black ball into the pocket.

"Good. Come, now let's move the table to a different location." Ding directed the confused Wang to pick up the heavy table. Together they moved it to another corner of the living room, next to a window. Then Ding scooped out the black ball, set it next to the pocket, and again picked up the white ball and set it down about ten centimeters away. "Think you can do it again?"

"Of course."

"Go for it."

Again, Wang easily made the shot.

Ding waved his hands. "Let's move it again." They lifted the table and set it down in a third corner of the living room. Ding set up the two balls as before. "Go."

"Listen, we—"

"Go!"

Wang shrugged helplessly. He managed to pocket the black ball a third time.

They moved the table two more times: once next to the door of the living room, and finally back to the original location. Ding set up the two balls twice more, and Wang twice more made his shot. By now both were slightly winded.

"Good, that's the conclusion of the experiment. Let's analyze the results." Ding lit a cigarette before continuing, "We ran the same experiment five times. Four of the experiments differed in both location and time. Two of the experiments were at the same location but different times. Aren't you shocked by the results?" He opened his arms exaggeratedly. "Five times! Every colliding experiment yielded the exact same result!"

"What are you trying to say?" Wang asked, gasping.

"Can you explain this incredible result? Please use the language of physics."

"All right . . . During these five experiments, the mass of the two balls never changed. In terms of their locations, as long as we're using the frame of reference of the tabletop, there was also no change. The velocity of the white ball striking the black ball also remained basically the same throughout. Thus, the transfer of momentum between the two balls didn't change. Therefore, in all five experiments, the result was the black ball being driven into the pocket."

Ding picked up a bottle of brandy and two dirty glasses from the floor. He filled both and handed one to Wang. Wang declined.

"Come on, let's celebrate. We've discovered a great principle of nature: The laws of physics are invariant across space and time. All the physical laws of human history, from Archimedes' principle to string theory, and all the scientific discoveries and intellectual fruits of our species are the by-products of this great law. Compared to us two theoreticians, Einstein and Hawking are mere applied engineers."

"I still don't understand what you're getting at."

"Imagine another set of results. The first time, the white ball drove the black ball into the pocket. The second time, the black ball bounced away. The third time, the black ball flew onto the ceiling. The fourth time, the black ball shot around the room like a frightened sparrow, finally taking refuge in your jacket pocket. The fifth time, the black ball flew away at nearly the speed of light, breaking the edge of the pool table, shooting through the wall, and leaving the Earth and the Solar System, just like Asimov once described.[13] What would you think then?"

---

13 *Author's Note:* See Isaac Asimov's short story "The Billiard Ball."

Ding watched Wang. After a long silence, Wang finally said, "This actually happened. Am I right?"

Ding drained both glasses in his hands. He stared at the pool table as though looking at a demon. "Yes. It happened. In the last few years, we finally obtained the necessary equipment for experimentally testing fundamental theories. Three expensive 'pool tables' have been constructed: one in North America, another in Europe, and the third you are familiar with, in Liangxiang. Your Nanotechnology Research Center earned a lot of money from it.

"These high-energy particle accelerators raised the amount of energy available for colliding particles by an order of magnitude, to a level never before achieved by the human race. Yet, with the new equipment, the same particles, the same energy levels, and the same experimental parameters would yield different results. Not only would the results vary if different accelerators were used, but even with the same accelerator, experiments performed at different times would give different results. Physicists panicked. They repeated the ultra-high-energy collision experiments again and again using the same conditions, but every time the result was different, and there seemed to be no pattern."

"What does this mean?" Wang asked. When he saw Ding staring at him without speaking, he added, "Oh, I'm in nanotech, and I also work with microscale structures. But that's orders of magnitude larger than the scale at which you do your work. Please educate me."

"It means that the laws of physics are not invariant across time and space."

"What does *that* mean?"

"I think you can deduce the rest. Even General Chang figured it out. He's really a smart man."

Wang looked outside the window thoughtfully. The lights of the city were so bright that the stars of the night sky were drowned out.

"It means that laws of physics that could be applied anywhere in the universe do not exist, which means that physics... also does not exist." Wang turned back from the window.

" 'I know what I'm doing is irresponsible. But I have no choice,' " Ding said. "That was the second half of her note. You just stumbled on the first half. Now can you understand her? At least a little?"

Wang picked up the white ball. He caressed it for a bit and put it back down. "For someone exploring the forefront of theory, that would indeed be a catastrophe."

"To accomplish something in theoretical physics requires one to have almost religious faith. It's easy to be led to the abyss."

As they said their farewells, Ding gave Wang an address. "If you have the time, please visit Yang Dong's mother. She and her mother always lived together, and she was the entirety of her mother's life. Now the old woman is all alone."

"Ding, you clearly know a lot more than I do. Can you tell me more? You really believe that the laws of physics are not invariant across time and space?"

"I don't know anything." Ding stared into Wang's eyes for a long time. Finally, he said, "But that is the question."

Wang knew that he was only finishing what the British colonel had begun to say: *To be, or not to be: that is the question.*

6

The Shooter and the Farmer

The next day was the start of the weekend. Wang got up early and left on his bicycle. As a hobby photographer, his favorite subjects were wildernesses free of human presence. But now that he was middle-aged, he no longer had the energy to engage in such indulgent travel and only shot city scenes.

Consciously or subconsciously, he usually chose corners of the city that held some aspect of the wild: a dried lakebed in a park, the freshly turned soil of a construction site, a weed struggling out of cracks in cement. In order to eliminate the busy colors of the city in the background, he only used black-and-white film. Unexpectedly, he had developed his own style and had gained some notice. His works had been selected for two exhibitions, and he was a member of the Photographers Association. Every time he went out to take pictures, he would ride his bike and wander around the city in search of inspiration and compositions that caught his fancy. Often he would be out all day.

Today, Wang felt strange. His photography style tended toward the classical, calm and dignified. But today he could not seem to get in the mood necessary for such compositions. In his mind, the city, as it awoke from its slumber, seemed to be built on quicksand. The stability was illusory. All night long, he had dreamt of those two billiard balls. They flew around a dark space without any pattern, the black one disappearing against the black background and only revealing its existence occasionally when it obscured the white ball.

Can the fundamental nature of matter really be lawlessness? Can the stability and order of the world be but a temporary dynamic equilibrium achieved in a corner of the universe, a short-lived eddy in a chaotic current?

Without realizing it, he found himself at the foot of the newly completed China Central Television building. He stopped at the side of the road and lifted his head to gaze up at this gigantic A-shaped tower, trying to recapture the feeling of stability. His gaze followed the sharp tip of the building, gleaming in the morning sunlight, pointing toward the blue, bottomless depths of the sky. Two words suddenly floated into his consciousness: "shooter" and "farmer."

When the members of the Frontiers of Science discussed physics, they often used the abbreviation "SF." They didn't mean "science fiction," but the two words "shooter" and "farmer." This was a reference to two hypotheses, both involving the fundamental nature of the laws of the universe.

In the shooter hypothesis, a good marksman shoots at a target, creating a hole every ten centimeters. Now suppose the surface of the target is inhabited by intelligent, two-dimensional creatures. Their scientists, after observing the universe, discover a great law: "There exists a hole in the universe every ten centimeters." They have mistaken the result of the marksman's momentary whim for an unalterable law of the universe.

The farmer hypothesis, on the other hand, has the flavor of a horror story: Every morning on a turkey farm, the farmer comes to feed the turkeys. A scientist turkey, having observed this pattern to hold without change for almost a year, makes the following discovery: "Every morning at eleven, food arrives." On the morning of Thanksgiving, the scientist announces this law to the other turkeys. But that morning at eleven, food doesn't arrive; instead, the farmer comes and kills the entire flock.

Wang felt the road beneath his feet shift like quicksand. The A-shaped building seemed to wobble and sway. He quickly brought his gaze back to the street.

To get rid of the anxiety, Wang forced himself to finish a roll of film. He returned home before lunch. His wife had taken their son out and wouldn't be back for a while. Usually, Wang would rush to develop the film, but today he wasn't in the mood. After a quick and simple lunch, he went to take a nap. Because he hadn't slept well the night before, by the time he woke up it was almost five. Finally remembering the roll of film he had shot, he went into the cramped darkroom he had converted from a closet.

The film developed. Wang began to look through the negatives to see if any shots were worth printing, but he saw something strange in the very first image. The shot was of a small lawn outside a large shopping center. The center of the negative held a line of tiny white marks, which, upon closer examination, turned out to be numbers: *1200:00:00*.

The second picture also had numbers: *1199:49:33*, as did the third: *1199:40:18*.

In fact, every picture in the roll had such numbers, until the thirty-sixth (and last) image: *1194:16:37*.

Wang's first thought was that something was wrong with the film. The camera he had used was a 1988 Leica

M2—entirely mechanical, which made it impossible for it to add a date stamp. Given the excellent lens and refined mechanical operation, it was considered a great professional camera even in this digital age.

After reexamining the negatives, Wang discovered another strange thing about the numbers: They seemed to adapt to the background. If the background was black, the numbers were white, and vice versa. The shift seemed designed to maximize the numbers' contrast for visibility. By the time Wang saw the sixteenth negative, his heart was beating faster, and a chill crept up his spine.

This shot was of a dead tree against an old wall. The wall was mottled, showing a pattern of alternating black and white patches on the negative. Given this background, either white or black numbers would have been hard to read. But in the picture, the numbers arranged themselves vertically to fit along the curve of the tree trunk, allowing the white numbers to show up against the dark coloring of the dead tree like a crawling snake.

Wang began to analyze the mathematical pattern in the numbers. At first he thought it was some kind of assigned numbering, but the difference between the numbers wasn't constant. He then guessed that the numbers represented time in the form of hours, minutes, and seconds. He took out his shooting diary, in which he recorded the exact time he took each picture down to the minute, and discovered the difference between two successive numbers on the photographs corresponded to the difference in time between when they were taken.

A countdown.

The countdown began with 1,200 hours. And now there were about 1,194 hours left, just under 50 days.

Now? No, at the moment I took the last photograph. Is the countdown still proceeding?

Wang walked out of the darkroom, loaded a new roll of film in the Leica, and began to snap random shots. He even walked onto the balcony for a few outdoor shots. Afterward, he took out the film and went back into the darkroom. In the developed roll, the numbers again appeared on every negative like ghosts. The first one was marked *1187:27:39*. The difference matched the passage of time between the last shot of the last roll and the first shot of this roll. After that, the number decreased by three or four seconds in each image: *1187:27:35, 1187:27:31, 1187:27:27, 1187:27:24 . . .* just like the intervals between the quick shots he had taken.

The countdown continued.

Wang again loaded a new roll of film. He snapped off the shots rapidly, even taking a few with the lens cap on. As he took out the roll of film, his wife and son returned. Before he went into the darkroom to develop the film, he loaded another roll of film in the Leica and handed it to his wife. "Here, finish the roll for me."

"What am I supposed to shoot?" His wife looked at him, amazed. He never allowed anyone to touch his camera, though she and their son had no interest in doing so either. In their eyes, it was a boring antique that cost more than twenty thousand yuan.

"Doesn't matter. Just shoot whatever you want." Wang stuffed the camera into her hands and ducked into the darkroom.

"All right. Dou Dou, why don't I take some pictures of you?" His wife aimed the camera at their son.

Wang's mind suddenly filled with the imagined sight of the ghostlike figures appearing over his son's face like a hangman's noose. He shuddered. "No, don't do that. Shoot something else."

The shutter clicked, and his wife had taken her first shot. "Why can't I press it again?" she asked. Wang taught her how to wind the film to advance it. "Like that. You have to do it after every shot." Then he ducked back into the darkroom.

"So complicated!" His wife, a doctor, couldn't understand why anyone would use such expensive but outdated equipment when ten- or even twenty-megapixel digital cameras were common. And he even used black-and-white film.

After the third roll of film developed, Wang held it up against the red light. He saw that the ghostlike countdown continued. The numbers showed up clearly on every randomly shot picture, including the few he had taken with the lens cap on: 1187:19:06, 1187:19:03, 1187:18:59, 1187:18:56 . . .

His wife knocked on the darkroom door and told him she was finished with the roll. Wang opened the door and took the camera from her. As he took out the roll, his hands trembled. Ignoring his wife's concerned look, he took the film back into the darkroom and shut the door. He worked fast and clumsily, spilling developer and fixer all over the ground. Soon the images were developed. He closed his eyes, silently praying, *Please don't appear. No matter what, please don't appear now. Don't make it my turn. . . .*

He examined the wet film with a magnifying glass. There was no countdown. The negatives held only the interior shots his wife had taken. She had used a slow shutter speed, and her amateurish operation left all the scenes blurry. But Wang thought these were the most enjoyable pictures he had ever seen.

Wang came out of the darkroom and let out a held breath.

He was covered in sweat. His wife was in the kitchen cooking, and his son was playing in his room. He sat on the sofa and thought the matter over more rationally.

First, the numbers, which precisely recorded the passage of time between shots and which showed signs of intelligence, could not possibly have been preprinted on the film. *Something* exposed them onto the film. But what? Did the camera have a malfunction? Had some mechanism been installed in the camera without his knowledge? He took off the lens and disassembled the camera. He examined the interior with a magnifying glass and checked every dustless component without discovering anything out of place. Then, considering that the numbers showed up even in the shots taken with the lens cap on, he realized the most likely light source was some kind of penetrating ray. But how was this technologically possible? Where was the source of the rays? How could they have been aimed?

At least given current technology, such power would be supernatural.

In order to see if the ghostly countdown had disappeared, Wang loaded another roll into the Leica, and again began to shoot randomly. When this roll was developed, Wang's short-lived calm was again shattered. He felt himself pushed to the precipice of madness. The countdown had returned. Based on the numbers, it had never stopped, just failed to display on the roll shot by his wife.

1186:34:13, 1186:34:02, 1186:33:46, 1186:33:35 . . .

Wang rushed out of the darkroom and continued through the door of the apartment. He knocked loudly on the door of his neighbor, retired Professor Zhang.

"Professor Zhang, do you have a camera? Not a digital one, but one that takes film!"

"A professional photographer like you wants to borrow my camera? What happened to your expensive one? I have only digital point-and-shoots. Are you okay? Your face looks so pale."

"Please, let me borrow it."

Zhang returned with a common Kodak digital camera. "Here you go. You can just delete the few pictures already on there."

"Thank you!" Wang seized the camera and rushed back home. He actually had three more film cameras and a digital one, but Wang thought it better to borrow a camera from someone else. He looked at his own camera lying on the sofa and the few rolls of film, paused in thought, and decided to reload the Leica with new film. He handed the borrowed digital camera to his wife, who was setting out dinner.

"Quick! Shoot another few pictures, like before."

"What are you doing? Look at your face! What's happening?"

"Don't worry about it. Shoot!"

She put down the dishes and came over to him, her eyes filled with both worry and fright.

Wang stuffed the Kodak into the hands of his six-year-old son, who was about to start eating dinner. "Dou Dou, come help Daddy. Push this button. Right, like that. That's one shot. Push it again. That's another shot. Keep on shooting like that. You can take pictures of anything you want."

The boy learned quickly. He was very interested and made rapid shots. Wang turned around and picked up the Leica from the couch, and began to shoot as well. The father and son kept on pressing the shutters as though they were mad. His wife, not knowing what to do as the flashes went off around her, began to cry.

82

"Wang Miao, I know that you've been under a lot of pressure lately, but please, I hope you haven't . . . ?"

Wang finished the roll in the Leica and grabbed the digital from his son. He thought for a moment, and then, in order to avoid his wife, went into the bedroom and took a few more shots with the digital. He used the optical finder instead of the LCD because he was afraid to see the results, though he was going to have to face them soon enough.

Wang took out the film from the Leica and went back into the darkroom. He shut the door and worked. After the film was developed, he examined the images carefully. Because his hands were shaking, he had to hold the magnifying glass with both hands. On the negatives, the countdown continued.

Wang rushed out of the darkroom and began to look through the digital images on the Kodak. On the LCD, he saw that the pictures his son had taken did not have the numbers, but in the pictures that he took, the countdown showed clearly and was synchronized with the numbers on the film.

By using different cameras, Wang was trying to eliminate problems with the camera or the film as possible explanations. But by allowing his son and his wife to take some pictures, he discovered an even stranger result: The countdown only appeared on the pictures he took!

Desperate, Wang picked up the pile of film rolls, like a tangled nest of snakes, like a bunch of ropes tied into an impossible knot.

He knew that he could not solve the mystery on his own. Who could he turn to? His old classmates from college and his colleagues at the Research Center were hopeless. Like him, they were all people with technical minds. Intuitively, he knew that this went beyond a technical problem. He thought of Ding Yi, but that man was now in a spiritual crisis of his own. Finally, he thought of the Frontiers of Science. These were deep thinkers who remained open-minded. So he dialed Shen Yufei's number.

"Dr. Shen, I have a problem. I must see you."

"Come over," Shen said, and hung up.

Wang was surprised. Shen was a woman of few words. Some in the Frontiers of Science jokingly called her the Female Hemingway. But the fact that she didn't even ask him what was wrong made Wang uncertain whether he should be comforted or even more anxious.

He stuffed the mess of film into a bag, and, taking the digital camera, rushed out of the apartment as his wife watched him anxiously. He could have driven, but even with the city being full of lights, he wanted to be with people. He called for a cab.

Shen lived in a luxury housing development reachable by one of the newer commuter rails. Here, the lights were much dimmer. The houses were set around a small artificial lake stocked with fish for the residents, and at night the place felt like a village.

Shen was clearly well off, but Wang could never figure out the source of her wealth. Neither her old research position nor her current job with a private company could earn that much income. But her house didn't show signs of luxury on the inside. It was used as a gathering place for the Frontiers of Science, and Wang always thought it resembled a small library with a meeting room.

In the living room, Wang saw Wei Cheng, Shen's husband. Wei was about forty years old and had the look of a staid, honest intellectual. Wang knew little about him other than his name. Shen hadn't said much when she introduced him. He didn't seem to have a job, since he stayed home all day. He never showed any interest in the Frontiers of Science discussions, but seemed used to the sight of so many scholars coming to their house.

But he wasn't idle. He appeared to be conducting some kind of research at home, always deep in thought. Whenever he met any visitor, he would greet them absentmindedly and then return to his room upstairs. Most of his day was spent there. One time, Wang glanced into his room through the half-open door and saw an astonishing sight: a powerful HP workstation. He was sure of what he saw because the workstation was the same model as the one he used at the Research Center: slate-gray chassis, model RX8620, four years old. It seemed very strange to own a machine costing more than a million yuan just for personal use. What was Wei Cheng doing with it all day?

"Yufei is a bit busy right now. Why don't you wait a while?" Wei Cheng walked upstairs. Wang tried to wait, but he found that he couldn't be still, so he followed Wei Cheng. Wei was about to enter his room with the workstation when he saw Wang behind him, but he didn't seem annoyed. He pointed to the room across from his. "She's in there."

Wang knocked on the door. It wasn't locked, and it opened a crack. Shen was seated in front of a computer, playing a game. He was surprised to see that she wore a V-suit.

The V-suit was a very popular piece of equipment among gamers, made up of a panoramic viewing helmet and a haptic feedback suit. The suit allowed the player to experience the sensations of the game: being struck by a fist, being stabbed by a knife, being burned by flames, and so on. It was also capable of generating feelings of extreme heat and cold, even simulating the sensation of being exposed in a snowstorm.

Wang walked behind her. As the game was displayed only on the inside of the panoramic viewing helmet, there were no colorful images on the computer monitor. Wang suddenly remembered Shi Qiang's comment about memorizing Web and e-mail addresses. He glanced at the monitor. The game site's URL caught his attention: www.3body.net.

Shen took off the helmet and stripped off the haptic feed-back suit. She put on her glasses, which appeared extra large against her thin face. Without any expression, she nodded at Wang and said nothing. Wang took out the mess of film rolls and began to explain his strange experience. Shen paid full attention to his story, picking up the rolls of film and only casually looking at them. This surprised Wang, but further confirmed for him that Shen wasn't completely igno-rant about what he was going through. He almost stopped speaking, but Shen kept on nodding at him, indicating that he should continue.

When he finished, Shen spoke for the first time. "How's the nanomaterial project you're leading proceeding?"

This non sequitur disoriented Wang. "The nanomaterial project? What does that have to do with this?" He pointed at the rolls of film.

Shen didn't answer, but continued to stare at him, waiting for him to answer her question. This was always her style, never wasting a single word.

"Stop your research," she said.

"What?" Wang wasn't sure he heard right. "What are you talking about?"

Shen remained silent.

"Stop? That's a key national project!"

Shen still said nothing, only looking at him calmly.

"You have to give me a reason."

"Just stop. Try it."

"What do you know? Tell me!"

"I've told you all I can."

"I can't stop the project. It's impossible!"

"Just stop. Try it."

That was the end of the conversation about the countdown. After that, no matter how hard Wang tried, Shen only repeated, "Just stop. Try it."

"I understand now," Wang said. "The Frontiers of Science isn't just a discussion group about fundamental theory, like you claimed. Its connection to reality is far more complicated than I had imagined."

"No. It's the opposite. Your impression is due to the fact that the Frontiers of Science concerns matters far more fundamental than you imagine."

Desperate, Wang got up to leave without saying good-bye. Mutely, Shen accompanied him to the door and watched as he got into the taxi.

Just then, another car drove up and braked to a hard stop in front of the door. A man got out. By the faint light leaking from the house, Wang recognized him immediately.

The man was Pan Han, one of the most prominent members of the Frontiers of Science. A biologist, he had successfully predicted the birth defects associated with long-term consumption of genetically modified foods. He had also predicted the ecological disasters that would come with cultivation of genetically modified crops. Unlike the prophets of doom who regularly warned of catastrophes without any particulars, Pan made predictions that always gave many specific details that later turned out to be correct.

His accuracy was such that there were rumors that he came from the future.

The other cause for his fame was that he had created China's first experimental community. Unlike the "return to nature" utopian groups in the West, his "Pastoral China" wasn't located in the wilderness, but in the midst of one of its largest cities. The community had no property of its own. Everything needed for daily life, including food, came from urban trash. Contrary to the predictions of many, Pastoral China not only survived, but thrived. Currently, it had more than three thousand permanent members, and countless others had joined for short stints to experience the lifestyle.

Based on these two successes, Pan's opinions on social issues had grown more and more influential. He believed that technological progress was a disease in human society. The explosive development of technology was analogous to the growth of cancer cells, and the results would be identical: the exhaustion of all sources of nourishment, the destruction of organs, and the final death of the host body. He advocated abolishing crude technologies such as fossil fuels and nuclear energy and keeping gentler technologies such as solar power and small-scale hydroelectric power. He believed in the gradual de-urbanization of modern metropolises by distributing the population more evenly in self-sufficient small towns and villages. Relying on the gentler technologies, he would build a new agricultural society.

"Is he in?" Pan asked Shen, pointing to the house.

Shen didn't answer, but blocked his progress.

"I have to warn him and also warn you. Do not force our hand." Pan's voice was cold.

Shen called to the taxi driver, "You can go now." After the taxi started, Wang couldn't hear any more of the conversation between Shen and Pan, but he glanced back and saw that Shen did not let Pan into the house.

By the time Wang arrived home, it was already after midnight. As Wang got out of the taxi, a black Volkswagen Santana braked to a stop next to him. The window rolled down and a cloud of smoke emerged. Shi Qiang's thick body filled the driver's seat.

"Professor Wang! Academician Wang![14] How've you been the last couple of days?"

"Are you following me? Don't you have anything better to do?"

"Now, don't misunderstand me. I could have just driven past you, but instead, I chose to be polite and stop to greet you. You're making being nice a thankless task." Shi revealed his trademark roguish smirk. "Well? Did you find out any useful information over there?"

"I've told you already, I don't want anything to do with you. Please leave me alone from now on."

"Fine." Shi started the car. "It's not like I'm going to starve without the overtime for doing this. I'd rather not have missed my soccer match."

Wang entered the apartment. His wife was already asleep. He could hear her tossing and turning in bed, mumbling anxiously. Her husband's strange behavior during the day was surely giving her bad dreams. Wang swallowed a few sleeping pills, lay down on the bed, and, after a long wait, fell asleep.

---

14 *Translator's Note:* This refers to Wang's status as a member of the Chinese Academy of Sciences.

His dreams were chaotic, but there was one constant: the ghostly countdown, suspended in midair. Even before he fell asleep, he had known he would dream of it. In his dreams, he attacked the countdown. Crazed, he tore at it, bit it, but every attempt failed to leave a mark. It continued to hang in the middle of his dream, steadily ticking away. Finally, just as the frustration became almost intolerable, he woke up.

Opening his eyes, he saw the ceiling, indistinct above him. The city lights outside the window cast a dim glow against it through the curtains. But one thing did follow him from dream into reality: the countdown. It was still hovering before his eyes. The numbers were thin, but very bright with a burning, white glow.

1180:05:00, 1180:04:59, 1180:04:58, 1180:04:57 . . .

Wang looked around, taking in the blurry shadows around the bedroom. He was now certain that he was awake, but the countdown did not disappear. He shut his eyes, and the countdown remained in the darkness of his vision, looking like mercury flowing against a black swan's feathers. He opened his eyes, rubbed them, and still the countdown did not go away. No matter how he moved his gaze, the numbers stayed at the center of it.

A nameless terror made Wang sit up. The countdown clung to him. He jumped off the bed, tore the curtains apart, and pushed the window open. The city, deep in sleep, was still brightly lit. The countdown hovered before this grand background like subtitles on a movie screen.

Wang felt he was suffocating. He let out a stifled scream. His wife, frightened awake, questioned him anxiously. He tried to force himself to be calm and comforted her, telling her that it was nothing. He lay back on the bed, closed his eyes, and spent the rest of his difficult night under the constant glow of the countdown.

In the morning, he tried to act normal in front of his family, but he could not fool his wife. She asked him whether his eyes were all right, whether he could see clearly.

After breakfast, Wang called the Research Center and asked for the day off. He drove to the hospital. Along the way, the countdown mercilessly hovered in front of the real world. It was able to adjust its brightness so that, no matter what the background, it showed up distinctly. Wang even tried to temporarily overwhelm the display by staring into the rising sun. But it was useless. The infernal numbers turned black and showed up against the orb of the sun like projected shadows, which made them even more frightening.

Tongren Hospital was very busy, but Wang was able to see a famous ophthalmologist who had gone to school with his wife. He asked the doctor to test him, without describing the symptoms. After careful examination of both eyes, the doctor told him they were functioning normally with no signs of any disease.

"There's something stuck in my vision. No matter where I look, it's always there." As Wang said this, the numbers hovered in front of the doctor's face.

1175:11:34, 1175:11:33, 1175:11:32, 1175:11:31 . . .

"Oh, you're talking about floaters." The doctor took out a prescription pad and began to write. "They're common at our age, the result of clouding in the lens. They're not easy to cure, but they're also not a big deal. I'll give you some iodine drops and vitamin D—it's possible that they'll go away, but don't get your hopes up too much. Really, they're nothing to worry about, as they don't affect your vision. You just have to get used to ignoring them."

"Floaters . . . Can you tell me what they look like?"

"There's no real pattern. It differs by person. For some, they appear as tiny black dots; for others, like tadpoles."

"What if someone sees a series of numbers?"

The doctor's pen stopped. "You see numbers?"

"Yes, right in the middle of the visual field."

The doctor pushed his pen and paper away, and looked at him sympathetically. "As soon as you came in, I could tell you'd been working too much. At the last class reunion, Li Yao told me you were under a lot of pressure at work. We have to be careful at our age. Our health is no longer what it used to be."

"You are saying this is due to psychological factors?"

The doctor nodded. "If it was anyone else, I'd suggest you go see a psychiatrist. But it's nothing serious, just exhaustion. Why don't you rest for a few days? Take a vacation. Go be with Yao and your kid—what's his name . . . Dou Dou, right? No worries. They'll go away soon."

1175:10:02, 1175:10:01, 1175:10:00, 1175:09:59 . . .

"Let me tell you what I see. It's a countdown! One second after another, it keeps on ticking precisely. Are you saying this is all in my head?"

The doctor gave him a tolerant smile. "You know how much the mind can affect vision? Last month we had a patient—a girl, maybe fifteen, sixteen. She was in class when she suddenly lost the ability to see, went completely blind. But all the tests showed that there was nothing wrong with her eyes physiologically. Finally, someone from the Department of Psychiatry treated her with psychotherapy for a month. All of a sudden, her vision returned."

Wang knew that he was wasting his time here. He got up. "All right, let's not talk about my eyes anymore. I have one last question: Do you know of any physical phenomenon that can operate from a distance and make people see visions?"

The doctor gave this some thought. "Yes, I do. A while ago I was part of the medical team for the Shenzhou 19 spacecraft. Some taikonauts engaged in extravehicular activities reported seeing flashes that didn't exist. The astronauts on the International Space Station reported similar experiences. It was because during periods of intense solar activity, high-energy particles struck against the retina, causing them to see flashes. But you're talking about numbers—a countdown, even. Solar activity can't possibly cause that."

Wang walked out of the hospital in a daze. The countdown continued to hover in his eyes, and he seemed to be following the numbers, following a ghost that would not leave him. He bought a pair of sunglasses and put them on so that others would not see his eyes wandering around as though he were sleepwalking.

Before entering the main lab at the Nanotechnology Research Center, Wang took off his sunglasses. Even so, his colleagues noticed his apparent mental state and gave him concerned looks.

Wang saw that the main reaction chamber in the middle of the lab was still in operation. The main compartment of the gigantic apparatus was a sphere with many pipes connected to it.

They had made small quantities of a new, ultrastrong nanomaterial that they'd given the code name "Flying Blade." But the samples so far were all made with molecular construction techniques—that is, using a nanoscale molecular probe to stack the molecules one by one, like laying out bricks for a wall. This method was very resource-intensive, and the results might as well have been the world's most precious jewels. It was impractical to produce large quantities this way.

At the moment, the lab was attempting to develop a catalytic reaction as a substitute for molecular construction so that large numbers of molecules would stack themselves into the right arrangement. The main reaction chamber could rapidly run through a large number of reactions using different molecular combinations. There were so many combinations that normal manual testing methods would have taken more than a hundred years. In addition, the apparatus augmented actual reactions with mathematical simulations. When the reaction reached a certain stage, the computer would build a mathematical model of it based on intermediate products and finish the remainder of the reaction via simulation. This greatly boosted the experimental efficiency.

When the lab director saw Wang, he hurried over and began to report a series of malfunctions with the main reaction chamber—a recent ritual whenever Wang arrived at work. By now the main reaction chamber had been in continuous operation for more than a year, and many sensors had lost sensitivity, resulting in measurement errors that required shutting down the apparatus for maintenance. But as the lead scientist on the project, Wang insisted that the machine would not be shut down until the third set of molecular combinations was finished. The technicians had no choice but to jury-rig more and more kludges onto the main reaction chamber to compensate. And now those kludges required their own kludges, a state of affairs that exhausted the project staff.

But the lab director carefully avoided the topic of shutting down the machine and temporarily halting the experiment, as he knew that such discussions tended to enrage Wang Miao. He just laid out the difficulties before Wang, though his unspoken desire was clear.

Engineers rushed around the main reaction chamber like doctors around a critical patient, trying to keep it going for a little longer. In front of the whole scene, the countdown appeared.

1174:21:11, 1174:21:10, 1174:21:09, 1174:21:08 . . .
Just stop. Try it. Shen's words came to Wang.

"How long would it take to completely overhaul the sensors?" Wang asked.

"Four or five days." Now that the lab director saw a ray of hope, he quickly added, "If we work fast, it will take only three days. I guarantee it, Chief Wang!"

I'm not giving in, Wang thought. *The equipment really needs maintenance, so the experiment must be temporarily stopped. This has nothing to do with anything else.* He turned to the lab director and focused on him through the hovering countdown. "Shut down the experiment and perform the maintenance. Follow the schedule you gave me."

"Absolutely, Chief Wang. I'll give you an updated schedule right away. We can stop the reaction this afternoon!"

"You can stop it right now."

The lab director stared at him in disbelief, but soon he was excited again, as if afraid to lose this opportunity. He picked up the phone and issued the order to stop the reaction. All the exhausted researchers and technicians grew excited, too. They immediately began the procedures to shut down the main reaction chamber, flipping a hundred complex switches. The various control screens became dark one after another, until finally, the main screen reflected the main reaction chamber's halted status.

Almost simultaneously, the countdown before Wang's eyes also stopped. The final number was *1174:10:07*. A few seconds later, the numbers flickered and disappeared.

As the world reemerged, free of the ghostly numbers, Wang let out a long breath, as though he had just struggled up from underwater. He sat down, drained, and realized that others were still watching him.

He turned to the lab director. "System maintenance is the responsibility of the Equipment Division. Why don't all of you in the research group take a break for a few days? I know everyone's been working hard."

"Chief Wang, you're tired, too. Chief Engineer Zhang can take care of things here. Why don't you go home and rest as well?"

"Yes, I *am* tired," Wang said.

After the lab director left, he picked up the phone and dialed Shen Yufei's number. She picked up after one ring.

"Who or what is behind this?" Wang asked. He tried to make his voice calm, but failed.

Silence.

"What will happen at the end of the countdown?"

More silence.

"Are you listening?"

"Yes."

"Why nanomaterials? This is not a particle accelerator. It's just applied research. Is it worth your attention?"

"Whether something is worth the attention is not for us to decide."

"That's enough!" Wang shouted into the phone. The terror and desperation of the last few days suddenly turned into uncontrollable rage. "Do you think these cheap tricks can fool me? Can stop technological progress? I admit that

96

I can't, for now, explain how you're doing it. But that's only because I haven't been able to peek behind the curtain of your shameful illusionist."

"You're saying you want to see the countdown on an even greater scale?"

Shen's question stunned Wang for a moment. He forced himself to be calm so he wouldn't fall into a trap. "Put away your set of tricks. So what if you show it at a bigger scale? It's still only an illusion. You can project a hologram into the sky, like what NATO did during the last war. With a powerful enough laser you can project an image onto the surface of the moon! The shooter and the farmer should be able to manipulate matters at a scale that humans cannot. For example, can you make the countdown appear on the surface of the sun?" Wang's mouth hung open. He had shocked himself with his own words. Unconsciously, he had named the two hypotheses that he ought to have avoided. He felt on the verge of falling into the same mental trap that had claimed the other victims.

Trying to seize the initiative, he continued, "I can't anticipate all your tricks, but even with the sun, perhaps your despicable illusionist can still somehow make the deception seem real. To give a demonstration that will really be convincing, you have to display it at an even larger scale."

"The question is whether you can take it," Shen said. "We're friends. I want to help you *avoid* Yang Dong's fate."

The mention of Yang's name made Wang shudder. But another surge of anger made him reckless. "Will you take up my challenge?"

"Of course."

"What are you going to do?"

"Do you have a computer connected to the Internet?

Okay, enter the following Web address: http://www.qsl.net/ bg3tt/zl/mesdm.htm. You got it open? Now, print it out and keep it with you."

Wang saw that the page was nothing more than a Morse code chart.

"I don't understand. This—"

"During the next two days, please find a place where you can observe the cosmic microwave background. For specifics, please check the e-mail I'll send you."

"What . . . are you going to do?"

"I know that your nanomaterial project has been stopped. Do you plan on restarting it?"

"Of course. Three days from now."

"Then the countdown will continue."

"At what scale will I see it?"

A long silence followed. This woman, who was acting as the spokesperson for some force beyond human understanding, blocked every exit Wang had.

"Three days from now—that's the fourteenth—between one and five in the morning, the entire universe will flicker for you."

7

Three Body: King Wen of Zhou and the Long Night

Wang dialed Ding Yi's number. Only when Ding picked up did he realize that it was already one in the morning.

"This is Wang Miao. I'm sorry to be calling so late."

"No problem. I can't sleep anyway."

"I have . . . seen something, and I'd like your help. Do you know if there are any facilities in China that are observing the cosmic microwave background?" Wang had the urge to talk to someone about what was going on, but he thought it best to not let too many people know about the countdown that only he could see.

"The cosmic microwave background? What made you interested in that? I guess you really have run into some problems. . . . Have you been to see Yang Dong's mother yet?"

"Ah—I'm sorry. I forgot."

"No worries. Right now, many scientists have . . . seen something, like you. Everyone's distracted. But I think it's still best if you go visit her. She's getting on in years, and she won't hire a caretaker. If there's some task around the home that she needs help with, please help her . . . . Oh, right, the cosmic microwave background. You can ask Yang's mother.

Before she retired, she was an astrophysicist. She's very familiar with such facilities in China."

"Good! I'll go after work today."

"Then I'll thank you in advance. I really can't face anything that reminds me of Yang Dong again."

After hanging up, Wang sat in front of his computer and printed out the simple Morse code chart. By now he was calm enough to turn his thoughts away from the countdown. He pondered the Frontiers of Science, Shen Yufei, and the computer game she had been playing. The only thing he knew for certain about Shen was that she wasn't the type to enjoy computer games. She spoke like a telegraph and gave him the impression that she was always extremely cold. It wasn't the kind of coldness that some people put on like a mask—hers suffused her all the way through.

Wang subconsciously thought of her as the long-obsolete DOS operating system: a blank, black screen, a bare "C:\>" prompt, a blinking cursor. Whatever you entered, it echoed back. Not one extra letter and not a single change. But now he knew that behind the "C:\>" was a bottomless abyss.

She's actually interested in a game? A game that requires a V-suit? She has no kids, which means she bought the V-suit for herself. The very idea is preposterous.

Wang entered the address for the game into the browser. It had been easy to memorize: www.3body.net. The site indicated that the game only supported access via V-suit. Wang remembered that the employee lounge at the Nanotechnology Research Center had a V-suit. He left the now-empty main lab and went to the security office to get the key. In the lounge, he passed the pool tables and the exercise machines and found the V-suit next to a computer. He struggled into the haptic feedback suit, put on the panoramic viewing helmet, and turned on the computer.

After entering the game, Wang found himself in the middle of a desolate plain at dawn. The plain was dun-colored, blurry, its details hard to make out. In the distance, there was a sliver of white light on the horizon. Twinkling stars covered the rest of the sky.

There was a loud explosion, and two red-glowing mountains crashed against the earth in the distance. The whole plain was bathed in red light. When the dust finally cleared from the sky, Wang saw two giant words erected between the sky and the earth: THREE BODY.

Next came a registration screen. Wang created the ID "Hairen," and logged in.[15]

The plain remained desolate, but now the compressors in the V-suit whirred to life, and Wang could feel gusts of cold air against his body. Before him appeared two walking figures, forming dark silhouettes against the dawn light. Wang ran after them.

He saw that both figures were male. They were dressed in long robes full of holes, covered by dirty animal hides. Each carried a short, wide bronze sword. One of them carried a narrow wooden trunk that was as long as half his height. He turned around to look at Wang. The man's face was as dirty and wrinkled as the hide he wore, but his eyes were sharp and lively, the pupils glinting in the early-morning glow.

---

15 *Translator's Note: Hairen* (海人) means "Man of the Sea." This is a play on Wang Miao's name (汪淼), which can be read to mean "sea."

"It's cold," he said.

"Yes, very cold."

"This is the Warring States Period," the man with the trunk on his back said. "I am King Wen of Zhou."

"I don't think King Wen belongs to the Warring States Period," Wang said.[16]

"He's survived until now," the other man said. "King Zhou of Shang is alive, too. I am a follower of King Wen. Indeed, that's my log-in ID: 'Follower of King Wen of Zhou.' He's a genius, you know?"[17]

"My log-in ID is 'Hairen.' What are you carrying on your back?"

King Wen put down the rectangular trunk and stood it up vertically. He opened one of the sides like a door and revealed five compartments within. By the faint light, Wang could see that every layer held a small mound of sand. Every compartment seemed to have sand falling into it from the compartment above, through a small hole.

"A type of sandglass. Every eight hours all the sand flows to the bottom. Flip it three times and you can measure a day. But often I forget to flip it, and I need Follower here to remind me."

"You seem to be on a very long journey. Is it necessary to carry such a bulky clock?"

"How else would we measure time?"

"A portable sundial would be much more convenient. Or else you could just look at the sun and know the approximate time."

---

16 *Translator's Note:* The Warring States Period lasted from 475 BC to 221 BC. But King Wen of Zhou reigned much earlier, from 1099 BC to 1050 BC. He is considered the founder of the Zhou Dynasty, which overthrew the corrupt Shang Dynasty.

17 *Translator's Note:* King Zhou of Shang reigned from 1075 BC to 1046 BC. The last king of the Shang Dynasty, he was a notorious tyrant in Chinese history.

King Wen and Follower stared at each other, and then turned as one to gaze at Wang, as though he was an idiot. "The sun? How can the sun tell us the time? We're in the midst of a Chaotic Era."

Wang was about to ask for the meaning of the strange term when Follower cried out piteously, "It's so cold! I'm going to die of the cold!"

Wang felt very cold as well. But in most games, taking off his V-suit would immediately cause his ID to be deleted by the system. He couldn't do that. He said, "When the sun comes out it will be warmer."

"Are you pretending to be some kind of oracle? Even King Wen cannot predict the future." Follower shook his head contemptuously.

"What does what I said have to do with predicting the future? Everyone can see that the sun will rise in about another hour or two." Wang pointed to the sliver of light above the horizon.

"This is a Chaotic Era!"

"What is a Chaotic Era?"

"Other than Stable Eras, all times are Chaotic Eras." King Wen answered the way he would have spoken to an ignorant child.

Indeed, the light over the horizon dimmed and soon disappeared. Night covered everything. The stars overhead shone even more brightly.

"So that was dusk instead of dawn?" Wang asked.

"It is morning. But the sun doesn't always rise in the morning. That's what a Chaotic Era is like."

Wang found the cold hard to take. "It looks like the sun won't rise for a long time." He shivered and pointed to the blurry horizon.

"What makes you think that? There's no way to be certain. I told you, this is a Chaotic Era." Follower turned to King Wen. "May I have some dried fish?"

"Absolutely not." King Wen's tone brooked no disagreement. "I barely have enough for myself. We must guarantee that *I* make it to Zhao Ge, not you."[18]

As they spoke, Wang noticed the sky brightening over another part of the horizon. He couldn't be sure of the compass directions, but he was sure the direction this time was different from last time. The sky grew brighter, and soon, the sun of this world rose. It was small and bluish in color, like a very bright moon. Wang still felt a bit of warmth, and could now see the landscape around him more clearly. But the day didn't last long. The sun traversed a shallow arc over the horizon and soon set. Night and the bone-chilling cold once more settled over everything.

The three travelers stopped in front of a dead tree. King Wen and Follower took out their bronze swords to chop the tree into firewood, and Wang gathered the firewood into a pile. Follower took out a piece of flint and struck it against a blade until the sparks caught. The fire soon warmed the front of Wang's V-suit, but his back remained cold.

"We should burn some of the dehydrated bodies," Follower said. "Then we'll have a roaring fire!"

"Put that thought out of your mind. Only the tyrant King Zhou would engage in that kind of behavior."

"We've seen so many dehydrated bodies scattered along the road here. They've been torn, and won't be revivable even when rehydrated. If your theory really works, what does it matter if we burn a few of them? We can even eat

---

18 *Translator's Note:* Zhao Ge was the capital of Shang China, where King Zhou held court.

some. How can a few lives compare to the importance of your theory?"

"Stop with that nonsense! We're scholars!"

After the fire burnt out, the three continued their journey. Since they were not speaking to each other much, the system sped up the passage of in-game time. King Wen flipped the sandglass on his back six times rapidly, indicating the lapse of two days. The sun never rose once, not even a hint of dawn over the horizon.

"It seems that the sun will never rise again," Wang said. He brought up the game menu to take a look at his health bar. Due to the extreme cold, it was steadily decreasing.

"Again, you're pretending you're some kind of oracle," Follower said. But this time he and Wang finished the thought together. "This is a Chaotic Era!"

Soon after this, however, dawn did appear over the horizon. The sky brightened rapidly, and the sun rose. Wang noticed that this time, the sun was gigantic. After just half of it rose, it took up at least one-fifth of the visible horizon. Waves of heat bathed them, and Wang felt refreshed. But when he glanced over at King Wen and Follower, he saw that both had terror on their faces as though they had seen a demon.

"Quick! Find shade!" Follower shouted. Wang ran after them. They ducked behind a large rock. The shadow cast by the rock gradually grew shorter and shorter. The earth around them glowed as though on fire. The permafrost beneath them soon melted, the steel-like hard surface turning into a sea of mud, roiled by waves of heat. Wang sweated profusely.

When the sun was directly overhead, the three covered their heads with the animal hides, but the bright light still shot through the holes and gaps like arrows. The three shifted around the rock until they were able to hide inside the new shadow that had just appeared on the other side.

After the sun set, the air remained hot and damp. The three sweat-drenched travelers sat on the rock. Follower spoke with dismay. "Traveling during a Chaotic Era is like walking through hell. I can't stand it anymore. Also, I haven't had anything to eat because you won't give me any dried fish and you won't let me eat the dehydrated bodies. What—"

"The only choice is to dehydrate you," King Wen said, fanning himself with a piece of hide.

"You won't abandon me afterwards, will you?"

"Of course not. I promise to bring you to Zhao Ge."

Follower stripped off his sweat-soaked robe and lay down nude on the muddy earth. In the last glow from the sun, already below the horizon, Wang saw water oozing out of Follower's body. He knew that it was no longer sweat. All the water in his body was being discharged and squeezed out. The water coalesced into a few small rivulets in the mud. His body turned soft and lost its shape like a melting candle.

Ten minutes later, all the water had been eliminated from his body. Follower was now a man-shaped piece of leather stretched out on the ground. His facial features had flattened and become indistinct.

"Is he dead?" Wang asked. He remembered seeing such man-shaped pieces of hide scattered along the road. Some were torn and incomplete. He supposed they were the dehydrated bodies Follower spoke of earlier as potential kindling.

"No," King Wen answered. He picked up Follower's skin, brushed the mud and dust off, laid him out on the rock, and rolled him up like a balloon with its air let out. "He'll recover soon enough, when we soak him in water. It's just like soaking dried mushrooms."

"Even his bones have turned soft?"

"Yes. His skeleton has turned into dried fibers. This makes him easy to carry."

"In this world, can everyone be dehydrated and rehydrated?"

"Of course. You can, too. Otherwise we could not survive the Chaotic Eras." King Wen handed the rolled-up Follower to Wang. "Carry him. If you abandon him on the road, he'll be burned or eaten."

Wang accepted the skin, a light roll. He held it under his arm, and it didn't feel too strange.

With Wang carrying the dehydrated Follower and King Wen carrying the sandglass, the two continued their arduous journey. Like the previous few days, the progress of the sun in this world followed no pattern. After a long, frigid night lasting several days' worth of time, a brief but scorching day might follow, and vice versa. The two relied on each other for survival. They lit fires to hold off the cold, and ducked into lakes to avoid the heat.

At least the game sped up the progress of time. A month in game time might pass in half an hour. This made the journey through the Chaotic Era at least tolerable for Wang.

One day, after a long night that lasted almost a week (as measured by the sandglass), King Wen suddenly shouted joyously as he pointed to the night sky.

"Flying stars! Two flying stars!"

Actually, Wang had already noticed the strange celestial bodies. They were bigger than stars, and showed up as disks about the size of ping-pong balls. They moved through the sky at a pace quick enough for the naked eye to detect the motion. But it was the first time two of them had appeared together.

King Wen explained, "When two flying stars appear, it means a Stable Era is about to begin."

"We've seen flying stars before."

"Yes, but only one at a time."

"Is two the most we'll see at once?"

"No. Sometimes three will appear, but no more than that."

"If three flying stars appear, does that herald an even better era?"

King Wen gave Wang a frightened look. "What are you talking about? Three flying stars . . . pray that such a thing never happens."

King Wen turned out to be right. The yearned-for Stable Era soon began. Sunrise and sunset began to follow a pattern. A day-night cycle began to stabilize around eighteen hours. The orderly alternation of day and night made the weather warm and mild.

"How long does a Stable Era last?" Wang asked.

"As short as a day or as long as a century. No one can predict how long one will last." King Wen sat on the sandglass, lifting his head to gaze at the noonday sun. "According to historical records, the Western Zhou Dynasty experienced a Stable Era lasting two centuries. How lucky to be born during such a time!"

"Then how long does a Chaotic Era last?"

"I already told you. Other than Stable Eras, all other times belong to Chaotic Eras. Each of them takes up the time not occupied by the other."

"So, this is a world in which there are no patterns?"

"Yes. Civilization can only develop in the mild climate of Stable Eras. Most of the time, humankind must collectively dehydrate and be stored. When a long Stable Era arrives, they collectively revive through rehydration. Then they proceed to build and produce."

"How can you predict the arrival and duration of each Stable Era?"

"Such a thing has never been done. When a Stable Era arrives, the king makes a decision based on intuition as to whether to engage in mass rehydration. Often, the people are revived, crops are planted, cities begin construction, life has just started—and then the Stable Era ends. Extreme cold and heat then destroy everything." King Wen now pointed at Wang, his eyes sparkling. "Now you know the goal of this game: to use our intellect and understanding to analyze all phenomena until we can know the pattern of the sun's movement. The survival of civilization depends on it."

"Based on my observations, there is no pattern to the sun's movement at all."

"That's because you do not understand the fundamental nature of the world."

"And you do?"

"Yes. This is why I'm going to Zhao Ge. I will present King Zhou with an accurate calendar."

"But I've seen no evidence on this trip that you can do such a thing."

"Predicting the sun's motion is only possible in Zhao Ge, for that is where yin and yang meet. Only the lots cast there are accurate."

The two continued on through the harsh conditions of another Chaotic Era, interrupted briefly by a short Stable Era, until they finally arrived in Zhao Ge.

Wang heard an unceasing roar that sounded like thunder. The sound was generated by the numerous giant pendulums that could be seen all over Zhao Ge, each tens of meters in height. The weight of each pendulum was a giant rock, suspended from a thick rope tied to a bridge that stretched between the tops of two slender stone towers.

All the pendulums were swinging as groups of soldiers in armor kept them in motion. Chanting incomprehensibly, they rhythmically pulled ropes attached to the giant stone weights, adding to the pendulums' arcs as they slowed. Wang noticed that all the pendulums swung in step. From far away, the sight was awe-inducing: It was as though numerous giant clocks had been erected over the earth, or colossal, abstract symbols had fallen from the sky.

The giant pendulums surrounded an even more enormous pyramid, standing like a tall mountain in the dark night. This was King Zhou's palace. Wang followed King Wen into a low door at the base of the pyramid, before which a few soldiers patrolled in the darkness, noiseless as ghosts. The door led to a long, narrow, dark tunnel going deep into the pyramid, with a few torches along the way.

As they walked, King Wen spoke to Wang. "During a Chaotic Era, the entire country is dehydrated. But King Zhou remains awake, a companion to the lifeless land. In order to survive during a Chaotic Era, one must live in thick-walled buildings like this one, as though one were living underground. It's the only way to avoid the extreme heat and cold."

After a long time in the tunnel, they finally arrived at the Great Hall at the center of the pyramid. Actually, the hall was not that big and reminded Wang of a cave. The man sitting on a dais and draped with a particolored hide was undoubtedly King Zhou. But what drew Wang's attention was a man dressed all in black. The black robe blended with the thick shadows in the Great Hall, and the pale white face seemed to float in air.

"This is Fu Xi."[19] King Zhou introduced the man in black to Wang and King Wen. He spoke as though Wang and King Wen had always been there, while the man in black was the newcomer. "He thinks that the sun is a temperamental god. When the god is awake, his moods are unpredictable, and thus we have a Chaotic Era. But when he's asleep, his breathing evens out, and thus we have a Stable Era. Fu Xi suggested that I build those pendulums you see out there and keep them in constant motion. He claims that the pendulums can have a hypnotic effect on the sun god and cause him to sink into a long slumber. But we can all see that so far, the sun god remains awake, though from time to time he seems to nap briefly."

King Zhou waved his hands, and servants brought over a clay pot and set it down on the small stone table before Fu Xi. Later, Wang found out that it was a pot of seasoned broth. Fu Xi sighed, lifted the pot, and drank in great gulps, the sound of his swallows echoing like the beating of a giant heart in the darkness. After he was halfway done with the contents, he poured the rest over his body. Then he threw down the pot and walked toward a large bronze cauldron suspended over a fire in the corner of the Great Hall. He climbed onto the edge of the cauldron and jumped in, stirring up a cloud of vapor.

"Ji Chang, sit down,"[20] King Zhou said. "We'll eat in just a little while." He pointed to the cauldron.

"Foolish witchcraft," King Wen said, glancing contemptuously at the cauldron.

"What have you learned about the sun?" King Zhou asked. Firelight flickered in his eyes.

---

19 *Translator's Note:* Fu Xi is the first of the Three Sovereigns, a Chinese mythological figure. He was one of the progenitors of the human race along with the goddess Nüwa.

20 *Translator's Note:* Ji Chang is King Wen's given name.

"The sun is not a god. The sun is yang, and the night is yin. The world proceeds on the balance between yin and yang. Though we cannot control the process, we can predict it." King Wen took out his bronze sword and drew a yin-yang symbol on the floor, dimly lit by the fire. Then, he carved the sixty-four hexagrams of the *I Ching* around the symbol, the whole composition resembling a calendar wheel. "My king, this is the code of the universe. With it, I can present your dynasty with an accurate calendar."

"Ji Chang, I need to know when the next long Stable Era will come."

"I will forecast it for you right now," King Wen said. He sat down in the middle of the yin-yang symbol, his legs curled under him. He raised his head to look up at the ceiling of the Great Hall, his gaze seeming to penetrate the thick stones of the pyramid, until it reached the stars. The fingers of his two hands began a series of rapid, complex movements, like components of a calculating machine. In the silence, only the soup in the cauldron in the corner made any noise, boiling and bubbling as though the shaman being cooked within was dream-talking in his sleep.

King Wen stood up in the middle of the yin-yang symbol. With his face still lifted to the ceiling, he said, "Next will be a Chaotic Era lasting forty-one days. Then comes a five-day Stable Era. Thereafter, there will be a twenty-three-day Chaotic Era followed by an eighteen-day Stable Era. Then we'll have an eight-day Chaotic Era. But when this Chaotic Era is over, my king, the long Stable Era you've been waiting for will begin. That Stable Era will last three years and nine months. The climate will be so mild that it will be a golden age."

"We have to verify your initial predictions first," King Zhou said, his face expressionless.

Wang heard a loud rumbling from above. A stone slab in the ceiling of the Great Hall slid open, revealing a square opening. Wang shifted his position and saw that the opening led to another tunnel going up through the center of the pyramid. At the end of the tunnel he could see a few twinkling stars.

Game time sped up. Every few seconds in real time, two soldiers flipped over the sandglass brought by King Wen, indicating the passing of eight hours in game time. The opening through the ceiling flickered with random lights, and once in a while a ray of sunlight from the Chaotic Era shot into the Great Hall. Sometimes the light was weak, like moonlight. Sometimes the light was very strong, and the incandescent white square cast against the ground glowed so brightly that the torches in the Great Hall paled in comparison.

Wang continued to count the flipping of the sandglass. By the time it had been flipped 120 times or so, the appearance of the sunlight through the square opening became regular. The first of the predicted Stable Eras had arrived.

After fifteen more flips of the sandglass, the flickering light through the opening became patternless again, the start of another Chaotic Era. Another Stable Era followed, and another Chaotic Era. The starting times and durations of the various eras were not exactly as King Wen had predicted, but they were close. After the conclusion of yet another eight-day Chaotic Era, the long Stable Era he predicted began.

Wang kept counting the flips of the sandglass. Twenty days passed, and the sunlight falling into the Great Hall maintained the precise rhythm. Game time slowed down to normal.

King Zhou nodded at King Wen. "I shall erect a monument for you, one even greater than this palace."

King Wen bowed deeply. "My king, awaken your dynasty and let it prosper!"

113

King Zhou stood up on the dais and opened his arms, as though he wanted to embrace the whole world. In a strange, otherworldly voice, he began to chant, "Re-hy-drate . . ."

As soon as the order was given, everyone in the Great Hall rushed to the door. Wang followed King Wen closely, and they exited the pyramid through the long tunnel they'd entered by. When they emerged, Wang saw the noonday sun bathing the land in warmth. In a passing breeze he seemed to smell the fragrances of spring. Together, King Wen and Wang walked to a nearby lake. The ice over the lake had melted, and sunlight danced between the gentle waves.

A column of soldiers shouted, "Rehydrate! Rehydrate!" as they ran toward a large stone building, shaped like a granary, next to the lake. On the road to Zhao Ge, Wang had seen many buildings like it, and King Wen had told him that these buildings were called dehydratories, warehouses where the dehydrated bodies could be stored. The soldiers opened the heavy stone doors of the dehydratory and carried out rolls of dusty skins. Each soldier walked to the lakeshore, and tossed them into the water. As soon as the skins touched the water, they began to unfurl and stretch out. Soon, the lake was covered by a layer of man-shaped floating skins, each rapidly absorbing the water and expanding. Gradually, all the man-shaped skin cutouts became fleshy bodies that gradually began to display signs of life. One by one, they struggled up out of the waist-deep water and stood up. Looking around at the sunny world with wide-open eyes, they appeared to have just awoken from a dream.

"Rehydrate!" one man cried out.

"Rehydrate! Rehydrate!" Other voices joyously echoed his.

Everyone climbed out of the lake and ran naked toward the dehydratory. They carried out more skins and tossed them into the water, and even more of the revived climbed out of the lake. The same scene repeated itself around every lake and pool. The entire world was coming back to life.

"Oh, heavens! My finger!"

Wang saw a man who had just been revived standing in the middle of the lake, holding up one hand and crying. The hand was missing its middle finger, and blood flowed from the wound into the water. Others, who had also just been revived, passed by him as they happily waded ashore, ignoring him.

"Count yourself lucky," one of them said to the man. "Some lost a whole arm or leg. Others had their heads chewed through by rats. If we hadn't been rehydrated in time, maybe all of us would have been eaten by the Chaotic Era rats."

"How long have we been dehydrated?" one of the revived asked.

"You can tell by looking at the thickness of the dust covering the palace. I just heard that the king is no longer the king from before. But I don't know if he's the old king's son or grandson."

It took eight days to complete the work of rehydration. All of the stored dehydrated bodies had been revived, and the world was given a new life. During these eight days, everyone enjoyed regular cycles of sunset and sunrise, each cycle precisely twenty hours long. Enjoying the springlike climate, everyone gave heartfelt praise to the sun and the gods who guided the world.

On the night of the eighth day, the bonfires scattered over the ground seemed even more numerous and denser than the stars in the sky. The ruins of cities and towns abandoned during the Chaotic Eras once again filled with noise and light. Like every mass rehydration in the past, the people were going to celebrate all night to welcome their new life after the next sunrise.

But the sun did not rise again.

Every kind of timepiece indicated that the time for sunrise had passed, but the horizon remained dark in every direction. Ten hours later, there was still no sign of the sun, not even the slightest hint of dawn. The endless night lasted through a whole day, then two days. Coldness now pressed toward the earth like a giant hand.

Inside the pyramid, King Wen knelt before King Zhou, pleading, "My king, please continue to have faith in me. This is but temporary. I have seen the yang of the universe gathering, and the sun will rise soon. The Stable Era and spring will continue!"

"Let's begin to heat the cauldron," King Zhou said, and sighed.

"Oh, King!" A minister stumbled through the cavelike entrance into the Great Hall. "There . . . there are three flying stars in the sky!"

Those in the Great Hall were stunned. The air seemed frozen. Only King Zhou remained impassive. He turned to Wang, to whom he had never deigned to speak before. "You still don't understand what the appearance of three flying stars means, do you? Ji Chang, why don't you tell him?"

"It indicates the arrival of a long period of extreme cold, cold enough to turn stone into dust." King Wen sighed.

"De-hy-drate . . ." King Zhou again chanted in that strange, otherworldly voice. Outside, people had already begun the process. They turned themselves back into dehydrated bodies to survive the long night that was coming. The lucky ones had time to be stacked in the dehydratories, but many were abandoned in the empty fields.

King Wen stood up slowly and walked toward the caul-dron over the roaring fire in the corner of the Great Hall. He climbed up the side and paused for a few seconds before jumping in. Perhaps he had seen the thoroughly cooked face of Fu Xi laughing at him from the soup.

"Keep the fire low," King Zhou ordered, his voice weak. Then he turned to the others. "You may exit if you wish. The game is no longer fun after it gets to this point."

A red EXIT sign showed up above the Great Hall's cavelike entrance. Players in the Great Hall streamed toward it, and Wang followed the crowd. Through the long tunnel, they finally emerged outside the pyramid. Heavy snow falling through the night air greeted them. The bone-chilling cold caused Wang to shiver, and a display in a corner of the sky indicated that game time had sped up again.

The snow continued without pause for ten days. By now the snowflakes were large and heavy, like pieces of solidified darkness. Someone whispered next to Wang, "The snow is now composed of frozen carbon dioxide, dry ice." Wang turned around and saw that the speaker was Follower.

After another ten days, the snowflakes turned thin and translucent. By the weak light from a few torches within the entrance to the long tunnel, the snowflakes gave off a faint blue glow, like pieces of dancing mica.

"Those snowflakes are now composed of solidified oxy-gen and nitrogen. The atmosphere is disappearing through deposition, which means it's near absolute zero above."

Snow gradually buried the pyramid. The lowest layers were composed of water snow, then dry ice, and finally, on top, snow made of oxygen and nitrogen. The night sky became especially clear, and the stars glowed like a field of silver bon-fires. A line of text appeared against the starry background:

The long night lasted forty-eight years. Civilization Number 137 was destroyed by the extreme cold. This civilization had advanced to the Warring States Period before succumbing.

The seed of civilization remains. It will germinate and again pro-gress through the unpredictable world of *Three Body*. We invite you to log on in the future.

Before exiting the game, Wang noticed the three flying stars in the sky. Revolving closely around each other, they seemed to perform a strange dance against the abyss of space.

8

Ye Wenjie

Wang took off the V-suit and panoramic viewing helmet. His shirt was soaked with sweat, as if he had just awoken from a nightmare. He left the Research Center, got into his car, and drove to the address given to him by Ding Yi: the house of Yang Dong's mother.

Chaotic Era, Chaotic Era, Chaotic Era . . .

The thought turned and turned in Wang's head. *Why would the path of the sun through the world of* Three Body *be devoid of regularity and pattern? Whether a planet's orbit is more circular or more elliptical, its motion around its sun must be periodic. Total irregularity in planetary motion is impossible. . . .*

Wang grew angry with himself. He shook his head, trying to chase away these thoughts. *It's only a game!*

But I lost.

Chaotic Era, Chaotic Era, Chaotic Era . . .

Damn it! Stop! Why am I thinking about this? Why?

Soon, Wang found the answer. He had not played any computer games for years, and the hardware for gaming had clearly advanced greatly in the interim. The virtual reality and multisensory feedback were all effects he had not experienced as a young student. But Wang also knew that the sense of realism in Three Body wasn't due to the interface technology.

He remembered taking a class in information theory as a third-year student in college. The professor had put up two pictures: One was the famous Song Dynasty painting *Along the River During the Qingming Festival,* full of fine, rich details; the other was a photograph of the sky on a sunny day, the deep blue expanse broken only by a wisp of cloud that one couldn't even be sure was there. The professor asked the class which picture contained more information. The answer was that the photograph's information content—its entropy— exceeded the painting's by one or two orders of magnitude.

Three Body was the same. Its enormous information content was hidden deep. Wang could feel it, but he could not articulate it. He suddenly understood that the makers of *Three Body* took the exact opposite of the approach taken by designers of other games. Normally, game designers tried to display as much information as possible to increase the sense of realism. But *Three Body*'s designers worked to compress the information content to disguise a more complex reality, just like that seemingly empty photograph of the sky.

Wang let his mind wander back to the world of *Three Body*.

Flying stars! The key must be in the flying stars. One flying star, two flying stars, three flying stars . . . what did they mean?

As he had that thought, he found himself at his destination.

At the foot of the apartment building, Wang saw a graying, thin woman, about sixty years old. She wore glasses and was struggling to go up the stairs with a basket of groceries. He guessed that this was the woman he had come to see.

A quick greeting confirmed his guess. She was Yang Dong's mother, Ye Wenjie. After hearing the purpose of Wang Miao's visit, she was grateful and appreciative. Wang was familiar with old intellectuals like her: The long years had ground away all the hardness and fierceness in their personalities, until all that was left was a gentleness like that of water.

Wang carried the grocery basket up the stairs for her. When they got to her apartment, it turned out to be not as quiet as he had expected: Three children were playing, the oldest about five, and the youngest barely walking. Ye told Wang that they were all the neighbors' kids.

"They like to play at my place. Today is Sunday, and their parents need to work overtime, so they left them to me. . . . Oh, Nan Nan, have you finished your picture? Oh, it looks great! Shall we give it a title? 'Ducklings in the Sun'? Sounds good. Let Granny write it for you. Then I'll put down the date: 'June 9th, by Nan Nan.' And what do you want to eat for lunch? Yang Yang, you want fried eggplant? Sure! Nan Nan, you want the snow peas like you had yesterday? No problem. How about you, Mi Mi? You want some meat-meat? Oh, no, your mom told me that you shouldn't eat so much meat-meat, not easy to digest. How about some fishie instead? Look at this big fishie Granny bought. . . ."

Wang observed Ye and the children, absorbed in their conversation. *She must want grandkids. But even if Yang Dong were alive, would she have had children?*

Ye took the groceries into the kitchen. When she reemerged, she said, "Xiao Wang, I'm going to soak the vegetables for a while." She had slipped effortlessly into addressing him by an affectionate diminutive. "These days, they use so much pesticide that when I feed the children, I have to soak the vegetables for at least two hours— Why don't you take a look in Dong Dong's room first?"

Her suggestion, tagged on at the end as though it was the most natural thing in the world, made Wang anxious. Clearly, she had figured out the real purpose of his visit. She turned around and went back into the kitchen without giving Wang another glance, and so avoided seeing his embarrassment. Wang was grateful that she was so considerate of his feelings.

Wang walked past the three happily playing children and entered the room that Ye had indicated. He paused in front of the door, seized by a strange feeling. It was as if he had returned to his dream-filled youth. From the depths of his memory arose a tingling sadness, fragile and pure like morning dew, tinged with a rosy hue.

Gently, he pushed the door open. The faint fragrance that filled the room was unexpected, the smell of the forest. He seemed to have entered the hut of a ranger: The walls were covered by strips of bark; the three stools were unadorned tree stumps; the desk was made from three bigger tree stumps pushed together. And then there was the bed, apparently lined with ura sedge from Northeast China, which the locals stuffed into their shoes to stay warm in the cold climate. Everything was rough-hewn and seemingly careless, without signs of aesthetic design. Yang Dong's job had earned her a high income, and she could have bought a home in some luxury development, but she chose to live here with her mother instead.

Wang walked up to the tree-stump desk. It was plainly furnished, and nothing on it betrayed a hint of femininity or scholarly interest. Maybe all such objects had been taken away, or maybe they had never been there. He noticed a black-and-white photograph in a wooden frame, a portrait of mother and daughter. In the picture, Yang Dong was just a little girl, and Ye Wenjie was crouching down so that they were the same height. A strong wind tangled the pair's long hair together.

The background of the photograph was unusual: The sky seemed to be seen through a large net held up by thick steel supporting structures. Wang deduced that it was some kind of parabolic antenna, so large that its edges were beyond the frame of the photograph.

In the picture, little Yang Dong's eyes gave off a fright that made Wang's heart ache. She seemed terrified by the world outside the picture.

Next, Wang noticed a thick notebook at the corner of the desk. He was baffled by the material the notebook was made of until he saw a line of childish writing scrawled across the cover: *Yang Dong's Birch-bark Notebook*. "Birch" was written in pinyin letters instead of using the character for it. The years had turned the silvery bark into a dull yellow. He reached out to touch the notebook, hesitated, and retracted his hand.

"It's okay," Ye said from the door. "Those are pictures Dong Dong drew when she was little."

Wang picked up the birch-bark notebook and gently flipped through it. Ye had dated each picture for her daughter, just like she had been doing for Nan Nan in the living room.

Wang saw that, based on the dates on the pictures, Yang Dong was three when she drew them. Normally, children of that age are able to draw humans and objects with clear shapes, but Yang Dong's pictures remained only messes of random lines. They seemed to express a kind of passionate anger and desperation born out of a frustrated desire to express something—not the sort of feeling one would expect in a child that young.

Ye slowly sat down on the edge of the bed, her eyes staring at the notebook, lost in thought. Her daughter had died here, ended her life while she slept. Wang sat next to her. He had never felt such a strong desire to share the burden of another's pain.

Ye took the birch-bark notebook from him and held it to her chest. In a low voice, she said, "I wasn't good at teaching Dong Dong in an age-appropriate manner. I exposed her too early to some very abstract, very extreme topics. When she first expressed an interest in abstract theory, I told her that field wasn't easy for women. She said, what about Madame Curie? I told her, Madame Curie was never really accepted as part of that field. Her success was seen as a matter of persistence and hard work, but without her, someone else would have completed her work. As a matter of fact, Wu Chien-Shiung went even further than Madame Curie.[21] But it really isn't a woman's field.

"Dong Dong didn't argue with me, but I later discovered that she really was different. For example, let's say I explained a formula to her. Other children might say, 'What a clever formula!' But she would say, 'This formula is so elegant, so beautiful.' The expression on her face was the same as when she saw a pretty wildflower.

"Her father left behind some records. She listened to all of them and finally picked something by Bach as her favorite, listening to it over and over. That was the kind of music that shouldn't have mesmerized a kid. At first I thought she picked

---

21 *Author's Note:* Chien-Shiung Wu was one of the most outstanding physicists of the modern era, with many accomplishments in experimental physics. She was the first to experimentally disprove the hypothetical "law of conservation of parity" and thereby lend support to the work of theoretical physicists Tsung-Dao Lee and Chen-Ning Yang.

it on a whim, but when I asked her how she felt about the music, she said that she could see in the music a giant building, a large, complex house. Bit by bit, the giant added to the structure, and when the music was over, the house was done. . . ."

"You were a great teacher for your daughter," Wang said.

"No. I failed. Her world was too simple, and all she had were ethereal theories. When they collapsed, she had nothing to lean on to keep on living."

"Professor Ye, I can't say that I agree with you. Right now, events are happening that are beyond our imagination. It's an unprecedented challenge to our theories about the world, and she's not the only scientist to have stumbled down that path."

"But she was a woman. A woman should be like water, able to flow over and around anything."

As Wang was about to leave, he remembered the other purpose for his visit. He mentioned to Ye his wish to observe the cosmic microwave background.

"Oh, that. There are two places in China that work on it. One is an observatory in Ürümqi—I think it's a project by the Chinese Academy of Sciences' Space Environment Observation Center. The other is very close by, a radio astronomy observatory located in the suburbs of Beijing, which is run by the Chinese Academy of Sciences and Peking University's Joint Center for Astrophysics. The one in Ürümqi does ground observation, and the one here just receives data from satellites, though the satellite data is more accurate and complete. I have a former student working there, and I can make a call for you." Ye found the phone number and dialed it. The ensuing conversation seemed to go smoothly.

"You're all set," Ye said as she hung up. "Let me give you the address. You can go over anytime. My student's name is Sha Ruishan, and he's going to be working the night shift tomorrow. . . . I don't think this is your field of research, right?"

"I work in nanotech. This is for . . . something else." Wang was afraid that Ye was going to ask more questions about why he sought this information, but she did not.

"Xiao Wang, you look a bit pale. How's your health?" she asked, her face full of concern.

"It's nothing. Please don't worry."

"Wait a moment." Ye took a small wooden box out of a cabinet. Wang saw from the label that it was ginseng. "An old friend from the base, a soldier, came to visit me a few days ago and brought this—take it, take it! It's cultivated, not very precious. I have high blood pressure and can't use it anyway. You can slice it thinly and make it into a tea. You look so pale that I'm sure you can use the enrichment. You're still young, but you have to watch your health."

Wang accepted the box, warmth filling his chest. His eyes moistened. It was as though his heart, stressed almost beyond the breaking point by the last few days, had been placed onto a pile of soft down feathers. "Professor Ye, I will come visit you often."

9

The Universe Flickers

Wang Miao drove along Jingmi Road until he was in Miyun County. From there he headed to Heilongtan, climbed up the mountain along a winding road, and arrived at the radio astronomy observatory of the Chinese Academy of Sciences' National Astronomical Center. He saw a line of twenty-eight parabolic antenna dishes, each with a diameter of nine meters, like a row of spectacular steel plants. At the end were two tall radio telescopes with dishes fifty meters in diameter, built in 2006. As he drove closer, Wang could not help but think of the background in the picture of Ye and her daughter.

But the work of Sha Ruishan, Ye's student, had nothing to do with these radio telescopes. Dr. Sha's lab was mainly responsible for receiving the data transmitted from three satellites: the Cosmic Background Explorer, COBE, launched in November of 1989 and about to be retired; the Wilkinson Microwave Anisotropy Probe, WMAP, launched in 2003; and Planck, the space observatory launched by the European Space Agency in 2009.

Cosmic microwave background radiation very precisely matched the thermal black body spectrum at a temperature of $2.7255\,K$ and was highly isotropic—meaning nearly uniform in every direction—with only tiny temperature fluctuations at the parts per million range. Sha Ruishan's job was to create a more detailed map of the cosmic microwave background using observational data.

The lab wasn't very big. Equipment for receiving satellite data was squeezed into the main computer room, and three terminals displayed the information sent by the three satellites.

Sha was excited to see Wang. Clearly bored with his long isolation and happy to have a visitor, he asked Wang what kind of data he wanted to see.

"I want to see the overall fluctuation in the cosmic microwave background."

"Can you . . . be more specific?"

"What I mean is . . . I want to see the isotropic fluctuation in the overall cosmic microwave background, between one and five percent," he said, quoting from Shen's email.

Sha grinned. Starting at the turn of the century, the Miyun Radio Astronomy Observatory had opened itself to visitors. In order to earn some extra income, Sha often played the role of tour guide or gave lectures. This was the grin he reserved for tourists, as he had grown used to their astounding scientific illiteracy. "Mr. Wang, I take it you're not a specialist in the field?"

"I work in nanotech."

"Ah, makes sense. But you must have some basic understanding of the cosmic microwave background?"

"I don't know much. I know that as the universe cooled after the big bang, the leftover 'embers' became the cosmic microwave background. The radiation fills the entire universe and can be observed in the centimeter wavelength range. I think it was back in the sixties when two Americans accidentally discovered the radiation when they were testing a supersensitive satellite reception antenna—"

"That's more than enough," Sha interrupted, waving his hands. "Then you must know that unlike the local variations we observe in different parts of the universe, the overall fluctuation in the cosmic microwave background is correlated with the expansion of the universe. It's a very slow change measured at the scale of the age of the universe. Even with the sensitivity of the Planck satellite, continuous observation for a million years might not detect *any* such shift. But you want to see a five percent fluctuation tonight? Do you realize what that would mean? The universe would flicker like a fluorescent tube that's about to burn out!"

And it will be flickering for me, Wang thought.

"This must be some joke from Professor Ye," Sha said.

"Nothing would please me more than to discover that it was a joke," Wang said. He was about to tell Sha that Ye didn't know the details of his request, but he was afraid that Sha would then refuse to help him.

"Well, since Professor Ye asked me to help you, let's do the observation. It's not a big deal. If you just need one percent precision, data from the antique COBE is sufficient." As he spoke, Sha typed quickly at the terminal. Soon a flat green line appeared on the screen. "This curve is the real-time measurement of the overall cosmic microwave background—oh, calling it a straight line would be more accurate. The temperature is 2.725 ± 0.002K. The error range is due to the Doppler effect from the motion of the Milky Way, which has already been filtered out. If the kind of fluctuation you anticipate—in excess of one percent—occurs, this line would turn red and become a waveform. I would bet that it's going to stay a flat green line until the end of the world, though.

If you want to see it show the kind of fluctuation observable by the naked eye, you might have to wait until long after the death of the sun."

"I'm not interfering in your work, am I?"

"No. Since you need such low precision, we can just use some basic data from COBE. Okay, it's all set. From now on, if such great fluctuations occur, the data will be automatically saved to disk."

"I think it might happen around one o'clock A.M."

"Wow, so precise! No problem, since I'm working the night shift, anyway. Have you had dinner yet? Good, then I'll take you on a tour."

The night was moonless. They walked along the row of antenna dishes, and Sha pointed to them. "Breathtaking, aren't they? It's too bad that they are all like the ears of a deaf man."

"Why?"

"Ever since construction was completed, interference has been unceasing in the observational bands. First, there were the paging stations during the eighties. Now, it's the scramble to develop mobile communications networks and cell towers. These telescopes are capable of many scientific tasks—surveying the sky, detecting variable radio sources, observing the remains of supernovae—but we can't perform most of them. We've complained to the State Regulatory Radio Commission many times, never with any results. How can we get more attention than China Mobile, China Unicom, China Netcom? Without money, the secrets of the universe are worth shit. At least my project only depends on satellite data and has nothing to do with these 'tourist attractions.'"

"In recent years, commercial operation of basic research has been fairly successful, like in high-energy physics. Maybe it would be better if the observatories were built in places farther away from cities?"

"It all comes down to money. Right now, our only choice is to find technical means to shield against interference. Well, it would be much better if Professor Ye were here. She accomplished a lot in this field."

So the topic of conversation turned to Ye Wenjie. And from her student, Wang finally learned about her life. He listened as Sha told of how she witnessed the death of her father during the Cultural Revolution, how she was falsely accused at the Production and Construction Corps, how she then seemed to disappear until her return to Beijing at the beginning of the nineties, when she began teaching astrophysics at Tsinghua, where her father had also taught, until her retirement.

"It was only recently revealed that she had spent more than twenty years at Red Coast Base."

Wang was stunned. "You mean, those rumors—"

"Most turned out to be true. One of the researchers who developed the deciphering system for the Red Coast Project emigrated to Europe and wrote a book last year. Most of the rumors you hear came out of that book. Many who participated in Red Coast are still alive."

"That is . . . a fantastical legend."

"Especially for it to happen during those years—absolutely incredible."

They continued to speak for a while. Sha asked the purpose behind Wang's strange request. Wang avoided giving a straight answer, and Sha didn't press. The dignity of a specialist did not allow Sha to express too much interest in a request that clearly went against his professional knowledge.

Then they went to an all-night bar for tourists and sat for two hours. As Sha finished one beer after another, his tongue loosened even more. But Wang became anxious, and his mind kept returning to that green line on the terminal in Sha's office. It was only at ten to one in the morning that Sha finally gave in to Wang's repeated pleas to go back to the lab.

The spotlights that had lit up the row of radio antennas had been turned off, and the antennas now formed a simple two-dimensional picture against the night sky like a series of abstract symbols. All of them gazed up at the sky at the same angle, as though waiting expectantly for something. The scene made Wang shudder despite the warmth of the spring evening. He was reminded of the giant pendulums in *Three Body*.

They arrived back at the lab at one. As they looked at the terminal, the fluctuation was just getting started. The flat line turned into a wave, the distance between one peak and the next inconstant. The line's color became red, like a snake awakening after hibernation, wriggling as its skin refilled with blood.

"It must be a malfunction in COBE!" Sha stared at the waveform, terrified.

"It's not a malfunction." Wang's tone was exceedingly calm. He had learned to control himself when faced with such sights.

"We'll know soon enough," Sha said. He went to the other two terminals and typed rapidly to bring up the data gathered by the other two satellites, WMAP and Planck.

Now three waveforms moved in sync across the three terminals, exactly alike.

Sha took out a notebook computer and rushed to turn it on. He plugged in a network cable and picked up the phone. Wang could tell from the one-sided conversation that he was trying to get in touch with the Ürümqi radio astronomy observatory. He didn't explain to Wang what he was doing, his eyes locked onto the browser window on the notebook. Wang could hear his rapid breathing.

A few minutes later, a red waveform appeared in the browser window, moving in step with the other three.

The three satellites and the ground-based observatory confirmed one fact: The universe was flickering.

"Can you print out the waveform?" Wang asked.

Sha wiped away the cold sweat on his forehead and nodded. He moved his mouse and clicked "Print." Wang grabbed the first page as soon as it came out of the laser printer, and, with a pencil, began to match the distance between the peaks with the Morse code chart he took out of his pocket.

short-long-long-long-long, short-long-long-long-long, long-long-long-long-long, long-long-long-short-short, long-long-long-short-short-short, short-short-long-long-long, short-long-long-long-long, long-long-long-short-short-short, short-short-short-long-long, long-long-short-short-short.

That's 1108:21:37, Wang thought.

short-long-long-long-long, short-long-long-long-long, long-long-long-long-long, long-long-long-short-short, long-long-long-short-short-short, short-short-long-long-long, short-long-long-long-long, long-long-long-short-short-short, short-short-short-long-long, long-short-short-short-short—that's 1108:21:36.

The countdown continued at the scale of the universe. Ninety-two hours had already elapsed, and only 1,108 hours remained.

Sha paced back and forth anxiously, pausing from time to time to look at the sequence of numbers Wang was writing down. "Can't you tell me what's going on?" he shouted.

"I can't possibly explain this to you, Dr. Sha. Trust me." Wang pushed away the pile of papers filled with waveforms. As he stared at the sequence of numbers, he said, "Maybe the three satellites and the observatory are all malfunctioning."

"You know that's impossible!"

"What if it's sabotage?"

"Also impossible! To simultaneously alter the data from three satellites and an observatory on Earth? You're talking about a supernatural saboteur."

Wang nodded. Compared to the idea of the universe flickering, he would prefer a supernatural saboteur. But Sha then deprived him of this last glimmer of hope. "It's easy to confirm this. If the cosmic microwave background is fluctuating this much, we should be able to see it with our own eyes."

"What are you talking about? The wavelength of the cosmic microwave background is seven centimeters. That's five orders of magnitude longer than the wavelength of visible light. How can we possibly see it?"

"Using 3K glasses."

"Three-K glasses?"

"It's a sort of science toy we made for the Capital Planetarium. With our current level of technology, we could take the six-meter horn antenna used by Penzias and Wilson almost half a century ago to discover the cosmic microwave background and miniaturize it to the size of a pair of glasses. Then we added a converter in the glasses to compress the detected radiation by five orders of magnitude so that seven-centimeter waves are turned into visible red light. This way, visitors can put on the glasses at night and observe the cosmic microwave background on their own. And now, we can use it to see the universe flicker."

"Where can I find these glasses?"

"At the Capital Planetarium. We made more than twenty pairs."

"I must get my hands on a pair before five."

Sha picked up the phone. The other side picked up only after a long while. Sha had to expend a lot of energy to convince the person awakened in the middle of the night to go to the planetarium and wait for Wang's arrival in an hour.

As Wang left, Sha said, "I won't go with you. What I've seen is enough, and I don't need any more confirmation. But I hope that you will explain the truth to me when you feel the time is right. If this phenomenon should lead to some research result, I won't forget you."

Wang opened the car door and said, "The flickering will stop at five in the morning. I'd suggest you not pursue it after this. Believe me, you won't get anywhere."

Sha stared at Wang for a long time and then nodded. "I understand. Strange things have been happening to scientists lately. . . ."

"Yes." Wang ducked into the car. He didn't want to discuss the subject any further.

"Is it our turn?"

"It's my turn, at least." Wang started the engine.

An hour later, Wang arrived at the new planetarium and got out of the car. The bright lights of the city penetrated the translucent walls of the immense glass building and dimly revealed its internal structure. Wang thought that if the architect had intended to express a feeling about the universe, the design was a success: The more transparent something was, the more mysterious it seemed. The universe itself was transparent; as long as you were sufficiently sharp-eyed, you

135

could see as far as you liked. But the farther you looked, the more mysterious it became.

The sleepy-eyed planetarium staffer was waiting by the door for Wang. He handed him a small suitcase and said, "There are five pairs of 3K glasses in here, all fully charged. The left button switches it on. The right dial is for adjusting brightness. I have a dozen more pairs upstairs. You can look as much as you like, but I'm going to take a nap now in the room over there. This Dr. Sha must be mental." He went into the dim interior of the planetarium.

Wang opened the suitcase on the backseat of his car and took out a pair of 3K glasses. It resembled the display inside the panoramic viewing helmet of the V-suit. He put the glasses on and looked around. The city looked the same as before, only dimmer. Then he remembered that he had to switch them on.

The city turned into many hazy glowing halos. Most were fixed, but a few flickered or moved. He realized that these were sources of radiation in the centimeter range, all now converted to visible light. At the heart of each halo was a radiation source. Because the original wavelengths were so long, it was impossible to see their shapes clearly.

He lifted his head and saw a sky glowing with a faint red light. Just like that, he was seeing the cosmic microwave background.

The red light had come from more than ten billion years ago. It was the remnants of the big bang, the still-warm embers of Creation. He could not see any stars. Normally, since visible light would be compressed to invisible by the glasses, each star should appear as a black dot. But the diffraction of centimeter-wave radiation overwhelmed all other shapes and details.

Once his eyes had grown used to the sight, Wang could see that the faint red background was indeed pulsing. The entire sky flickered, as if the universe was but a quivering lamp in the wind.

Standing under the flashing dome of the night sky, Wang suddenly felt the universe shrink until it was so small that only he was imprisoned in it. The universe was a cramped heart, and the red light that suffused everything was the translucent blood that filled the organ. Suspended in the blood, he saw that the flickering of the red light was not periodic—the pulsing was irregular. He felt a strange, perverse, immense presence that could never be understood by human intellect.

Wang took off the 3K glasses and sat down weakly on the ground, leaning against the wheel of his car. The city at night gradually recovered the reality of visible light. But his eyes roamed, trying to capture other sights. By the entrance of the zoo across the street, there was a row of neon lights. One of the lights was about to burn out and flickered irregularly. Nearby, a small tree's leaves trembled in the night breeze, twinkling without pattern as they reflected streetlight. In the distance, the red star atop the Beijing Exhibition Center's Russian-style spire reflected the light from the cars passing below, also twinkling randomly. . . .

Wang tried to interpret the flickers as Morse code. He even felt that the wrinkles in the flags flapping next to him and the ripples in the puddle on the side of the road might be sending him messages. He struggled to understand all the messages, and felt the passing of the countdown, second by second.

He didn't know how long he stayed there. The planetarium staffer finally emerged and asked him whether he was done. But when he saw Wang's face, sleep disappeared from the staffer's eyes and was replaced by fear. He packed up the

3K glasses, stared at Wang for a few seconds, and quickly left with the suitcase.

Wang took out his mobile and dialed Shen Yufei's number. She picked up right away. Perhaps she was also suffering from insomnia.

"What happens at the end of the countdown?" Wang asked.

"I don't know." She hung up.

What can it be? Maybe my own death, like Yang Dong's.

Or maybe it will be a disaster like the great tsunami that swept through the Indian Ocean more than a decade ago. No one will connect it to my nanotech research. Could it be that every previous great disaster, including the two World Wars, was also the result of reaching the end of ghostly countdowns? Could it be that every time there was someone like me, who no one thought of, who bore the ultimate responsibility?

Or maybe it signals the end of the whole world. In this perverse world, that would be a relief.

One thing was certain. No matter what was at the end of the countdown, in the remaining one thousand or so hours, the possibilities would torture him cruelly, like demons, until he suffered a complete mental breakdown.

Wang ducked back into the car and left the planetarium. Just before dawn, the roads were relatively empty. But he didn't dare to drive too fast, feeling that the faster the car moved, the faster the countdown would go. When a glimmer of light appeared in the eastern sky, he parked and walked around aimlessly. His mind was empty of thoughts: Only the countdown pulsed against the dim red background of cosmic radiation. He seemed to have turned into nothing but a simple timer, a bell that tolled for he knew not whom.

The sky brightened. He was tired, so he sat down on a bench.

When he lifted his head to see where his subconscious had brought him, he shivered.

He sat in front of St. Joseph's Church at Wangfujing. In the pale white light of dawn, the church's Romanesque vaults appeared as three giant fingers pointing out something in space for him.

As Wang got up to leave, he was held back by a snippet of hymnal music. It wasn't Sunday, so it was likely a choir rehearsal. The song was "Come, Gracious Spirit, Heavenly Dove." As he listened to the solemn, sacred music, Wang Miao once again felt that the universe had shrunk until it was the size of an empty church. The domed ceiling was hidden by the flashing red light of the background radiation, and he was an ant crawling through the cracks in the floor. He felt a giant, invisible hand caressing his trembling heart, and he was once again a helpless babe. Something deep in his mind that had once held him up softened like wax and collapsed. He covered his eyes and began to cry.

Wang's cries were interrupted by laughter. "Hahaha, another one bites the dust!"

He turned around.

Captain Shi Qiang stood there, blowing out a mouthful of white smoke.

10

Da Shi

Shi sat down next to Wang and handed him his car keys. "You parked right at the intersection at Dongdan. If I had arrived just a minute later, the traffic cops would have had it towed."

Da Shi, if I had known you were following me, I would have been comforted, Wang thought, switching to Shi Qiang's familiar nickname in his mind, though self-respect made him hold back the words. He accepted a cigarette from Da Shi, lit it, and took his first drag since he quit several years ago.

"So how's it going, buddy? Finding it hard to bear? I said you couldn't handle it. And you insisted on playing the tough guy."

"You wouldn't understand." Wang took several more deep puffs.

"Your problem is, you understand too well. . . . Fine, let's go grab a bite."

"I'm not hungry."

"Then we'll go drinking! My treat."

Wang got into Da Shi's car and they drove to a small restaurant nearby. It was still early, and the place was deserted.

"Two orders of quick-fried tripe, and a bottle of *er guo*

tou!"[22] Da Shi shouted, without even looking up. He was obviously a regular here.

As he stared at the two plates filled with black slices of tripe, Wang's empty stomach began to churn, and he thought he was going to be sick. Da Shi ordered him some warm soymilk and fried pancakes, and Wang forced himself to eat some.

Then they drank shots of *er guo tou*. He began to feel lightheaded, and his tongue loosened. Gradually, he recounted the events of the last three days to Da Shi, even though he knew that Da Shi probably knew everything already—maybe Da Shi even knew more than he did.

"You're saying that the universe was . . . winking at you?" Da Shi asked, as he slurped down strips of tripe like noodles.

"That's a very appropriate metaphor."

"Bullshit."

"Your lack of fear is based on your ignorance."

"More bullshit. Come, drink!"

Wang finished another shot. Now the world was spinning around him, and only the tripe-chomping Shi Qiang across from him remained stable. He said, "Da Shi, have you ever . . . considered certain ultimate philosophical questions? For example, where does Man come from? Where does Man go? Where does the universe come from? Where does the universe go? Et cetera."

"Nope."

"Never?"

"Never."

"You must see the stars. Aren't you awed and curious?"

"I never look at the sky at night."

---

22 *Translator's Note: Er guo tou* is a distilled liquor made from sorghum, sometimes called "Chinese vodka."

"How is that possible? I thought you often worked the night shift?"

"Buddy, when I work at night, if I look up at the sky, the suspect is going to escape."

"We really have nothing to say to each other. All right. Drink!"

"To be honest, even if I were to look at the stars in the sky, I wouldn't be thinking about your philosophical questions. I have too much to worry about! I gotta pay the mortgage, save for the kid's college, and handle the endless stream of cases. . . . I'm a simple man without a lot of complicated twists and turns. Look down my throat and you can see out my ass. Naturally, I don't know how to make my bosses like me. Years after being discharged from the army, my career is going nowhere. If I weren't pretty good at my job, I would have been kicked out a long time ago. . . . You think that's not enough for me to worry about? You think I've got the energy to gaze at stars and philosophize?"

"You're right. All right, drink up!"

"But, I did indeed invent an ultimate rule."

"Tell me."

"Anything sufficiently weird must be fishy."

"What . . . what kind of crappy rule is that?"

"I'm saying that there's always someone behind things that don't seem to have an explanation."

"If you had even basic knowledge of science, you'd know it's impossible for any force to accomplish the things I experienced. Especially that last one. To manipulate things at the scale of the universe—not only can you not explain it with our current science, I couldn't even imagine how to explain it *outside* of science. It's more than supernatural. It's super-I-don't-know-what. . . ."

"I'm telling you, that's bullshit. I've seen plenty of weird things."

"Then tell me what I should do next."

"Keep on drinking. And then sleep."

"Fine."

Wang Miao had no idea how he got back into his car. He tumbled into the backseat and fell into a dreamless slumber. He didn't think that he was asleep for long, but when he opened his eyes, the sun was already near the horizon in the west.

He got out of the car. Even though the alcohol that morning had made him weak, he did feel better. He saw that he was at one corner of the Forbidden City. The setting sun shone on the ancient palace and turned into bright gold ripples in the moat. In his eyes, the world became once again classical and stable.

Wang sat until it got dark, enjoying the peace that had been missing from his life. The black Volkswagen Santana that he was now so familiar with pulled out of the traffic streaming through the street and braked to a stop right in front of him. Shi Qiang got out of the car.

"Slept well?" Da Shi growled.

"Yes. What next?"

"Who? You? Go have dinner. Then drink a little more. Then sleep again."

"Then what?"

"Then? Don't you have to go to work tomorrow?"

"But the countdown . . . there's only 1,091 hours left."

"Fuck the countdown. Your first priority right now is to make sure you can stand straight and not collapse into a heap. Then we can talk about other things."

143

"Da Shi, can you tell me something about what's really going on? I'm begging you."

Da Shi stared at Wang a while. Then he laughed. "I've said the very same thing to General Chang several times. We're in the same boat, you and I. I'll be honest: I know fucking shit. My pay grade is too low, and they tell me nothing. Sometimes I think this is a nightmare."

"But you must know more than I."

"Fine. I'll tell you what little I know." Da Shi pointed to the shore of the moat around the Forbidden City. The two found a spot and sat down.

It was now night, and traffic flowed ceaselessly behind them like a river. They watched their shadows lengthening and shortening over the moat.

"In my line of work, it's all about putting together many apparently unconnected things. When you piece them together the right way, you get the truth. For a while now, strange things have been happening.

"For example, there's been an unprecedented wave of crimes against academia and science research institutions. Of course you know about the explosion at the Liangxiang accelerator construction site. There was also the murder of that Nobel laureate . . . the crimes were all unusual: not for money, not for revenge. No political background, just pure destruction.

"Other strange things didn't involve crimes. For example, the Frontiers of Science and the suicides of those academics. Environmental activists have also become extra bold: protest mobs at construction sites to stop nuclear power plants and hydroelectric dams, experimental communities 'returning to nature,' and other apparently trivial matters . . . . Do you go to the movies?"

144

"No, not really."

"Recent big-budget films all have rustic themes. The setting is always green mountains and clear water, with handsome men and pretty women of some indeterminate era living in harmony with nature. To use the words of the directors, they 'represent the beautiful life before science spoiled nature.' Take *Peach Blossom Spring*: it's clearly the sort of film that no one wants to see. But they spent hundreds of millions to make it. There was also this science fiction contest with a top reward of five million for the person who imagined the most disgusting possible future. They spent another few hundred million to turn the winning stories into movies. And then you've got all these strange cults popping up everywhere, where every cult leader seems to have a lot of money. . . ."

"What does that last bit have to do with everything you mentioned before?"

"You have to connect all the dots. Of course I didn't need to busy myself with such concerns before, but after I was transferred from the crime unit to the Battle Command Center, it became part of my job. Even General Chang is impressed by my talent for connecting the dots."

"And your conclusion?"

"Everything that's happening is coordinated by someone behind the scenes with one goal: to completely ruin scientific research."

"Who?"

"I have no idea. But I can sense the plan, a very comprehensive, intricate plan: damage scientific research installations, kill scientists, drive scientists like you crazy and make you commit suicide—but the main goal is to misdirect your thoughts until you're even more foolish than ordinary people."

"Your last statement is really perceptive."

"At the same time, they want to ruin science's reputation in society. Of course some people have always engaged in anti-science activities, but now it's coordinated."

"I believe it."

"*Now* you believe me. So many of you scientific elites couldn't figure it out, and I, having gone only to vocational school, had the answer? Ha! After I explained my theory, the scholars and my bosses all ridiculed it."

"If you had told me your theory back then, I'm sure I wouldn't have laughed at you. Take those frauds who practice pseudoscience—do you know who they're most afraid of?"

"Scientists, of course."

"No. Many of the best scientists can be fooled by pseudoscience and sometimes devote their lives to it. But pseudoscience is afraid of one particular type of people who are very hard to fool: stage magicians. In fact, many pseudo-scientific hoaxes were exposed by stage magicians. Compared to the bookworms of the scientific world, your experience as a cop makes you far more likely to perceive such a large-scale conspiracy."

"Well, there're plenty of people smarter than me. People in positions of power are well aware of the plot. When they ridiculed me at first, it was only because I wasn't explaining my theory to the right people. Later on, my old company commander—General Chang—had me transferred. But I'm still not doing anything other than running errands. . . . That's it. Now you know as much as I do."

"Another question: What does this have to do with the military?"

"I was baffled, too. I asked them, and they said that now that there's a war, of course the military would be involved. I was like you, thinking that they were talking nonsense.

But no, they weren't joking. The army really is on high alert. There are twenty-some Battle Command Centers like ours around the globe. And above them there's another level of command structure. But no one knows the details."

"Who's the enemy?"

"No idea. NATO officers are now stationed in the war room of the PLA General Staff Department, and a bunch of PLA officers are working out of the Pentagon. Who the fuck knows who we're fighting?"

"This is all so bizarre. Are you sure it's all true?"

"A bunch of my old buddies from the army are now generals, so I know a few things."

"The media has no idea about any of this?"

"Ah, that's another thing. All the countries are keeping a tight lid on this, and they've been successful so far. I can guarantee you that the enemy is incredibly powerful. Those in charge are terrified! I know General Chang very well. He's the sort who's afraid of nothing, not even the sky falling, but I can tell that he's worried about something much worse right now. They're all scared out of their wits, and they have no confidence that we'll win."

"If what you say is true, then we should all be frightened."

"Everyone is afraid of something. The enemy must be, too. The more powerful they are, the more they have to lose to their fears."

"What do you think the enemy is afraid of?"

"You! Scientists! The odd thing is that the less practical your research is, the more they're afraid of you—like abstract theories, the kind of thing Yang Dong worked on. They are more frightened of such work than you are of the universe winking at you. That's why they're so ruthless. If killing you would solve the problem, you'd all be dead by now. But the

147

most effective technique remains disrupting your thoughts. When a scientist dies, another will take his place. But if his thoughts are confused, then science is over."

"You're saying they're afraid of fundamental science?"

"Yes, fundamental science."

"But my research is very different in nature from Yang Dong's. The nanomaterial I work on isn't fundamental science. It's just a very strong material. What's the threat to them?"

"You're a special case. Usually, they don't bother those engaged in applied research. Maybe the material you're developing really scares them."

"Then what should I do?"

"Go to work and keep up your research. That's the best way to strike back at them. Don't worry about that shitty countdown. If you want to relax a bit after work, play that game. If you can beat it, that might help."

"That game? *Three Body*? You think it's connected to all this?"

"Definitely connected. I know that several specialists at the Battle Command Center are playing it, too. It's no ordinary game. Someone like me, fearless out of ignorance, can't play it. It has to be someone knowledgeable like you."

"Anything else?"

"No. But if I find out more I'll let you know. Keep your phone on, buddy. Keep your head screwed on straight, and if you get scared again, just remember my ultimate rule."

Da Shi drove away before Wang had a chance to thank him.

11

Three Body:
Mozi and Fiery Flames

Wang Miao returned home, stopping on the way to buy a
V-suit. His wife told him that people from work had been
trying to get ahold of him all day.

Wang turned on his phone, checked his messages, and
returned a few calls. He promised he'd be at work tomorrow.
At dinner, he followed Da Shi's advice and drank some more.

But he didn't feel sleepy. After his wife went to bed, he sat
in front of the computer, put on his new V-suit, and logged
into *Three Body*.

Desolate plain at dawn.

Wang stood in front of King Zhou's pyramid. The snow
that had once covered it was gone, and the blocks of stone
were pockmarked by erosion. The ground was now a different color. In the distance were a few massive buildings
that Wang guessed were dehydratories, but they were of a
different design than the ones he had seen last time.

Everything told him that eons had passed.

By the faint dawn light, Wang looked for the entrance.
When he found it, he saw that the opening had been sealed

by blocks of stone. But next to it, there was now a staircase carved into the pyramid leading all the way to the apex. He looked up and saw that the top had been flattened into a platform. The pyramid, once Egyptian in style, now resembled an Aztec one.

Wang climbed up the stairs and reached the apex. The platform looked like an ancient astronomical observatory. In one corner was a telescope several meters high, and next to it were a few smaller telescopes. In another corner were a few strange instruments that reminded him of ancient Chinese armillary spheres, models of objects in the sky.

His attention was drawn to the large copper sphere in the center of the platform. Two meters in diameter, it was set on top of a complex machine. Propelled by countless gears, the sphere slowly rotated. Wang noticed that the direction and speed of its rotation constantly shifted. Below the machine was a large square cavity. By the faint torchlight within, Wang saw a few slavelike figures pushing a spoked, horizontal wheel, which provided the power to the machine above.

A man walked toward Wang. Like King Wen when Wang had first encountered him, the man had his back against the sliver of light on the horizon, and he appeared to Wang as a pair of bright eyes floating in the darkness. He was slender and tall, dressed in a flowing black robe, his hair carelessly knotted on top of his head with a few strands waving in the wind.

"Hello," the man said. "I'm Mozi."[23]

"Hello, I'm Hairen."

"Ah, I know you!" Mozi grew excited. "You were a follower of King Wen back in Civilization Number 137."

---

23 *Translator's Note:* Mozi was the founder of the Mohist school of philosophy during the Warring States Period. Mozi himself emphasized experience and logic, and was known as an accomplished engineer and geometer.

"I did follow him here. But I never believed his theories."

"You're right." Mozi nodded at Wang solemnly. Then he moved closer. "During the three hundred and sixty-two thousand years you've been away, civilization has been reborn four more times. These civilizations struggled to develop through the irregular alternation of Chaotic Eras and Stable Eras. The shortest-lived one got only halfway through the Stone Age, but Civilization Number 139 broke a record and developed all the way to the Steam Age."

"You're saying that people from that civilization found the laws governing the sun's motion?"

Mozi laughed and shook his head. "Not at all. They were just lucky."

"But the effort to do so has never ceased?"

"Of course not. Come, let us see the efforts of the last civilization." Mozi led Wang to a corner of the observatory platform. The ground spread out beneath them like an ancient piece of leather. Mozi aimed one of the smaller telescopes at a target on the ground and gestured for Wang to look. Wang looked through the eyepiece and saw a strange sight: a skeleton. In the dawn light it gave off a snow-white glint and appeared to be very refined.

Astonishingly, the skeleton stood on its own. Its posture was graceful and elegant. One hand was held below the chin, as though stroking a long-missing beard. Its head tilted slightly up, as though questioning sky and earth.

"That's Confucius," Mozi said. "He believed that everything had to fit *li,* the Confucian conception of order and propriety, and nothing in the universe could be exempt from it. He created a system of rites and hoped to predict the motion of the sun with it."

"I can imagine the result."

"Right you are. He calculated how the sun would follow the rites, and predicted a five-year Stable Era. And you know what? There was indeed a Stable Era . . . lasting a month."

"And then one day the sun just didn't come out?"

"No, the sun rose that day as well. It rose to the middle of the sky, and then went out."

"What? Went out?"

"Yes. It gradually dimmed, became smaller, and then went out all of a sudden. Night fell. Oh, the cold. Confucius stood there and froze into a column of ice. And there he remains."

"Was there anything remaining in the sky after the sun went out?"

"A flying star appeared in that location, like a soul left behind after the sun died."

"You're sure that the sun really disappeared suddenly, and the flying star appeared just as suddenly?"

"Yes, absolutely. You can check the historical annals. It was clearly recorded."

"Hmmm . . ." Wang thought hard about this information. He had already formed some vague ideas about the workings of the world of *Three Body*. But this bit of news from Mozi overturned all his theories. "How can it be . . . sudden?" he muttered in annoyance.

"We're now in the Han Dynasty—I'm not sure if it's the Western Han or the Eastern Han."

"You've stayed alive until now?"

"I have a mission: observing the precise movements of the sun. Those shamans, metaphysicians, and Daoists are all useless. Like those proverbial bookish men who could not even tell types of grains apart, they do not labor with their hands, and know nothing practical. They have no ability to do experiments, and they're immersed in their mysticism all day long. But I'm different. I know how to make things." He pointed to the numerous instruments on the platform.

"Do you think these can lead you to your goal?" Wang nodded specifically at the giant copper sphere.

"I have theories, too, but they're not mystical. They're derived from a large number of observations. First, do you know what the universe is? It's a machine."

"That's not very insightful."

"Let me be more specific: The universe is a hollow sphere floating in the middle of a sea of fire. There are numerous tiny holes in the surface of the sphere, as well as a large one. The light from the sea of flames shines through these holes. The tiny ones are stars, and the large one is the sun."

"That's a very interesting model." Wang looked at the giant copper sphere again and guessed at its purpose. "But there's a problem with your theory. When the sun rises or sets, we can see its motion against the background of fixed stars. But in your hollow sphere, all the holes remain in fixed positions relative to each other."

"Correct! That's why I've modified my model. The universal sphere is made of two spheres, one inside the other. The sky we can see is the surface of the inner sphere. The outer sphere has one large hole while the inner sphere has many small holes. The light coming through the hole in the outer sphere is reflected and scattered many times in the space between the two spheres, filling it with light. Then the light comes in through the tiny holes in the inner sphere, and that's how we see the stars."

"What about the sun?"

"The sun is the result of the large hole in the outer sphere being projected onto the inner one. The projection is so bright that it penetrates the inner sphere like the shell of an egg, and that is how we see the sun. Around the spot of light, the scattered light rays are also very bright, and can be seen through the inner shell. That is why we can see a clear sky during the day."

"What is the force that propels the two spheres in their irregular motion?"

"It's the force of the sea of fire outside the two spheres."

"But the sun's brightness and size change over time. In your double-shell model, the sun's size and brightness ought to be fixed. Even if the brightness of the flames in the sea of fire is inconstant, the size of the hole would not be."

"Your conception of this model is too simplistic. As conditions in the sea of fire shift and change, the two shells will expand and shrink. This leads to changes in the size and brightness of the sun."

"What about the flying stars?"

"Flying stars? Why do you care about them? They're not important. Maybe just some random dust flying about the inside of the universal spheres."

"No, I think the flying stars are extremely important. Otherwise, how does your model explain the sudden extinguishing of the sun during the time of Confucius?"

"That's a rare exception. Maybe it was because a dark spot or cloud in the sea of fire just happened to pass over the big hole in the outer shell."

Wang pointed to the large copper sphere. "This must be your model, then?"

"Yes. I built a machine to replicate the universe. The complex gears that move the sphere simulate the forces from the sea of fire. The laws governing such motion are based on the distribution of flames in the sea of fire and the currents within it. I deduced them from hundreds of years of observations."

"Can this sphere contract and expand?"

"Of course. Right now it's slowly contracting."

Wang used the handrail at the edge of the platform as a fixed visual reference. He found Mozi's assertion to be true.

"And there's an inner shell inside this sphere?"

"Of course. The inner shell moves within the outer shell through another complex set of mechanisms."

"Truly a skillfully designed machine!" Wang's praise was heartfelt. "But I don't see a large hole in the outer shell to cast the sun's light onto the inner shell."

"There is no hole. On the inner surface of the outer shell I have installed a source of light to simulate the hole. The light source is made of the luminescent material gathered from hundreds of thousands of fireflies. I used a cool light because the inner shell is made of translucent plaster, which is not a good heat conductor. This way, I can avoid the problem of too much heat accumulating inside the sphere that we would have with a regular source of light. The observer can then stay inside for a long time."

"There's a person inside the sphere?"

"Yes. A clerk stands on top of a shelf with a wheeled base that is kept at the center of the sphere. After we set up the model universe to correspond to the current state of the real universe, the motion of the model thereafter should be an accurate simulation of the future, including the motion of the sun. After the clerk records the movements of the sun, we will have a precise calendar. This is the dream of hundreds of civilizations before us.

"And it looks like you have come at an opportune time. According to the model universe, a four-year-long Stable

Era is about to begin. Emperor Wu of Han has just issued the order to rehydrate based on my prediction. Let's wait for sunrise!"

Mozi brought up the game's interface and slightly increased the rate of passage of game time. A red sun rose above the horizon, and the numerous frozen lakes and ponds scattered over the plain began to melt. These lakes had been covered by dust and had merged into the dun ground, but now they turned into numerous mirrors, as though the earth had opened many eyes. From up so high, Wang couldn't see the details of rehydration, but he could see more and more people gathered on the shores of the lakes like swarms of ants coming out of their nests in spring. The world had once again been revived.

"Do you not want to join this wonderful life?" Mozi asked, pointing to the ground below. "When women are first revived, they crave love. There is no reason for you to stay here any longer. The game is over. I am the winner."

"As a piece of machinery, your model universe is indeed incomparable. But as for its predictions . . . . May I use your telescope to observe something?"

"Please." Mozi gestured at the large telescope.

Wang walked up to the instrument and paused. "How can I use it to observe the sun?"

Mozi retrieved a black, circular piece of glass. "Use this smoked glass filter." He inserted it in front of the eyepiece.

Wang aimed the telescope at the sun, now halfway up the sky. He was impressed by Mozi's imagination. The sun did indeed look like a hole through which a sea of fire could be seen, a small view into a much larger whole.

But as he examined the image in the telescope more closely, he realized that the sun was different from the sun he was used to in real life. The sun here had a small core. He imagined the sun as an eye. The core was like the eye's pupil, and though it was small, it was bright and dense. The layers surrounding it, by contrast, appeared insubstantial, wispy, gaseous. The fact that he could see through the outside layers to the core indicated that those layers were transparent or translucent, and the light from those layers was likely just scattered light from the core.

The details in the image of the sun stunned Wang. He was once again assured that the game designers had hidden a vast amount of data within the superficially simple images, just waiting to be revealed by players.

As Wang pondered the meaning of the sun's structure, he became excited. Because time in the game was now passing quickly, the sun was already in the west. Wang stood, adjusted the telescope to aim at the sun again, and tracked it until it dipped below the horizon.

Night fell, and the bonfires across the plains mirrored the sky full of stars. Wang took off the smoked glass filter and continued to scan the skies. He was most interested in the flying stars, and shortly found two. He only had time to observe one of them briefly before it was dawn again. So he inserted the filter and continued to observe the sun. . . .

In this manner Wang performed astronomical observations for more than ten days, enjoying the thrill of discovery. Indeed, the fact that time within the game had been sped up helped with the observations, as the motion of celestial bodies became more apparent.

On the seventeenth day of the Stable Era, five hours after the predicted time for sunrise, the world was still under cover of dark night. Multitudes thronged at the foot of the pyramid, their innumerable torches flickering in the chill wind.

"The sun will probably not rise again. It is like at the end of Civilization Number 137," Wang said to Mozi.

Mozi stroked his beard and smiled confidently. "Do not fret. The sun will rise soon, and the Stable Era will continue. I've already learned the secret of the motion of the universal machine. My predictions cannot be wrong."

As though confirming Mozi's words, the sky over the horizon brightened with dawn's first light. The crowd around the pyramid shouted in joy.

The silvery light brightened far more rapidly than usual, as though the rising sun wanted to make up for lost time. Soon, the light covered half the sky, even though the sun was still below the horizon. The world was already as bright as midday.

Wang looked toward the horizon and saw it giving off a blinding glare. The glowing horizon arched upward and became a curve that spread from one edge of his visual field to the other. He soon realized that he wasn't seeing the horizon, but the edge of the rising sun, an incomparably immense sun.

After his eyes adjusted to the bright light, the horizon reappeared in its old place. Wang saw columns of black smoke rising in the distance, especially clear against the glowing background of the solar disk. A fast horse rushed toward the pyramid from the direction of the rising sun, the dust from its hooves forming a distinct line across the plains.

The crowd parted before the horse, and Wang heard the rider scream at the top of his lungs: "Dehydrate! Dehydrate!"

Following the rider was a herd of cattle, horses, and other animals. Their bodies were on fire and they moved across the ground like a burning carpet.

Half of the gigantic sun's disk was now above the horizon, taking up much of the sky. The earth seemed to slowly sink down against a brilliant wall. Wang could clearly make out the fine structures on the surface of the sun: eddies and surging waves filling the sea of flames; sunspots floating along random paths like ghosts; the corona lazily spreading out like golden sleeves.

On the ground, both those who had already dehydrated and those who hadn't began to burn like countless logs thrown into the belly of a furnace. The flames that consumed them were even brighter than glowing charcoal in a furnace, but were quickly extinguished.

The giant sun continued to rise and soon filled most of the sky. Wang looked up and felt his perspective shift. Suddenly he was no longer looking up, but down. The surface of the giant sun became a fiery earth, and he felt himself falling toward this brilliant hell.

Lakes and ponds began to evaporate, and puffs of white steam rose up like mushroom clouds. They rose, spilled open, and dispersed, covering the ashes of the dead.

"The Stable Era will continue. The universe is a machine. I created this machine. The Stable Era will continue. The universe . . ."

Wang turned his head. The voice belonged to Mozi, who was already on fire. His body was encased within a column of tall, orange flame, and his skin crinkled and turned into charcoal. But his two eyes still shone with a light that was distinct from the fire consuming him. His two hands, already burning pieces of charcoal, held up the cloud of swirling ashes that had once been his calendar.

Wang was burning up as well. He lifted his two hands and saw two torches.

The sun briskly moved to the west, revealing the sky behind it. It soon fell below the horizon, and the ground seemed to rise against the brilliant wall this time. A dazzling sunset swiftly turned to night, as though a pair of giant hands had pulled a black cloth over a world that had turned to ash.

The earth glowed with a dim red light like a piece of charcoal just retrieved from a furnace. For a brief moment, Wang saw the stars, but soon steam and smoke hid the sky and covered everything on the red-glowing earth. The world sank into a dark chaos. A red line of text appeared:

> Civilization Number 141 fell into ruin in flames. This civilization had advanced to the Eastern Han Period.
> The seed of civilization remains. It will germinate and again pro-gress through the unpredictable world of *Three Body*. We invite you to log on in the future.

Wang took off the V-suit. After his mind had calmed down a bit, he again had the thought that *Three Body* was deliberately pretending to be merely illusory, while in fact possessing some deep reality. The real world in front of him, on the other hand, had begun to seem like the superficially complex, but in truth rather simple, *Along the River During the Qingming Festival*.

The next day, Wang went to the Nanotechnology Research Center. Other than some minor confusion due to his absence the day before, everything was normal. He found work to be an effective tranquilizer. As long as he was absorbed by it, he was no longer bothered by his nightmarish worries. He deliberately kept himself constantly busy the whole day and left the lab only after it was dark.

As soon as Wang left the Research Center building, the nightmarelike feeling caught up to him. He felt like the starry sky was a magnifying glass that covered the world, and he was a tiny insect below the lens with nowhere to hide.

He had to find something to occupy himself. Then he thought of Yang Dong's mother Ye Wenjie and drove to her home.

Ye was alone at home. When Wang entered, she was sitting on the sofa reading. Wang noticed that her eyes were both myopic and presbyopic, and she had to switch glasses both when she read and when she looked at something far away. She was very happy to see Wang, and said that he looked much better than the last time he had come to see her.

Wang chuckled. "It's all because of your ginseng."

Ye shook her head. "What I gave you wasn't very good. We used to be able to find really high-quality wild ginseng around the base. I once found one about this long. . . . I wonder what it's like there now. I heard that it's deserted. Well, I guess I'm really getting old. These days, I'm always thinking about the past."

"I heard that you suffered a lot during the Cultural Revolution."

"You heard it from Ruishan, didn't you?" Ye waved her hand, as though trying to wave away a strand of spider silk. "In the past, it's all in the past. . . . Last night, Ruishan called me. He was in such a hurry that I had a hard time understanding him. All I got was that something seemed to have happened to you. Xiao Wang, let me tell you: By the time you're my age, you'll realize that everything you once thought mattered so much turns out to mean very little."

"Thank you," Wang said. He once again felt the warmth that he had missed. In his current state, his mental stability depended on two pillars: this old woman, who had weathered so many storms and become as gentle as water, and Shi Qiang, the man who feared nothing because he knew nothing.

Ye continued. "As far as the Cultural Revolution is concerned, I was pretty lucky. Just when I thought I had nowhere to go, I found a place where I could survive."

"You mean Red Coast Base?"

Ye nodded.

"That was truly an incredible project. I used to think it was just made-up rumors."

"Not rumors. If you want, I can tell you some of what I experienced."

The offer made Wang a little worried. "Professor Ye, I'm only curious. You don't need to tell me if it's not appropriate."

"It's no big deal. Let's just imagine that I'm looking for someone to hear me talk."

"You could go visit the senior center. You wouldn't be lonely if you went there occasionally."

"Many of those retirees were my colleagues back at the university, but somehow I just can't mix with them. Everyone likes to reminisce, but no one wants to listen, and everyone feels annoyed when someone else tells a story. You're the only one who's interested in Red Coast."

"But for you to tell me about those things . . . isn't that prohibited?"

"That's true—it's still classified. But after that book was published, many others who were there also began to tell their stories, so they're like open secrets. The person who wrote that book was very irresponsible. Even if we put aside his agenda, the content of that book was often inaccurate. I should at least correct those errors."

Then Ye Wenjie began to tell Wang about what happened to her during her years at Red Coast.

12

Red Coast II

Ye wasn't given a real job immediately after entering Red Coast Base. Under the watchful eyes of a security guard, she was only allowed to perform a few technical tasks.

Back when she was still a second-year in college, Ye had already known the professor who would end up being her thesis advisor. He had told Ye that to do astrophysics research, it was useless to excel at theory without knowledge of experimental methods and observational skills—at least, that was true in China. This was very different from her father's view, but Ye tended to agree with her professor. She had always felt that her father was too theoretical.

Her advisor was one of the pioneers of Chinese radio astronomy. Under his influence, Ye developed a great interest in radio astronomy as well. Thus, she taught herself electrical engineering and computer science, the foundation for experiments and observations in the field. During the two years when she was a graduate student, the two of them had tested China's first small-scale radio telescope and had accumulated a great deal of experience in the area.

She hadn't expected the knowledge would one day be useful at Red Coast Base.

Eventually, Ye was assigned to the Transmission

Department to maintain and repair equipment. She quickly became an indispensable part of their operations.

Initially, this confused her a bit. She was the only person at the base who wasn't in a military uniform. And given her political status, everyone kept their distance. She had no way to ward off the loneliness other than devoting herself to work. However, this wasn't enough to explain why they relied on her so much. This was, after all, a key defense project. How could the technical staff here be so mediocre that she, who had not majored in engineering and who had no real working experience, easily took over their jobs?

She learned the reason soon enough. Contrary to appearances, the base's staff was composed of the best technical officers from the Second Artillery Corps. She could study all her life and have no hope of catching up to those excellent electrical and computer engineers. But the base was remote, the conditions were poor, and the main research work of the Red Coast Project was already completed. All that was left was maintenance and operation, so there was little opportunity for achieving any interesting technical results. Most people did not want to be indispensable, because they understood that in highly classified projects like this, once someone was put into a core technical position, it would be very difficult for him to be transferred out. Thus, all of them tried to deliberately hide their technical competence as they went about their jobs.

Yet, they couldn't appear *too* incompetent. So if the supervisor said to go east, they would work hard to move west, purposely playing the fool. Their hope was to put the following thought into the supervisor's head: *This man is working hard, but he's limited in his skills. There's no point in keeping him, because he'll only get in the way.* Many really did successfully obtain transfers through this method.

Under such conditions, Ye gradually became a key technician at the base. But the other reason that she could achieve this position puzzled her, and for that she could find no explanation: Red Coast Base—at least the parts that she had contact with—had no real advanced technology at all.

Over time, as Ye continued to work at the Transmission Department, the restrictions on her were gradually relaxed, and even the security guard assigned to watch her was called off. She was allowed to touch most components of Red Coast's systems, and could read the relevant technical documents. Of course, there were still areas forbidden to her. For example, she wasn't allowed near the computer control systems. However, Ye discovered that the impact of those systems on Red Coast was far smaller than she had imagined. For instance, the Transmission Department's computers consisted of three machines even more primitive than DJS130.[24] They used cumbersome magnetic core memory and paper input tape, and their longest uptime did not exceed fifteen hours. She also saw that the precision of Red Coast's targeting system was very low, probably not even on par with that of an artillery cannon.

One day, Commissar Lei came to speak with Ye. By this time, Yang Weining and Lei Zhicheng had swapped places in her eyes. During those years, Yang, as the highest-ranked technical officer, did not enjoy a high political status, and outside of technical matters he had little authority. He had to be careful with his subordinates, and had to speak politely even to the sentries, lest he be deemed to have an intellectual's resistant attitude toward thought reform and collaboration

---

24 *Translator's Note:* This was a Chinese 16-bit minicomputer modeled on the American Data General Nova.

with the masses. Thus, whenever he encountered difficulties in his work, Ye became his punching bag. But as Ye gained importance as a technical staff member, Commissar Lei gradually shed his initial rudeness and coldness and became kind toward her.

Commissar Lei said, "Wenjie, by now you're pretty familiar with the transmission system. This is also Red Coast's offensive component, its principal part. Can you give me your views of the system as a whole?"

They were sitting at the lip of the steep cliff on Radar Peak, the most secluded spot on the base. The cliff seemed to drop straight off into a bottomless abyss. At first, the spot had frightened Ye, but now she liked to come here by herself.

Ye wasn't sure how to answer Commissar Lei's question. She was only responsible for maintaining and repairing equipment and knew nothing about Red Coast as a whole, including its operation, targets, and so on. Indeed, she wasn't allowed to know. She wasn't even permitted to be present at the transmission. She pondered the question, began to speak, and stopped herself.

"Go ahead, speak your mind," Commissar Lei said. He ripped out a blade of grass next to him and played with it absent-mindedly.

"It . . . is just a radio transmitter."

"That's right, just a radio transmitter." The commissar nodded, satisfied. "Do you know about microwave ovens?"

Ye shook her head.

"They are a luxury plaything of the capitalist West. Food is heated by the energy generated from absorbing microwave radiation. At my previous research station, in order to precisely test the high-temperature aging of certain components, we imported one. After work, we would use it to warm *mantou*

166

bread, bake a potato, that sort of thing. It's very interesting: The inside heats up first while the outside remains cold."

Commissar Lei stood up and paced back and forth. He was so close to the edge of the cliff that it made Ye nervous.

"Red Coast is a microwave oven, and its heating targets are the enemy's space vessels. If we can apply microwave radiation at a specific power level of one-tenth of a watt to one watt per square centimeter, we'll be able to disable or destroy many electronic components of satellite communications, radar, and navigation systems."

Ye finally understood. Even though Red Coast was only a radio transmitter, that didn't mean it was conventional. The most surprising aspect was its transmission power: as high as twenty-five megawatts! This wasn't just more powerful than all communication transmissions, but also all radar transmissions. Red Coast relied on a set of gigantic capacitors. Because the power requirements were so high, the transmission circuits were also different from conventional designs. Ye now understood the purpose of such ultrahigh power in the system, but something seemed wrong right away. "The emission from the system seems to be modulated."

"That's right. However, the modulation is unlike that used in conventional radio communications. The purpose isn't to add information, but to use shifting frequencies and amplitudes to penetrate possible shielding by the enemy. Of course, those are still experimental."

Ye nodded. Many of her questions had now been answered.

"Recently, two target satellites were launched from Jiuquan. The test attacks by Red Coast were completely successful. Temperature inside the satellites reached nearly a thousand degrees, and all instruments and photographic equipment onboard were destroyed. In future wars, Red

Coast can effectively strike at the enemy's communication and reconnaissance satellites, like the KH-8 spy satellites on which the American Imperialists rely, as well as the KH-9, which are about to be launched. The lower-orbit spy satellites of the Soviet Revisionists are even more vulnerable. If necessary, we even have the capacity to destroy the Salyut space station of the Soviet Revisionists and the Skylab station that American Imperialists plan on launching next year."

"Commissar! What are you telling her?" Someone spoke behind Ye. She turned and saw that it was Yang Weining, who stared at Commissar Lei severely.

"This is for work," Commissar Lei said, and then left. Yang glanced at Ye without saying anything and followed Lei. Ye was left all by herself.

He's the one who brought me here, but he still doesn't trust me, a disconsolate Ye thought. She was worried about Commissar Lei. At the base, Lei had more authority than Yang, since the commissar had the final vote on most important matters, but the way he rushed away with Yang seemed to indicate that he felt the chief engineer had caught him doing something wrong. This convinced Ye that Lei had made a personal decision to tell her about the true purpose of the Red Coast Project.

What will happen to him as a result of this decision? As she gazed at Commissar Lei's burly back, Ye felt a wave of gratitude. For her, trust was a luxury that she dared not wish for. Compared to Yang, Lei was closer to her image of a real military officer, possessing a soldier's frank and forthright manners. Yang, on the other hand, was nothing more than a typical intellectual of the period: cautious, timid, seeking only to protect himself. Even though Ye understood him, the wide gulf already between them grew wider.

The next day, Ye was transferred out of the Transmission Department and assigned to the Monitoring Department. At first, she thought this was related to the events of the day before, an attempt to move her away from the core of Red Coast. But after arriving at the Monitoring Department, she realized that *this* was more like the heart of Red Coast. Even though the two departments shared some resources, such as the antenna, the technology level of the Monitoring Department was far more advanced.

The Monitoring Department had a very sophisticated and sensitive radio receiver. A ruby-based traveling-wave maser[25] amplified the signals received by the gigantic antenna, and in order to minimize interference, the core of the reception system was immersed in liquid helium at -269 degrees Celsius. Periodically, a helicopter came to replenish the supply of liquid helium. The reception system was thus capable of picking up very faint signals. Ye couldn't help but imagine how wonderful it would be to use the equipment for radio astronomy research.

The Monitoring Department's computer system was also much bigger and more complex than the one at the Transmission Department. The first time she entered the main computer room, Ye saw a row of cathode ray tube displays. She was stunned to see programming code scrolling across each of them, and the operators were free to edit and test the code using the keyboard. When she learned programming in college, the source code was always written on the grids of special programming paper, then transferred to paper tape using a typewriter. She had heard of input using a keyboard and screen, but this was the first time she had seen it.

---

25 *Translator's Note:* A maser is like a laser, but for electromagnetic radiation, typically microwaves, not in the visible light range.

The software available astonished her even more. She learned about something called FORTRAN, which allowed you to program using a language close to natural language. You could even type mathematical equations directly into the code! Programming in it was several times more efficient than programming in machine code. And then there was something called a database, which allowed for easy storage and manipulation of vast amounts of data.

Two days later, Commissar Lei sought Ye out for another talk. This time, they were in the main computer room of the Monitoring Department, in front of the row of green-glowing screens. Yang Weining sat close by, not part of their conversation, but also not willing to leave, which made Ye very uncomfortable.

"Wenjie," Commissar Lei began, "let me explain the work of the Monitoring Department to you. Simply put, the goal is to keep an eye on enemy activities in space, including intercepting communications between enemy space vessels and the ground, and between the space vessels themselves; collaborating with our telemetry, tracking, and command centers to determine the orbits of enemy space vessels and provide data for Red Coast's combat systems. In other words, the eyes of Red Coast are here."

Yang interrupted, "Commissar Lei, I don't think what you're doing is a good idea. There's no need to tell her these things."

Ye glanced at Yang and anxiously said, "Commissar, if it's not appropriate for me to know, then—"

"No, no, Wenjie." The commissar held up a hand to stop Ye from speaking. He turned to Yang. "Chief Yang, I'm going to tell you the same thing I did before. This is for work. For Wenjie to perform her duties better, she must be told the purpose of her work."

Yang stood up. "I will report this to our superiors."

"That is your right, of course. But do not fret, Chief Yang. I will assume responsibility for all consequences."

Yang got up and left with a bitter expression.

"Don't mind him. That's just the way Chief Yang is." Commissar Lei chuckled and shook his head. Then he stared at Ye and his tone became solemn. "Wenjie, when we first brought you to the base, the goal was simple. Red Coast's monitoring systems often had interference caused by electromagnetic radiation from solar flares and sunspots. Fortuitously, we saw your paper and realized that you had researched solar activity. Among Chinese scholars, your predictive model turned out to be the most accurate, so we wanted to ask for your help in solving this problem.

"But after you came, you showed very strong abilities, so we decided to give you more responsibilities. My thought was this: assign you first to the Transmission Department, then the Monitoring Department. This way, you'd gain a comprehensive understanding of Red Coast as a whole and we could wait and see where to assign you after that.

"Of course, as you can see, this plan has met with some resistance. But I have trust in you, Wenjie. Let me be clear: Until now, the trust placed in you has been mine, personally. I hope that you can continue to work hard and earn the trust of the organization as a whole."

Commissar Lei placed a hand on Ye's shoulder. She felt the warmth and strength conveyed through it. "Wenjie, let me tell you my sincere hope: One day, I'd like to call you *Comrade Ye*."

Lei stood up and strode away in the confident manner of a soldier. Ye's eyes were filled with tears. Seen through them, the code on the screen became flickering flames. This was the first time she had cried since the death of her father.

As Ye familiarized herself with the work of the Monitoring Department, she discovered that she was far less successful here than at the Transmission Department. The computer science knowledge she had was outdated, and she had to learn the software techniques from scratch. Even though Commissar Lei trusted her, the restrictions on her were severe. She was allowed to view the software source code, for example, but was forbidden from touching the database.

On a day-to-day basis, Ye was mainly supervised by Yang. He became even ruder to her, and would get angry at her for the smallest things. Commissar Lei talked to him about it multiple times without effect. It seemed that Yang became filled with a nameless anxiety as soon as he saw Ye.

Gradually, as Ye encountered more and more unexplainable matters in her work, she came to realize that the Red Coast Project was far more complex than she had imagined.

One day, the monitoring system intercepted a transmission that, after being deciphered by the computer, turned out to be a few satellite photographs. The blurry images were sent to the General Staff Department's Surveying and Mapping Bureau for interpretation. They turned out to be images of important military targets in China, including the naval harbor at Qingdao and several key factories of the Third Front program.[26] Analysis confirmed that these images came from the KH-9 American reconnaissance system.

The first KH-9 satellite had just been launched. Although it mainly relied on recoverable film capsules for intelligence gathering, it was also being used to test out the more advanced technique of radio transmission of digital images. Due to the

---

26 *Translator's Note:* The Third Front program was a secret, military-led industrialization effort during the Cultural Revolution that built factories in China's interior, where they would be less vulnerable to American and Soviet attacks.

technology's immaturity, the satellite transmitted at a low frequency, which increased its range of reception sufficiently for it to be intercepted by Red Coast. And because it was only a test, the encryption was not very secure and could be broken.

The KH-9 was without a doubt an important monitoring target, as it presented a rare opportunity to gather more information about American satellite reconnaissance systems. Yet, after the third day, Yang Weining ordered a change in the frequency and direction of monitoring and abandoned the target. Ye found the decision incomprehensible.

Another event also shocked her. Even though she was now in the Monitoring Department, sometimes the Transmission Department still needed her. One time, she accidentally saw the frequency settings for a few upcoming transmissions. She discovered that the designated frequencies for transmissions 304, 318, and 325 were lower than microwave range and could not result in any heating effect in the target.

One day, an officer summoned Ye to the main base administrative office out of the blue. From the officer's tone and expression, Ye knew that something had gone wrong.

As she walked into the office, the scene before her seemed familiar: All the senior officers of the base were present, along with two officers she didn't know. However, she could tell at a glance that they were from higher up in the chain of command.

Everyone's icy stares focused on her, but the sensitivity she had developed over the stormy years informed her that she wasn't the one in big trouble today. She was at most a sideshow. She saw Commissar Lei sitting in a corner with a dejected look.

He's finally going to pay for trusting me, she thought. At once, she decided that she would do whatever she could to save him. She would take responsibility for everything, even lie if necessary.

But Commissar Lei was the first to speak, and what he said was completely unexpected. "Ye Wenjie, I must make it clear at the start that I do not agree with what is about to be done. The decision was made by Chief Engineer Yang after requesting instructions from our superiors. He alone will be responsible for all consequences."

Commissar Lei turned to look at Yang, who nodded solemnly. Lei continued, "In order to better utilize your skills at Red Coast Base, Chief Engineer Yang repeatedly requested permission from our superiors to abandon the cover story we've been using with you. Our comrades from the Army Political Department"—he indicated the two officers Ye didn't know—"were sent to investigate your work situation. Finally, with the approval of our superiors, we've decided to inform you of the true nature of the Red Coast Project."

Only after a long pause did Ye finally understand Commissar Lei's meaning: He had been lying to her all along.

"I hope you will treasure this opportunity and work hard to redeem your sins. After this, you must behave with the utmost propriety. Any reactionary behavior will be severely punished!" Commissar Lei stared at Ye. He was a completely different person from the image Ye had formed of him. "Are we clear? Good. Now Chief Yang can explain."

The others left, leaving only Yang and Ye.

"If you don't want this, there's still time."

Ye discerned the weight behind these words. She now understood Yang's anxiety whenever he had seen her the last few weeks. To make full use of her skills, it was necessary for her to know the truth about Red Coast. However, this choice would extinguish the last ray of hope she had of ever leaving

Radar Peak. Once she said yes, she really would spend the rest of her life at Red Coast Base.

"I agree," Ye said, softly, but resolutely.

Thus, on this early summer evening, as the wind howled through the giant parabolic antenna, and as the forest rustled over the Greater Khingan Mountains in the distance, Yang Weining explained to Ye Wenjie the true nature of Red Coast.

It was a fairy tale for the ages, even more incredible than the commissar's lies.

13

Red Coast III

SELECTED DOCUMENTS FROM
THE RED COAST PROJECT

These documents were declassified three years after Ye Wenjie told Wang Miao the inside story of Red Coast and provide background information for what she told him.

I.

A Question Largely Ignored by Trends in Fundamental World Scientific Research

(Originally published in Internal Reference, XX/XX/196X)

[**Abstract**] Based on modern and contemporary history, there are two ways in which the results of fundamental scientific research can be converted into practical applications: gradualistic mode and saltatory mode.

Gradualistic mode: theoretical, fundamental results are gradually applied to technology; advances accumulate until they reach a breakthrough. Recent examples include the development of space technology.

Saltatory mode: theoretical, fundamental results rapidly become applied technology, leading to a technological leap. Recent examples include the appearance of atomic weapons. Until the forties, some of the foremost physicists still thought it would never be possible to release the energy of the atom. But atomic weapons then appeared within a very short period. We define a technology leap to occur when fundamental science is converted to applied technology across a great span in an extremely brief time interval.

Currently, both NATO and the Warsaw Pact are intensely active in fundamental research and investing heavily in it. One or more technological leaps can occur at any time. Such an occurrence will pose a major threat to our strategic planning.

This article argues that our focus is currently on the gradualistic mode of technology development and insufficient attention is paid to the possibility of technology leaps. Starting from a higher vantage point, we should develop a comprehensive strategy and set of principles so that we can respond appropriately when technological leaps occur.

Fields where technological leaps are most likely:

Physics: [omitted]

Biology: [omitted]

Computer Science: [omitted]

The Search for Extraterrestrial Intelligence (SETI): Of all fields, this is the one in which the possibility for a technology leap is greatest. If a leap occurs in this field, the impact will exceed the sum of technology leaps in the other three fields.

[Full Text][omitted]

[Instructions from Central Leadership] Distribute this article to appropriate personnel and organize discussion groups. The article's views will not be to the liking of some, but let's not rush to label the author. The key is to appreciate the author's long-term thinking. Some comrades cannot see beyond the ends of their noses, possibly because of the greater political environment, possibly because of their arrogance. This is not good. Strategic blind spots are extremely dangerous.

In my view, of the four fields where technology leaps may occur, we have given the least thought to the last one. It's worth some attention, and we should systematically analyze the matter in depth.

Signed: XXX Date: XX/XX/196X

II.

Research Report on the Possibility of Technology Leap Due to the Search for Extraterrestrial Intelligence

1. Current International Research Trends [**Summary**]

    (1) The United States and other NATO states: The scientific case and the necessity for SETI are generally accepted, and strong academic support exists.

    Project Ozma: In 1960, the National Radio Astronomy Observatory at Green Bank, West Virginia, searched for extraterrestrial intelligence with a radio telescope 26 meters in diameter. The project examined the stars Tau Ceti and Epsilon Eridani for 200 hours using ranges near the 1.420 gigahertz frequency. Project Ozma II, which will involve more targets and a broader frequency range, is planned for 1972.

    Probes: The Pioneer 10 and Pioneer 11 probes, each of which will carry a metal plaque containing information about civilization on Earth, are scheduled for launch in 1972. The Voyager 1 and Voyager 2 probes, each of which will carry a metal audio record, are scheduled for launch in 1977.

The Arecibo Observatory in Puerto Rico: Constructed in 1963, this is an important instrument for SETI. Its effective energy collection area is about 20 acres, which is greater than the sum of the collecting areas of all other radio telescopes in the world. When combined with its computer system, it can simultaneously monitor 65,000 channels and is also capable of ultrahigh-energy transmissions.

(2) The Soviet Union: Few sources of intelligence are available, but there are indications that large investments have been made in the field. Compared to NATO countries, the research seems to be more systematic and long term. Based on certain isolated information channels, plans are currently under way to build a global-scale very-long-baseline interferometry (VLBI) aperture-synthesis radio telescope system. Once the system is completed, it will possess the world's most powerful deep-space exploration capabilities.

2. Preliminary Analysis of Social Patterns of Extraterrestrial Civilizations Using a Materialist Conception of History [omitted]

3. Preliminary Analysis of the Influence of Extraterrestrial Civilizations on Human Social and Political Trends [omitted]

4. Preliminary Analysis of the Influence on Current International Patterns Due to Possible Contact with Extraterrestrial Civilizations

(1) Unidirectional contact (only receiving messages sent by extraterrestrial intelligence): [omitted]

(2) Bidirectional contact (exchange of messages with extraterrestrial intelligence and direct contact): [omitted]

5. The Danger and Consequences of Superpowers Making Initial Contact with Extraterrestrial Intelligence and Monopolizing Such Contact

(1) Analysis of consequences of American Imperialists and NATO making initial contact with extraterrestrial intelligence and monopolizing such contact: [still classified]

(2) Analysis of consequences of Soviet Revisionists and Warsaw Pact making initial contact with extraterrestrial intelligence and monopolizing such contact: [still classified]

[Instructions from Central Leadership] Others have already sent their messages out into space. It's dangerous if extraterrestrials only hear their voices. We should speak up as well. Only then will they get a complete picture of human society. It's not possible to get the truth by only listening to one side. We must make this happen, and quickly.

Signed: XXX Date: XX/XX/196X

III.

Research Report on the Initial Phase of the Red Coast Project (XX/XX/196X)

TOP SECRET

Number of Copies: 2

Summary Document: Central Document Number XXXXXX, forwarded to the Commission for Science, Technology, and Industry for National Defense, the

Chinese Academy of Sciences, and the Central Planning Commission, Department of National Defense; disseminated at the XXXXXX Conference and the XXXXXX Conference; partially disseminated at the XXXXXX Conference.

Topic Serial Number: 3760

Code Name: "Red Coast"

1. Goal [**Summary**]

To search for the possible existence of extraterrestrial intelligence and to attempt contact and exchange.

2. Theoretical Study of the Red Coast Project

(1) Searching and Monitoring

Monitoring frequency range: 1,000 MHz to 40,000 MHz

Monitoring channels: 15,000

Key frequencies to monitor:

Hydrogen atom frequency at 1,420 MHz

Hydroxyl radical radiation frequency at 1,667 MHz

Water molecule radiation frequency at 22,000 MHz

Monitoring target range: a sphere centered around Earth with a radius of 1,000 light-years, containing approximately 20 million stars. For a list of targets, please see Appendix 1.

(2) Message Transmission

Transmission frequencies: 2,800 MHz, 12,000 MHz, 22,000 MHz

Transmission power: 10–25 megawatts

Transmission targets: a sphere centered around Earth with a radius of 200 light-years, containing approximately 100,000 stars. For a list of targets, please see Appendix 2.

(3) Development of the Red Coast Self-Interpreting Code System

Guiding principle: using universal, basic mathematical and physical laws, construct an elemental linguistic code that can be understood by any civilization that has mastered basic algebra, Euclidean geometry, and the laws of classical mechanics (nonrelativistic physics).

Using the elemental code above and supplemented with low-resolution images, gradually build up to a full linguistic system. Languages supported: Chinese and Esperanto.

The entire system's information content should be 680 KB. Transmission times at the 2,800 MHz, 12,000 MHz, and 22,000 MHz channels are 1,183 minutes, 224 minutes, and 132 minutes respectively.

3. Implementation Plan for the Red Coast Project

(1) Preliminary Design for the Red Coast Monitoring and Searching System [**still classified**]

(2) Preliminary Design for the Red Coast Transmission System [**still classified**]

(3) Preliminary Site-Selection Plan for Red Coast Base [**omitted**]

(4) Preliminary Thoughts on the Formation of Red Coast Force from within the Second Artillery Corps [**still classified**]

4. Content of Message Transmitted by Red Coast [**Summary**]

Overview of Earth (3.1 KB), overview of life on Earth (4.4 KB), overview of human society (4.6 KB), basic world history (5.4 KB).

Total information content: 17.5 KB.

The entire message will be sent after transmitting

the self-interpreting code system. Transmission times of message at the 2,800 MHz, 12,000 MHz, and 22,000 MHz channels are 31 minutes, 7.5 minutes, and 3.5 minutes, respectively.

The message will be carefully vetted by a multidisciplinary review to ensure that it will not give away the Earth's coordinates relative to the Milky Way. Among the three channels, transmission at the higher-frequency 12,000 MHz and 22,000 MHz channels should be minimized to reduce the likelihood that the source of transmission may be precisely ascertained.

IV.
Message to Extraterrestrial Civilizations
First Draft [Complete Text]

Attention, you who have received this message! This message was sent out by a country that represents revolutionary justice on Earth! Before this, you may have already received other messages sent from the same direction. Those messages were sent by an imperialist superpower on this planet. That superpower is struggling against another superpower for world domination so that it can drag human history backwards. We hope you will not listen to their lies. Stand with justice, stand with the revolution!

[Instructions from Central Leadership] This is utter crap! It's enough to put up big-character posters[27]

---

27 *Translator's Note:* Hand-written posters using large Chinese characters have become associated with the Cultural Revolution in the popular imagination. However, they have a long history in China as tools of propaganda as well as protest both before and after the Cultural Revolution.

everywhere on the ground, but we should not send them into space. The Cultural Revolution leadership should no longer have any involvement with Red Coast. Such an important message must be composed carefully. It's probably best to have it drafted by a special committee and then discussed and approved by a meeting of the Politburo.

Signed: XXX Date: XX/XX/196X

Second Draft [omitted]

Third Draft [omitted]

Fourth Draft [Complete Text]

We extend our best wishes to you, inhabitants of another world.

After reading the following message, you should have a basic understanding of civilization on Earth. By dint of long toil and creativity, the human race has built a splendid civilization, blossoming with a multitude of diverse cultures. We have also begun to understand the laws governing the natural world and the development of human societies. We cherish all that we have accomplished.

But our world is still flawed. Hate exists, as does prejudice and war. Because of conflicts between the forces of production and the relations of production, wealth distribution is extremely uneven, and large portions of humanity live in poverty and misery.

Human societies are working hard to resolve the difficulties and problems they face, striving to create a better future for Earth civilization. The country that sent this message is engaged in this effort. We are dedicated to building an ideal society, where the labor and value of every member of the human race are fully respected, where everyone's material and spiritual needs are fully met, so that civilization on Earth may become more perfect.

With the best of intentions, we look forward to establishing contact with other civilized societies in the universe. We look forward to working together with you to build a better life in this vast universe.

V.
Related Policies and Strategies

1. Consideration of Policies and Strategies After Reception of Message from Extraterrestrial Intelligence [omitted]

2. Consideration of Policies and Strategies After Establishing Contact with Extraterrestrial Intelligence [omitted]

[Instructions from Central Leadership] It's important to take the time out of our busy schedules to do something entirely unrelated to our immediate needs. This project has allowed us to give some thought to issues we have never had time for. Indeed, we can think through them only when we take a sufficiently high vantage point. This alone is enough to justify the Red Coast Project.

How wonderful it will be if the universe really contains other intelligences and other societies! Bystanders have the clearest view. Someone truly neutral will then be able to comment on whether we're the heroes or villains of history.

Signed: XXX Date: XX/XX/196X

14

Red Coast IV

"Professor Ye," Wang Miao said, "I have a question. Back then, SETI was marginalized research. Why did the Red Coast Project have such a high security rating?"

"That question was asked during the very first phases of the Red Coast Project, and continued to be asked until the end. But now you should know the answer. We can only be impressed by the foresight of the top decision-maker responsible for the Red Coast Project."

"Yes, he thought far ahead." Wang nodded gravely.

Wang knew that it was only within the last couple of years that serious and systematic consideration had been given to the question of how and to what degree human societies would be influenced by establishing contact with extraterrestrial intelligence, but the research had rapidly gained interest, and the conclusions were shocking.

Naïve, idealistic hopes had been shattered. Scholars found that, contrary to the happy wishes of most people, it was not a good idea for the human race as a whole to make contact with extraterrestrials. The impact of such contact on human society would be divisive rather than uniting, and would exacerbate rather than mitigate the conflicts between different cultures. In summary, if contact were to occur, the internal divisions within Earth civilization would be magnified and likely lead to disaster. The most shocking conclusion of all was that the impact would have nothing at all to do with the degree and type of contact (unidirectional or bidirectional), or the form and degree of advancement of the alien civilization.

This was the theory of "contact as symbol" proposed by sociologist Bill Mathers of RAND Corporation in his book, *The 100,000-Light-Year Iron Curtain: SETI Sociology*. Mathers believed that contact with an alien civilization is only a symbol or a switch. Regardless of the content of the encounter, the results would be the same.

Suppose that the nature of the contact is such that only the existence of extraterrestrial intelligence is confirmed, with no other substantive information—what Mathers called elementary contact. The impact would be magnified by the lens of human mass psychology and culture until it resulted in huge, substantive influences on the progress of civilization. If such contact were monopolized by one country or political force, the significance would be comparable to an overwhelming advantage in economic and military power.

"How did Red Coast end?"

"You can probably guess."

Wang nodded again. Of course he understood that, had Red Coast succeeded, the world today would be very different. To comfort Ye, he said, "It's still too early to tell if it succeeded or not. The radio waves sent out by Red Coast haven't gone very far in the universe yet."

Ye shook her head. "The farther the signals travel, the weaker they become, and the less likely that any extraterrestrial civilization will receive them. Of course, if aliens have already detected the Earth's existence and its oxygen-rich atmosphere and decided to focus powerful equipment specifically at us, the story would be different. But, in general, research shows that in order for extraterrestrials to detect our signals, we must broadcast at a power level equal to the energy output of a midsized star.

"Soviet astrophysicist Nicolai Kardashev once proposed that civilizations can be divided into three types based on the power they can command—for communication purposes, let's say. A Type I civilization can muster an amount of energy equivalent to the total energy output of the Earth. Based on his estimates, the energy output of the Earth is about 10^{15} to 10^{16} watts. A Type II civilization can marshal the energy equivalent to the output of a typical star—10^{26} watts. A Type III civilization's communication energy can reach 10^{36} watts, approximately equal to the energy output of a galaxy. Civilization on Earth is currently about a Type 0.7, not even a full Type I. And the transmissions from Red Coast used only about one ten-millionth of the amount of power the Earth could muster. Our call was like the buzzing of a mosquito in the sky. No one could hear it."

"But if Kardashev's Type II and Type III civilizations really exist, we should be able to hear *them*."

"We never heard anything during the twenty years that Red Coast was in operation."

"Indeed. Given Red Coast and SETI, could all our efforts ultimately have proven only one thing: In the entire universe, only the Earth has intelligent life?"

Ye gave a light sigh. "Theoretically, there may never be a definitive answer to that question. But my sense, and the sense of everyone who went through Red Coast, is that that is the case."

"It's too bad that Red Coast was decommissioned. Once

it was built, it should have been kept running. It was a truly great enterprise."

"Red Coast's decline was gradual. At the beginning of the eighties, there was a large-scale renovation. Mainly, the transmission and monitoring computer systems were partially upgraded. The transmission system was automated, and the monitoring system incorporated two IBM minicomputers. The data processing capability became far more advanced, and it was able to simultaneously monitor forty thousand channels.

"But later, as people gained perspective, they had a better appreciation of the difficulty of the search for extraterrestrial intelligence, and the leadership lost interest in Red Coast. The first change was reducing the base's security rating. The consensus was that the extreme secrecy around Red Coast was unnecessary, and the security detail at the base was reduced from a company to a squad, until eventually only a group of five security guards were left. Also, after that renovation, although Red Coast remained administratively within the Second Artillery Corps, management of its scientific activities was turned over to the Chinese Academy of Sciences' Astronomy Institute, and it took on some research projects that had nothing to do with the search for extraterrestrial intelligence or the military."

"I believe you achieved most of your scientific accomplishments during that time."

"Initially, Red Coast also took on some radio astronomy projects. At the time, it was the largest radio telescope in the country. Later, as other radio astronomy observatories were built, Red Coast's research turned to the observation and analysis of solar electromagnetic activity. For this, they added a solar telescope. The mathematical model we built for solar electromagnetic activity was at the forefront of the field back then, and had many practical applications. With these later research results, the large amount invested in Red Coast had at least a little return.

"Actually, much of the credit should be given to Commissar Lei. Of course he had his own agenda. He realized that as a political officer in a technical unit, his future wasn't bright. Before joining the army, he had studied astrophysics as well, so he wanted to return to doing science. The research projects that Red Coast took on outside of the search for extraterrestrial intelligence were all due to his efforts."

"I doubt that he could have returned to technical work so easily after spending so much time as a political commissar. Back then, you still hadn't been politically rehabilitated. It looks to me like all he did was to put his name on your research results."

Ye smiled forgivingly. "Without Lei, Red Coast Base would have been finished even earlier. After Red Coast was designated for conversion to civilian use, the military basically abandoned it. Eventually, the Chinese Academy of Sciences couldn't maintain the funds necessary for Red Coast's operation, and it was shut down."

Ye didn't talk much about her daily life at Red Coast Base, and Wang didn't ask. Four years after entering the base, she married Yang Weining. Everything just happened naturally, without any drama. Later, an accident at the base killed both Yang and Lei, and Yang Dong was born after her father's death. The mother and daughter only left Radar Peak in the mid-eighties, when Red Coast Base was finally decommissioned. Ye later returned to Tsinghua, her alma mater, to teach astrophysics until retirement. All this Wang had heard from Sha Ruishan at the Miyun Radio Astronomy Observatory.

"The search for extraterrestrial intelligence is a unique

discipline. It has a profound influence on the researcher's perspective on life." Ye spoke in a drawn-out voice, as though telling stories to a child. "In the dead of the night, I could hear in my headphones the lifeless noise of the universe. The noise was faint but constant, more eternal than the stars. Sometimes I thought it sounded like the endless winter winds of the Greater Khingan Mountains. I felt so cold then, and the loneliness was indescribable.

"From time to time, I would gaze up at the stars after a night shift and think that they looked like a glowing desert, and I myself was a poor child abandoned in the desert. . . . I thought that life was truly an accident among accidents in the universe. The universe was an empty palace, and humankind the only ant in the entire palace. This kind of thinking infused the second half of my life with a conflicted mentality: Sometimes I thought life was precious, and everything was so important; but other times I thought humans were insignificant, and nothing was worthwhile. Anyway, my life passed day after day accompanied by this strange feeling, and before I knew it, I was old. . . ."

Wang wanted to comfort this old woman who had devoted her life to a lonely but great enterprise, but Ye's last speech caused him to sink into the same sorrowful mood. He found that he had nothing to say except, "Professor Ye, someday I'll go with you to visit the ruins of Red Coast Base."

Ye slowly shook her head. "Xiao Wang, I'm not like you. I'm getting on in years, and my health isn't what it used to be. It's hard to predict the future. I live my life day to day."

Looking at the silvery head of hair on Ye Wenjie, Wang knew she was thinking of her daughter again.

15

Three Body: Copernicus, Universal Football, and Tri-Solar Day

After leaving Ye's home, Wang Miao couldn't calm down. The events of the last two days and the history of Red Coast, two seemingly unconnected strands, now twisted together, made the world unfamiliar overnight.

Once he was home, in order to escape this mood, Wang turned on the computer, put on the V-suit, and logged on to *Three Body* for the third time.

The attempt to adjust his state of mind worked. By the time the log-in screen appeared, Wang seemed like a different person, one filled with an unexplainable excitement. Unlike the first two times, this time Wang came with a purpose: He was going to reveal the secret of the world of *Three Body*.

He created a new log-in ID appropriate for his new role: Copernicus.

Once logged in, Wang again stood on that broad, desolate plain, facing the strange dawn of the world of *Three Body*. A colossal pyramid appeared in the east, but right away Wang knew it was no longer the pyramid of King Zhou of Shang or Mozi. It had a Gothic-style apex, stabbing straight into the morning sky, recalling St. Joseph's Church at Wangfujing. But if that church were placed next to this pyramid, it would be nothing more than an entrance booth. He saw many buildings in the distance that were apparently dehydratories, but also now built in the Gothic style, with tall, sharp steeples, as though the ground had grown numerous spikes.

Wang saw a door on the side of the pyramid, lit from within by flickering lights. He walked over. Inside the tunnel was a row of statues of the gods of Olympus holding up torches, their surfaces blackened by smoke. He entered the Great Hall and saw that it was even dimmer than the entrance tunnel. Two silver candelabra on top of a long marble table provided a drowsy light.

Several men were seated around the table. The dim light allowed Wang to see only the outlines of their faces. Their eyes were hidden in the shadows of their deep eye sockets, but Wang could still feel their gazes focusing on him. The men seemed to be dressed in medieval robes. On closer examination, one or two of them had simpler robes, more like Classical Greek chitons. At one end of the table was a thin, tall man. The golden crown on top of his head was the only thing that glittered in the Great Hall other than the candles. With some effort, Wang saw by the dim candlelight that his robe was different from the others': it was red.

Wang realized that the game displayed a distinct world for each player. This world, based on the European High Middle Ages, was chosen by the software based on his ID.

"You're late. The meeting has been going on for a while," the gold-crowned, red-robed man said. "I'm Pope Gregory."

Wang tried to recall what little he knew of European

history in the Middle Ages so that he could deduce the level of advancement of this civilization based on the name. But then he remembered how wildly anachronistic historical references could be in the world of *Three Body* and decided the effort wasn't worth it.

"I'm Aristotle. You changed your ID, but we all recognize you. In the previous two civilizations, you traveled to the East." The speaker was the man with the Greek chiton. He had a head of white curls.

"Yes." Wang nodded. "There, I witnessed the destruction of two civilizations, one by extreme cold, another by a blazing sun. I also saw the great efforts the scholars of the East expended in trying to master the laws governing the sun's motion."

"Ha!" The sound came from a man with a goatee that curled upward. He was even thinner than the pope. "Eastern scholars tried to understand the secrets of the sun's motion through meditation, epiphany, or even dreams. Utterly laughable!"

"This is Galileo," said Aristotle. "He advocates understanding the world through observation and experiment. He is an unimaginative thinker, but his results demand our attention."

"Mozi also conducted experiments and observation," Wang said.

Galileo snorted. "Mozi's way of thinking was still Eastern. He was nothing more than a mystic dressed as a scientist. He never took his own observation data seriously, and he constructed his model based on subjective speculation. Ridiculous! I feel sorry for his refined equipment. We're different. Based on large amounts of observational data and experiments, we make strict, logical deductions to build a model of the universe. Then we go back to experimentation and observation to test it."

"That's correct." Wang nodded. "That's also my way of thinking."

"Have you brought a calendar as well, then?" The pope's tone was mocking.

"I don't have a calendar. I only brought a model built upon observation data. But I must make it clear that even if the model is correct, it's not certain that by using it one can master the precise details of the sun's motion and create a calendar. However, it's a necessary step."

A few lonely claps echoed throughout the Great Hall. The applause came from Galileo. "Excellent, Copernicus, excellent. Your pragmatic way of thinking, adapted to the experimental, scientific approach, is lacking in most scholars. Based on this alone, your theory is worth listening to."

The pope nodded at Wang. "Go ahead."

After calming himself and walking to the other end of the long table, Wang said, "It's actually pretty simple. The reason why the sun's motion seems patternless is because our world has three suns. Under the influence of their mutually perturbing gravitational attraction, their movements are unpredictable—the three-body problem. When our planet revolves around one of the suns in a stable orbit, that's a Stable Era. When one or more of the other suns move within a certain distance, their gravitational pull will snatch the planet away from the sun it's orbiting, causing it to wander unstably through the gravitational fields of the three suns. That's a Chaotic Era. After an uncertain amount of time, our planet is once again pulled into a temporary orbit and another Stable Era begins. This is a football game at the scale of the universe. The players are the three suns, and our planet is the football."

A few hollow laughs rang out in the Great Hall. "Burn him to death," the pope said impassively. The two soldiers standing at the door in rusty armor started toward Wang like two clumsy robots.

"Burn him." Galileo sighed. "I had hopes for you, but you're nothing more than another mystic or warlock."

"Such men are a public nuisance," Aristotle agreed.

"At least let me finish!" Wang shoved away the iron gauntlets of the two soldiers.

"Have you seen three suns? Or know anyone who has?" Galileo asked.

"Everyone has seen them."

"Then, other than the sun that appears during Chaotic Eras and Stable Eras, where are the other two?"

"The sun that we see at different times may not be the same: It's only one of the three suns. When the other two are far away, they look like flying stars."

"You lack basic scientific training," Galileo said, shaking his head. "The sun must move continuously to a distant spot. It cannot jump over the intervening space. According to your hypothesis, there should be another observable situation: The sun must get smaller than it usually appears but bigger than a flying star, and gradually shrink into a flying star as it moves farther away. But we've never seen the sun behave that way."

"Since you have scientific training, you ought to have some knowledge of the sun's structure."

"That's my proudest discovery. The sun is made of a sparse but expansive gaseous outer layer and a dense and hot inner core."

"Very true," said Wang. "But you apparently haven't discovered the special optical interaction between the sun's gaseous outer layer and our planet's atmosphere. It's a phenomenon akin to polarization or destructive interference. As a result, when we view the sun from within our atmosphere and it gets a certain distance from us, the gaseous outer layer suddenly becomes completely transparent and invisible, and all we can see is its bright inner core. The sun then appears to be only the size of the inner core, a flying star.

"This phenomenon has confused every researcher in every civilization throughout history, and prevented them from discovering the existence of the three suns. Now you understand why the appearance of three flying stars heralds a long period of extreme cold: because all three suns are far away."

A brief silence followed as everyone pondered this. Aristotle was the first to speak. "You lack basic training in logic. It's true that we can sometimes see three flying stars, and that's always accompanied by destructive periods of extreme cold. But based on your theory, we should also sometimes see three normal-sized suns in the sky. This has never happened. In all the records of all the civilizations, this has never occurred!"

"Wait!" A man wearing a strangely shaped hat and a long beard stood up and spoke for the first time. "I'm Leonardo da Vinci. There may be such historical records. One civilization saw two suns and was immediately destroyed by their combined heat, but the record was very vague."

"We're talking about three suns, not two!" Galileo shouted. "According to his theory, three suns must appear sometime, just like three flying stars."

"Three suns *have* appeared," Wang said, utterly calm. "And people have seen them. But those who saw such a great sight could not leave behind any information about them because seeing three suns would mean that they had at most a few seconds left to live. They had no chance to escape or survive. Tri-solar days are the most terrifying catastrophes for our world. On such days, the surface of the planet would turn into a smelting furnace in a second, and the heat would be enough to melt rocks. After the destruction caused by a tri-solar day, an eon would pass before the reappearance of life and civilization. This is yet another reason why there's no historical record of them."

Silence. Everyone stared at the pope.

"Burn him," the pope said, gently. The smile on his face was a little familiar to Wang: the smile of King Zhou of Shang.

The Great Hall came alive, and everyone seemed to be preparing for a celebration. Galileo and some others joyfully carried a stake out of a dark corner. They pulled off the charcoal-black body still tied to the stake and cast it aside before fastening it in an upright position. Another group happily piled firewood around the stake. Only Leonardo ignored the commotion. He sat at the table, pondering, and occasionally using a pen to calculate something on the table.

"Giordano Bruno," Aristotle said, pointing at the black-ened body. "Like you, he came here and spewed nonsense."

"Use a low fire," the pope said, his voice weak.

Two soldiers started to tie Wang Miao to the stake using asbestos ropes. Wang used the hand that was still free to point at the pope. "You are nothing more than a program. As for the rest of you, you're either programs or idiots. I will log back on!"

"You cannot return. You will disappear forever from the world of *Three Body*." Galileo cackled.

"Then you *must* be a program. A normal person would certainly understand the basics of the Internet. The most the game can do is record my MAC address. I can just switch computers and create a new ID. I'll announce myself when I'm back."

"The system has recorded your retinal scan through the V-suit," Leonardo said, looking up at Wang. Then he returned to his calculations.

Wang Miao was seized by a nameless terror. He shouted, "Don't do this! Let me go! I'm telling the truth!"

"If you're telling the truth, then you won't be burnt to death. The game rewards those who are on the right path." As Aristotle grinned, he took out a silver Zippo lighter, flipped it in his hand in a complicated fashion, and then flicked it on.

As he was about to light the firewood piled around Wang, a bright red light filled the entrance tunnel, followed by a wave of heat and smoke. A horse dashed out of the light and into the Great Hall. Its body was already on fire, and as it galloped, the wind whipped it into a ball of flames. The rider, a knight in heavy armor that glowed red from the heat, dragged a line of white smoke behind him.

"The world has ended! The world has ended! Dehydrate! Dehydrate!" As the knight shouted, the animal under him fell down and turned into a bonfire. The knight was thrown some distance and rolled all the way to the stake, where he stopped moving. White smoke continued to pour out of openings in the armor. The sizzling grease from the dead man inside oozed out on the ground and caught fire, giving the armor a pair of burning wings.

Everyone in the Great Hall streamed toward the entrance tunnel and squeezed into it, disappearing in the red light from outside. Wang Miao struggled with all his strength until he was freed from the ropes. He dodged the burning knight and horse, dashed through the empty Great Hall, and ran down the sweltering tunnel until he emerged outside.

The ground glowed red like a piece of iron in a black-smith's furnace. Bright rivulets of lava snaked across the dim red earth, forming a net of fire that stretched to the horizon. Countless thin pillars of flame erupted toward the sky: The dehydratories were burning. The dehydrated bodies inside gave the fire a strange bluish glow.

Not far from him, Wang saw a dozen or so small pillars of flame of the same color. These were the people who had just run out of the pyramid: the pope, Galileo, Aristotle, and Leonardo. The fiery pillars around them were translucent blue, and he could see their faces and bodies slowly deform-ing in the flame. They focused their gazes on Wang, who had just emerged. Holding the same pose and lifting their arms toward the sky, they chanted in unison, "Tri-solar day—"

Wang looked up and saw three gigantic suns slowly spinning around an invisible origin, like an immense three-bladed fan blowing a deadly wind toward the world below. The three suns took up almost the entire sky, and as they drifted toward the west, half of the formation sank below the horizon. The giant fan continued to spin, a bright blade occasionally shooting above the horizon to give the dying world another brief sunrise and sunset. After a sunset, the ground glowed dim red, and the sunrise a moment later flooded everything with its glaring, parallel rays.

Once the three suns had completely set, the thick clouds that had formed from all the evaporated water still reflected their glow. The sky burned, displaying a hellish, maddening beauty.

After the last light of destruction finally disappeared and the clouds only glowed with a faint red luminescence reflect-ed from the hellish fire on the ground, a few lines of giant text appeared:

Civilization Number 183 was destroyed by a tri-solar day. This civilization had advanced to the Middle Ages.

After a long time, life and civilization will begin again, and progress once more through the unpredictable world of *Three Body*.

But in this civilization, Copernicus successfully revealed the basic structure of the universe. The civilization of *Three Body* will take its first leap. The game has now entered the second level.

We invite you to log on to the second level of *Three Body*.

16

The Three-Body Problem

As soon as Wang logged out of the game, the phone rang.

It was Shi Qiang, who said it was urgent that he come down to Shi's office at the Criminal Division. Wang glanced at his watch: It was three in the morning.

Wang arrived at Da Shi's chaotic office and saw that it was already filled with a dense cloud of cigarette smoke. A young woman police officer who shared the office fanned the smoke away from her nose with a notebook. Da Shi introduced her as Xu Bingbing, a computer specialist from the Information Security Division.

The third person in the office surprised Wang. It was Wei Cheng, the reclusive, mysterious husband of Shen Yufei from the Frontiers of Science. Wei's hair was a mess. He looked up at Wang, but seemed to have forgotten they had met.

"I'm sorry to bother you, but at least it looks like you weren't asleep," Da Shi said. "I have to deal with something that I haven't told the Battle Command Center yet, and I need your advice." He turned to Wei Cheng. "Tell him what you told me."

"My life is in danger," Wei said, his face wooden.

"Why don't you start from the beginning?"

"Fine. I will. Don't complain about me being long-winded.

Actually, I've often thought about talking to someone lately. . . ." Wei turned to look at Xu Bingbing. "Don't you need to take notes or something?"

"Not right now," Da Shi said, not missing a beat. "You didn't have anyone to talk to before?"

"No, that's not it. I was too lazy to talk. I've always been lazy."

Wei Cheng's story

I've been lackadaisical since I was a kid. When I lived at boarding school, I never washed the dishes or made the bed. I never got excited about anything. Too lazy to study, too lazy to even play, I dawdled my way through the days without any clear goals.

But I knew that I had some special talents others lacked. For example, if you drew a line, I could always draw another line that would divide it into the golden ratio: 1.618. My classmates told me that I should be a carpenter, but I thought it was more than that, a kind of intuition about numbers and shapes. But my math grades were just as bad as my grades in other classes. I was too lazy to bother showing my work. On tests, I just wrote out my guesses as answers. I got them right about eighty to ninety percent of the time, but I still got mediocre scores.

When I was a second-year student in high school, a math teacher noticed me. Back then, many high school teachers had impressive academic credentials, because during the Cultural Revolution many talented scholars ended up teaching in high schools. My teacher was like that.

One day, he kept me after class. He wrote out a dozen or so numerical sequences on the blackboard and asked me to

203

write out the summation formula for each. I wrote out the formulas for some of them almost instantaneously and could tell at a glance that the rest of them were divergent.

My teacher took out a book, The Collected Cases of Sherlock Holmes. He turned to one story— "A Study in Scarlet," I think. There's a scene in it where Watson sees a plainly dressed messenger downstairs and points him out to Holmes. Holmes says, "Oh, you mean the retired sergeant of marines?" Watson is amazed by how Holmes could deduce the man's history, but Holmes can't articulate his reasoning and has to think for a while to figure out his chain of deductions. It was based on the man's hand, his movements, and so on. He tells Watson that there is nothing strange about this: Most people would have difficulty explaining how they know two and two make four.

My teacher closed the book and said to me, "You're just like that. Your derivation is so fast and instinctive that you can't even tell how you got the answer." Then he asked me, "When you see a string of numbers, what do you feel? I'm talking about feelings."

I said, "Any combination of numbers appears to me as a three-dimensional shape. Of course I can't describe the shapes of numbers, but they really do appear as shapes."

"Then what about when you see geometric figures?" The teacher asked.

I said, "It's just the opposite. In my mind there are no geometric figures. Everything turns into numbers. It's just like if you get really close to a picture in the newspaper and everything turns into little dots."

The teacher said, "You really have a natural gift for math, but . . . but . . ." He added a few more "but"s, pacing back and forth as though I was a difficult problem that he didn't know how to handle. "But people like you don't cherish your gift." After thinking for a while, he seemed to give up, saying, "Why don't you sign up for the district math competition next month? I'm not going to tutor you. I'd just be wasting my time with your sort. But when you give your answers, make sure to write out your derivations."

So I went to the competition. From the district level up through the International Mathematics Olympiad in Budapest, I won first place each time. After I got back, I was accepted by a top college's math program without having to go through the entrance examination. . . .

You're not bored by my talking all this time? Ah, good. Well, to make sense of what happened later, I have to tell you all this. That high school math teacher was right. I didn't cherish my talent. Bachelor's, master's, Ph.D.—I never put much effort into any of them, but I did manage to get through them all. However, once I graduated and went back to the real world, I realized that I was completely useless. Other than math, I knew nothing. I was half asleep when it came to the complexities of relationships between people. The longer I worked, the worse my career. Eventually I became a lecturer at a college, but I couldn't survive there either. I just couldn't take teaching seriously. I'd write on the blackboard, "easy to prove," and my students would still struggle for a long while. Later, when they began to eliminate the worst teachers, I was fired.

By then I was sick of everything. I packed a bag and went to a Buddhist temple deep in the mountains somewhere in southern China.

Oh, I didn't go to become a monk. Too lazy for that. I just wanted to find a truly peaceful place to live for a while. The abbot there was my father's old friend—very intellectual, but became a monk in his old age. The way my father told it, at *his level, this was about the only way out. The abbot asked me to stay. I told him, "I want to find a peaceful, easy way to just muddle through the rest of my life." The abbot said, "This place isn't really peaceful. There are lots of tourists, and many pilgrims too. The truly peaceful can find peace in a bustling city. And to attain that state, you need to empty yourself." I said, "I'm empty enough. Fame and fortune are nothing to me. Many of the monks in this temple are worldlier than me." The abbot shook his head and said, "No, emptiness is not nothingness. Emptiness is a type of existence. You must use this existential emptiness to fill yourself."*

His words were very enlightening to me. Later, after I thought about it a bit, I realized that it wasn't Buddhist philosophy at all, but was more akin to some modern physics theories. The abbot also told me he wasn't going to discuss Buddhism with me. His reason was the same as my high school teacher's: With my sort, he'd just be wasting his time.

That first night, I couldn't sleep in the tiny room in the temple. I didn't realize that this refuge from the world would be so uncomfortable. My blanket and sheet both became damp in the mountain fog, and the bed was so hard. In order to make myself sleep, I tried to follow the abbot's advice and fill myself with "emptiness."

In my mind, the first "emptiness" I created was the infinity of space. There was nothing in it, not even light. But soon I knew that this empty universe could not make me feel peace. Instead, it filled me with a nameless anxiety, like a drowning man wanting to grab on to anything at hand.

So I created a sphere in this infinite space for myself: not too big, though possessing mass. My mental state didn't improve, however. The sphere floated in the middle of "emptiness"— in infinite space, anywhere could be the middle. The universe had nothing that could act on it, and it could act on nothing. It hung there, never moving, never changing, like a perfect interpretation for death.

I created a second sphere whose mass was equal to the first one's. Both had perfectly reflective surfaces. They reflected each other's images, displaying the only existence in the universe other than itself. But the situation didn't improve much. If the spheres had no initial movement—that is, if I didn't push them at first—they would be quickly pulled together by their own gravitational attraction. Then the two spheres would stay together and hang there without moving, a symbol for death. If they did have initial movement and didn't collide, then they would revolve around each other under the influence of gravity. No matter what the initial conditions, the revolutions would eventually stabilize and become unchanging: the dance of death.

I then introduced a third sphere, and to my astonishment, the situation changed completely. Like I said, any geometric figure turns into numbers in the depths of my mind. The sphereless, one-sphere, and two-sphere universes all showed up as a single equation or a few equations, like a few lonesome leaves in late fall. But this third sphere gave "emptiness" life. The three spheres, given initial movements, went through complex, seemingly never-repeating movements. The descriptive equations rained down in a thunderstorm without end.

Just like that, I fell asleep. The three spheres continued to dance in my dream, a patternless, never-repeating dance. Yet, in the depths of my mind, the dance did possess a rhythm; it was just that its period of repetition was infinitely long. This mesmerized me. I wanted to describe the whole period, or at least a part of it.

*The next day I kept on thinking about the three spheres danc-
ing in "emptiness." My attention had never been so completely
engaged. It got to the point where one of the monks asked the
abbot whether I was having mental health issues. The abbot
laughed and said, "Don't worry. He has found emptiness."
Yes, I had found emptiness. Now I could be at peace in a bustling city. Even in the midst of a noisy crowd, my heart would
be completely tranquil. For the first time, I enjoyed math. I
felt like a libertine who has always fluttered carelessly from
one woman to another suddenly finding himself in love.*

*The physics principles behind the three-body problem[28]
are very simple. It's mainly a math problem.*

"Didn't you know about Henri Poincaré?" Wang Miao interrupted Wei to ask.[29]

*At the time, I didn't. Yes, I know that someone studying
math should know about a master like Poincaré, but I didn't
worship masters and I didn't want to become one, so I didn't
know his work. But even if I had, I would have continued to
pursue the three-body problem.*

---

28 *Author's Note:* How three bodies would move under the influence of their
    mutual gravitational attractions is a traditional problem in classical mechanics
    that arises naturally in the study of celestial mechanics. Many have worked
    on it since the sixteenth century. Euler, Lagrange, and more recent researchers
    (aided by computers) have all found solutions for special cases of the three-
    body problem. Karl F. Sundman later proved the existence of a general
    solution to the three-body problem in the form of a convergent infinite series,
    but the series converges so slowly that it is practically useless.

29 *Translator's Note:* Poincaré showed that the three-body problem exhibited
    sensitive dependence on initial conditions, which we would now understand
    as characteristic of chaotic behavior.

Everyone seems to believe that Poincaré proved that the three-body problem couldn't be solved, but I think they're mistaken. He only proved sensitive dependence on initial conditions, and that the three-body system couldn't be solved by integrals. But sensitivity is not the same as being completely indeterminable. It's just that the solution contains a greater number of different forms. What's needed is a new algorithm.

Back then, I thought of one thing: Have you heard of the Monte Carlo method? Ah, it's a computer algorithm often used for calculating the area of irregular shapes. Specifically, the software puts the figure of interest in a figure of known area, such as a circle, and randomly strikes it with many tiny balls, never targeting the same spot twice. After a large number of balls, the proportion of balls that fall within the irregular shape compared to the total number of balls used to hit the circle will yield the area of the shape. Of course, the smaller the balls used, the more accurate the result.

Although the method is simple, it shows how, mathematically, random brute force can overcome precise logic. It's a numerical approach that uses quantity to derive quality. This is my strategy for solving the three-body problem. I study the system moment by moment. At each moment, the spheres' motion vectors can combine in infinite ways. I treat each combination like a life form. The key is to set up some rules: which combinations of motion vectors are "healthy" and "beneficial," and which combinations are "detrimental" and "harmful." The former receive a survival advantage while the latter are disfavored. The computation proceeds by eliminating the disadvantaged and preserving the advantaged. The final combination that survives is the correct prediction for the system's next configuration, the next moment in time.

"It's an evolutionary algorithm," Wang said.

"It's a good thing I invited you along." Shi Qiang nodded at Wang.

Yes. Only much later did I learn that term. The distinguishing feature of this algorithm is that it requires ultralarge amounts of computing power. For the three-body problem, the computers we have now aren't enough.

Back then, in the temple, I didn't even have a calculator. I had to go to the accounting office to get a blank ledger and a pencil. I began to build the math model on paper. This required a lot of work, and in no time at all I went through more than a dozen ledgers. The monks in charge of accounts were angry with me, but because the abbot wished it, they found me more paper and pen. I hid the completed calculations under my pillow, and threw the scratch paper into the incense burner in the yard.

One evening, a young woman suddenly dashed into my room. This was the first time a woman had shown up at my place. She clutched a few pieces of paper with burnt edges, the scratch paper I had thrown out.

"They tell me these are yours. Are you studying the three-body problem?" Behind her wide glasses, her eyes seemed to be on fire.

The woman surprised me. The math I used was unconventional, and my derivations took large leaps. But the fact that she could tell the subject of my study from a few pieces of scratch paper showed that she had unusual math talent and that she, like me, was very devoted to the three-body problem.

I didn't have a good impression of the tourists and pilgrims.

The tourists had no idea what they were looking at, only running around to snap pictures. As for the pilgrims, they looked much poorer than the tourists, and all seemed to be in a state of numbness, their intellect inhibited. But this woman was different. She looked like an academic. Later I found out that she had come with a group of Japanese tourists.

Without waiting for my answer, she added, "Your approach is brilliant. We've been searching for a method like this that could turn the difficulty of the three-body problem into a matter of massive computation. Of course, it would require a very powerful computer."

I told her the truth. "Even if we were to use all the computers in the world, it wouldn't be enough."

"But you must have an adequate research environment, and there's nothing like that here. I can give you the use of a supercomputer. I can also give you a minicomputer. Let's leave together tomorrow morning."

The woman, of course, was Shen Yufei. Like now, she was concise and authoritarian, but she was more attractive then. I'm naturally a cold person. I had less interest in women than the monks around me. This woman who didn't adhere to conventional ideas about femininity was different, though. She attracted me. Since I had nothing to do anyway, I agreed right away.

That night, I couldn't sleep. I draped a shirt over my shoulders and walked out into the yard. In the distance, I saw Shen in the dim temple hall. She knelt before the Buddha with lit joss sticks, and all her movements seemed full of piety. I approached noiselessly, and as I came by the door to the temple hall, I heard her whisper a prayer: "Buddha, please help my Lord break away from the sea of misery."

I thought I must have heard wrong, but she chanted the prayer again.

"*Buddha, please help my Lord break away from the sea of misery.*"

I didn't understand religion and had no interest in any of them, but I really couldn't think of any prayer odder than this one. "*What are you saying?*" I blurted.

Shen ignored me. She kept her eyes barely closed, her hands clasped together in front of her, as though watching her prayer rise with the incense smoke toward the Buddha. After a long while, she finally opened her eyes and turned toward me. "*Go to sleep. We have to get up early.*" She didn't even look at me.

"*This 'Lord' you mentioned, is he part of Buddhism?*" I asked.

"*No.*"

"*Then . . . ?*"

Shen said nothing, just hurried away. I didn't get a chance to ask anything else. I repeated the prayer to myself over and over, and it seemed to grow even stranger. Eventually, I became frightened. I rushed over to the abbot's room and knocked on his door.

"*What does it mean if someone prays to the Buddha to help another Lord?*" I then told him the details of what I saw.

The abbot silently looked at the book in his hand, but he was thinking about what I said, not reading. Then he said, "*Please leave me for a bit. Let me think.*"

I turned and left, knowing that it was unusual. The abbot was very learned. Usually, he could answer any question about religion, history, and culture without having to think. I waited outside the door for about the time it took to smoke a cigarette, and the abbot called for me.

"*I think there's only one possibility.*" His expression was grim.

"*What? What could it be? Could there be some religion*

212

whose god needs worshippers to pray to the gods of other religions to save it?"

"Her Lord really exists."

This response confused me. "Then . . . the Buddha doesn't exist?" As soon as I said it I realized how rude it sounded. I apologized.

The abbot slowly waved his hand at me. "I told you, the two of us can't talk about Buddhism. The existence of the Buddha is a kind of existence that you cannot comprehend. But the Lord she's talking about exists in a way that you can understand . . . . I can say no more concerning this matter. All I can do is counsel you against leaving with her."

"Why?"

"It's just a feeling. I feel that behind her are things that you and I cannot imagine."

I left the abbot's room and walked through the temple toward my room. The night had a full moon. I looked up at it and thought it a silvery, strange eye that gazed down at me, the light suffused with an eerie chill.

The next day, I did leave with Shen—I couldn't stay in the temple the rest of my life, after all. But I didn't think that over the next few years, I would live the life of my dreams. Shen fulfilled her promise. I had a minicomputer and a comfortable environment. I even left the country several times to use supercomputers—not time-sharing, but having the whole CPU to myself. She had a lot of money, though I didn't know where it came from.

Later, we got married. There wasn't much love or passion, just mutual convenience. We both had things we wanted to get done. As for me, the few years after that could be described as a single day. My time passed peacefully. In her house, I was taken care of and did not have to worry about food or cloth-

ing, so that I could devote myself to the study of the three-body problem. Shen never interfered with my life. The garage had a car that I could drive anywhere. I'm sure she wouldn't even have minded if I brought another woman home. She only paid attention to my research, and the only thing we talked about day to day was the three-body problem.

"Do you know what else Shen has been up to?" Shi Qiang asked.

"Just the Frontiers of Science. She's busy with it all the time. Lots of people show up every day."

"She didn't ask you to join?"

"Never. She never even talks to me about it. I don't care, either. That's just the way I am. I don't want to care about anything. She knows it, and says I'm an indolent man without any sense of purpose. The organization doesn't suit me and would interfere with my research."

"Have you made any progress with the three-body problem?" Wang asked.

Compared with the general state of the field, my progress could be said to be a breakthrough. Some years ago, Richard Montgomery of UCSC and Alain Chenciner of Université Paris Diderot discovered another stable, periodic solution to the three-body problem.[30] Under appropriate initial conditions, the three bodies will chase each other around a fixed figure-eight curve. After that, everyone was keen to find such special stable configurations, and every discovery was greeted with joy. Only three or four such configurations have been found so far.

---

30 *Translator's Note:* For details, please see Alain Chenciner and Richard Montgomery, "A remarkable periodic solution of the three-body problem in the case of equal masses," *Annals of Mathematics*, 152 (2000), 881–901.

But my evolutionary algorithm has already discovered more than a hundred stable configurations. Drawings of their orbits would fill a gallery with postmodern art, but that's not my goal. The real solution to the three-body problem is to build a mathematical model so that, given any initial configuration with known vectors, the model can predict all subsequent motion of the three-body system. This is also what Shen Yufei craves.

But my peaceful life ended yesterday.

"This is the crime you're reporting?" Shi Qiang asked.

"Yes. A man called yesterday and told me that if I didn't cease my research, I would be killed."

"Who was he?"

"I don't know."

"Phone number?"

"Don't know. Caller ID showed nothing."

"Anything related to report?"

"Don't know."

Da Shi laughed and tossed his cigarette butt into an ashtray. "You went on and on forever, and in the end all you have to report is one line and a few 'I don't know's?"

"If I hadn't gone on like that, would you have understood the import of that call? Also, if that were all, I wouldn't have come here. I'm lazy, remember? But there was another thing: It was the middle of the night—I don't know if it was today or yesterday—and I was in bed. As I was drifting halfway between sleep and wakefulness, I felt something cold moving on my face. I opened my eyes and saw Shen Yufei, and I almost died of fright."

"What's so frightening about seeing your wife in the middle of the night?"

"She stared at me in a way that I had never seen. The light from outside fell on her face, and she looked like a ghost. She held something in her hand: a gun! Moving the barrel over my face, she told me that I had to continue working on the three-body problem. Otherwise she'd kill me."

"Oh, now this is getting interesting." Da Shi gave a satisfied nod. He lit another cigarette.

"Interesting? Look, I've nowhere to go. That's why I came to you."

"Tell us exactly what she said."

"She said: 'If you succeed in solving the three-body problem, you will be the savior of the world. If you stop now, you'll be a sinner. If someone were to save or destroy the human race, then your possible contribution or sin would be exactly twice as much as his.'"

Da Shi blew out a thick cloud of smoke and stared at Wei Cheng until he squirmed. He pulled a notepad out of the mess on his desk and picked up a pen. "You wanted us to take notes, right? Repeat what you just said."

Wei did.

Wang said, "What she said is indeed strange. What does she mean by exactly twice as much?"

Wei blinked. "This seems pretty serious. When I came, the officer on duty immediately sent me to see you. It looks like you've already been paying attention to Shen and me."

Da Shi nodded. "Let me ask you something else: Do you think the gun your wife held was real?" He saw that Wei didn't know how to answer. "Could you smell gun oil?"

"Yes, there was definitely an oily smell."

"Good." Da Shi, who had been sitting on his desk, jumped off. "Finally we have an opening. Suspected illegal possession of firearms is enough to justify a search. I'll leave the paperwork until tomorrow, because we have to move right away."

He turned to Wang. "No rest for the weary. I have to ask you to come and advise me some more." Then he turned to Xu Bingbing, who'd been silent the whole time. "Bingbing, right now I have only two men on duty, and that's not enough. I know the Information Security Division isn't used to fieldwork, but I need you to come along."

Xu nodded, glad to leave the smoke-filled office.

In addition to Da Shi and Xu, the team for conducting the search consisted of Wang Miao, Wei Cheng, and two other officers from the Criminal Division. The six of them rode through the predawn darkness in two police cars, heading toward Wei's neighborhood at the edge of the city.

Xu and Wang were in the backseat. As soon as the car started, she whispered to Wang, "Professor Wang, your reputation in *Three Body* is very high."

Somebody mentioned Three Body *in the real world!* Wang was excited, right away feeling close to this young woman in a police uniform. "Do you play?"

"I'm responsible for monitoring and tracking it. An unpleasant task."

Wang anxiously asked, "Can you tell me its background? I really want to know."

In the faint light coming through the car window, Wang saw Xu give a mysterious smile. "We want to know as well. But all its servers are outside the country. The system and firewall are very secure and hard to penetrate. We don't know much, but we can be sure it's not operated for profit. The software quality is uncommonly high, and the amount of information contained in it even more unusual. It doesn't even seem like a game."

"Have there been any . . ." Wang carefully picked the right words. ". . . *supernatural* signs?" Wang's night had been filled with coincidences: He had been called in to discuss the three-body problem with Wei Cheng immediately after he solved the *Three Body* game. And now Xu was telling him she was monitoring the game. Something didn't seem right.

"We don't think so. Many from all around the world participate in the game's development. Their collaboration method seems similar to popular open-source practices, like the kind used to make the Linux operating system. But they're definitely using some very advanced development tools. As for the content of the game, who knows where they're getting it? It does seem a bit . . . supernatural, like you said. *However,* we still believe in Captain Shi's famous rule: All this must be the work of people. Our tracking efforts are effective, and we'll have results soon."

The young woman was not experienced in lying, and her last remark made Wang realize that she was hiding much of the truth from him. "His 'rule' is famous now?" Wang looked at Da Shi, who was in the driver's seat.

When they reached the house, the sun had not yet risen. It was about the same time of night that Wang had seen Shen playing *Three Body*. A second-story window was lit, but all the other windows were dark.

As soon as Wang got out of the car, he heard noises coming from upstairs. It sounded like something was slapping against the wall. Da Shi, who had just gotten out of the car himself, immediately became alert. He kicked open the yard gate and rushed into the house with an agility surprising for his burly frame, his three colleagues close behind.

Wang and Wei followed them into the house. They went upstairs and entered the room with a light on, their shoes splashing in a pool of blood. Shen lay in the middle of the room, blood still oozing from two bullet wounds in her chest. A third bullet had gone through her left brow, causing her whole face to be covered in red. Not far from her, a gun lay in a crimson pool.

As Wang entered, Da Shi and one of the other officers rushed out and entered the dark room across the hall. The window there was open, and Wang heard the sound of a car starting outside. A male police officer began to make a phone call. Xu Bingbing stood a little ways apart, watching anxiously. She, like Wang and the others, had probably never seen a scene like this.

A moment later, Da Shi returned. He put his gun back in its holster and said to the officer holding the phone, "A black Volkswagen Santana with only one man. I couldn't get the license plate number. Tell them to block all entrances to the fifth ring road. Shit. He might actually get away."

Da Shi looked around and saw the bullet holes in the wall. He glanced at the shell casings scattered on the ground and added, "The man got off five shots, and three hit her. She shot twice—both misses." Then he crouched down to examine the body with the other officer. Xu stood farther away, stealing a glance at Wei Cheng next to her. Da Shi also looked up at him.

On Wei's face was a trace of shock and a trace of sorrow, but only a trace. His usual wooden expression didn't break. He was far calmer than Wang.

"You don't seem bothered by this," Da Shi said to Wei. "They probably came to kill you."

Wei gave a ghastly grin. "What can I do? Even now, I still don't know anything about her. I've told her many times to keep life simple. I'm thinking of the abbot's counsel to me that night. But . . . eh."

Da Shi stood up and walked over to stand in front of Wei. He took out a cigarette and lit it. "I think you still have some things you haven't told us."

"Some things I was too lazy to talk about."

"Then you'd better work harder now!"

Wei thought for a moment and said, "Today—no, yesterday afternoon—she argued with a man in the living room. It's that Pan Han, the famous environmentalist. They had argued a few times before, in Japanese, as though afraid to have me listen in. But yesterday they didn't care at all and argued in Chinese. I overheard a few snatches."

"Try to tell us exactly what you heard."

"Fine. Pan Han said, 'Although we seem like fellow travelers on the surface, in reality we're irreconcilable enemies.' Shen said, 'Yes, you're trying to use our Lord's power against the human race.' Pan said, 'Your understanding is not completely unreasonable. We want our Lord to come to this world, to punish those who have long deserved it. However, you're working to prevent our Lord's coming, and that's why we can't tolerate you. If you don't stop, we'll *make* you stop!' Shen said, 'The commander was blind to allow you to join the organization!' Pan said, 'Speaking of, can you tell whether the commander sides with the Adventists or the Redemptionists? Does the commander want humanity eliminated or saved?' Pan's words briefly silenced Shen, and the two didn't argue so loudly anymore. I couldn't hear anything else."

"What did the man who threatened you on the phone sound like?"

"You're asking if he sounded like Pan Han? I don't know. He was speaking very softly, and I couldn't tell."

Several more police cars arrived, sirens blaring. A group of white-gloved policemen came upstairs with cameras, and the house hummed with activity. Da Shi told Wang to go back and get some rest.

Instead, Wang walked into the room with the minicomputer to find Wei. "Can you give me an outline of your three-body evolutionary algorithm? I want to . . . introduce it to some people. I know my request is abrupt. If you can't, don't worry about it."

Wei took out a CD and handed it to Wang. "It's all on here: the whole model and additional documentation. Do me a favor and publish it under your own name. That would be a big help."

"No, no! How could I do that?"

Wei pointed at the disk in Wang's hand and said, "Professor Wang, I noticed you the first time you came here. You're a good man, a man with a sense of responsibility. That's why I'm counseling you to stay away from this. The world is about to change. Everyone should try to live out the rest of their lives in peace. That would be best. Don't worry too much about other matters. It's all useless anyway."

"You seem to know even more than you let on."

"I spent every day with her. It's impossible to have no inkling."

"Then why not tell the police?"

Wei smiled contemptuously. "The police are worthless. Even if God were here, it wouldn't do any good. The entire human race has reached the point where no one is listening to their prayers."

Wei was standing next to an east-facing window. Through the glass, beyond the distant cityscape, the sky was brightening with the first light of dawn. For some reason, the light reminded Wang of the strange dawn he saw each time he logged on to *Three Body*.

"In reality, I'm not so detached. I haven't been able to sleep the last few nights. Every morning when I see the sunrise, it feels like sunset." He turned to Wang, and after a long pause, added, "And it's all because God, or the Lord she talked about, can't even protect Himself anymore."

17

Three Body: Newton,
Von Neumann, the First
Emperor, and Tri-Solar Syzygy

The start of the second level of *Three Body* wasn't too different than the first: still the strange, cold dawn, still that colossal pyramid. But this time, the pyramid was back in the Egyptian style.

Wang heard the crisp sound of metal striking against metal. The clashing only highlighted the silence of the chilly dawn. Searching for the source, he saw two dark shadows flickering at the foot of the pyramid. In the dim light, metallic glints flashed between the shadows: a swordfight.

Once his eyes had adjusted, Wang saw the figures more clearly. Based on the shape of the pyramid, this should be someplace in *Three Body*'s version of the East, but the two fighters were Europeans dressed in a sixteenth- or seventeenth-century style. The shorter one ducked below a swinging sword and his silvery wig fell to the ground. After a few more thrusts and parries, another man appeared around the corner of the pyramid and ran toward the fighters. He tried to get the two to stop, but the swinging blades whistling through the air prevented him from getting close.

He shouted, "Stop! Don't you two have anything better to do? Where's your sense of responsibility? If civilization has no future, what good is this supposed bit of glory you're fighting over?"

Both swordfighters ignored him, concentrating on the duel. The taller one suddenly cried out in pain, and his sword fell to the ground with a clang. He turned and ran, holding his wounded arm. The other gave chase for a few steps and spat in the direction of the loser.

"Shameless!" He bent down to pick up his wig. As he straightened up, he saw Wang. Pointing in the direction of the escapee, he said, "He dared to claim that he invented calculus!" He put on his wig, put a hand over his heart, and bowed courteously to Wang. "Isaac Newton, at your service."

"Then the one who ran away must be Leibniz?" Wang asked.

"Indeed, an unscrupulous man. I don't really care about this little claim to fame. Inventing the three laws of mechanics has already made me the greatest, God excepted. From planetary motion to cell division, everything follows the three great laws. Now, with the powerful mathematical tool that is calculus, it will only be a matter of time before we master the pattern of the motion of the three suns."

"It's not that simple," said the man who had tried to stop the fight. "Have you considered the amount of calculation that's needed? I saw the differential equations you listed, and I don't think an analytical solution is possible, only a numerical one. However, the calculating capacity required is such that even if all of the world's mathematicians worked without pause, they'd still not be able to complete them by the time the world ended. Of course, if we can't figure out the pattern of the suns' movements soon, the end of the world will not be too far away." He bowed at Wang as well, a more modern bow. "Von Neumann."

"Didn't you bring us thousands of miles to the East specifically to solve the problem of calculating these equations?" Newton asked. Then he turned to Wang. "Norbert Wiener and that degenerate who just ran away also came with us. We encountered some pirates near Madagascar. Wiener fought the pirates by himself so that the rest of us could escape, and he died valiantly."

"Why did you have to come to the East to build a computer?" Wang asked Von Neumann.

Von Neumann and Newton looked at each other, puzzled. "A computer? A *computing machine*! Such a thing exists?"

"You don't know about computers? Then what did you have in mind for completing the vast amount of calculations?"

Von Neumann stared at Wang with wide-open eyes, as though his question made no sense. "Using people, of course. Other than people, what else in the world is capable of performing calculations?"

"But you just said that all the mathematicians in the world wouldn't be enough."

"Instead of mathematicians, we'll use common laborers. But we need many of them, at least thirty million. We'll do mathematics using human wave tactics."

"Common laborers? Thirty million?" Wang was amazed. "But if I recall correctly, this is an age when ninety percent of the population are illiterate. Yet you want to find thirty million people who understand calculus?"

"Have you heard the joke about the Army of Sichuan?" Von Neumann took out a thick cigar, bit off the end, and lit it. "Some soldiers were being drilled, but because they had no education, they couldn't even follow the drill instructor's simple orders to march LEFT-RIGHT-LEFT. So the instructor came up with a solution: He had every soldier wear a straw shoe on the left foot and a cloth shoe on the right. When they marched, he shouted"—here he switched to a Sichuan accent—"STRAW-CLOTH-STRAW-CLOTH. . . . That's the kind of soldier we need. Except we need thirty million of them."

Hearing this modern joke, Wang knew that the man before him wasn't a program but a real person, and almost certainly Chinese.

"It's hard to imagine such a large army," Wang said, shaking his head.

"That's why we've come to see Qin Shi Huang, the First Emperor." Newton pointed at the pyramid.

"He's still in charge?" Wang looked around. He saw that the soldiers guarding the entrance to the pyramid really were equipped with the simple leather armor and *ji*-style halberds of the Qin Dynasty. The anachronistic mix of historical elements in *Three Body* no longer surprised him.

"The whole world is going to be under his rule because he has an army of more than thirty million preparing to conquer Europe. All right, let's go see him." Von Neumann turned to Newton. "Drop the sword." Newton obeyed.

The three of them entered the pyramid, and just as they were about to emerge from the tunnel into the Great Hall, a guard insisted that they strip off all their clothes. Newton objected. "We're famous scholars. No one of our stature would carry hidden weapons!"

As the two sides explored this stalemate, a deep, male voice came from the Great Hall. "Is it the foreigner who discovered the three laws of motion? Let him and his companions in."

They entered the Great Hall. The First Emperor was pacing back and forth, his robe and his famous long sword both dragging along the ground. As he turned to gaze at the three scholars, Wang realized that his eyes were the same as the eyes of King Zhou of Shang and Pope Gregory.

"I already know the purpose of your visit. You're Europeans. Why not go find Caesar? His empire is vast. Surely he can find you thirty million men."

"But my most honored Emperor, do you know what kind of army he has? Do you know what shape his empire is in? In the magnificent eternal city of Rome, even the river that flows through the city has been heavily polluted. Do you know the cause?"

"Military industrial production?"

"No, Great Emperor, it's the vomit from Romans after their binge and purge feasts. When the nobles attend the feasts, stretchers have already been prepared for them under the tables. When they've eaten so much that they can no longer move, the servants carry them home. The entire empire has sunk into a quagmire of extravagance from which they cannot extricate themselves. Even if Caesar could organize an army of thirty million, it would not have the quality and strength necessary to perform this great calculation."

"I am aware of that," Qin Shi Huang said. "But Caesar is waking up and reinvigorating his army. The wisdom of Westerners is terrifying. You are not more intelligent than the men of the East, but you can see the right path. For example, Copernicus could figure out that there are three suns, and *you* could come up with your three laws. These are very impressive accomplishments. We here in the East cannot, for now, match them. I don't possess the ability to conquer Europe. My ships are not good enough, and the

227

supply lines cannot be maintained for long enough to go over land."

"That's why your empire must continue to develop, Great Emperor!" Von Neumann seized the opportunity. "If you can master the pattern of the suns' movements, you will be able to make the most of each Stable Era, and also avoid the damage brought by each Chaotic Era. This way, your progress will be much faster than Europe's. Believe us, we're scholars. As long as we can use the three laws of motion and calculus to accurately forecast the movements of the suns, we do not care who conquers the world."

"Of course I need to predict the suns' movements. But if you want me to gather thirty million men, you must at least demonstrate for me how such calculations would be conducted."

"Your Imperial Majesty, please give me three soldiers. I will demonstrate." Von Neumann grew excited.

"Three? Only three? I can easily give you three thousand." Qin Shi Huang glanced at Von Neumann, distrustful.

"Your Imperial Majesty, you mentioned just now the defect in the Eastern mind when it comes to scientific thinking. This is because you have not realized that even the complicated objects of the universe are made from the simplest elements. I only need three."

Qin Shi Huang waved his hand and three soldiers came forward. They were all very young. Like other Qin soldiers, they moved like order-obeying machines.

"I don't know your names," Von Neumann said, tapping the shoulders of two of the soldiers. "The two of you will be responsible for signal input, so I'll call you 'Input 1' and 'Input 2.'" He pointed to the last soldier. "You will be responsible for signal output, so I'll call you 'Output.'" He shoved the soldiers to where he wanted them to stand. "Form a triangle. Like this. Output is the apex. Input 1 and Input 2 form the base."

"You could have just told them to stand in the Wedge Attack Formation," Qin Shi Huang said, glancing at Von Neumann contemptuously.

Newton took out six small flags: three white, three black. Von Neumann handed them out to the three soldiers so that each held a black flag and a white flag. "White represents 0; black represents 1. Good. Now, listen to me. Output, you turn around and look at Input 1 and Input 2. If they both raise black flags, you raise a black flag as well. Under all other circumstances, you raise the white flag."

"I think you should use some other color," Qin Shi Huang said. "White means surrender."

The excited Von Neumann ignored him. He shouted orders at the three soldiers. "Begin operation! Input 1 and Input 2, you can raise whichever flag you want. Good. Raise! Good. Raise again! Raise!"

Input 1 and Input 2 raised their flags three times. The first time they were black-black, the second time white-black, and the third time black-white. Output reacted correctly each time, raising the black flag once and the white one twice.

"Very good. Your Imperial Majesty, your soldiers are very smart."

"Even an idiot would be capable of that. Tell me, what are they really doing?" Qin Shi Huang looked baffled.

"The three soldiers form a computing component. It's a type of gate, an AND gate." Von Neumann paused to let the emperor digest this information.

Qin Shi Huang said impassively, "I'm not impressed. Continue."

Von Neumann turned to the three soldiers again. "Let's form another component. You, Output: if you see either Input 1 or Input 2 raise a black flag, you raise the black flag. There are three situations where that will be true: black-black, white-black, black-white. When it's white-white, you raise the white flag. Understand? Good lad, you're really clever. You're the key to the correct functioning of the gate. Work hard, and the emperor will reward you! Let's begin operation. Raise! Good, raise again! Raise again! Perfect. Your Imperial Majesty, this component is called an OR gate."

Then, Von Neumann used the three soldiers to form a NAND gate, a NOR gate, an XOR-gate, an XNOR-gate, and a tristate gate. Finally, using only two soldiers, he made the simplest gate, a NOT gate, or an inverter: Output always raised the flag that was opposite in color from the one raised by Input.

Von Neumann bowed to the emperor. "Now, Your Imperial Majesty, all the gate components have been demonstrated. Aren't they simple? Any three soldiers can master the skills after one hour of training."

"Don't they need to learn more?" Qin Shi Huang asked.

"No. We can form ten million of these gates, and then put the components together into a system. This system will then be able to carry out the calculations we need and work out those differential equations for predicting the suns' movements. We could call the system . . . um . . ."

"A computer," Wang said.

"Ah, good!" Von Neumann gave Wang a thumbs-up. "Computer—that's a great name. The entire system is a large machine, the most complex machine in the history of the world."

The passage of in-game time sped up. Three months went by.

Qin Shi Huang, Newton, Von Neumann, and Wang all stood on the platform at the apex of the pyramid. This platform was similar to the one where Wang had met Mozi. It was filled with astronomical instruments, some of which were of recent European design. Below them, a magnificent phalanx of thirty million Qin soldiers was arrayed on the ground. The entire formation fit inside a square six kilometers on each side. As the sun rose, the phalanx remained still like a giant carpet made of thirty million terra-cotta warriors. But when a flock of birds wandered above the phalanx, the birds immediately felt the potential for death from below and scattered anxiously in chaos.

Wang performed some computations in his head and realized that even if the entire population of Earth were arranged into such a phalanx, the whole formation would fit inside the Huangpu District of Shanghai. Though it was powerful, the phalanx also revealed the fragility of civilization.

Von Neumann said, "Your Imperial Majesty, your army is truly matchless. In an extremely short time, we have completed such complex training."

Qin Shi Huang held on to the hilt of his long sword. "Even though the whole is complex, what each soldier must do is very simple. Compared to the training they went through to learn how to break the Macedonian Phalanx, this is nothing."

Newton added, "And God blessed us with two consecutive Stable Eras to get them trained and ready."

"Even in a Chaotic Era, my army continues to train. They will finish your calculations even if it's a Chaotic Era." Qin Shi Huang glanced over the phalanx with pride in his eyes.

"Then, Your Imperial Majesty, please give the great order!" Von Neumann's voice trembled with excitement.

Qin Shi Huang nodded. A guard ran over, grabbed the hilt of the emperor's sword, and stepped backwards. The bronze sword was so long that it was impossible for the emperor himself to pull it out of the scabbard. The guard knelt and handed the sword to the emperor. Qin Shi Huang lifted the sword to the sky, and shouted: "Computer Formation!"

Four giant bronze cauldrons at the corners of the platform came to life simultaneously with roaring flames. A group of soldiers standing on the sloping side of the pyramid facing the phalanx chanted in unison: "Computer Formation!"

On the ground below, colors in the phalanx began to shift and move. Complicated and detailed circuit patterns appeared and gradually filled the entire formation. Ten minutes later, the army had made a thirty-six kilometer square computer motherboard.

Von Neumann pointed to the gigantic human circuit below the pyramid and began to explain, "Your Imperial Majesty, we have named this computer Qin I. Look, there in the center is the CPU, the core computing component, formed from your five best divisions. By referencing this diagram, you can locate the adders, registers, and stack memory. The part around it that looks highly regular is the memory. When we built that part, we found that we didn't have enough soldiers. But luckily, the work done by the elements in this component is the simplest, so we trained each soldier to hold more colored flags. Each man can now complete the work that initially required twenty men. This allowed us to increase the memory capacity to meet the minimum requirements for running the Qin 1.0 operating system. Observe also the open passage that runs through the entire formation, and the light cavalry waiting for orders in that passage: That's the system bus, responsible for transmitting information between the components of the whole system.

"The bus architecture is a great invention. New plug-in components, which can be made from up to ten divisions, can quickly be added to the main operation bus. This allows Qin I's hardware to be easily expanded and upgraded. Look further still—you might have to use the telescope for this—and there's the external storage, which we call the 'hard drive' at Copernicus's suggestion. It's formed by three million soldiers with more education than most. When you buried all those scholars alive after you unified China, it's a good thing you saved these ones! Each of them holds a pen and a notepad, and they're responsible for recording the results of the calculations. Of course, the bulk of their work is to act as virtual memory and store intermediate calculation results. They're the bottleneck for the speed of computation. And, finally, the part that's closest to us is the display. It's capable of showing us in real time the most important parameters of the computation."

Von Neumann and Newton carried over a large scroll, tall as a man, and spread it open before Qin Shi Huang. When they reached the scroll's end, Wang's chest tightened, remembering the legend of the assassin who hid a dagger in a map scroll that he then displayed to the emperor. But the imaginary dagger did not appear. Before them was only a large sheet of paper filled with symbols, each the size of a fly's head. Packed so densely, the symbols were as dazzling to behold as the computer formation on the ground below.

"Your Imperial Majesty, this is the Qin 1.0 operating system we developed. The software for doing the calculations will run on top of it. That below"—Von Neumann pointed to the human-formation computer—"is the hardware. What's on this paper is the software. The relationship between hardware and software is like that between the *guqin* zither and sheet music."

He and Newton then spread open another scroll, just as large. "Your Imperial Majesty, this is the software for using numerical methods to solve those differential equations. After entering the motion vectors of the three suns at a particular moment obtained by astronomical observation, the software's operation will give us a prediction for the suns' subsequent motion at any moment in the future. Our first computation will calculate all the suns' positions for the next two years. Each set of output values will be one hundred and twenty hours apart."

Qin Shi Huang nodded. "Good. Begin."

Von Neumann lifted both hands above his head and solemnly chanted: "As ordered by the great emperor, turn on the computer! System self-test!"

A row of soldiers standing halfway down the face of the pyramid repeated the order using flag signals. In a moment, the motherboard made of thirty million men seemed to turn into a lake filled with sparkling lights. Tens of millions of tiny flags waved. In the display formation closest to the base of the pyramid, a progress bar made of numerous green flags slowly advanced, indicating the percentage of the self-test that had been completed. Ten minutes later, the progress bar reached its end.

"Self-test complete! Begin boot sequence! Load operating system!"

Below, the light cavalry on the main bus that passed through the entire human-formation computer began to move swiftly. The main bus soon turned into a turbulent river. Along the way, the river fed into numerous thin tributaries,

234

infiltrating all the modular subformations. Soon, the ripple of black and white flags coalesced into surging waves that filled the entire motherboard. The central CPU area was the most tumultuous, like gunpowder on fire.

But suddenly, as though the powder had been exhausted, the movements in the CPU slackened and eventually stopped. Starting with the CPU in the center, the stillness spread in every direction, like a sea being frozen over. Finally, the entire motherboard came to a stop, with only a few scattered components flashing lifelessly in infinite loops. The center of the display formation blinked red.

"System lockup!" a signal officer called out. Shortly after, the reason for the malfunction was determined: There was an error with the operation of one of the gates in the CPU status register.

"Restart system!" Von Neumann ordered confidently.

"Wait!" Newton stopped the signal officer. He turned with an insidious expression and said to Qin Shi Huang, "Your Imperial Majesty, in order to improve system stability, you should take certain maintenance measures with respect to faulty components."

Qin Shi Huang grasped his sword and said, "Replace the malfunctioning component and behead all the soldiers who made up that gate. In the future, any malfunctions will be dealt with the same way!"

Von Neumann glanced at Newton, disgusted. They watched as a few riders dashed into the motherboard with their swords unsheathed. After they "repaired" the faulty component, the order to restart was given. This time, the operation went very smoothly. Twenty minutes later, *Three Body*'s Von Neumann architecture human-formation computer had begun full operations under the Qin 1.0 operating system.

"Run solar orbit computation software 'Three Body 1.0'!" Newton screamed at the top of his lungs. "Start the master computing module! Load the differential calculus module! Load the finite element analysis module! Load the spectral method module! Enter initial condition parameters . . . and begin calculation!"

The motherboard sparkled as the display formation flashed with indicators in every color. The human-formation computer began the long computation.

"This is really interesting," Qin Shi Huang said, pointing to the spectacular sight. "Each individual's behavior is so simple, yet together, they can produce such a complex, great whole! Europeans criticize me for my tyrannical rule, claiming that I suppress creativity. But in reality, a large number of men yoked by severe discipline can also produce great wisdom when bound together as one."

"Great First Emperor, this is just the mechanical operation of a machine, not wisdom. Each of these lowly individuals is just a zero. Only when someone like you is added to the front as a one can the whole have any meaning." Newton's smile was ingratiating.

"Disgusting philosophy!" Von Neumann said as he glanced at Newton. "If, in the end, the results computed in accordance with your theory and mathematical model don't match reality, then you and I aren't even zeroes."

"Indeed. If that turns out to be the case, you will be nothing!" Qin Shi Huang turned and left the scene.

Time passed quickly. The human-formation computer operated for a year and four months. Subtracting out the time spent to adjust the programming, the actual processing time was approximately a year and two months. During this time, processing had to be stopped twice due to extremely bad weather in Chaotic Eras. But the computer stored the data at the time of each shutdown, and was able to resume calculations successfully after the pauses. By the time Qin Shi Huang and the European scholars ascended the pyramid again, the first phase of the computation was complete. The results precisely described the orbits of the three suns for the next two years.

It was a chilly dawn. The torches that had kept the motherboard lit through the night were extinguished. After the final calculation, Qin I entered standby mode. The turbulent waves over the motherboard settled into light ripples.

Von Neumann and Newton presented the scroll with the results of the computation to Qin Shi Huang. Newton said, "Great First Emperor, the calculations were completed three days ago. We waited until now to present the results to you because they show that the long night is about to be over. We'll soon welcome the first sunrise of a long Stable Era, which will last more than a year. Judging by the orbital parameters, the climate will be extremely mild and comfortable. Please revive your empire and order everyone to be rehydrated."

"Ever since the start of this computation, my empire has never been dehydrated," Qin Shi Huang said in a huff, grabbing the scroll. "I've devoted all the resources of the Qin Empire to maintain the operation of the computer, and we've run out of stored supplies. For this computer, countless people have died of hunger, cold, and heat." Qin pointed into the distance with the scroll. By the dim dawn light, they could see tens of white lines radiating from the edges of the motherboard in every direction, disappearing over the horizon. These were the supply routes from every corner of the empire.

"Your Imperial Majesty, you will find that the sacrifices are worth it," Von Neumann said. "After mastering the orbits of the suns, Qin will develop by leaps and bounds, and will grow many times more powerful than before."

"According to the calculations, the sun is about to rise. Great First Emperor, prepare to receive your glory!"

As if in response to Newton's words, a sliver of red sun peeked over the horizon, bathing the pyramid and the human-formation computer in a golden light. A wave of joyous cries rose from the motherboard.

A man hurried toward them. He was running so fast that, as he knelt down, he couldn't catch his breath. He was the emperor's astronomy minister.

"Sire, the calculations were in error. Disaster is about to befall us!"

"What are you babbling about?" Without even waiting for the emperor to speak, Newton kicked the man. "Don't you see that the sun is rising at the exact moment predicted by our precise calculations?"

"But . . ." The minister half straightened, one hand pointing at the sun. "How many suns do you see?"

Everyone gazed at the rising sun, confused. "Minister, you received a proper Western education and obtained a doctorate from the University of Cambridge," Von Neumann said. "You must at least know how to count. Of course there's only one sun in the sky. And the temperature is very comfortable."

"No. There are three!" The minister cried, tears flowing from his face. "The other two are behind that one!"

Everyone stared at the sun again, still confused.

"The Imperial Observatory has confirmed that right now we are experiencing the extremely rare phenomenon of a tri-solar syzygy. The three suns are in a straight line, moving around our planet at the same angular speed! Thus, our planet and the three suns are in a straight line with our world at the end!"

"You're certain that the observation is not in error?" Newton grabbed the collar of the astronomy minister.

"Absolutely certain. The observation was conducted by the Western astronomers of the Imperial Observatory, including Kepler and Herschel. They're using the largest telescope in the world, imported from Europe."

Newton let go of the minister and stood up. Wang saw that his face was pale, but his expression was one of pure joy. He clasped his two hands in front of his chest and said to Qin Shi Huang, "Oh Greatest, Most Honorable Emperor, this is the most propitious sign of them all! Now that the three suns are orbiting around our planet, your empire is the center of the universe. This is God's reward for our efforts. Let me check the calculations one more time. I will prove this!"

While the rest remained stunned, Newton slipped away. Later, others would report that Sir Isaac had stolen a horse and left for parts unknown.

An anxiety-filled moment of silence later, Wang suddenly said, "Your Imperial Majesty, please unsheathe your sword."

"What do you want?" Qin Shi Huang asked, baffled. But he gestured at the soldier by his side, and the soldier pulled the sword out of its scabbard.

Wang said, "Please try to swing it."

Qin Shi Huang held the sword and waved it around. His expression turned to one of surprise. "Oh, why is it so light?"

"The game's V-suit cannot simulate the feeling of

diminished gravity. Otherwise we'd feel that we're much lighter as well."

"Look! Down there! Look at the horses, and the men!" Someone cried out. Everyone looked down and saw a column of cavalry moving at the foot of the pyramid. All the horses seemed to be floating. Each horse drifted over a long distance before the four hooves struck ground again. They also saw several running men. With each step, the men leapt a dozen meters, falling slowly back to the ground. On top of the pyramid, a soldier tried to jump up, and easily reached the height of three meters.

"What is going on?" Qin Shi Huang looked at the soldier slowly falling back down.

"Sire, the three suns are over our planet in a straight line, so their gravitational forces are added together. . . ." The astronomy minister tried to explain, but discovered that his two feet had already left the ground and he was now horizontal. The others were also floating in the air, leaning at different angles. Like a bunch of men who had fallen into water without knowing how to swim, they clumsily waved their limbs, trying to stabilize themselves but colliding into each other instead.

The ground they had just left now cracked open like a spiderweb. The cracks grew fast, and, accompanied by thunderous crashes and sky-obscuring dust, the pyramid below them broke into its constituent blocks. Through the slowly drifting gigantic blocks, Wang saw the Great Hall below come apart. The large cauldron that had once cooked Fu Xi and the iron stake to which he had once been bound were both adrift.

The sun rose to the middle of the sky. Everything that floated—men, colossal blocks of stone, astronomical instruments, bronze cauldrons—began to rise slowly, then accelerated. Wang glanced at the human-formation computer and saw a nightmarish sight: The thirty million men who had formed the motherboard were floating away from the earth and rising, like a swarm of ants sucked up by a vacuum cleaner. The ground they left behind clearly displayed the marks of the motherboard circuits. The set of intricate, complex markings that could only be taken in from a great height would become an archaeological site that would confuse the next *Three Body* civilization, in the distant future.

Wang looked up. The sky was obscured by a strangely mottled layer of clouds. The clouds were made of dust, stones, humans, and other odds and ends. The sun sparkled behind them. In the far distance, Wang saw a long range of transparent mountains also rising up. The mountains were crystal clear, and changed shapes as they sparkled—they were formed from the ocean, which was also being attracted into space.

Everything on the surface of the *Three Body* world rose toward the sun.

Wang looked around and saw Von Neumann and Qin Shi Huang. As he drifted, Von Neumann shouted at Qin Shi Huang, but there was no sound. A small set of subtitles appeared: *I figured it out! Electronic elements! We can use electronic elements to make gate circuits and combine them into computers! Such computers will be many times faster and take up much less space. I estimate that a small building will be sufficient. . . . Your Imperial Majesty, are you listening?*

Qin Shi Huang swung his long sword at Von Neumann. The latter kicked at a giant block of stone drifting nearby and dodged out of the way. The long sword struck the stone, causing sparks to fly, and broke itself into two pieces. Right after, the giant block of stone collided with another, with Qin Shi Huang in the middle. Stone chips and flesh and blood scattered everywhere, an appalling sight.

But Wang did not hear the noise made by colliding stones. Around him it was completely silent. Because the atmosphere was gone, there was no more sound. As the bodies drifted, their blood boiled in the vacuum and their inner organs were vomited out, until they turned into strange blobs surrounded by crystalline clouds made from the liquid they exuded. Also, due to the lack of an atmosphere, the sky turned pitch black. Everything that had floated into space from the Three Body world reflected the sunlight and formed a brilliant, starry cloud in space. The cloud then turned into a giant vortex, spiraling toward its final resting place: the sun.

Wang now saw the sun changing shape. He understood that he was actually seeing the other two suns, both peeking out from behind the first sun. From this perspective, the three stacked suns formed a bright eye in the universe.

Against the background of the three suns in syzygy, text appeared:

Civilization Number 184 was destroyed by the stacked gravitational attractions of a tri-solar syzygy. This civilization had advanced to the Scientific Revolution and the Industrial Revolution.

In this civilization, Newton established nonrelativistic classical mechanics. At the same time, due to the invention of calculus and the Von Neumann architecture computer, the foundation was set for the quantitative mathematical analysis of the motion of three bodies.

After a long time, life and civilization will begin once

more, and progress through the unpredictable world of
Three Body.

We invite you to log on again.

Just as Wang logged out of the game, a stranger called. The
voice on the phone was that of a very charismatic man.
"Hello! First, we thank you for giving us your real number.
I'm a system administrator for the *Three Body* game."

Wang was both excited and anxious.

"Please tell us your age, education, employer, and position. You didn't fill those out when you registered."

"What do they have to do with the game?"

"When you've reached this level, you must provide these
pieces of information. If you refuse, *Three Body* will be
permanently closed to you."

Wang answered the administrator's questions truthfully.

"Very good, Professor Wang. You satisfy the conditions
for continuing in *Three Body*."

"Thank you. Can I ask you a few questions?"

"You may not. But tomorrow night there will be a meet-
up for *Three Body* players. We welcome you to attend." The
administrator gave Wang an address.

18

Meet-up

The location for the *Three Body* players' meet-up was a small, out-of-the-way coffee shop. Wang had always imagined game meet-ups would be lively events full of people, but this meet-up consisted of only seven players, including himself. Like Wang, the other six did not look like gaming enthusiasts. Only two were relatively young. Another three, including a woman, were middle-aged. There was also an old man who appeared to be in his sixties or seventies.

Wang had originally thought that as soon as they met they'd begin a lively discussion of *Three Body*, but he was wrong. The profound but strange content of *Three Body* had had a psychological impact on the participants. All the players, including Wang himself, couldn't bring it up easily. They only made simple self-introductions. The old man took out a refined pipe, filled it with tobacco, and smoked as he strolled around, admiring the paintings on the walls. The others sat silently, waiting for the meet-up organizer to show up. They had all come early.

Actually, of the six, Wang already knew two. The old man was a famous scholar who had made his name by imbuing Eastern philosophy with the content of modern science. The strangely dressed woman was a famous writer, one of those rare novelists who wrote in an avant-garde style but still had many readers. You could start one of her books on any page.

Of the two middle-aged men, one was a vice president at China's largest software company, plainly and casually dressed so that his status wasn't obvious at all; and the other was a high-level executive at the State Power Corporation. Of the two young men, one was a reporter with a major media outlet, and the other was a doctoral student in the sciences. Wang now realized that a considerable number of *Three Body* players were probably social elites like them.

The meet-up organizer showed up not long after. Wang's heart began to beat faster as soon as he saw the man: it was Pan Han, prime suspect for the murder of Shen Yufei. He took out his phone when no one was looking and texted Shi Qiang.

"Haha, everyone got here early!" Pan greeted them in a relaxed manner, as though nothing was wrong. Appearing in the media, he usually looked disheveled, like a vagrant, but today, he was dressed sharply in a suit and dress shoes. "You're just like I imagined. *Three Body* is intended for people in your class because the common crowd cannot appreciate its meaning and mood. To play it well requires knowledge and understanding that ordinary people do not possess."

Wang sent out his text: *Spotted Pan Han. At Yunhe Coffee Shop in Xicheng District.*

Pan continued. "Everyone here is an excellent *Three Body* player. You have the best scores and are devoted to it. I believe that *Three Body* is already an important part of your lives."

"It's part of what keeps me alive," the young doctoral student said.

"I saw it by accident on my grandson's computer," the old philosopher said, lifting his pipe stem. "The young man abandoned it after a few tries, saying it was too abstruse.

But I was attracted to it. I find it strange, terrible, but also beautiful. So much information is hidden beneath a simple representation."

A few players nodded at this description, including Wang himself.

Wang received Da Shi's reply text: *We also see him. No worries. Carry on. Play the fanatic in front of them, but not so much that you can't pull it off.*

"Yes," the author agreed, and nodded. "I like the literary elements of *Three Body*. The rises and falls of two hundred and three civilizations evoke the qualities of epics in a new form."

She mentioned 203 civilizations, but Wang had only experienced 184. This told Wang that *Three Body* progressed independently for each player, possibly with different worlds.

"I'm a bit sick of the real world," the young reporter said. "*Three Body* is already my second reality."

"Really?" Pan asked, interested.

"Me too," the software company vice president said. "Compared to *Three Body*, reality is so vulgar and unexciting."

"It's too bad that it's only a game," said the power company executive.

"Very good," Pan said. Wang noticed his eyes sparkling with excitement.

"I have a question that I think everyone wants to know the answer to," Wang said.

"I know what it is. But you might as well ask."

"*Is Three Body* only a game?"

The other players nodded. Clearly the question was also on their minds.

Pan stood up and said solemnly, "The world of *Three Body*, or Trisolaris, really does exist."

"Where is it?" several players asked in unison.

After looking at each of them in turn, Pan sat down and spoke. "Some questions I can answer. Others I cannot. But if you are meant to be with Trisolaris, all your questions will be answered someday."

"Then . . . does the game really portray Trisolaris accurately?" the reporter asked.

"First, the ability of Trisolarans to dehydrate through its many cycles of civilization is real. In order to adapt to the unpredictable natural environment and avoid extreme environmental conditions unsuitable for life, they can completely expel the water in their bodies and turn into dry, fibrous objects."

"What do Trisolarans look like?"

Pan shook his head. "I don't know. I really don't. In every cycle of civilization, the appearance of Trisolarans is different. However, the game does portray something else that really existed on Trisolaris: the Trisolaran-formation computer."

"Ha! I thought that was the most unrealistic aspect," the software company vice president said. "I conducted a test with more than a hundred employees at my company. Even if the idea worked, a computer made of people would probably operate at a speed slower than manual computation."

Pan gave a mysterious smile. "You're right. But suppose that of the thirty million soldiers forming the computer, each one is capable of raising and lowering the black and white flags a hundred thousand times per second, and suppose also that the light cavalry soldiers on the main bus can run at several times the speed of sound, or even faster. Then the result would be very different.

"You asked about the appearance of the Trisolarans just now. According to some signs, the bodies of the Trisolarans

247

who formed the computer were covered by a purely reflective surface, which probably evolved as a response to survival under extreme conditions of sunlight. The mirrorlike surface could be deformed into any shape, and they communicated with each other by focusing light with their bodies. This kind of light-speech could transmit information extremely rapidly and was the foundation of the Trisolaran-formation computer. Of course, this was still a very inefficient machine, but it was capable of completing calculations that were too difficult to be performed manually. The computer did in fact make its first appearance in Trisolaris as formations of people, before becoming mechanical and then electronic."

Pan stood up and paced behind the players. "As a game, *Three Body* only borrows the background of human society to simulate the development of Trisolaris. This is done to give players a familiar environment. The real Trisolaris is very different from the world of the game, but the existence of the three suns is real. They're the foundation of the Trisolaran environment."

"Developing this game must have cost an enormous amount of effort," the vice president said. "But the goal is clearly not profit."

"The goal of *Three Body* is very simple and pure: to gather those of us who have common ideals," Pan said.

"What ideals do we have in common, exactly?" Wang immediately regretted the question. He wondered whether asking it sounded hostile.

Pan studied everyone meaningfully, and then added in a soft voice, "How would you feel if Trisolaran civilization were to enter our world?"

"I would be happy." The young reporter was the first to break the silence. "I've lost hope in the human race after

248

what I've seen in recent years. Human society is incapable of self-improvement, and we need the intervention of an outside force."

"I agree!" the author shouted. She was very excited, as though finally finding an outlet for pent-up feelings. "The human race is hideous. I've spent the first half of my life unveiling this ugliness with the scalpel of literature, but now I'm even sick of the work of dissection. I yearn for Trisolaran civilization to bring real beauty to this world."

Pan said nothing. That glint of excitement appeared in his eyes again.

The old philosopher waved his pipe, which had gone out. He spoke with a serious mien. "Let's discuss this question with a bit more depth: What is your impression of the Aztecs?"

"Dark and bloody," the author said. "Blood-drenched pyramids lit by insidious fires seen through dark forests. Those are my impressions."

The philosopher nodded. "Very good. Then try to imagine: If the Spanish Conquistadors did not intervene, what would have been the influence of that civilization on human history?"

"You're calling black white and white black," the soft-ware company vice president said. "The Conquistadors who invaded the Americas were nothing more than murderers and robbers."

"Even so, at least they prevented the Aztecs from developing without bound, turning the Americas into a bloody, dark great empire. Then civilization as we know it wouldn't have appeared in the Americas, and democracy wouldn't have thrived until much later. Indeed, maybe they wouldn't have appeared at all. This is the key to the question: No matter what the Trisolarans are like, their arrival will be good news for the terminally ill human race."

"But have you thought through the fact that the Aztecs were completely destroyed by the Western invaders?" the power company executive asked. He looked around, as though seeing these people for the first time. "Your thoughts are very dangerous."

"You mean profound!" the doctoral student said, raising a finger. He nodded vigorously at the philosopher. "I had the same thought, but I didn't know how to express it. You said it so well!"

After a moment of silence, Pan turned to Wang. "The other six have all given their views. What about you?"

"I stand with them," Wang said, pointing to the reporter and the philosopher. He kept his answer simple. *The less said the better.*

"Very good," Pan said. He turned to the software company vice president and the power company executive. "The two of you are no longer welcome at this meet-up, and you are no longer appropriate players for *Three Body*. Your IDs will be deleted. Please leave now. Thank you."

The two stood up and looked at each other; then glanced around, confused, and left.

Pan held out his hand to the remaining five, shaking each person's hand in turn. Then he said, solemnly, "We are comrades now."

19

Three Body: Einstein,
the Pendulum Monument,
and the Great Rip

The fifth time Wang Miao logged on to *Three Body*, it was dawn as usual, but the world was unrecognizable.

The great pyramid that had appeared the first four times had been destroyed by the tri-solar syzygy. In its place was a tall, modern building, whose dark gray shape was familiar to Wang: the United Nations Headquarters.

In the distance were many more tall buildings, apparently dehydratories. All had completely reflective mirror surfaces. In the dawn light they appeared as giant crystal plants growing out of the ground.

Wang heard a violin playing something by Mozart. The playing wasn't very practiced, but there was a special charm to it, as though saying: *I play for myself.* The violinist was a homeless old man sitting on the steps in front of the UN Headquarters, his fluffy silver hair fluttering in the wind. Next to his feet was an old top hat containing some scattered change.

Wang suddenly noticed the sun. But it rose in the opposite direction from the dawn light, and the patch of the sky around it was still completely dark.

The sun was very large, its half-risen disk taking up a third of the horizon. Wang's heart beat faster: Such a large sun could only mean another great catastrophe. But when Wang turned around, the old man continued to play as though nothing odd was happening. His silver hair shone brilliantly in the sun, as though it was on fire.

The sun was silvery, just like the old man's hair. It cast a pale white light over the ground, but Wang couldn't feel any warmth from the light. He gazed at the sun, which had now completely risen. On the giant silver disk he could pick out lines like wood grains: mountain ranges.

Wang realized that the disk did not emit light. It only reflected the light from the real sun, which was on the other side of the sky, below the horizon. What had risen wasn't a sun at all, but a giant moon. The giant moon moved briskly up the sky at a pace that could be detected by the naked eye. In the process, it gradually waned from a full to a half moon, and then a crescent. The old man's soothing violin strains drifted on the cold morning breeze. The majestic sight of the universe was like the music made material. Wang was intoxicated.

The giant crescent now fell into the dawn light and grew much brighter. When only two glowing tips remained above the horizon, Wang imagined them as the tips of the horns of a titanic bull rushing toward the sun.

"Honored Copernicus, rest your busy feet here a while," the old man said, after the giant moon had set. "Then after you've appreciated some Mozart, perhaps I can have some lunch."

"If I'm not mistaken . . ." Wang looked at the face full of wrinkles. The wrinkles were long and their curves gentle, as though they were trying to create a kind of harmony.

"You're not. I'm Einstein, a pitiful man full of faith in God, though abandoned by Him."

"What is that giant moon? I've never seen it the previous times I was here."

"It's already cooled off."

"What?"

"The big moon. When I was little it was still hot. When it rose to the middle of the sky, I could see the red glow from the central plains. But now it's cold. . . . Haven't you heard about the great rip?"

"No. What's that?"

Einstein sighed and shook his head. "Let's not speak of it. Forget the past. My past, civilization's past, the universe's past—all of it too painful to recall."

"How did you get to be like this?" Wang searched in his pocket and found some change. He bent over and dropped the money into the hat.

"Thank you, Mr. Copernicus. Let's hope that God doesn't abandon you, though I don't have much faith in that. I feel that the model you and Newton and the others created in the East with the help of the human-formation computer was very close to being correct. But the little bit of error left was like an uncrossable chasm for Newton and the others.

"I've always believed that without me, others would have discovered special relativity eventually. But general relativity is different. The bit that Newton lacked was the effect on planetary orbit from the gravitationally induced curvature of space-time described by general relativity. Though the error caused by it was small, its impact on the results of the computation was fatal. Adding the correction factor for perturbation from space-time curvature to the classical equations would yield the right mathematical model. The amount of computational power required far exceeds what you accomplished in the East, but is easily provided by modern computers."

"Have the results of the computation been confirmed by astronomical observations?"

"If that had occurred, do you think I'd be here? But from the perspective of aesthetics, I must be right and the universe must be wrong. God abandoned me, then others abandoned me as well. I'm wanted nowhere. Princeton dismissed me as a professor. UNESCO wouldn't even have me as a science consultant. Before, even if they had begged on their knees, I wouldn't have wanted the position. I even thought of going to Israel to be president, but they changed their minds and said I was nothing but a fraud. . . ."

Einstein began playing again, picking up right where he had stopped. After listening to him for a while, Wang strode toward the UN building.

"There's no one in there," Einstein said, still playing. "All the members of the General Assembly session are behind the building attending the Pendulum Initiation Ceremony."

Wang walked around the building and was greeted by a breathtaking sight: a colossal pendulum that seemed to stretch between the sky and the earth. In fact, Wang had seen it peeking out from behind the building, but he didn't know what he was seeing.

The pendulum resembled those constructed by Fu Xi to hypnotize the sun god during the Warring States Period, back when Wang Miao first logged on to *Three Body*. But the pendulum before him had been completely modernized. The two pillars holding up the pendulum were made of metal, each as tall as the Eiffel Tower. The weight was also made of metal, streamlined, with a smooth, mirrorlike, electroplated surface. The pendulum line, made of some ultrastrong material, was so thin as to be almost invisible, and the weight seemed to float in the air between the two towers.

Below the pendulum was a crowd of people dressed in suits, probably the leaders of the various countries attending the General Assembly session. They gathered in small cliques and talked amongst themselves quietly, as though waiting for something.

"Ah, Copernicus, the man who crossed five eras!" someone shouted. The others welcomed him.

"You're one of those who saw the pendulums of the Warring States Period with your own eyes!" A friendly man shook and held Wang's hand. Someone introduced the man as the secretary general of the UN, from Africa.

"Yes, I did see them," Wang said. "But why are we building another one now?"

"It's a monument for Trisolaris, as well as a tombstone." The secretary general looked up at the pendulum. From down here, it appeared as big as a submarine.

"A tombstone? For who?"

"For an aspiration, a striving that lasted through almost two hundred civilizations: the effort to solve the three-body problem, to find the pattern in the suns' movements."

"Is the effort over?"

"Yes. As of now, it's completely over."

Wang hesitated for a moment before taking out a stack of papers, Wei Cheng's three-body mathematical model. "I . . . I came here for this. I brought a mathematical model that solves the three-body problem. I have reason to believe it will likely work."

As soon as Wang said this, the crowd around him lost interest. They returned to their cliques to continue their conversations. He noticed that a few even shook their heads and laughed as they left him. The secretary general took the document and, without even glancing at it, handed it to a slender man wearing glasses standing next to him. "Out of respect for your famed reputation, I'll have my science advisor take a look. Indeed, everyone here has shown you respect. If anyone else had said what you said, they'd be laughing at him."

The science advisor flipped through the document. "Evolutionary algorithm? Copernicus, you're a genius. Anyone who can come up with such an algorithm is a genius. This requires not only superior math skills, but also imagination."

"You seem to be suggesting that someone has already created such a mathematical model?"

"Yes. There are dozens of other mathematical models. Of those, more than half are more advanced than yours. They've all been implemented and run on computers. During the past two centuries, such massive computation became the principal activity of this world. Everyone waited for the results as if waiting for Judgment Day."

"And?"

"We have definitively proven that the three-body problem has no solution."

Wang gazed up at the massive pendulum overhead. In the dawn light, it was crystal bright. Its deformed mirrorlike surface reflected everything around it like the eye of the world. In this place, in a distant age separated from the here and now by many civilizations, he and King Wen had passed through a forest of giant pendulums on their way to the palace of King Zhou. Just like that, history had made a long circuit and returned to its starting place.

The science advisor said, "It's just like we guessed long ago: The three-body system is a chaotic system. Tiny perturbations can be endlessly amplified. Its patterns of movement essentially cannot be mathematically predicted."

256

Wang felt his scientific knowledge and system of thought become a blur in a single moment. In their place was unprecedented confusion. "If even an extremely simple arrangement like the three-body system is unpredictable chaos, how can we have any faith in discovering the laws of the complicated universe?"

"God is a shameless old gambler. He has abandoned us!" The speaker was Einstein, waving his violin. Wang didn't know when he had shown up.

The secretary general slowly nodded. "Yes, God is a gambler. The only hope for Trisolaran civilization is to gamble as well."

By now, the giant moon was rising again from the dark side of the horizon. Its large, silvery image was reflected by the surface of the pendulum weight. The light wriggled strangely, as though the weight and the moon had developed a mysterious sympathy together.

"This civilization seems to have developed to a very advanced state," Wang said.

"Yes. We've mastered the energy of the atom and reached the Information Age." The secretary general didn't seem to be too impressed by his own words.

"Then there is hope: Even if it's impossible to know the pattern of the suns' movements, civilization can continue to develop until it reaches a stage where it can survive the Chaotic Eras by protecting itself against the devastating catastrophes of those eras."

"People once thought as you do. That was one of the motivating forces pushing Trisolaran civilization to tenaciously come back again and again. But the moon made us realize the naïveté of such an idea." The secretary general pointed to the rising giant moon. "This is probably the first time you've seen this moon. Actually, since it's about a quarter of the size of our planet, it's no longer a moon, but a companion to our world in a double planet system. It resulted from the great rip."

"The great rip?"

"The disaster that destroyed the last civilization. Compared to the civilizations before it, they had ample warning of the disaster. Based on surviving records, the astronomers of Civilization 191 detected a frozen flying star early on."

Wang's heart clenched as he heard the last phrase. A frozen flying star was a terrible omen for Trisolaris. When a flying star, or a distant sun, seems to come to a complete stop against the background starfield, then the sun's and the planet's motion vectors are aligned. This has three possible interpretations: the sun and the planet are moving in the same direction at the same speed; the sun and the planet are moving apart from each other; and the sun and the planet are moving toward each other. Before Civilization 191, this last possibility was purely theoretical, a disaster that had never occurred. But the population's fear of it and their vigilance did not diminish, so much so that "frozen flying star" became an extremely unlucky phrase in many Trisolaran civilizations. A single flying star remaining still was sufficient to terrify everyone.

"And then three flying stars froze simultaneously. The people of Civilization 191 stood on the ground, gazing up helplessly at the three frozen flying stars, at the three suns falling directly toward their world. A few days later, one of the suns moved to a distance where its outer gaseous layer became visible. In the middle of a tranquil night, the star suddenly turned into a blazing sun. Separated by intervals of thirty hours or so, the other two suns also appeared in quick succession. This was not a normal kind of tri-solar day. By the time the last flying star turned into a sun, the first sun had already swept past the planet at extremely close range. Right after that, the other two suns swept past Trisolaris at even closer ranges, well within the planet's Roche limit[31], such that the tidal forces imposed on Trisolaris by the three suns exceeded the force of the planet's gravitational self-attraction. The first sun shook the deepest geological structure of the planet; the second sun tore open a great rift in the planet that went straight to the core; and the third sun ripped the planet into two pieces."

The secretary general pointed at the giant moon overhead. "That's the smaller piece. There are still ruins from Civilization 191 on it, but it's a lifeless world. It was the most terrible disaster in the entire history of Trisolaris. After the planet was torn apart, the two irregularly shaped pieces each returned to spherical form under self-gravitation. The dense, searing planetary core material gushed to the surface, and the oceans boiled over the lava. The continents drifted over the magma like icebergs. As they collided, the ground became as soft as the ocean. Massive mountain ranges tens of thousands of meters high rose in an hour and disappeared just as quickly.

"For a while, the two ripped-apart pieces were still connected by streams of molten lava that coalesced into a space-spanning river. Then the lava cooled and turned into rings around the planets, but because of perturbations from the planets, the rings were unstable. The rocks that formed them fell back to the surface in a rain of giant stones that

---

31 *Author's Note:* Roche limit: Édouard Roche, French astronomer, was the first to calculate the theoretical distance between two celestial bodies such that the smaller body will be torn apart by tidal forces from the larger body. The Roche limit is usually expressed as a function of the densities of the bodies and the equatorial radius of the larger body.

lasted several centuries. . . . Can you imagine what kind of hell that was? The ecological destruction caused by this catastrophe was the most severe in all of history. All life on the companion planet went extinct, and the mother planet almost became a lifeless waste as well. But in the end, the seeds of life managed to germinate here, and as the geology of the mother planet settled down, evolution began its tottering steps in new oceans and on new continents, until civilization reappeared for the one hundred and ninety-second time. The entire process took ninety million years.

"Trisolaris's place in the universe is even more grim than we had imagined. What will happen the next time frozen flying stars occur? Very likely, our planet will not just skim past the edge of the sun, but will plunge into the fiery sea of the sun itself. Given enough time, this possibility will become certainty.

"This was originally just a frightening speculation, but a recent astronomical discovery has caused us to lose all hope for the fate of Trisolaris. The researchers had intended to recover the history of the formation of the stars and the planets based on signs in this stellar system. Instead, they discovered that, in the distant past, the Trisolaran stellar system had *twelve* planets. Yet, now only this one remains.

"There is only one explanation: The other eleven planets have all been consumed by the three suns! Our world is nothing more than the sole survivor of a Great Hunt. The fact that civilization has been reincarnated a hundred and ninety-two times is only a kind of luck. Also, after further study, we discovered the phenomenon of 'breathing' by the three stars."

"The stars breathe?"

"It's only a metaphor. You discovered the gaseous outer layer of the suns, but you didn't know that this gaseous layer expands and contracts over cycles lasting eons, like breathing. When the gaseous layer expands, its thickness can grow by more than a dozen times. This greatly increases the diameter of the sun, like a giant mitt that can catch planets more easily. When a planet passes by a sun at close range, it will enter the sun's gaseous layer. Friction will cause it to lose speed, and finally, like a meteor, it will fall into the blazing sea of the sun, dragging a long, fiery tail.

"The study results show that in the long history of the Trisolaran stellar system, every time the suns' gaseous layers expanded, one or two planets were consumed. The other eleven planets all fell into a fiery sea during times when the gaseous layers were at their greatest. Right now, the gaseous layers of the three suns are in a contracted stage—otherwise our planet would have already fallen into one of them the last time they skimmed past. But scholars predict that the next expansion will occur in one thousand years."

"We can't stay in this terrible place anymore," Einstein said, crouched down on the ground like an old beggar.

The secretary general nodded. "We can't stay here any longer. The only path left for Trisolaran civilization is to gamble with the universe."

"How?" Wang asked.

"We must leave the Trisolaran stellar system and fly into the wide open sea of stars. We must find in the galaxy a new world to emigrate to."

Wang heard a grinding noise. He saw that the giant weight of the pendulum was being pulled up by a thin cable whose other end was attached to an elevated winch. As it rose to its highest point, a great waning crescent moon descended slowly in the sky behind it.

The secretary general solemnly announced, "Start the pendulum."

The elevated winch released the cable tied to the pendulum, and the weight noiselessly fell along a smooth arc. Initially, it fell slowly, but then it accelerated, reaching maximum speed at the bottom of the arc. As it sliced through the air, the sound of the wind was deep and resonant. By the time the noise disappeared, the pendulum had followed the arc to its highest point on the other side, and, after pausing for a moment, began its backward swing.

Wang felt the great force generated by the movement of the pendulum, as though the ground was shaken by its swings. Unlike a pendulum in the real world, this giant pendulum's period was not stable, but changed constantly. This was due to the continually shifting gravitational attraction of the giant moon. When the giant moon was on this side of the planet, its gravity partially canceled out the gravity of the planet, causing the pendulum to lose weight. When it was on the other side of the planet, its gravity was added to the gravity of the planet, causing the pendulum's weight to increase, almost to the level it would have had before the great rip.

As he gazed up at the awe-inspiring swings of the Trisolaran Pendulum Monument, Wang asked himself, *Does it represent the yearning for order, or the surrender to chaos?* Wang also thought of the pendulum as a gigantic metal fist, swinging eternally against the unfeeling universe, noiselessly shouting out Trisolaran civilization's indomitable battle cry. . . .

As Wang Miao's eyes blurred with tears, he saw a line of text appear against the background of the swinging pendulum:

Four hundred and fifty-one years later, Civilization 192 was destroyed by the fiery flames of twin suns appearing together. It had reached the Atomic Age and the Information Age.

Civilization 192 was a milestone in Trisolaran civilization. It finally proved that the three-body problem had no solution. It gave up the useless effort that had already lasted through 191 cycles and set the course for future civilizations. Thus, the goal of *Three Body* has changed.

The new goal is: Head for the stars; find a new home.

We invite you to log on again.

After logging out of *Three Body*, Wang felt exhausted, the same way he did after each previous session. But this time, he only rested half an hour before logging in again.

This time, against the pitch-black background, an unexpected line of text appeared:

The situation is urgent. The *Three Body* servers are about to be shut down. Please log on freely during the remaining time. *Three Body* will now go directly to the final scene.

20

Three Body: Expedition

The chilly dawn revealed a bare landscape. There was no pyramid, no United Nations Headquarters, no sign of the Pendulum Monument. Only a dark desert extended to the horizon, just as Wang had seen the first time he had logged in.

But Wang soon realized that he was wrong. What he thought were numerous stones arrayed across the desert were not stones at all, but human heads. The ground was filled with a densely packed crowd.

From where he stood on a small hill, Wang could see no end to the sea of people. He estimated the number of individuals within his view alone to be in the hundreds of millions. All the Trisolarans on the planet were probably gathered here.

The silence of hundreds of millions created a suffocating sense of strangeness. *What are they waiting for?* Wang looked around and noticed everyone was gazing up at the sky.

Wang lifted his face and found the starry sky had been transformed to an astonishing sight: The stars were arrayed in a square formation! However, Wang soon realized that the stars in the formation were in a synchronous orbit above the planet, moving together against the dimmer, more distant background of the Milky Way.

The stars in the formation closest to the direction of dawn were also the brightest, shining with a silver light that cast shadows on the ground. The brightness decreased as one moved away from that edge. Wang counted more than thirty stars along each edge of the formation, which meant a total of more than a thousand stars. The slow movement of the obviously artificial formation against the starry universe exuded a solemn power.

A man standing next to him nudged him lightly and spoke in a low voice, "Ah, Great Copernicus, why have you come so late? Three cycles of civilizations have passed, and you've missed many great enterprises."

"What is that?" Wang asked, pointing at the formation in the sky.

"The Trisolaran Interstellar Fleet. It's about to begin its expedition."

"Trisolaran civilization has already achieved the capacity for interstellar flight?"

"Yes. All those magnificent ships can reach one-tenth the speed of light."

"That is a great accomplishment, as far as I understand it, but it still seems too slow for interstellar flight."

"The journey of a thousand miles begins with the first step. The key is finding the right target."

"What's the fleet's destination?"

"A star with planets about four light-years away—the closest star to the Trisolaran system."

Wang was surprised. "The closest star to us is also about four light-years away."

"You?"

"The Earth."

"Oh, that's not very surprising. In most regions of the Milky

Way, the distribution of stars is fairly even. It's the result of star clusters acting under the influence of gravity. The distance between most stars is between three and six light-years."

A loud, joyous cry erupted from the crowd. Wang looked up and saw that every star in the square formation was rapidly growing brighter. This was due to the light emitted by the ships themselves. Their combined illumination soon overwhelmed the dawn, and one thousand stars became one thousand little suns. Trisolaris was bathed in glorious daylight, and the crowd raised their hands and formed an endless prairie of uplifted arms.

The Trisolaran Fleet began to accelerate, solemnly gliding across the dome of the sky, skimming past the giant, just-risen moon's tip, casting a dim blue glow against the moon's mountains and plains.

The joyous cry subsided. The people of Trisolaris mutely gazed as their hope gradually shrunk in the western sky. They would not know the outcome of the launch in their lifetimes, but four or five hundred years from now, their descendants would receive the news from a new world, the beginning of a new life for Trisolaran civilization. Wang stood with them, silently gazing, until the phalanx of a thousand stars shrank into a single star, and until that star disappeared in the western night sky. Then the following text appeared:

The Trisolaran Expedition to the new world has begun. The fleet is still in flight. . . .

Three Body is over. When you have returned to the real world, if you remain true to the promise you've made, please attend the meet-up of the Earth-Trisolaris Organization. The address will be in the follow-up e-mail you receive.

PART III

SUNSET FOR
HUMANITY

21

Rebels of Earth

There were many more attendees this time than at the last *Three Body* meet-up. They met at the employee cafeteria of a chemical plant. The factory had already been moved elsewhere, and the interior of the building, which was about to be demolished, was worn out but spacious. About three hundred people were gathered here, and Wang Miao noticed many familiar faces: celebrities and elites of various fields; famous scientists, writers, politicians, and so on.

The first thing to attract Wang's attention was the strange device at the center of the cafeteria. Three silver spheres, each slightly smaller than a bowling ball, hovered and swirled over a metal base. Wang guessed the device was probably based on magnetic levitation. The orbits of the three spheres were completely random: a real-life version of the three-body problem.

The others didn't pay much mind to the artistic portrayal of the three-body problem. Instead, they focused on Pan Han, who was standing on top of a broken table in the middle of the cafeteria.

"Did you murder comrade Shen Yufei?" a man asked.

"Yes," Pan said, perfectly calm. "It's because the Adventists have traitors like her in our midst that the Organization faces the crisis it does today."

"Who gave you the right to kill?"

"I did it out of a sense of duty to the Organization."

"Duty? I think you've always had malice in your heart!"

"What do you mean by that?"

"What has the Environment Branch done under your leadership? Your charge is to exploit and create environmental problems to make the population loathe science and modern industry. But in reality, you've only used our Lord's technology and predictions to gain riches and fame for yourself!"

"Do you think I became famous for myself? To my eyes, the entire human race is a pile of garbage. Why would I care what they think? But if I'm not famous, how do I direct and channel their thinking?"

"You always pick the easy tasks. What you've done could have been better accomplished by regular environmentalists. They're more sincere and passionate than you, and with just a little guidance, we could easily take advantage of their actions. Your Environment Branch should be creating environmental disasters and then exploiting them. For example, disseminating poison in reservoirs, leaking toxic waste from chemical plants . . . have you done any of those? No, not a single one!"

"We had devised numerous programs and plans, but the commander vetoed them all. Anyway, such acts would have been stupid, at least until recently. The Biology and Medicine Branch once created a catastrophe from the overuse of antibiotics, but that was soon detected. And the rash actions of the European Detachment almost drew attention to us."

"Talk about drawing attention to us—you just murdered someone!"

"Listen to me, comrades! Sooner or later, it would have been unavoidable. You must already know that the governments of the world are preparing for war. In Europe and North America, they're already cracking down on the Organization. Once the crackdown begins here, the Redemptionists will no doubt side with the government. So our first priority is to purge the Redemptionists from the Organization."

"That is not within your authority."

"Of course the commander must decide. But, comrades, I can tell you right now that the commander is an Adventist!"

"Now you're just making things up. Everyone knows the scope of the commander's power. If the commander really is an Adventist, then the Redemptionists would have been purged long ago."

"Maybe the commander knows something we don't. Perhaps that's what the meeting today is about."

After this, the crowd's attention turned away from Pan Han to the crisis before them. A famous scientist who had won the Turing Award jumped onto the table and began to speak. "The time for talk is over. Comrades, what should be our next step?"

"Start a global rebellion!"

"Then we're asking to be killed."

"Long live the spirit of Trisolaris! We shall persevere like the stubborn grass that resprouts after every wildfire!"

"A rebellion will finally reveal our existence to the world. As long as we have an appropriate plan of action, I'm sure many people will support us."

This last remark came from Pan Han, and many applauded.

Someone yelled, "The commander is here!" The crowd parted to form a path.

Wang looked up and felt dizzy. The world turned white and black in his eyes, and the only spot of color was the person who had just appeared.

Surrounded by a group of young bodyguards, the commander in chief of the Earth-Trisolaris rebels, Ye Wenjie, walked steadily into the crowd.

Ye stood in the middle of the space the crowd cleared for her, raised a bony fist, and—with a resolve and strength that Wang could not believe she possessed—said, "Eliminate human tyranny!"

The crowd responded in a way that had clearly been rehearsed countless times: "The world belongs to Trisolaris!"

"Hello, comrades," Ye said. Her voice returned to the gentleness that Wang knew. It was only now that he could be sure that it was really her. "I haven't been well lately, and haven't spent much time with all of you. But now the situation is urgent, and I know everyone is under a great deal of pressure, so I've come to see you."

"Commander, take care of yourself," someone in the crowd said. Wang could hear the heartfelt concern.

Ye said, "Before we move on to more important matters, let's take care of one small detail. Pan Han—" She kept her eyes on the crowd even as she called his name.

"Here, Commander." Pan emerged from the crowd. Earlier, he had tried to lose himself in the throng. He appeared calm, but the terror in his heart was obvious. The commander had not called him *comrade,* a bad sign.

"You committed a severe violation of the Organization's rules." Ye spoke without looking at Pan. Her voice remained kind, as though talking to a child who had been naughty.

"Commander, the Organization is facing a crisis of survival! If we don't take decisive measures and cleanse the traitors and enemies within, we will lose everything!"

Ye looked up at Pan, her eyes affectionate. But his breath stopped for a few seconds. "The ultimate goal and ideal of

272

the ETO *is* to lose everything. Everything that now belongs to the human race, including us."

"Then you must be an Adventist! Commander, please openly declare this to be true, because it's very important. Am I right, comrades? Very important!" he shouted, and waved an arm as he looked around. But the crowd remained mute.

"This request is not yours to make. You have seriously violated our code of conduct. If you want to make an appeal, now is the time. Otherwise, you must bear the responsibility." Ye spoke slowly, enunciating every word, as though afraid the child she was teaching had trouble understanding.

"I went intending to eliminate Wei Cheng, that math prodigy. The decision was made by Comrade Evans and ratified by the committee unanimously. If he really succeeds in creating a mathematical model of the three-body problem that gives a complete solution, our Lord will not come, and the great enterprise of Trisolaris on Earth will be ruined. I only shot at Shen Yufei since she shot at me first. I was acting in self-defense."

Ye nodded. "Let us believe you. This is, after all, not the most important issue. I hope we can continue to trust you. Now, please repeat the request you made to me just now."

Pan was stunned for a second. That she had moved on didn't seem to relax him. "I . . . asked that you openly declare yourself to be an Adventist. After all, the action plan of the Adventists is also your ideal."

"Then repeat the plan of action."

"Human society can no longer rely on its own power to solve its problems. It can also no longer rely on its own power to restrain its madness. Therefore, we ask our Lord to come to this world, and with Its power, forcefully watch over us and transform us, so as to create a brand-new, perfect human civilization."

"Are the Adventists loyal believers in this plan?"

"Of course! Commander, please do not believe false rumors."

"It's not a false rumor!" a man shouted. He made his way to the front. "I'm Rafael, from Israel. Three years ago, my fourteen-year-old son died in an accident. I had his kidney donated to a Palestinian girl suffering kidney failure as an expression of my hope that the two peoples could live together in peace. For this ideal, I was willing to give my life. Many, many Israelis and Palestinians sincerely strove toward the same goal by my side. But all this was useless. Our home remained trapped in the quagmire of cycles of vengeance.

"Eventually, I lost hope in the human race and joined the ETO. Desperation turned me from a pacifist into an extremist. Also, probably because I donated so much money to the Organization, I became a core member of the Adventists. Let me tell you now, the Adventists have their own secret agenda.

"And it is this: The human race is an evil species. Human civilization has committed unforgivable crimes against the Earth and must be punished. The ultimate goal of the Adventists is to ask our Lord to carry out this divine punishment: the destruction of all humankind."

"The real program of the Adventists is already an open secret," someone shouted.

"But what you don't know is that this was not a program they evolved into. It was the goal set out at the very beginning; it's been the life-long dream of Mike Evans, the mastermind behind the Adventists. He lied to the Organization and fooled everyone, including the commander! Evans has been working toward this goal from the very start. He turned the Adventists into a kingdom of terror populated by extreme environmentalists and madmen who hated the human race."

"I didn't know Evans's real thoughts until much later," Ye

said. "Still, I tried to patch over the differences to allow the ETO to remain whole. But some of the other acts committed by Adventists lately have made the effort impossible."

Pan said, "Commander, the Adventists are the core of ETO. Without us, there is no Earth-Trisolaris Movement."

"But this is no excuse for you to monopolize all communications between our Lord and the Organization."

"We built the Second Red Coast Base; of course we should operate it."

"The Adventists took advantage of this and committed an unforgivable betrayal of the Organization: You intercepted the messages from our Lord to the Organization and passed on only a small portion of them. Even those, you distorted. Also, through the Second Red Coast Base, you sent a large amount of information to our Lord without the Organization's approval."

Silence descended over the meeting like a monstrous thing. Wang's scalp began to tingle.

Pan did not answer. His expression became cold, as if to say, *Finally, it has happened.*

"There is much evidence of the Adventists' betrayal. Comrade Shen Yufei was one of the witnesses. Though she belonged to the core group of Adventists, in her heart, she remained a resolute Redemptionist. You only discovered this recently, and she already knew too much. When Evans sent you, he wanted you to kill two people, not one."

Pan looked around, apparently reassessing the situation. His gesture didn't go unnoticed by Ye.

"You can see that most people attending this meeting are comrades from the Redemptionist faction. I trust that the few Adventists who are here will stand on the side of the Organization. But men like Evans and you can no longer be saved. To protect the program and ideals of the ETO, we must completely solve the problem of the Adventists."

Silence returned. A few moments later, one of the bodyguards near Ye, a young woman, smiled. She walked toward Pan Han casually.

Pan's face changed. He stuck a hand inside the lapel of his jacket, but the young woman dashed quicker than the eye could follow. Before anyone could react, she wrapped one of her slender arms around Pan's neck, placed her other hand on top of his head, and, by applying her unexpected strength at just the right angle, she twisted Pan's head 180 degrees with practiced ease. The cracks from his cervical vertebrae breaking stood out against the complete silence.

The young woman's hands immediately let go, as though Pan's head was too hot. Pan fell to the ground, and the gun that had killed Shen Yufei slid under the table. His body still spasmed, and his eyes remained open, his tongue sticking out. But his head no longer moved, as though it were never a part of the rest of his body. Several men came and dragged him away, the blood oozing from his mouth leaving a long trail.

"Ah, Xiao Wang, you're here too. How have you been?" Ye's gaze fell on Wang Miao. She smiled kindly at him and nodded. Then she turned to the others. "This is Professor Wang, a member of the Chinese Academy of Sciences and my friend. He researches nanomaterials. This is the first technology our Lord wishes to extinguish from the Earth."

No one looked at Wang, and Wang had no strength to express himself in any way. He had to pull at the sleeve of the man next to him so that he wouldn't fall, but the man lightly brushed his hand away.

"Xiao Wang, why don't I continue to tell you the story of Red Coast from last time? All the comrades here can listen too. This is not a waste of time. In this extraordinary moment, it is a fine time to review the history of our Organization."

"Red Coast. . . . You weren't done?" Wang asked foolishly.

Ye slowly approached the three-body model, seemingly absorbed by the swirling silver spheres. Through the broken window, the setting sun's light fell on the model, and the flying spheres intermittently reflected the light onto the rebel commander, like sparks from a bonfire.

"No. I've only just started," Ye said softly.

22

Red Coast V

Since she entered Red Coast Base, Ye Wenjie had never thought of leaving. After she learned the real purpose of the Red Coast Project, top-secret information that even many mid-level cadres at the base didn't know, she cut off her spiritual connection to the outside world and devoted herself to her work. Thereafter, she became even more deeply embedded in the technical core of Red Coast, and began to take on more important research topics.

Commissar Lei never forgot that it was Chief Yang who first trusted Ye, but Lei was happy to assign important topics to her. Given Ye's status, she had no rights to the results of her research. And Lei, who had studied astrophysics, was a political officer who was also an intellectual, rare at the time. Thus he could take credit for all of Ye's research results and papers, and cast himself as an exemplary political officer with both technical acumen and revolutionary zeal.

The Red Coast Project had initially requisitioned Ye because of a paper on an attempted mathematical model of the sun she had published in the *Journal of Astrophysics* as a graduate student. Compared to the Earth, the sun was a far simpler physical system, made almost entirely of hydrogen and helium. Though its physical processes were violent, they were relatively straightforward, only fusing hydrogen into helium. Thus, it was likely that a mathematical model of the sun could describe it rather precisely. The paper was basic, but Lei and Yang saw in it a hope for a solution to a technical difficulty faced by the Red Coast monitoring system.

Solar outages, a common problem in satellite communications, had always plagued the Red Coast monitoring operations.

When the Earth, an artificial satellite, and the sun are in a straight line, the line of sight from the ground-based antenna to the satellite will have the sun as its background. The sun is a giant source of electromagnetic radiation, and, as a result, satellite transmissions to the ground will be overwhelmed by interference from the solar radiation. This problem could not be completely solved, even in the twenty-first century.

The interference that Red Coast had to deal with was similar, but the source of interference (the sun) was between the source of the transmission (outer space) and the ground-based receiver. Compared to communication satellites, the solar outages suffered by Red Coast were more frequent and more severe. Red Coast Base as constructed was also much more modest than its original design, such that the transmission and monitoring systems shared the same antenna. This made the times available for monitoring even more precious, and solar outages even more of a problem.

Lei and Yang's idea for eliminating interference was very simple: ascertain the frequency spectrum and characteristics of solar radiation in the monitored range, and then filter it out digitally. Both of them were technical, and at that time, when the ignorant often led the knowledgeable, that was a rare bit of fortune. But Yang wasn't a specialist in astrophysics, and Lei had taken the path of becoming a political officer, which prevented him from accruing in-depth technical know-how. In reality, electromagnetic radiation from the sun is only stable within the limited range from near-ultraviolet to mid-infrared (including visible light). In other ranges, the radiation is quite volatile and unpredictable.

To set the right expectations, Ye made it clear in her first research report that during periods of intense solar activity—sunspots, solar flares, coronal mass ejections, and so on—it was impossible to eliminate solar interference. Thus, her research target was limited to radiation within the frequency ranges monitored by Red Coast during periods of normal solar activity.

Research conditions at the base weren't too bad. The library could obtain foreign-language materials related to the topic, including timely European and American academic journals. In those years, this was no easy feat. Ye also could use the military phone line to connect to the two groups conducting solar science research within the Chinese Academy of Sciences and obtain their observation data by fax.

After half a year of study, Ye saw no glimpse of hope. She quickly discovered that within the frequency ranges monitored by Red Coast, solar radiation fluctuated unpredictably. By analyzing large amounts of observed data, Ye discovered a puzzling mystery. Sometimes, during one of the sudden fluctuations in solar radiation, the surface of the sun was calm. Since hundreds of thousands of kilometers of solar material would absorb any shortwave and microwave radiation originating from the core of the sun, the radiation must have come from activities on its surface, so there should have been observable surface activity when these fluctuations occurred. If there were no corresponding surface disturbances, what caused these sudden changes to the narrow frequency ranges? The more she thought about it, the more mysterious it seemed.

Eventually Ye ran out of ideas and decided to give up.

In her last report, she conceded that she could not solve the problem. This shouldn't have been a big deal. The military had asked several groups within universities and the Chinese Academy of Sciences to research the same issue, and all of those efforts had failed. But Yang wanted to try one more time, relying on Ye's extraordinary talent.

Lei's agenda was even simpler: He just wanted Ye's paper. The research topic was highly theoretical and would show off his expertise and skill. Now that the chaos in society was finally subsiding, the demands on cadres were also changing. There was an acute need for men like him, politically mature and academically accomplished. Of course he would have a bright future. As to whether the problem of interference from solar outages could be solved, he didn't really care.

But in the end, Ye didn't hand in her report. She thought that if the research project were terminated, the base library would stop receiving foreign language journals and other research materials, and she would no longer have access to such a rich trove of astrophysics references. So she nominally continued her research, while in reality she focused on refining her mathematical model of the sun.

One night, Ye was, as usual, the only person in the cold reading room of the base library. On the long table in front of her, a pile of documents and journals were spread open. After completing a set of tedious and cumbersome matrix calculations, she blew on her hands to warm them, and picked up the latest issue of the *Journal of Astrophysics* to take a break. As she flipped through it, a brief note about Jupiter caught her attention:

Last issue, in "A New, Powerful Radiation Source Within the Solar System," Dr. Harry Peterson of Mount Wilson

Observatory published a set of data accidentally obtained while observing Jupiter's precession on June 12 and July 2, during which strong electromagnetic radiation was detected, lasting 81 seconds and 76 seconds, respectively. The data included the frequency ranges of the radiation as well as other parameters. During the radio outbursts, Peterson also observed certain changes in the Great Red Spot. This discovery drew a lot of interest from planetary scientists. In this issue, G. McKenzie's article argues that it was a sign of fusion starting within Jupiter's core. In the next issue we will publish Inoue Kumoseki's article, which attributes the Jovian radio outbursts to a more complicated mechanism—the movements of internal metallic hydrogen plates—and gives a complete mathematical description.

Ye clearly remembered the two dates noted in the paper. During those windows, the Red Coast monitoring system had also received strong interference from solar outages. She checked the operations diary and confirmed her memory. The times were close, but the solar outages had occurred sixteen minutes and forty-two seconds after the arrival of the Jovian radio outbursts on Earth.

The sixteen minutes and forty-two seconds are critical! Ye tried to calm her wild heartbeat, and asked the librarian to contact the National Observatory to obtain the ephemeris of the Earth's and Jupiter's positions during those two time periods.

She drew a big triangle on the blackboard with the sun, the Earth, and Jupiter at the vertices. She marked the distances along the three edges, and wrote down the two arrival times next to the Earth. From the distance between the Earth and

Jupiter it was easy to figure out the time it took for the radio outbursts to travel between the two. Then she calculated the time it would take the radio outbursts to go from Jupiter to the sun, and then from the sun to the Earth. The difference between the two was exactly sixteen minutes and forty-two seconds.

Ye referred to her solar structure mathematical model and tried to find a theoretical explanation. Her eyes were drawn to her description of what she called "energy mirrors" within the solar radiation zone.

Energy produced by reaction within the solar core is initially in the form of high-energy gamma rays. The radiation zone, the region of the sun's interior that surrounds the core, absorbs these high-energy photons and re-emits them at a slightly lower energy level. After a long period of successive absorption and re-emission (a photon might take a thousand years to leave the sun), gamma rays become x-rays, extreme ultraviolet, ultraviolet, then eventually turn into visible light and other forms of radiation.

Such were the known facts about the sun. But Ye's model led to a new result: As solar radiation dropped through these different frequencies on its way through the radiation zone, there were boundaries between the subzones for each type of radiation. As energy crossed each boundary, the radiation frequency stepped down a grade sharply. This was different from the traditional view that the radiation frequency lowered gradually as energy passed from the core outwards. Her calculations showed that these boundaries would reflect radiation coming from the lower-frequency side, which was why she named the boundaries "energy mirrors."

Ye had carefully studied these membranelike boundary surfaces suspended in the high-energy plasma ocean of the sun and discovered them to be full of wonderful properties. One of the most incredible characteristics she named "gain reflectivity." However, the characteristic was so bizarre that it was hard to confirm, and even Ye herself didn't quite believe it was real. It seemed more likely an artifact of some error in the dizzying, complex calculations.

But now, Ye made the first step in confirming her guess about the gain reflectivity of solar energy mirrors: The energy mirrors not only reflected radiation coming from the lower-frequency side, but amplified it. All the mysterious sudden fluctuations within narrow frequency bands that she had observed were in fact the result of other radiation coming from space being amplified after reflecting off an energy mirror in the sun. That was why there were no observable disturbances on the surface of the sun.

This time, after the Jovian radio outbursts reached the sun, they were re-emitted, as if by a mirror, after being amplified about a hundred million times. The Earth received both sets of emissions, before and after the amplification, separated by sixteen minutes and forty-two seconds.

The sun was an amplifier for radio waves.

However, there was a question: The sun must be receiving electromagnetic radiation from space every second, including radio waves emitted by the Earth. Why were only some of the waves amplified? The answer was simple: In addition to the selectivity of the energy mirrors for frequencies they would reflect, the main reason was the shielding effect of the solar convection zone. The endlessly boiling convection zone situated outside the radiation zone was the outermost liquid layer of the sun. The radio waves coming from space must first penetrate the convection zone to reach the energy mirrors in the radiation zone, where they would be amplified and reflected back out. This meant that in order to reach the energy mirrors, the waves would have to be more powerful than a threshold value. The vast majority of Earth-based radio sources could not cross this threshold, but the Jovian radio outburst did—

And Red Coast's maximum transmission power also exceeded the threshold.

The problem with solar outages was not resolved, but another exciting possibility presented itself: Humans could use the sun as a superantenna, and, through it, broadcast radio waves to the universe. The radio waves would be sent with the power of the sun, hundreds of millions of times greater than the total usable transmission power on Earth.

Earth civilization had a way to transmit at the level of a Kardashev Type II civilization.

The next step was to compare the waveforms of the two Jovian radio outbursts with the waveforms of the solar outages received by Red Coast. If they matched, then her guess would receive further confirmation.

Ye made her request to the base leadership to contact Harry Peterson and obtain the waveform records of the two Jovian radio outbursts. This was not easy. It was difficult to find the right communication channels, and numerous bureaucracies required layers of formal paperwork. Any error could lead to her being suspected of acting as a foreign spy. So Ye had to wait.

But there was a more direct way to prove the hypothesis: Red Coast itself could transmit radio waves directly at the sun at a power level exceeding the threshold value.

Ye again made her request to the base leadership. But she didn't dare to give her real reason—it was too fantastic, and she would have been turned down for certain. Instead, she explained that she wanted to do an experiment for her solar research: The Red Coast transmission system would be used as a solar exploration radar whose echoes could be analyzed to obtain some information about solar radiation. Lei and Yang both had deep technical backgrounds, and wouldn't have been easily fooled, but the experiment described by Ye did have real precedents in Western solar research. In fact, her suggestion was technically easier than the radar exploration of terrestrial planets already being conducted.

"Ye Wenjie, you're getting out of line," said Commissar Lei. "Your research should be focused on theory. Do we really need to go to so much trouble?"

Ye begged, "Commissar, it's possible that a big discovery will be made. Experiments are absolutely necessary. I just want to try it once, please?"

Chief Yang said, "Commissar Lei, maybe we should try once. It doesn't seem to be too difficult operationally. Receiving the echoes after transmission would take—"

"Ten, fifteen minutes," Lei said.

"Then Red Coast has just enough time to switch from transmission mode to monitoring mode."

Lei shook his head again. "I know that it's technically and operationally feasible. But you . . . eh, Chief Yang, you just lack the sensitivity for this kind of thing. You want to aim a superpowerful radio beam at the red sun. Have you thought about the political symbolism of such an experiment?"[32]

Yang and Ye were both utterly stunned, but they did not think Lei's objection ridiculous. Just the opposite: They were horrified that they themselves had not thought of it. During

---

32 *Translator's Note:* Chairman Mao was often compared to the "red sun," especially during the years of the Cultural Revolution.

those years, finding political symbolism in everything had reached absurd levels. The research reports Ye turned in had to be carefully reviewed by Lei so that even technical terms related to the sun could be repeatedly revised to remove political risk. Terms like "sunspots" were forbidden.[33] An experiment that sent a powerful radio transmission at the sun could of course be interpreted in a thousand positive ways, but a single negative interpretation would be enough to bring political disaster on everyone. Lei's reason for refusing to allow the experiment was truly unassailable.

Ye didn't give up, though. In fact, as long as she didn't take excessive risk, it wasn't difficult to accomplish her goal. The Red Coast transmitter was ultra-high-powered, but all of its components were domestically produced during the Cultural Revolution. As the quality of the components was not up to par, the fault rate was very high. After every fifteenth transmission, the entire system had to be overhauled, and after each overhaul, there would be a test transmission. Few people attended these tests, and the targets and other parameters were arbitrarily selected.

One time when she was on duty, Ye was assigned to work during one of the test transmissions after an overhaul. Because a test transmission omitted many operational steps, only Ye and five others were present. Three of them were low-level operators who knew little about the principles behind the equipment. The remaining two were a technician and an engineer, both exhausted and not paying much attention after two days of overhaul work. Ye first adjusted the test transmission power to exceed the threshold value for her

33 *Translator's Note:* The Chinese term for "sunspot" (太阳黑子) literally means "solar black spots." Black, of course, was the color of counter-revolutionaries.

gain-reflective solar energy mirror theory, using the maximum power of the Red Coast transmission system. Then she set the frequency to the value most likely to be amplified by the energy mirror. And under the guise of testing the antenna's mechanical components, she aimed it at the setting sun in the west. The content of the transmission remained the same as usual.

This was a clear afternoon in the autumn of 1971. Afterwards, Ye recalled the event many times but couldn't remember any special feelings except anxiety, a desire for the transmission to be completed quickly. First, she was afraid to be discovered by her colleagues. Even though she had thought of some excuses, it was still unusual to use maximum power for a test transmission, because doing so would wear down the components. In addition, the Red Coast transmission system's positioning equipment was never designed to be aimed at the sun. Ye could feel the eyepiece growing hot. If it burnt out she would be in real trouble.

As the sun set slowly in the west, Ye had to manually track it. The Red Coast antenna seemed like a giant sunflower at that moment, slowly turning to follow the descending sun. By the time the red light indicating transmission completion lit up, she was already soaked in sweat.

She glanced around. The three operators at the control panel were shutting down the equipment piece by piece in accordance with the instructions in the operating manual. The engineer was drinking a glass of water in a corner of the control room, and the technician was asleep in his chair. No matter how historians and writers later tried to portray the scene, the reality at the time was completely prosaic.

The transmission completed, Ye rushed out of the control room and dashed into Yang Weining's office. Catching her breath, she said, "Tell the base station to begin monitoring the twelve thousand megahertz channel!"

"What are we receiving?" Chief Yang looked in surprise at Ye, strands of hair stuck to her sweaty face. Compared to the highly sensitive Red Coast monitoring system, the conventional military-grade radio—normally used by the base for communicating with the outside—was only a toy.

"Maybe we'll get something. There's no time to change the Red Coast systems to monitoring mode!" Normally, warming up and switching over to the monitoring system required a little more than ten minutes. But right now the monitoring system was also being overhauled. Many modules had been taken apart and remained unassembled, rendering them inoperable in the short term.

Yang stared at Ye for a few seconds, and then picked up the phone and ordered the communications office to follow Ye's direction.

"Given the low sensitivity of that radio, we can probably only receive signals from extraterrestrials on the moon."

"The signal comes from the sun," Ye said. Outside the window, the sun's edge was already approaching the mountains on the horizon, red as blood.

"You used Red Coast to send a signal to the sun?" Yang asked anxiously.

Ye nodded.

"Don't tell anyone else. This must never happen again. Never!" Yang looked behind him to be sure there was no one at the door.

Ye nodded again.

"What's the point? The echo wave must be extremely weak, far outside the sensitivity of a conventional radio."

"No. If my guess is right, we should get an extremely

strong echo. It will be more powerful than . . . I can hardly imagine. As long as the transmission power exceeds a certain threshold, the sun can amplify the signal a hundred million–fold."

Yang looked at Ye strangely. Ye said nothing. They both waited in silence. Yang could clearly hear Ye's breath and heartbeat. He hadn't paid much attention to what she had said, but the feelings he had buried in his heart for many years resurfaced. He could only restrain himself, waiting.

Twenty minutes later, Yang picked up the phone, called the communications office, and asked a few simple questions.

He put the phone down. "They received nothing."

Ye let out a long-held breath and eventually nodded.

"That American astronomer responded, though." Yang took out a thick envelope covered with customs stamps and handed it to Ye. She tore the envelope open and scanned Harry Peterson's letter. The letter said that he had not imagined that there would be colleagues in China studying planetary electromagnetism, and that he wished to collaborate and exchange more information in the future. He had also sent two stacks of paper: the complete record of the waveforms of the radio outbursts from Jupiter. They were clearly photocopied from the long signal recording tape, and would have to be pieced together.

Ye took the dozens of sheets of photocopier paper and started lining them up in two columns on the floor. Halfway through the effort she gave up any hope. She was very familiar with the waveforms of the interference from the two solar outages. They didn't match these two.

Ye slowly picked up the photocopies from the floor. Yang crouched down to help her. When he handed the stack of paper to this woman he loved with all his heart, he saw her smile. The smile was so sad that his heart trembled.

"What's wrong?" he asked, not realizing that he had never spoken to her so softly.

"Nothing. I'm just waking up from a dream." Ye smiled again. She took the stack of photocopies and the envelope and left the office. She went back to her room, picked up her lunch box, and went to the cafeteria. Only *mantou* buns and pickles were left, and the cafeteria workers told her impatiently that they were closing. So she had no choice but to carry her lunch box outside and walk next to the lip of the cliff, where she sat down on the grass to chew the cold *mantou*.

The sun had already set. The Greater Khingan Mountains were gray and indistinct, just like Ye's life. In this gray life, a dream appeared especially colorful and bright. But one always awoke from a dream, just like the sun—which, though it would rise again, brought no fresh hope. In that moment Ye saw the rest of her life suffused with an endless grayness. With tears in her eyes, she smiled again, and continued to chew the cold *mantou*.

Ye didn't know that at that moment, the first cry that could be heard in space from civilization on Earth was already spreading out from the sun to the universe at the speed of light. A star-powered radio wave, like a majestic tide, had already crossed the orbit of Jupiter.

Right then, at the frequency of 12,000 MHz, the sun was the brightest star in the entire Milky Way.

23

Red Coast VI

The next eight years were among the most peaceful of Ye Wenjie's life. The horror experienced during the Cultural Revolution gradually subsided, and she was finally able to relax a little. The Red Coast Project completed its testing and breaking-in phases, settling down into routine operation. Fewer and fewer technical problems remained, and both work and life became regular.

In peace, what had been suppressed by anxiety and fear began to reawaken. Ye found that the real pain had just begun. Nightmarish memories, like embers coming back to life, burned more and more fiercely, searing her heart. For most people, perhaps time would have gradually healed these wounds. After all, during the Cultural Revolution, many people suffered fates similar to hers, and compared to many of them, Ye was relatively fortunate. But Ye had the mental habits of a scientist, and she refused to forget. Rather, she looked with a rational gaze on the madness and hatred that had harmed her.

Ye's rational consideration of humanity's evil side began the day she read *Silent Spring*. As she grew closer to Yang Weining, he was able to get her many classics of foreign-language philosophy and history under the guise of gathering technical research materials. The bloody history of humanity shocked her, and the extraordinary insights of the philosophers also led her to understand the most fundamental and secret aspects of human nature.

Indeed, even on top of Radar Peak, a place the world almost forgot, the madness and irrationality of the human race were constantly on display. Ye saw that the forest below the peak continued to fall to the deranged logging by her former comrades. Patches of bare earth grew daily, as though those parts of the Greater Khingan Mountains had had their skin torn off. When those patches grew into regions and then into a connected whole, the few surviving trees seemed rather abnormal. To complete the slash-and-burn plan, fires were lit on the bare fields, and Radar Peak became the refuge for birds escaping the fiery inferno. As the fires raged, the sorrowful cries of birds with singed feathers at the base never ceased.

The insanity of the human race had reached its historical zenith. The Cold War was at its height. Nuclear missiles capable of destroying the Earth ten times over could be launched at a moment's notice, spread out among the countless missile silos dotting two continents and hidden within ghostlike nuclear-powered ballistic missile submarines patrolling deep under the sea. A single *Lafayette*- or Yankee-class submarine held enough warheads to destroy hundreds of cities and kill hundreds of millions, but most people continued their lives as if nothing was wrong.

As an astrophysicist, Ye was strongly against nuclear weapons. She knew this was a power that should belong only to the stars. She knew also that the universe had even more terrible forces: black holes, antimatter, and more. Compared to those forces, a thermonuclear bomb was nothing but a tiny candle. If humans obtained mastery over one of those other forces, the world might be vaporized in a moment. In the face of madness, rationality was powerless.

Four years after entering Red Coast Base, Ye and Yang married. Yang truly loved her. For love, he gave up his future.

The fiercest stage of the Cultural Revolution was over, and the political climate had grown somewhat milder. Yang wasn't persecuted, exactly, for his marriage. However, because he married a woman who had been deemed to be a counter-revolutionary, he was viewed as politically immature and lost his position as chief engineer. The only reason that he and his wife were allowed to stay on the base as ordinary technicians was because the base could not do without their technical skills.

Ye accepted Yang's proposal mainly out of gratitude. If he hadn't brought her into this safe haven in her most perilous moment, she would probably no longer be alive. Yang was a talented man, cultured and with good taste. She didn't find him unpleasant, but her heart was like ashes from which the flame of love could no longer be lit.

As she pondered human nature, Ye was faced with an ultimate loss of purpose and sank into another spiritual crisis. She had once been an idealist who needed to give all her talent to a great goal, but now she realized that all that she had done was meaningless, and the future could not have any meaningful pursuits, either. As this mental state persisted, she gradually felt more and more alienated from the world. She didn't belong. The sense of wandering in the spiritual wilderness tormented her. After she made a home with Yang, her soul became homeless.

One night, Ye was working the night shift. This was the loneliest time. In the deep silence of midnight, the universe revealed itself to its listeners as a vast desolation. What Ye disliked most was seeing the waves that slowly crawled across the display, a visual record of the meaningless noise Red Coast picked up from space. Ye felt this interminable wave was an abstract view of the universe: one end connected to the endless past, the other to the endless future, and in the middle only the ups and downs of random chance—without life, without pattern, the peaks and valleys at different heights like uneven grains of sand, the whole curve like a one-dimensional desert made of all the grains of sand lined up in a row, lonely, desolate, so long that it was intolerable. You could follow it and go forward or backward as long as you liked, but you'd never find the end.

On this day, however, Ye saw something odd when she glanced at the waveform display. Even experts had a hard time telling with the naked eye whether a waveform carried information. But Ye was so familiar with the noise of the universe that she could tell that the wave that now moved in front of her eyes had something extra. The thin curve, rising and falling, seemed to possess a soul. She was certain that the radio signal before her had been modulated by intelligence.

She rushed to another terminal and checked the computer's rating of the signal's recognizability: AAAAA. Before this, no radio signal received by Red Coast ever garnered a recognizability rating above C. An A rating meant the likelihood that the transmission contained intelligent information was greater than 90 percent. A rating of AAAAA was a special, extreme case: It meant the received transmission used the exact same coding language as Red Coast's own outbound transmission.

Ye turned on the Red Coast deciphering system. The software attempted to decipher any signal whose recognizability rating was above B. During the entire time that the Red Coast

Project had been running, it had never been invoked even once in real use. Based on test data, deciphering a transmission suspected of being a message might require a few days or even a few months of computing time, and the result would be failure more than half the time. But this time, as soon as the file containing the original transmission was submitted, the display showed that the deciphering was complete.

Ye opened the resulting document, and, for the first time, a human read a message from another world.

The content was not what anyone had imagined. It was a warning repeated three times.

> Do not answer!
> Do not answer!!
> Do not answer!!!

Still caught up by the dizzying excitement and confusion, Ye deciphered a second message.

> This world has received your message.
> I am a pacifist in this world. It is the luck of your civilization that I am the first to receive your message. I am warning you: Do not answer! Do not answer!! Do not answer!!!
> There are tens of millions of stars in your direction. As long as you do not answer, this world will not be able to ascertain the source of your transmission.
> But if you do answer, the source will be located right away. Your planet will be invaded. Your world will be conquered!
> Do not answer! Do not answer!! Do not answer!!!

As she read the flashing green text on the display, Ye was no longer capable of thinking clearly. Her mind, inhibited by shock and excitement, could only understand this: No more than nine years had passed since the time she had sent the message to the sun. Then the source of this transmission must be around four light-years away. It could only have come from the closest extra-solar stellar system: Alpha Centauri.[34]

The universe was not desolate. The universe was not empty. The universe was full of life! Humankind had cast their gaze to the end of the universe, but they had no idea that intelligent life already existed around the stars closest to them!

Ye stared at the waveform display: The signal continued to stream from the universe into the Red Coast antenna. She opened up another interface and began real-time deciphering. The messages began to show up immediately on the screen.

During the next four hours, Ye learned of the existence of Trisolaris, learned of the civilization that had been reborn again and again, and learned of their plan to migrate to the stars.

At four in the morning, the transmission from Alpha Centauri ended. The deciphering system continued to run uselessly and emitted an unceasing string of failure codes. The Red Coast monitoring system was once again only hearing the noise of the universe.

But Ye was certain that what she had just experienced was not a dream.

---

34 *Translator's Note:* Alpha Centauri, though appearing to the naked eye as a single star, is actually a double-star system (Alpha Centauri A and Alpha Centauri B). A third star, called Proxima Centauri and invisible to the naked eye, is probably gravitationally associated with the double-star system. The Chinese name for the objects (半人马座三星) makes it clear that the "star" is really a system of three stars.

The sun really was an amplifying antenna. But why had her experiment eight years ago not received any echoes? Why had the waveforms of Jupiter's radio outbursts not matched the later radiation from the sun? Later, Ye came up with many reasons. It was possible that the base communication office couldn't receive radio waves at that frequency, or maybe the office did receive the echo but it sounded like noise and so the operator thought it was nothing. As for the waveforms, it was possible that when the sun amplified the radio waves, it also added another wave to it. It would likely be a periodic wave that could be easily filtered out by the alien deciphering system, but to her unaided eye, the waveform from Jupiter and from the sun would appear very different. Years later, after Ye had left Red Coast, she would manage to confirm her last guess: The sun had added a sine wave.

She looked around alertly. There were three others in the main computer room. Two of the three were chatting in a corner, while the last was napping before a terminal. In the data analysis section of the monitoring system, only the two terminals in front of her could view the recognizability rating of a signal and access the deciphering system.

Maintaining her composure, she worked quickly and moved all of the received messages to a multiply-encrypted, invisible subdirectory. Then she copied over a segment of noise received a year ago as a substitute for the transmission received during the last five hours.

Finally, from the terminal, she placed a short message into the Red Coast transmission buffer.

Ye got up and left the monitoring main control room. A chilly wind blew against her feverish face. Dawn had just brightened the eastern sky, and she followed the dimly lit pebble-paved path to the transmission main control room.

Above her, the Red Coast antenna lay open, silently, like a giant palm toward the universe. The dawn turned the guard at the door into a silhouette, and as usual, he did not pay attention to Ye as she entered.

The transmission main control room was much dimmer than the monitoring main control room. Ye passed through rows of cabinets to stand in front of the control panel and flipped more than a dozen switches with practiced ease to warm up the transmission system. The two men on duty next to the control panel looked up at her with sleepy eyes, and one turned to glance at the clock. Then one of them went back to his nap while the other flipped through a well-thumbed newspaper. At the base, Ye had no political status, but she did have some freedom in technical matters. She often tested the equipment before a transmission. Although she was early today—the transmission wasn't scheduled to occur until three hours later—warming up a bit early wasn't that unusual.

What happened next was the longest half hour of her life. During this time, Ye adjusted the transmission frequency to the optimal frequency for amplification by the solar energy mirror, and increased the transmission power to maximum. Then, putting her eyes to the eyepiece of the optical positioning system, she watched the sun rise above the horizon, activated the positioning system for the antenna, and slowly aligned it with the sun. As the gigantic antenna turned, the rumbling noise shook the main control room. One of the men on duty looked at Ye again, but said nothing.

The sun was now completely above the horizon. The crosshair of the Red Coast positioning system was aimed at its upper edge to account for the time it would take for the radio wave to travel to the sun. The transmission system was ready.

The Transmit button was a long rectangle—very similar

to the Space key on a computer keyboard, except that it was red.

Ye's hand hovered two centimeters above it.

The fate of the entire human race was now tied to these slender fingers.

Without hesitation, Ye pressed the button.

"What are you doing?" one of the men on duty asked, still sleepy.

Ye smiled at him and said nothing. She pressed a yellow button to stop the transmission. Then she moved the control stick until the antenna was pointed elsewhere. She left the control panel and walked away.

The man looked at his watch. It was time to get off work. He picked up the diary and thought about recording Ye's operation of the transmission system. It was, after all, out of the ordinary. But then he looked at the paper tape and saw that she had transmitted for no more than three seconds. He tossed the diary back, yawned, put on his army cap, and left.

The message that was winging its way to the sun said, *Come here! I will help you conquer this world. Our civilization is no longer capable of solving its own problems. We need your force to intervene.*

The newly risen sun dazzled Ye Wenjie. Not too far from the door of the main control room, she collapsed onto the lawn in a faint.

When she woke up, she found herself in the base clinic. Next to her bed sat Yang, watching her with concern, like that time many years ago on the helicopter. The doctor told Ye to be careful and get plenty of rest.

"You are pregnant," he said.

24

Rebellion

After Ye Wenjie finished recounting the history of her first contact with Trisolaris, the abandoned cafeteria remained silent. Many present were apparently just hearing the complete story for the first time. Wang was deeply absorbed by the narrative and temporarily forgot about the danger and terror he faced. Unable to stop himself, he asked, "How did the ETO then develop to its present scale?"

Ye replied, "I'd have to start with how I got to know Evans. . . . But every comrade here already knows that part of history, so we shouldn't waste time on it now. I can tell you later. However, whether we'll have such an opportunity depends on you. . . . Xiao Wang, let's talk about your nanomaterial."

"This . . . Lord that you talk about. Why is it so afraid of nanomaterial?"

"Because it can allow humans to escape gravity and engage in space construction at a much larger scale."

"The space elevator?" Wang suddenly understood.

"Yes. If ultrastrong nanomaterials could be mass produced, then that would lay the technical foundation for building a space elevator from the ground up to a geostationary point in space. For our Lord, this is but a tiny invention; but for humans on Earth, its meaning would be significant.

With this technology, humans could easily enter near-Earth space and build up large-scale defensive structures. Thus, this technology must be extinguished."

"What is at the end of the countdown?" Wang asked the question that frightened him the most.

Ye smiled. "I don't know."

"But trying to stop me is useless! This is not basic research. Based on what we've already found out, someone else can figure out the rest." Wang's voice was loud but anxious.

"Yes, it is rather useless. It's far more effective to confuse the researchers' minds. But, like you point out, we didn't stop the progress in time. After all, what you do is applied research. Our technique is far more effective against basic research. . . ."

"Speaking of basic research, how did your daughter die?"

The question silenced Ye for a few seconds. Wang noticed that her eyes dimmed almost imperceptibly. But she then resumed the conversation. "Indeed, compared to our Lord, who possesses peerless strength, everything we do is meaningless. We're just doing whatever we can."

Just as she finished speaking, several loud booms rang out and the doors to the cafeteria broke open. A team of soldiers holding submachine guns rushed in. Wang realized that they were not armed police, but the real army. Noiselessly they proceeded along the walls and soon surrounded the rebels of the ETO. Shi Qiang was the last to enter. His jacket was open, and he held the barrel of a pistol so that the grip was like the head of a hammer.

Da Shi looked around arrogantly, then suddenly dashed forward. His hand flashed and there was the dull thud of metal striking against a skull. An ETO rebel fell to the ground, and the gun that he was trying to draw tumbled to fall some distance away. Several soldiers began to shoot at the ceiling, and dust and debris fell. Someone grabbed Wang Miao and pulled him away from the ETO ranks until he was safe behind a row of soldiers.

"Drop all your weapons onto the table! I swear I'm going to kill the next son of a bitch who tries anything." Da Shi pointed at the submachine guns arrayed behind him. "I know that none of you is afraid to die, but we're not afraid either. I'm going to say this up front: Normal police procedures and laws don't apply to you. Even the human laws of warfare no longer apply to you. Since you've decided to treat the entire human race as your enemy, there's no longer anything we wouldn't do to you."

There was some commotion among the ETO members, but no one panicked. Ye's face remained impassive. Three people suddenly rushed out of the crowd, including the young woman who had twisted Pan Han's neck. They ran toward the three-body sculpture, and each grabbed one of the spheres and held it in front of his or her chest.

The young woman raised the bright metal sphere before her with both hands, as though she were getting ready to start a gymnastics routine. Smiling, she said, "Officers, we hold in our hands three nuclear bombs, each with a yield of about one point five kilotons. Not too big, since we like small toys. This is the detonator."

Everyone in the cafeteria froze. The only one who moved was Shi Qiang. He put his gun back into the holster under his left arm and placed his hands together calmly.

"Our demand is simple: Let the commander go," the young woman said. "Then we can play whatever game you want." Her tone suggested that she wasn't afraid of Shi Qiang and the soldiers at all.

"I stay with my comrades," Ye said, calmly.

"Can you confirm her claim?" Da Shi asked an officer next to him, an explosives expert.

The officer threw a bag in front of the three ETO members holding the spheres. One of the ETO fighters picked up the bag and took out a spring scale, a bigger version of the ones some customers brought to street markets to verify the portions measured by vendors. He placed his metal sphere into the bag, attached it to the spring scale, and held it aloft. The gauge extended about halfway and stopped.

The young woman chuckled. The explosives expert also laughed, contemptuously.

The ETO member took out the sphere and tossed it on the ground. Another ETO fighter picked up the scale and the bag and repeated the procedure with his sphere, and ended up also tossing the sphere to the ground.

The young woman laughed once more and picked up the bag herself. She loaded her sphere into the bag, hung it on the hook of the scale, and the gauge immediately dropped to its bottom, the spring in the scale having been fully extended.

The smile on the explosives expert's face froze. He whispered to Da Shi, "Damn! They really do have one."

Da Shi remained impassive.

The explosives expert said, "We can at least confirm that there are heavy elements—fissile material—inside. We don't know if the detonation mechanism works."

The flashlights attached to the soldiers' guns focused on the young woman holding the nuclear bomb. While she held the destructive power of 1.5 kilotons of TNT in her hands, she smiled brightly, as though enjoying applause and praise on a spotlit stage.

"I have an idea: Shoot the sphere," the explosives expert whispered to Da Shi.

"Won't that set off the bomb?"

"The conventional explosives around the outside will go off, but the explosion will be scattered. It won't lead to the kind of precise compression of the fissile material in the center necessary for a nuclear explosion."

Da Shi stared at the nuclear woman, saying nothing.

"How about snipers?"

Almost imperceptibly, Da Shi shook his head. "There's no good position. She's sharp as a tack. As soon as she's targeted by a sniper scope, she'll know."

Da Shi strode forward. He pushed the crowd apart and stood in the middle of the empty space.

"Stop," the young woman warned Da Shi, staring at him intently. Her right thumb was poised over the detonator. Her face was no longer smiling in the flashlight beams.

"Calm down," Da Shi said, standing about seven or eight meters from her. He took an envelope from his pocket. "I have some information you'll definitely want to know. Your mother has been found."

The young woman's feverish eyes dimmed. At that moment her eyes were truly windows to her soul.

Da Shi took two steps forward. He was now no more than five meters from her. She raised the bomb and warned him with her eyes, but she was already distracted. One of the two ETO members who had tossed away fake bombs strode toward Da Shi to take the envelope from him. As the man blocked the woman's view of Da Shi, he drew his gun with a lightning-fast motion. The woman only saw a flash by the ear of the man trying to take the letter from Da Shi before the bomb in her hands exploded.

After hearing the muffled explosion, Wang saw nothing before his eyes but darkness. Someone dragged him out of

305

the cafeteria. Thick, yellow smoke poured out of the door, and a cacophony of shouting and gunshots came from inside. From time to time, people rushed through the smoke and out of the cafeteria.

Wang got up and tried to go back into the cafeteria, but the explosives expert grabbed him around the waist and stopped him.

"Careful. Radiation!"

The chaos eventually subsided. More than a dozen ETO fighters were killed in the gunfight. The rest—more than two hundred, including Ye Wenjie—were arrested. The explosion had turned the nuclear woman into a bloody mess, but she was the only casualty of the aborted bomb. The man who had tried to take the letter from Da Shi was severely injured, but since his body had shielded Da Shi, his wounds were light. However, like everyone else who remained in the cafeteria after the explosion, Shi suffered severe radiation contamination.

Through the small window of an ambulance, Wang stared at Da Shi, who was lying inside. A wound on Da Shi's head continued to ooze blood. The nurse who was dressing the wound wore transparent protective gear. Da Shi and Wang could only talk through their mobile phones.

"Who was that young woman's mother?" Wang asked.

Da Shi grinned. "Fucked if I know. Just a guess. A girl like that most likely has mother issues. After doing this for more than twenty years, I'm pretty good at reading people."

"I bet you're happy to be proven right. There really was someone behind all this." Wang forced himself to smile, hoping Da Shi could see it.

"Buddy, you're the one who was right!" Da Shi laughed, shaking his head. "I would never have thought that actual fucking aliens would be involved!"

25

The Deaths of Lei Zhicheng and Yang Weining

INTERROGATOR: Name?

YE WENJIE: Ye Wenjie.

INTERROGATOR: Birth date?

YE: June 1943.

INTERROGATOR: Employment?

YE: Professor of Astrophysics at Tsinghua University. Retired in 2004.

INTERROGATOR: In consideration of your health, you may stop the interrogation temporarily at any time.

YE: Thank you. I'm fine.

INTERROGATOR: We're only conducting a regular criminal investigation now and won't get into more sensitive matters. We would like to finish quickly. We hope you'll cooperate.

YE: I know what you're referring to. Yes, I'll cooperate.

INTERROGATOR: Our investigation revealed that while you were working at Red Coast Base, you were suspected of murder.

YE: I did kill two people.

INTERROGATOR: When?

YE: The afternoon of October 21, 1979.

INTERROGATOR: Names of the victims?

YE: Base Commissar Lei Zhicheng, and my husband, Base Engineer Yang Weining.

INTERROGATOR: Explain your motive for murder.

YE: Can I . . . assume that you understand the relevant background?

INTERROGATOR: I know the basics. If something is unclear I'll ask you.

YE: Good. On the day when I received the extraterrestrial communication and replied, I learned that I wasn't the only one to get the message. Lei did as well.

Lei was a typical political cadre of the time, so he possessed an extremely keen sense for politics and saw everything through an ideological lens. Unbeknownst to most of the technical staff at Red Coast Base, he ran a small program in the background on the main computer. This program constantly read from the transmission and reception buffers and stored the results in a hidden encrypted file. This way, there would be a copy of everything Red Coast sent and received that only he could read. It was from this copy that he discovered the extraterrestrial message.

On the afternoon after I sent my message toward the rising sun, and shortly after I learned that I was pregnant at the base clinic, Lei called me to his office, and I saw that his terminal displayed the message from Trisolaris that I had received the night before. . . .

"Eight hours have passed since you received the first message. Instead of making a report, you deleted the original message and maybe hid a copy. Isn't that right?"

I kept my head down and did not reply.

"I know your next move. You plan to reply. If I hadn't discovered this in time, you could have ruined all human civilization! Of course I'm not saying that we're afraid of an interstellar invasion. Even if we assumed the worst and that really did happen, the outer space invaders would surely drown in the ocean of the people's righteous war!"

I realized then that he didn't know that I'd already replied. When I placed the answer into the transmission buffer, I didn't use the regular file interface. Luckily, this got around his monitoring program.

"Ye Wenjie, I knew you were capable of something like this. You've always held a deep hatred toward the Party and the people. You would seize any opportunity for revenge. Do you know the consequences of your actions?"

Of course I knew, so I nodded. Lei was silent for a moment. But what he said next was unexpected. "Ye Wenjie, I have no pity for you at all. You've always been a class enemy who views the people as your adversaries. But I've served many years with Yang. I cannot bear to see him ruined along with you, and I certainly cannot allow his child to be ruined as well. You're pregnant, aren't you?"

What he said wasn't idle speculation. During that era, my deeds would certainly have implicated my husband if revealed, regardless of whether he had anything to do with them.

Lei kept his voice very low. "Right now, only you and I know what happened. What we must do is to minimize the impact of your actions. Pretend that it never happened and never mention it to anyone, including Yang. I'll take care of the rest. As long as you cooperate, you can avoid the disastrous consequences."

I immediately knew what Lei was after. He wanted to

become the first man to discover extraterrestrial intelligence. It really was a great opportunity to get his name into the history textbooks.

I assented. Then I left his office. I'd already decided everything.

I took a small wrench and went to the equipment closet for the processing module of the receiver. Because I often needed to inspect the equipment, no one paid attention. I opened the main cabinet and carefully loosened the bolt that secured the ground wire to the bottom. The interference on the receiver suddenly increased and the ground resistance went up from 0.6 ohms to 5 ohms. The technician on duty thought it was a problem with the ground wire, because that kind of malfunction happened a lot. It was an easy diagnosis. He would never have guessed that the problem was at this end, at the top of the ground wire, because this end was securely fastened, out of the way, and I told him that I had just inspected it.

The top of Radar Peak had an unusual geological feature: a layer of clay more than a dozen meters thick—poor conductivity—covered it. When the ground wire wasn't buried deeply, ground resistance was invariably too high. However, the ground wire couldn't be sunk too deep, either, because the clay layer had a strong corrosive effect, and after a while, it would corrode the middle section of the ground wire. In the end, the only solution was to drape the ground wire over the lip of the cliff until the tip was below the clay layer, and then bury the ground terminal into the cliff at that point. Even so, the grounding wasn't very stable, and the resistance was often excessive. Whenever such problems occurred, the trouble always involved the part of the wire going into the cliff. Whoever was assigned to repair it would have to go over the edge of the cliff, dangling on ropes.

The technician on duty informed the maintenance squad of the issue. One of the soldiers in the squad tied a rope to an iron post and then rappelled down the cliff. After half an hour down below, he climbed back up, soaked in sweat, saying that he couldn't find the malfunction. It seemed that the next monitoring session would have to be delayed. There was no choice but to inform the Base Command Center. I waited by the iron post at the top of the cliff. Very soon, just as I had planned, Lei Zhicheng came back with that soldier.

To be honest, Lei was very dedicated to his job and faithfully followed the demands placed on political officers during that era: Become a part of the masses and always be on the front line. Maybe it was all for show, but he really was a good performer. Whenever there was some difficult and perilous work at the base, he was sure to volunteer. One of the tasks that he performed more than anyone else was to repair the ground wire, a task both dangerous and tiring. Even though this job wasn't particularly demanding technically, it did benefit from experience. There were many causes of malfunction: a loose contact due to exposure to open air—difficult to detect—or possibly the location where the ground wire went into the cliff was too dry. The volunteer soldiers responsible for external maintenance were all new, and none had much experience. So I had guessed that Lei would most likely show up.

He put on the safety harness and went over the cliff edge on the rope, as though I didn't exist. I made some excuse to get rid of the soldier who brought him so that I was the only one left on the cliff. Then I took a short hacksaw out of my pocket. It was made from a longer saw blade broken into three pieces and then stacked together. With the stacked blades, any cut I made would be particularly ragged, and it would not be obvious later that the rope was cut through with a tool.

Just then, my husband, Yang Weining, showed up.

After I explained to him what had happened, he looked over the cliff edge. Then he said that to inspect the ground terminal in the cliff face required digging, and the work would be too much for just Lei. He wanted to go down to help, so he put on the safety harness left by that other soldier. I asked him to use another rope, but he said no—the rope that Lei was on was thick and sturdy and could easily bear the weight of two. I insisted, so he told me to go get the rope. By the time I rushed back to the cliff with the rope, he had already gone down over the side. I poked my head over the edge and saw that he and Lei had already finished their inspection and were climbing back up. Lei was in the front.

There would never be another chance. I took out my hacksaw and cut through the rope.

INTERROGATOR: I want to ask a question, but I won't record the answer. How did you feel at the time?

YE: Calm. I did it without feeling anything. I had finally found a goal to which I could devote myself. I didn't care what price had to be paid, either by me or by others. I also knew that the entire human race would pay an unprecedented price for this goal. This was a very insignificant beginning.

INTERROGATOR: All right. Continue.

YE: I heard two or three surprised cries, and then the sound of bodies slamming against the rocks at the cliff bottom. After a while, I saw that the stream at the foot of the cliff had turned red. . . . That's all I'll say about that.

INTERROGATOR: I understand. This is the record. Please check it over carefully. If there are no errors, please sign it.

26

No One Repents

The deaths of Lei and Yang were treated as accidents. Everybody at the base knew that Ye and Yang were a happy couple, and no one suspected her.

A new commissar came to the base, and life returned to its habitual peace. The tiny life inside Ye grew bigger every day, and she also felt the world outside change.

One day, the security platoon commander asked Ye to come to the gatehouse at the entrance to the base. When she entered the gatehouse, she was surprised to see three children: two boys and a girl, about fifteen or sixteen. They all wore old coats and dog fur hats, obviously locals. The guard on duty told her that they came from the village of Qijiatun. They had heard that the people on Radar Peak were learned and had come to ask some questions related to their studies.

Ye wondered how they dared to come onto Radar Peak. This was a restricted military zone, and the guards were authorized to warn intruders only once before shooting. The guard saw that Ye was puzzled and explained that they had just received orders that Red Coast Base's security rating had been reduced. The locals were allowed onto Radar Peak as long as they stayed outside the base. Several local peasants had already come yesterday to bring vegetables.

One of the children took out a worn-out middle school physics textbook. His hands were dirty and cracked like tree bark. In a thick Northeastern accent, he asked a simple physics question: The textbook said that a body in free fall is under constant acceleration but will always reach a terminal velocity. They had been thinking about this for several nights and could not understand why.

"You walked all this way just to ask this?" Ye asked.

"Teacher Ye, don't you know that they've restarted the exam?" the girl said excitedly.

"The exam?"

"The National College Entrance Exam! Whoever studies hard and gets the best score gets to go to college! It began two years ago. Didn't you know?"

"There's no need for recommendations anymore?"

"No. Anyone can take the exam. Even the children of the Five Black Categories in the village can take it."[35]

Ye was stunned. This change left her with mixed feelings. Only after a while did she realize that the children were still waiting with their books held up. She hurriedly answered their question, explaining that it was due to air resistance reaching equilibrium against the force of gravity. Then she promised that if they encountered any difficulties in their studies in the future, they could always come to her for help.

Three days later, seven children came to seek Ye. In addition to the three who had come last time, there were four more from villages located even farther away. The third time, fifteen children came to find her, and even a teacher at a small-town high school came along.

---

35 *Translator's Note:* The Five Black Categories, the targets of the Cultural Revolution, were five political identities used during the revolution: landlords, rich farmers, counter-revolutionaries, "bad elements," and right-wingers.

Because there was a shortage of teachers, he had to teach physics, math, and chemistry, and he came to ask Ye for some help on teaching. The man was over fifty years old, and his face was already full of wrinkles. He was very nervous in front of Ye, and spilled books everywhere. After they left the gatehouse, Ye heard him say to the students: "Children, that was a *scientist*. A real, bona fide *scientist*!"

After that, children would come to her for tutoring every few days. Sometimes there were so many of them that the gatehouse couldn't accommodate them all. With the permission of the officers in charge of base security, the guards would escort them to the cafeteria. There, Ye put up a small blackboard and taught the children.

It was dark by the time Ye got off work on the eve of Chinese New Year, 1980. Most people at the base had already left Radar Peak for the three-day holiday, and it was quiet everywhere. Ye returned to her room. This was once the home of her and Yang Weining, but now it was empty, her only companion the unborn child within her. In the night outside, the cold wind of the Greater Khingan Mountains screamed, carrying with it the faint sound of firecrackers going off in the village of Qijiatun. Loneliness pressed down on Ye like a giant hand, and she felt herself being crushed; compressed until she was so small that she disappeared into an invisible corner of the universe. . . .

Just then, someone knocked on her door. When she opened it, Ye first saw the guard, and then, behind him, the fire of several pine branch torches flickering in the cold wind. The torches were held aloft by a crowd of children, their faces bright red from the cold, and icicles hung from their hats. When they came into her room, they seemed to bring the cold air in with them. Two of the boys, thinly dressed, had

315

suffered the most. They had taken off their thick coats and wrapped them around something that they carried in their arms. Unwrapping the coats revealed a large pot, the fermented cabbage and pork dumplings inside still steaming hot.

That year, eight months after she sent her signal toward the sun, Ye went into labor. Because the baby was malpositioned and her body was weak, the base clinic couldn't handle her case and had to send her to the nearest town hospital.

This became one of the hardest times in Ye's life. After enduring a great deal of pain and losing a large amount of blood, she sank into a coma. Through a blur she could only see three hot, blinding suns slowly orbiting around her, cruelly roasting her body. This state lasted for some time, and she hazily thought it was probably the end for her. It was her hell. The fire of the three suns would torment her and burn her forever. This was punishment for her betrayal, the betrayal that exceeded all others. She sank into terror: not for her, but for her unborn child—was the child still in her? Or had she already been born into this hell to suffer eternally with her?

She didn't know how much time had passed. Gradually the three suns moved farther away. After a certain distance, they suddenly shrank and turned into crystalline flying stars. The air around her cooled, and her pain lessened. She finally awoke.

Ye heard a cry next to her. Turning her head with great effort, she saw the baby's pink, wet, little face.

The doctor told Ye that she had lost more than 2,000 ml of blood. Dozens of peasants from Qijiatun had come to donate blood to her. Many of the peasants had children who Ye had tutored, but most had no connection to her at all, having only heard her name from the children and their parents. Without them, she would certainly have died.

Ye's living situation became a problem after the birth of her child. The difficult birth had damaged her health. It was impossible for her to stay at the base with the baby all by herself, and she had no relatives who could help. Just then, an old couple living in Qijiatun came to talk to the base leaders and explained that they could take Ye and her baby home with them and take care of them. The old man used to be a hunter and also gathered some herbs for traditional medicine. Later, after the forest around the area was lost to logging, the couple had turned to farming, but people still called him Hunter Qi out of habit. They had two sons and two daughters. The daughters were married and had moved out. One of the sons was a soldier away from home, and the other was married and lived with them. The daughter-in-law had also just given birth.

Ye still hadn't been rehabilitated politically, and the base leadership was unsure about this suggested solution. But in the end, there was no other way, and so they allowed the couple to take Ye and the baby home from the hospital on a sled.

Ye lived for more than half a year with this peasant family in the Greater Khingan Mountains. She was so weak after giving birth that her milk did not come in. During this time, the baby girl, Yang Dong, was breastfed by all the women of the village. The one who nursed her the most was Hunter Qi's daughter-in-law, called Feng. Feng had the strong, solid frame of the women of the Northeast. She ate sorghum every day, and her large breasts were full of milk even though she was feeding two babies at the same time. Other nursing women in Qijiatun also came to feed Yang Dong. They liked her, saying that the baby had the same clever air as her mother.

Gradually, Hunter Qi's home became the gathering place for all the women of the village. Old and young, matrons and maidens, they all liked to stop by when they had nothing else going on. They admired Ye and were curious about her, and she found that she had many women's topics to discuss with them.

On countless days, Ye held Yang Dong and sat with the other women of the village in the yard, surrounded by birch posts. Next to her was a lazy black dog and the playing children, bathing in the warm sunlight. She paid attention especially to the women with the copper tobacco pipes. Leisurely, they blew smoke out of their mouths, and the smoke, filled with sunlight, gave off a silvery glow much like the fine hairs on their plump limbs. One time, one of them handed her the long-stemmed cupronickel pipe and told her it would make her feel better. She took only two hits before she became dizzy, and they laughed about it for several days.

As for the men, Ye had little to say to them. The matters that occupied them all day also seemed outside her understanding. She gathered that they were interested in planting some ginseng for cash while the government seemed to be relaxing policies a little, but they didn't quite have the courage to try. They all treated Ye with great respect and were very polite toward her. She didn't pay much attention to this at first. But after a while, after observing how those men roughly beat their wives and flirted outrageously with the widows in the village, saying things that made her blush, she finally realized how precious their respect was. Every few days, one of them would bring a hare or pheasant he had caught to Hunter Qi's home. They also gave Yang Dong strange and quaint toys that they'd made with their own hands.

In Ye's memory, these months seemed to belong to

someone else, like a segment of another life that had drifted into hers like a feather. This period condensed in her memory into a series of classical paintings—not Chinese brush paintings but European oil paintings. Chinese brush paintings are full of blank spaces, but life in Qijiatun had no blank spaces. Like classical oil paintings, it was filled with thick, rich, solid colors. Everything was warm and intense: the heated *kang* stove-beds lined with thick layers of ura sedge, the Guandong and Mohe tobacco stuffed in copper pipes, the thick and heavy sorghum meal, the sixty-five-proof *baijiu* distilled from sorghum—all of these blended into a quiet and peaceful life, like the creek at the edge of the village.

Most memorable to Ye were the evenings. Hunter Qi's son was away in the city selling mushrooms—the first to leave the village to earn money elsewhere, so she shared a room in his house with Feng. Back then, there was no electricity in the village, and every evening, the two huddled around a kerosene lamp. Ye would read while Feng did her needlework. Ye would lean closer and closer to the lamp without noticing, and her bangs would often get singed, at which point the two of them would glance up and smile at each other. Feng, of course, never had this happen to her. She had very sharp eyes, and could do detailed work even in the dim light from heating charcoal. The two babies, not even half a year old, would be sleeping together on the *kang* next to them. Ye loved to watch them sleep, their even breathing the only sound in the room.

At first, Ye did not like sleeping on the heated *kang*, and often got sick, but she gradually got used to it. As she slept, she would imagine herself becoming a baby sleeping in someone's warm lap. The person who held her wasn't her father or mother, or her dead husband. She didn't know who it was.

The feeling was so real that she would wake up with tears on her face.

One time, she put down her book and saw that Feng was holding the cloth shoe she was stitching over her knee and staring into the kerosene lamp without moving. When she realized that Ye was looking at her, Feng asked, "Sister, why do you think the stars in the sky don't fall down?"

Ye examined Feng. The kerosene lamp was a wonderful artist and created a classical painting with dignified colors and bright strokes: Feng had her coat draped over her shoulders, exposing her red belly-band, and a strong, graceful arm. The glow from the kerosene lamp painted her figure with vivid, warm colors, while the rest of the room dissolved into a gentle darkness. Close attention revealed a dim red glow, which didn't come from the kerosene lamp, but the heating charcoal on the ground. The cold air outside sculpted beautiful ice patterns on the windowpanes with the room's warm, humid air.

"You're afraid of the stars falling down?" Ye asked softly.

Feng laughed and shook her head. "What's there to be afraid of? They're so tiny."

Ye did not give her the answer of an astrophysicist. She only said, "They're very, very far away. They can't fall."

Feng was satisfied with this answer, and went back to her needlework. But Ye could no longer be at peace. She put down her book and lay down on the warm surface of the *kang,* closing her eyes. In her imagination, the rest of the universe around their tiny cottage disappeared, just the way the kerosene lamp hid most of the room in darkness. Then she substituted the universe in Feng's heart for the real one. The night sky was a black dome that was just large enough to cover the entirety of the world. The surface of the dome was inlaid with countless stars shining with a crystalline silver light, none of which was bigger than the mirror on the old wooden table next to the bed. The world was flat and extended very far in each direction, but ultimately there was an edge where it met the sky. The flat surface was covered with mountain ranges like the Greater Khingan Mountains, and with forests dotted with tiny villages, just like Qijiatun. . . . This toy-box-like universe comforted Ye, and gradually it shifted from her imagination into her dreams.

In this tiny mountain hamlet deep in the Greater Khingan Mountains, something finally thawed in Ye Wenjie's heart. In the frozen tundra of her soul, a tiny, clear lake of melt-water appeared.

Ye eventually returned to Red Coast Base with Yang Dong. Another two years passed, divided between anxiety and peace. Ye then received a notice: Both she and her father had been politically rehabilitated. Soon after, a letter arrived for her from Tsinghua, stating that she could return to teach right away. Accompanying the letter was a sum of money: the back pay owed to her father after his rehabilitation. Finally, at base meetings, her supervisors could call her *comrade*.

Ye faced all these changes with equanimity, showing no sign of excitement or elation. She had no interest in the outside world, only wanting to stay at the quiet, out-of-the-way Red Coast Base. But for the sake of Yang Dong's education, she finally left the base that she had once thought would be her home for the rest of her life, and returned to her alma mater.

Leaving the mountains, Ye felt spring was everywhere. The cold winter of the Cultural Revolution really was over, and everything was springing back to life. Even though the calamity had just ended, everything was in ruins, and count-less men and women were licking their wounds. The dawn of a new life was already evident. Students with children of their own appeared on college campuses; bookstores sold out of famous literary works; technological innovation became the focus in factories; and scientific research now enjoyed a sacred halo. Science and technology were the only keys to opening the door to the future, and people approached science with the faith and sincerity of elementary school students. Though their efforts were naïve, they were also down-to-earth. At the first National Conference on Science, Guo Moruo, president of the Chinese Academy of Sciences, declared that it was the season of rebirth and renewal for China's battered science establishment.

Was this the end of the madness? Were science and ratio-nality really coming back? Ye asked herself these questions repeatedly.

Ye never again received any communication from Trisolaris. She knew that she would have to wait at least eight years to hear that world's response to her message, and after leaving the base, she no longer had any way of receiving extraterrestrial replies.

It was such an important thing, and yet she had done it all by herself. This gave her a sense of unreality. As time passed, that sense grew ever stronger. What had happened resembled an illusion, a dream. Could the sun really amplify radio signals? Did she really use it as an antenna to send a message about human civilization into the universe? Did she really receive a message from the stars? Did that blood-hued morning, when she had betrayed the entire human race, really happen? And those murders . . .

Ye tried to numb herself with work so as to forget

the past—and almost succeeded. A strange kind of self-protective instinct caused her to stop recalling the past, to stop thinking about the communication she had once had with another civilization. Her life passed this way, day after day, in tranquility.

After she had been back at Tsinghua for a while, Ye took Dong Dong to see her grandmother, Shao Lin. After her husband's death, Shao had soon recovered from her mental breakdown and found ways to survive in the tiny cracks of politics. Her attempts to chase the political winds and shout the right slogans finally paid off, and later, during the "Return to Class, Continue the Revolution" phase, she went back to teaching.[36]

But then Shao did something that no one expected. She married a persecuted high-level cadre from the Education Ministry. At that time, the cadre still lived in a "cowshed" for reform through labor.[37] This was part of Shao's long-term plan. She knew that the chaos in society could not last long. The young rebels who were attacking everything in sight had no experience in managing a country. Sooner or later, the persecuted and sidelined old cadres would be back in power.

Her gamble paid off. Even before the end of the Cultural Revolution, her husband was partially restored to his old

---

36 *Translator's Note:* During the initial phase of the Cultural Revolution, all classes ceased at colleges and elementary, junior high, and high schools as older students became Red Guards. The resulting chaos finally caused the leadership in Beijing to ask students to return to class in late 1967 and continue the revolution in a more controlled manner.

37 *Translator's Note:* "Cowsheds" were locations set up by work units (factories, schools, towns, etc.) during the early phases of the Cultural Revolution to detain the counter-revolutionary "Monsters and Demons" (reactionary academic authorities, rightists, the Five Black Categories, etc.) at the work unit.

position. After the Third Plenary Session of the Eleventh CPC Central Committee,[38] he was soon promoted to the level of a deputy minister. Based on this background, Shao Lin also rose quickly as intellectuals became favored again. After becoming a member of the Chinese Academy of Sciences, she very wisely left her old school and was promoted to be the vice president of another famous university.

Ye Wenjie saw this new version of her mother as the very model of an educated woman who knew how to take care of herself. There was not a hint of the persecution that she went through. She enthusiastically welcomed Ye and Dong Dong, inquired after Ye's life during those years with concern, exclaimed that Dong Dong was so cute and smart, and meticulously directed the cook in preparing Ye's favorite dishes. Everything was done with skill, practice, and the appropriate level of care. But Ye could clearly detect an invisible wall between her mother and herself. They carefully avoided sensitive topics and never mentioned Ye's father.

After dinner, Shao Lin and her husband accompanied Ye and Dong Dong down to the street to say good-bye. Then Shao Lin returned home while the deputy minister asked to have a word with Ye. In a moment, the deputy minister's kind smile turned to frost, as though he had impatiently pulled off his mask.

"We're happy to have you and the child visit in the future under one condition: Do not try to pursue old historical debts. Your mother bears no responsibility for your father's death. She was a victim as well. Your father clung to his own faith in a manner that was not healthy and walked all the

---

38 *Translator's Note:* This meeting marked the beginning of the "Reform and Opening Up" policy and was seen as the moment when Deng Xiaoping became the leader of China.

way down a blind alley. He abandoned his responsibility to his family and caused you and your mother to suffer."

"You have no right to speak of my father," Ye said, anger suffusing her voice. "This is between my mother and me. It has nothing to do with you."

"You're right," Shao Lin's husband said coldly. "I'm only passing on a message from your mother."

Ye looked up at the residential apartment building reserved for high-level cadres. Shao Lin had lifted a corner of the curtain to peek down at them. Without a word, Ye bent down to pick up Dong Dong and left. She never returned.

Ye searched and searched for information about the four female Red Guards who had killed her father, and eventually managed to locate three of them. All three had been sent down to the countryside[39] and then returned, and all were unemployed. After Ye got their addresses, she wrote a brief letter to each of them, asking them to meet her at the exercise grounds where her father had died. Just to talk.

Ye had no desire for revenge. Back at Red Coast Base, on that morning of the transmission, she had gotten revenge against the entire human race, including those Red Guards. But she wanted to hear these murderers repent, wanted to see even a hint of the return of humanity.

That afternoon after class, Ye waited for them on the exercise grounds. She didn't have much hope, and was almost

---

39 Translator's Note: In the later years of the Cultural Revolution, privileged, educated urban youths were sent down to the poor, mountainous countryside to live with and learn from the farmers there. Many of these so-called "Rusticated Youths" were former Red Guards, and some commentators believe that the policy was instituted by Chairman Mao to restore order by removing the rebels, who had gotten out of control, from the cities.

certain that they wouldn't show up. But at the time of the appointment, the three old Red Guards came.

Ye recognized them from a distance because they were all dressed in now-rare green military uniforms. When they came closer, she realized that the uniforms were likely the same ones they had worn at that mass struggle session. The clothes had been laundered until their color had faded, and they had been conspicuously patched. Other than the uniforms, the three women in their thirties no longer resembled the three young Red Guards who had looked so valiant on that day. They had lost not only youth, but also something else.

The first impression Ye had was that, though the three had once seemed to be carved out of the same mold, they now looked very different from each other. One had become very thin and small, and her uniform hung loose on her. Already showing her age, her back was bent and her hair had a yellow tint. Another had become thick framed, so that the uniform jacket she wore could not even be buttoned. Her hair was messy and her face dark, as though the hardship of life had robbed her of any feminine refinement, leaving behind only numbness and rudeness. The third woman still had hints of her youthful appearance, but one of her sleeves was now empty and hung loose as she walked.

The three old Red Guards stood in front of Ye in a row— just like they had stood against Ye Zhetai—trying to recapture their long-forgotten dignity. But the demonic spiritual energy that had once propelled them was gone. The thin woman's face held a mouselike expression. The thickset woman's face showed only numbness. The one-armed woman gazed up at the sky.

"Did you think we wouldn't dare to show up?" the thick-set woman asked, her tone trying to be provocative.

"I thought we should see each other. There should be some closure to the past," Ye said.

"The past is finished. You should know that." The thin woman's voice was sharp, as though she was always frightened of something.

"I meant spiritual closure."

"Then you want to hear us repent?" the thick woman asked.

"Don't you think you should?"

"Then who will repent to us?" the one-armed woman asked.

The thickset woman said, "Of the four of us, three had signed the big-character poster at the high school attached to Tsinghua. Revolutionary tours, the great rallies in Tiananmen, the Red Guard Civil Wars, First Red Headquarters, Second Red Headquarters, Third Red Headquarters, Joint Action Committee, Western Pickets, Eastern Pickets, New Peking University Commune, Red Flag Combat Team, The East is Red—we went through every single milestone in the history of the Red Guards from birth to death."

The one-armed woman took over. "During the Hundred-Day War at Tsinghua, two of us were with the Jinggang Mountain Corps, and the other two were with the April Fourteenth Faction. I held a grenade and attacked a home-made tank from the Jinggang Mountain faction. My arm was crushed by the treads on the tank. My blood and muscle and bones were ground into the mud. I was only fifteen years old."[40]

---

40 *Translator's Note*: The Hundred-Day War at Tsinghua University was one of the most violent Red Guard civil wars during the Cultural Revolution. Fought between two Red Guard factions, it lasted from April 23 to July 27 in 1968. Mêlée weapons, guns, grenades, mines, cannons, etc. were all used. In the end, eighteen people died, more than eleven hundred were wounded, and more than thirty were permanently disabled.

"Then, we were sent to the wilderness!" The thickset woman raised her arms. "Two of us were sent to Shaanxi, the other two to Henan, all to the most remote and poorest corners. When we first went, we were still idealistic, but that didn't last. After a day of laboring in the fields, we were so tired that we couldn't even wash our clothes. We lay in leaky straw huts and listened to wolves cry in the night, and gradually we woke from our dreams. We were stuck in those forgotten villages and no one cared about us at all."

The one-armed woman stared at the ground numbly. "While we were down in the countryside, sometimes, on a trail across the barren hill, I'd bump into another Red Guard comrade or an enemy. We'd look at each other: the same ragged clothes, the same dirt and cow shit covering us. We had nothing to say to each other."

The thickset woman stared at Ye. "Tang Hongjing was the girl who gave your father the fatal strike with her belt. She drowned in the Yellow River. There was a flood that carried off a few of the sheep kept by the production team. So the Party secretary called to the sent-down students, 'Revolutionary youths! It's time to test your mettle!' And so, Hongjing and three other students jumped into the river to save the sheep. It was early spring, and the surface of the river was still covered by a thin layer of ice. All four died, and no one knew if it was from drowning or freezing. When I saw their bodies . . . I . . . I . . . can't fucking talk about this anymore." She covered her eyes and sobbed.

The thin woman sighed, tears in her eyes. "Then, later, we returned to the city. But so what if we're back? We still have nothing. Rusticated youths who have returned don't lead very good lives. We can't even find the worst jobs. No job, no money, no future. We have nothing."

Ye had no words.

The one-armed woman said, "There was a movie called *Maple* recently. I don't know if you've seen it. At the end, an adult and a child stand in front of the grave of a Red Guard who had died during the faction civil wars. The child asks the adult, 'Are they heroes?' The adult says no. The child asks, 'Are they enemies?' The adult again says no. The child asks, 'Then who are they?' The adult says, 'History.'"

"Did you hear that?" The thickset woman waved an arm excitedly at Ye. "History! History! It's a new age now. Who will remember us? Who will think of us, including you? Everyone will forget all this completely!"

The three old Red Guards departed, leaving only Ye on the exercise grounds. More than a dozen years ago, on that rainy afternoon, she had stood alone here as well, gazing at her dead father. The old Red Guard's final remark echoed endlessly in her mind. . . .

The setting sun cast a long shadow from Ye's slender figure. The small sliver of hope for society that had emerged in her soul had evaporated like a drop of dew in the sun. Her tiny sense of doubt about her supreme act of betrayal had also disappeared without a trace.

Ye finally had her unshakable ideal: to bring superior civilization from elsewhere in the universe into the human world.

27

Evans

Half a year after her return to Tsinghua, Ye took on an important task: the design of a large radio astronomy observatory. She and the task force traveled around the country to find the best site for the observatory. The initial considerations were purely technical. Unlike traditional astronomy, radio astronomy didn't have as many demands on atmospheric quality, but required minimal electromagnetic interference. They traveled to many places and finally picked a place with the cleanest electromagnetic environment: a remote, hilly area in the Northwest.

The loess hills here had little vegetation cover. Rifts from erosion made the slopes look like old faces full of wrinkles. After selecting a few possible sites, the task force stayed for a brief rest at a village where most of the inhabitants still lived in traditional cave dwellings. The village's production team leader recognized Ye as an educated person and asked her whether she knew how to speak a foreign language. She asked him which foreign language, and he said he didn't know. However, if she did know a foreign tongue, he would send someone up the hill to call down Bethune, because the production team needed to discuss something with him.[41]

"Bethune?" Ye was amazed.

"We don't know the foreigner's real name, so we just call him that."

"Is he a doctor?"

"No. He's planting trees up in the hills. Has been at it for almost three years."

"Planting trees? What for?"

"He says it's for the birds. A kind of bird that he says is almost extinct."

Ye and her colleagues were curious and asked the production team leader to bring them for a visit. They followed a trail until they were on top of a small hillock. The team leader showed them a place among the barren loess hills. Ye felt it brighten before her eyes. There was a slope covered by green forests, as though an old, yellowing canvas had been accidentally blessed with a splash of green paint.

Ye and the others soon saw the foreigner. Other than his blond hair and green eyes and tattered jeans and a jacket that reminded her of a cowboy, he didn't look too different from the local peasants who had labored all their lives. Even his skin had the same dark hue from the sun as the locals. He didn't show much interest in the visitors. He introduced himself as Mike Evans without mentioning his nationality, but his English was clearly American-accented. He lived in a simple two-room adobe hut, which was filled with tools for planting trees: hoes, shovels, saws for pruning tree branches, and so on, all of which were locally made and crude.

---

41 *Translator's Note:* Norman Bethune (1890–1939) was a Canadian surgeon who served with the Chinese Communists in their fight against the Japanese invasion force during World War II. As one of the few Westerners who showed friendship to the Chinese Communists, Bethune became a Chinese hero known to the elderly and children alike.

The dust that permeated the Northwest lay in a thin layer over his simple and rough-hewn bed and kitchen implements. A pile of books, most of which dealt with biology, sat on his bed. Ye noticed a copy of Peter Singer's *Animal Liberation*. The only sign of modernity was a small radio set, hooked up to an external D battery. There was also an old telescope.

Evans apologized for not being able to offer them anything to drink. He hadn't had coffee for a while. There was water, but he only had one cup.

"May we ask what you're really doing here?" one of Ye's colleagues asked.

"I want to save lives."

"Save . . . save the locals? It's true that the ecological conditions here—"

"Why are you all like this?" Evans suddenly became furious. "Why does one have to save *people* to be considered a hero? Why is saving other species considered insignificant? Who gave humans such high honors? No, humans do not need saving. They're already living much better than they deserve."

"We heard that you are trying to save a type of bird."

"Yes, a swallow. It's a subspecies of the northwestern brown swallow. The Latin name is very long, so I won't bore you with it. Every spring, they follow ancient, established migratory paths to return from the south. They nest only here, but as the forest disappears year after year, they can no longer find the trees in which to build their nests. When I discovered them, the species had less than ten thousand individuals left. If the trend continues, within five years it will be extinct. The trees I've planted now provide a habitat for some of them, and the population is rising again. I must plant more trees and expand this Eden."

Evans allowed Ye and the others to look through his

telescope. With his help, they finally saw a few tiny black birds darting through the trees.

"Not very pretty, are they? Of course, they're not as crowd-pleasing as giant pandas. Every day on this planet some species that doesn't draw the attention of humans goes extinct."

"Did you plant all of these trees by yourself?"

"Most of them. Initially I hired some locals to help, but soon I ran out of money. Saplings and irrigation all cost a lot—but you know something? My father is a billionaire. He is the president of an international oil company, but he will not give me any more funding, and I don't want to use his money anymore."

Now that Evans had opened up, he seemed to want to pour his heart out. "When I was twelve, a thirty-thousand-ton oil tanker from my father's company ran aground along the Atlantic coast. More than twenty thousand tons of crude oil spilled into the ocean. At the time, my family was staying at a coastal vacation home not too far from the site of the accident. After my father heard the news, the first thing he thought of was how to avoid responsibility and minimize damage to the company.

"That afternoon, I went to see the hellish coast. The sea was black, and the waves, under the sticky, thick film of oil, were smooth and weak. The beach was also covered by a black layer of crude oil. Some volunteers and I searched for birds on the beach that were still alive. They struggled in the sticky oil, looking like black statues made out of asphalt, only their eyes proving that they were still alive. Those eyes staring out of the oil still haunt my dreams to this day. We soaked those birds in detergent, trying to get rid of the oil stuck to their bodies. But it was extremely difficult: crude oil was infused into their feathers, and if you brushed a little too hard, the feathers would come off with the oil. . . . By that evening, most of the birds had died. As I sat on the black beach, exhausted and covered in oil, I stared at the sun setting over a black sea and felt like it was the end of the world.

"My father came up behind me without my noticing. He asked me if I still remembered the small dinosaur skeleton. Of course I remembered. The nearly complete skeleton had been discovered during oil exploration. My father spent a large sum to buy it, and installed it on the grounds of my grandfather's mansion.

"My father then said, 'Mike, I've told you how dinosaurs went extinct. An asteroid crashed into the Earth. The world first became a sea of fire, and then sank into a prolonged period of darkness and coldness. . . . One night, you woke from a nightmare, saying that you had dreamt that you were back in that terrifying age. Let me tell you now what I wanted to tell you that night: If you really lived during the Cretaceous Period, you'd be fortunate. The period we live in now is far more frightening. Right now, species on Earth are going extinct far faster than during the late Cretaceous. Now is truly the age of mass extinctions! So, my child, what you're seeing is nothing. This is only an insignificant episode in a much vaster process. We can have no sea birds, but we can't be without oil. Can you imagine life without oil? Your last birthday, I gave you that lovely Ferrari and promised you that you could drive it after you turned fifteen. But without oil, it would be a pile of junk metal and you'd never drive it. Right now, if you want to visit your grandfather, you can get there on my personal jet and cross the ocean in a dozen hours or so. But without oil, you'd have to tumble in a sailboat for more than a month. . . . These are the rules of the game of civilization: The first priority is to guarantee the existence of the human race and their comfortable life. Everything else is secondary.'

"My father placed a great deal of hope in me, but in the end I didn't turn out the way he wanted. In the days after that, the eyes of those drowned birds always followed me and determined my life. When I was thirteen, my father asked me what I wanted to do when I grew up. I said I wanted to save lives. My dream wasn't that great. I only wanted to save a species near extinction. It could be a bird that wasn't very pretty, a drab butterfly, or a beetle that no one would even notice. Later, I studied biology, and became a specialist on birds and insects. The way I see it, my ideal is worthy. Saving a species of bird or insect is no different from saving humankind. 'All lives are equal' is the basic tenet of Pan-Species Communism."

"What?" Ye wasn't sure she had heard the last term correctly.

"Pan-Species Communism. It's an ideology I invented. Or maybe you can call it a faith. Its core belief is that all species on Earth are created equal."

"That is an impractical ideal. Our crops are also living species. If humans are to survive, that kind of equality is impossible."

"Slave owners must also have thought that about their slaves in the distant past. And don't forget technology— there will be a day when humanity can manufacture food. We should lay down the ideological and theoretical foundation long before that. Indeed, Pan-Species Communism is a natural continuation of the Universal Declaration of Human Rights. The French Revolution was two hundred years ago, and we haven't even taken a step beyond that. From this we can see the hypocrisy and selfishness of the human race."

"How long do you intend to stay here?"

"I don't know. I'm prepared to devote my life to the task. The feeling is beautiful. Of course, I don't expect you to understand."

Evans seemed to lose interest. He said that he had to go back to work, so he picked up a shovel and a saw and then left. When he said good-bye, he glanced at Ye again, as though there was something unusual about her.

On the way back, one of Ye's colleagues recited from Chairman Mao's essay "Remembering Bethune": " 'Noble-minded and pure, a man of moral integrity and above vulgar interests.' " He sighed. "There really are people who can live like that."

Others also expressed their admiration and conflicted feelings. Ye seemed to be speaking to herself as she said, "If there were more men like him, even just a few more, things would have turned out differently."

Of course, no one understood what she really meant.

The task force leader turned the conversation back to their work. "I think this site isn't going to work. Our superiors won't approve it."

"Why not? Of the four possible sites, this has the best electromagnetic environment."

"What about the human environment? Comrades, don't just focus on the technical side. Look at how poor this place is. The poorer a village, the craftier the people. Do you understand? If the observatory were located here, there would be trouble between the scientists and the locals. I can imagine the peasants thinking of the astronomy complex as a juicy piece of meat that they can take bites from."

This site was indeed not approved, and the reason was just what the task force leader had said.

Three years passed without Ye hearing anything more about Evans.

But one spring day, Ye received a postcard from Evans with only a single line: "Come here. Tell me how to go on."

Ye rode the train for a day and a night, and then switched to a bus for many hours until she arrived at the village nestled in the remote hills of the Northwest.

As soon as she climbed onto that small hillock, she saw the forest again. Because the trees had grown, it now seemed far denser, but Ye noticed that the forest had once been much bigger. Newer parts that had grown in the past few years had already been cut.

The logging was in full swing. In every direction, trees were falling. The entire forest seemed like a mulberry leaf being devoured by silkworms on all sides. At the current rate, it would disappear soon. The workers doing the logging came from two nearby villages. Using axes and saws, they cut down those barely grown trees one by one, and then dragged them off the hill using tractors and ox carts. There were many loggers, and fights frequently erupted among them.

The fall of each small tree didn't make much sound, and there was no loud buzzing from chain saws, but the almost-familiar scene made Ye's chest tighten.

Someone called out to her—that production team leader, now the village chief. He recognized Ye. When she asked him why they were cutting down the forest, he said, "This forest isn't protected by law."

"How can that be? The Forestry Law has just been promulgated."

"But who ever gave Bethune permission to plant trees here? A foreigner coming here to plant trees without approval would not be protected by any law."

337

"You can't think that way. He was planting on the barren hills and didn't take up any arable land. Also, back when he started, you didn't object."

"That's true. The county actually gave him an award for planting the trees. The villagers originally planned to cut down the forest in a few more years—it's best to wait until the pig is fat before slaughtering it, am I right? But those people from Nange Village can't wait any longer, and if my village doesn't join in, we won't get any."

"You must stop immediately. I will go to the government to report this!"

"There's no need." The village chief lit a cigarette and pointed to a truck loading the cut trees in the distance. "See that? That's from the deputy secretary of the County Forestry Bureau. And there are also people here from the town police department. They've carried off more trees than anyone else! I told you, these trees have no status and aren't protected. You'll never find anyone who cares. Also, comrade, aren't you a college professor? What does this have to do with you?"

The adobe hut looked the same, but Evans wasn't inside. Ye found him in the woods holding an ax and carefully pruning a tree. He had obviously been at it for a while, his posture full of exhaustion.

"I don't care if this is meaningless. I can't stop. If I stop I'll fall apart." Evans cut down a crooked branch with a practiced swing.

"Let's go together to the county government. If they won't do anything, we'll go up to the provincial government. Someone will stop them." Ye looked at Evans with concern.

Evans stopped and stared at Ye in surprise. Light from the setting sun slanted through the trees and made his eyes sparkle. "Ye, do you really think I'm doing this because of this forest?" He laughed and shook his head, then dropped the ax. He sat down, his back against a tree. "If I want to stop them, it'd be easy. I just returned from America. My father died two months ago, and I inherited most of his money. My brother and sister only got five million each. This wasn't what I expected at all. Maybe in his heart, he still respected me. Or maybe he respected my ideals. Not including fixed assets, do you know how much money I have at my disposal? About four point five billion dollars. I could easily ask them to stop and get them to plant more trees. I could make all the loess hills within sight be covered by quick-growth forest. But what would be the point?

"Everything you see before you is the result of poverty. But how are things any better in the wealthy countries? They protect their own environments, but then shift the heavily polluting industries to the poorer nations. You probably know that the American government just refused to sign the Kyoto Protocol. . . . The entire human race is the same. As long as civilization continues to develop, the swallows I want to save and all the other swallows will go extinct. It's just a matter of time."

Ye sat silently, gazing at the rays of light cast among the trees by the setting sun, listening to the noise from the loggers. Her thoughts returned to twenty years ago, to the forests of the Greater Khingan Mountains, where she had once had a similar conversation with another man.

"Do you know why I came here?" Evans continued. "The seeds of Pan-Species Communism had sprouted long ago in the ancient East."

"You're thinking of Buddhism?"

"Yes. The focus of Christianity is Man. Even though all the species were placed into Noah's Ark, other species were never given the same status as humans. But Buddhism is focused on saving all life. That was why I came to the East. But . . . it's obvious now that everywhere is the same."

"Yes, that's true. Everywhere, people are the same."

"What can I do now? What is the purpose of my life? I have four point five billion dollars and an international oil company. But what good is all that? Humans have surely invested more than forty-five billion dollars in saving species near extinction. And probably more than four hundred and fifty billion has already been spent on saving the environment from degradation. But what's the use? Civilization continues to follow its path of destruction of all life on Earth except humans. Four point five billion is enough to build an aircraft carrier, but even if we build a thousand aircraft carriers, it would be impossible to stop the madness of humanity."

"Mike, this is what I wanted to tell you. Human civilization is no longer capable of improving by its own strength."

"Can there be any source of power outside of humanity? Even if God once existed, He died long ago."

"Yes, there are other powers."

The sun had set and the loggers had left. The forest and the loess hills were silent. Ye now told Evans the whole story of Red Coast and Trisolaris. Evans listened quietly, and the loess hills and the forest in dusk seemed to listen as well. When Ye was finished, a bright moon rose from the east and cast speckled shadows on the forest floor.

Evans said, "I still can't believe what you just told me. It's too fantastic. But luckily, I have the resources to confirm this. If what you told me is true"—he extended his hand and spoke the words that every new member of the future ETO would have to say upon joining—"let us be comrades."

28

The Second Red Coast Base

Three more years passed. Evans seemed to have disappeared. Ye didn't know if he really was somewhere in the world working to confirm her story, and had no idea how he would confirm it. Even though, by the scale of the universe, a gap of four light-years was as close as touching, it was still a distance that was unimaginably far for fragile life. The two worlds were like the source and mouth of a river that crossed space. Any connections between them would be extremely attenuated.

One winter, Ye received an invitation from a not-very-prominent university in Western Europe to be a visiting scholar for half a year. After she landed at Heathrow for her interview, a young man came to meet her. They didn't leave the airport, but instead turned back to the landing strip. There, he escorted her onto a helicopter.

As the helicopter roared into the foggy air over England, time seemed to rewind and Ye experienced déjà vu. Many years ago, when she first rode in a helicopter, her life was transformed. Where would fate bring her now?

"We're going to the Second Red Coast Base."

The helicopter passed the coastline and continued toward the heart of the Atlantic. After half an hour, the helicopter descended toward a huge ship in the ocean. As soon as Ye saw the ship, she thought of Radar Peak. Only now did she realize that the shape of the peak did resemble a giant ship. The Atlantic appeared like the forest of the Greater Khingan Mountains, but the thing that reminded her most of Red Coast Base was the huge parabolic antenna erected in the middle of the ship, which resembled a round sail. The ship was modified from a sixty-thousand-ton oil tanker, like a floating steel island. Evans had built his base on a ship—maybe it was so that it would always be at the best position for transmission and reception, or maybe it was to hide from detection. Later, she learned that the ship was called *Judgment Day*.

Ye stepped off the helicopter and heard a familiar howl. It was caused by the giant antenna slicing through the wind over the sea. The sound again drew her thoughts to the past. On the broad deck below the antenna, about two thousand people stood in a dense crowd.

Evans walked up to her and solemnly said, "Using the frequency and coordinates you provided, we received a message from Trisolaris. We've confirmed everything you told me."

Ye nodded calmly.

"The great Trisolaran Fleet has already set sail. Their target is this solar system, and they will arrive in four hundred and fifty years."

Ye remained calm. Nothing could surprise her anymore.

Evans pointed to the crowd behind him. "You're looking at the first members of the Earth-Trisolaris Organization. Our ideal is to invite Trisolaran civilization to reform human civilization, to curb human madness and evil, so that the Earth can once again become a harmonious, prosperous, sinless world. More and more people identify with our ideal, and our organization is growing rapidly. We have members all over the world."

"What can I do?" Ye asked in a soft voice.

"You will become the commander in chief of the Earth-Trisolaris Movement. This is the wish of all ETO fighters."

Ye remained silent for a few seconds. Then she nodded slowly. "I'll do my best."

Evans raised a fist and shouted at the crowd, "Eliminate human tyranny!"

Accompanied by the sound of crashing waves and the wind howling against the antenna, the ETO fighters shouted as one, "The world belongs to Trisolaris!"

This was the day that the Earth-Trisolaris Movement formally began.

29

The Earth-Trisolaris Movement

The most surprising aspect of the Earth-Trisolaris Movement was that so many people had abandoned all hope in human civilization, hated and were willing to betray their own species, and even cherished as their highest ideal the elimination of the entire human race, including themselves and their children.

The ETO was called an organization of spiritual nobles. Most members came from the highly educated classes, and many were elites of the political and financial spheres. The ETO had once tried to develop membership among the common people, but these efforts all failed. The ETO concluded that the common people did not seem to have the comprehensive and deep understanding of the highly educated about the dark side of humanity. More importantly, because their thoughts were not as deeply influenced by modern science and philosophy, they still felt an overwhelming, instinctual identification with their own species. To betray the human race as a whole was unimaginable for them. But intellectual elites were different: Most of them had already begun to consider issues from a perspective outside the human race. Human civilization had finally given birth to a strong force of alienation.

As astounding as the speed of the ETO's growth had been, the number of members did not tell the whole story of the ETO's strength. Because most of its members had high social status, they held a lot of power and influence.

As commander in chief of the ETO rebels, Ye was only their spiritual leader. She did not participate in the details of the organization's operation, didn't know how the ETO grew so large, and wasn't even aware of the exact number of members.

In order to grow fast, the organization operated semi-openly, but the governments of the world never paid much attention to the ETO. The ETO knew that they would be protected by the governments' conservatism and lack of imagination. In those organs wielding the powers of the state, no one took the ETO's proclamations seriously, thinking that they were like other extremists who spewed nonsense. And because of its members' social status, governments always treated it carefully. By the time it was recognized as a threat, the rebels were already everywhere. It was only when the ETO began to develop an armed force that some national security organs began to notice it and realized how unusual it was. Consequently, it was only within the last two years that they had begun to attack the ETO effectively.

The members of the ETO were not of a single mind. Within the organization were complicated factions and divisions of opinion. Mainly, they fell into two factions.

The Adventist group was the purest, most fundamentalist strand of the ETO, comprised mainly of believers in Evans's Pan-Species Communism. They had completely given up hope in human nature. This despair began with the mass extinctions of the Earth's species caused by modern civilization. Later, other Adventists based their hatred of the human race on other foundations, not limited to issues such as the environment or warfare. Some raised their hatred to very abstract, philosophical levels. Unlike how they would be imagined later, most of them were realists, and did not place too much hope in the alien civilization they served either. Their betrayal was based only on their despair and hatred of the human race. Mike Evans gave the Adventists their motto: We don't know what extraterrestrial civilization is like, but we know humanity.

The Redemptionists didn't appear until long after the ETO's founding. This group's nature was a religious organization, and the members were believers in the Trisolaran faith.

A civilization outside the human race would doubtlessly greatly attract the highly educated classes, and it was easy for them to develop many beautiful fantasies about such a civilization. The human race was a naïve species, and the attraction posed by a more advanced alien civilization was almost irresistible. To make an imperfect analogy: Human civilization was like a young, unworldly person walking alone across the desert of the universe, who has found out about the existence of a potential lover. Though the person could not see the potential lover's face or figure, the knowledge that the other person existed somewhere in the distance created lovely fantasies about the potential lover that spread like wildfire. Gradually, as fantasies about that distant civilization grew more and more elaborate, the Redemptionists developed spiritual feelings toward Trisolaran civilization. Alpha Centauri became Mount Olympus in space, the dwelling place of the gods; and so the Trisolaran religion—which really had nothing to do with religion on Trisolaris—was born. Unlike other human religions, they worshipped something that truly existed. Also unlike other human religions, it was the Lord who was in crisis, and the duty of salvation fell on the shoulders of the believer.

The main path of spreading Trisolaran culture to society was the *Three Body* game. The ETO invested enormous effort to develop this massive piece of software. The initial goals were twofold: one, to proselytize the Trisolaran religion; and two, to allow the tentacles of the ETO to spread from the highly educated intelligentsia to the lower social strata, and recruit younger ETO members from the middle and lower classes.

Using a shell that drew elements from human society and history, the game explained the culture and history of Trisolaris, thus avoiding alienating beginners. Once a player had advanced to a certain level and had begun to appreciate Trisolaran civilization, the ETO would establish contact, examine the player's sympathies, and finally recruit those who passed the tests to be members of the ETO. But *Three Body* didn't attract much notice, because the game required too much background knowledge and in-depth thinking, and most young players didn't have the patience or skill to discover the shocking truth beneath its apparently common surface. Those who were attracted by it were still mostly intellectuals.

Most of those who became Redemptionists got to know Trisolaran civilization through the *Three Body* game, and so *Three Body* could be said to be the cradle of the Redemptionists.

While the Redemptionists developed religious feelings toward Trisolaran civilization, they were also not as extreme as the Adventists in their attitude toward human civilization. Their ultimate ideal was to save the Lord. In order to allow the Lord to continue to exist, they were willing to sacrifice the human world to some degree. But most of them believed that the ideal solution would be to find a way to allow the Lord to continue to live in the Trisolaris stellar system and avoid the invasion of the Earth. Naïvely, they believed that solving the three-body problem would achieve this goal, saving both Trisolaris and the Earth. Admittedly, perhaps this thought wasn't all that naïve. Trisolaran civilization itself had thought so through many eons. The effort to solve the three-body problem was a thread that ran through several hundreds of cycles of Trisolaran civilization. Most Redemptionists with some in-depth math and physics knowledge had attempted the three-body problem, and even after knowing that the problem was mathematically unsolvable as posed, the effort did not cease, because solving the three-body problem had become a religious ritual of their faith. Even though the Redemptionists had many first-class physicists and mathematicians, research in this area never yielded any important results. It took someone like Wei Cheng, a prodigy who had no connection to the ETO or the Trisolaran faith, to accidentally come up with a breakthrough in which the Redemptionists placed much hope.

The Adventists and the Redemptionists were always in sharp conflict. The Adventists believed that the Redemptionists were the greatest threat to the ETO. This view wasn't without reason: It was only through some Redemptionists who had a sense of duty that the governments of the world gradually came to understand the shocking background of the ETO rebels. The two factions were of approximately equal strength within the organization, and the armed forces of both had developed to the point of starting a civil war. Ye Wenjie used her authority and reputation to try to patch over the division between the two, but the result was never ideal.

As the ETO movement continued to develop, a third faction appeared: the Survivors. After confirming the existence of the alien invasion fleet, surviving that war became a most natural human desire. Of course, that war wouldn't occur for another 450 years, and had nothing to do with those living today, but many people hoped that if humans *did* lose, at least their descendants who were alive in four and a half centuries could live on. Serving the Trisolaran invaders would clearly help with this goal. Compared to the other two factions, the Survivors tended to come from the lower social classes, and most were from the East, and especially from China. Their numbers were still small, but they were growing rapidly. As Trisolaran culture continued to spread, they would become a force that could not be ignored in the future.

The ETO members' alienation developed variously from the faults of human civilization itself, the yearning and adoration for a more advanced civilization, and the strong desire for one's descendants to survive that final war. These three powerful motives propelled the ETO movement to develop rapidly.

By then, the extraterrestrial civilization was still in the depths of space, more than four light-years away, separated from the human world by a long journey of four and a half centuries. The only thing they had sent to the Earth was a radio transmission.

Bill Mathers's "contact as symbol" theory thus received chillingly perfect confirmation.

30

Two Protons

INTERROGATOR: We will now begin today's investigation. We hope you'll cooperate again as you did last time.

YE WENJIE: You already know everything I know. In fact, by now there are many things that I'd like to learn from you.

INTERROGATOR: I don't think you've told us everything. First, we want to know this: Among the messages that Trisolaris sent to Earth, what were the contents of those portions that the Adventists intercepted and withheld?

YE: I can't tell you. They have a tight organization. I only know that they did withhold some messages.

INTERROGATOR: Change of subject. After the Adventists monopolized communications with Trisolaris, did you build a third Red Coast Base?

YE: I did have such a plan. But we only built a receiver, and then construction stopped. The equipment and the base were all dismantled.

INTERROGATOR: Why?

YE: Because there were no more messages coming from Alpha Centauri. There was nothing on any frequency. I think you've already confirmed this.

INTERROGATOR: Yes. In other words—at least as of four years ago—Trisolaris decided to terminate all communications with Earth. This makes the messages intercepted by the Adventists even more important.

YE: True. But there's really nothing more I can tell you about them.

INTERROGATOR: *(pausing a few seconds)* Then let's find some topic where you can tell me more. Mike Evans lied to you, is that right?

YE: You could put it that way. He never revealed to me the thoughts buried deep in his heart, and only expressed his sense of duty toward the other species on this planet. I never realized that this sense of duty had caused his hatred of human civilization to develop to such extremes that he could make the destruction of the human race his ultimate ideal.

INTERROGATOR: Let's look at the current composition of the ETO. The Adventists would like to destroy the human race by means of an alien power; the Redemptionists worship the alien civilization as a god; the Survivors wish to betray other humans to buy their own survival. None of these is in line with your original ideal of using the alien civilization as a way to reform humanity.

YE: I started the fire, but I couldn't control how it burnt.

INTERROGATOR: You had a plan to eliminate the Adventists from within the ETO, and you even began to implement this plan. But *Judgment Day* is the core base and command center for the Adventists, and Mike Evans and other Adventist leaders usually reside there. Why didn't you attack the ship first? Most of the armed forces of the Redemptionists are loyal to you, and you should have enough firepower to sink it or capture it.

YE: It's because of the messages from the Lord that they intercepted. All those messages are stored in the Second Red

Coast Base, on some computer on *Judgment Day*. If we attacked that ship, the Adventists could erase all the messages when they realized that loss was imminent. Those messages are too important for us to risk losing them. For Redemptionists, losing those messages would be as if Christians lost the Bible or Muslims lost the Koran. I think you are faced with the same problem. The Adventists are holding the Lord's messages hostage, and that is why *Judgment Day* has remained unmolested so far.

INTERROGATOR: Do you have any advice for us?

YE: No.

INTERROGATOR: You also call Trisolaris your "Lord." Does this mean that you've also developed religious feelings for Trisolaris like the Redemptionists? Are you already a follower of the Trisolaran faith?

YE: Not at all. It's just a habit. . . . I do not wish to discuss it further.

INTERROGATOR: Let's get back to those intercepted messages. Maybe you don't know the exact contents, but surely you must have heard rumors of some of the details?

YE: Probably only baseless rumors.

INTERROGATOR: Such as?

YE: . . .

INTERROGATOR: Did Trisolaris transfer certain technologies to the Adventists, technologies more advanced than current human technology?

YE: Not likely. Because such technology would risk falling into your hands.

INTERROGATOR: One last question, and also the most important: Until now, has Trisolaris sent only radio waves to the Earth?

YE: Almost true.

INTERROGATOR: Almost?

YE: The current Trisolaran civilization is capable of space travel at one-tenth the speed of light. This technology leap occurred a few decades ago in Earth years. Before that point, their maximum speed had hovered around one-thousandth the speed of light. The tiny probes that they sent to the Earth have not even completed one-hundredth of the journey between there and here.

INTERROGATOR: Then I have a question. If the Trisolaran Fleet that had been launched is capable of flight at one-tenth the speed of light, it should take only forty years to reach the solar system. So why do you say that it would take more than four hundred years?

YE: Here's the thing. The Trisolaran Interstellar Fleet is composed of incredibly massive spaceships. Accelerating them is a slow process. One-tenth the speed of light is only their maximum speed, but they cannot cruise at this speed for long before decelerating as they approach the Earth. Also, the source of propulsion for the Trisolaran ships is matter-antimatter annihilation. In front of each ship is a large magnetic field shaped like a funnel to collect antimatter particles from space. This collection process is slow, and only after a long wait can it gather enough antimatter to allow the ship to accelerate for a brief period. Thus, the fleet's acceleration occurs in spurts, interspersed by long periods of coasting to collect fuel. This is why the time it takes the Trisolaran Fleet to reach the solar system is ten times longer than the flight time of a small probe.

INTERROGATOR: Then what did you mean by "almost" just now?

YE: We're talking about the speed of space flight within a certain context. Outside this context, even backward human beings are capable of accelerating certain objects to close to the speed of light.

INTERROGATOR: *(a pause)* By "context," do you mean at the macro scale? At a micro scale, humans can already use high-energy particle accelerators to speed up subatomic particles to near the speed of light. These particles are the "objects" you meant, correct?

YE: You're very clever.

INTERROGATOR: *(points to his earpiece)* I have the world's foremost scientists behind me.

YE: Yes, I meant subatomic particles. Six years ago, in the distant Trisolaran stellar system, Trisolaris accelerated two hydrogen nuclei to near the speed of light and shot them toward the solar system. These two hydrogen nuclei, or protons, arrived at the solar system two years ago, then reached the Earth.

INTERROGATOR: Two protons? They only sent two protons? That's almost nothing.

YE: *(laughs)* You also said "almost." That's the limit of Trisolaran power. They can only accelerate something as small as a proton to near the speed of light. So over a distance of four light-years, they can only send two protons.

INTERROGATOR: At the macroscopic level, two protons are nothing. Even a single cilium on a bacterium would include several billion protons. What's the point?

YE: They're a lock.

INTERROGATOR: A lock? What are they locking?

YE: They are sealing off the progress of human science. Because of the existence of these two protons, humanity will not be able to make any important scientific developments during the four and a half centuries until the arrival of the Trisolaran Fleet. Evans once said that the day of arrival of the two protons was also the day that human science died.

INTERROGATOR: That's . . . too fantastic. How can that be?

YE: I don't know. I really don't know. In the eyes of Trisolaran civilization, we're probably not even primitive savages. We might be mere bugs.

It was near midnight by the time Wang Miao and Ding Yi walked out of the Battle Command Center. They had been invited to listen to Ye's interrogation due to Wang's involvement in the case and Ding Yi's connection to Ye's daughter.

"Do you believe what Ye Wenjie said?" Wang asked.

"Do you?"

"Many things that have happened recently are incredible. But for two protons to block all progress of human science? That seems . . ."

"Let's focus on one thing first. The Trisolarans were able to shoot two protons at the Earth from four light-years away and they both reached the target! That accuracy is incredible! There are numerous obstacles between there and here: interstellar dust, for example. And both the solar system and the Earth are moving. It would require more precision than shooting a mosquito here from Pluto. The shooter is beyond imagination."

Wang's heart clenched when he heard "shooter." "What do you think this means?"

"I don't know. In your impression, what do subatomic particles such as neutrons and protons look like?"

"They would just look like a point. Though the point has internal structure."

"Luckily, the image in my head is more realistic than

yours." As Ding spoke, he tossed his cigarette butt away. "What do you think that is?" He pointed at the butt.

"A cigarette filter."

"Good. Looking at that tiny thing from this distance, how would you describe it?"

"It's practically just a point."

"Right." Ding walked over and picked up the butt. In front of Wang's eyes he tore it open and revealed the yellowed spongy material inside. Wang smelled burnt tar. Ding continued, "Look, if you spread this little thing open, the adsorbent surface area can be as large as a living room." He tossed the filter away. "Do you smoke pipes?"

"I no longer smoke anything."

"Pipes use another type of more advanced filter. You can get one for three yuan. The diameter is about the same as a cigarette filter, but it's longer: a small paper tube filled with active charcoal. If you take out all the active charcoal, it will look like a little pile of black particles, like mouse droppings. But added together, the adsorbent surface formed by the tiny holes inside is as large as a tennis court. This is why active charcoal is so adsorbent."

"What are you trying to say?" Wang asked, listening intently.

"The sponge or active charcoal inside a filter is three-dimensional. Their adsorbent surfaces, however, are two-dimensional. Thus, you can see how a tiny high-dimensional structure can contain a huge low-dimensional structure. But at the macroscopic level, this is about the limit of the ability for high-dimensional space to contain low-dimensional space. Because God was stingy, during the big bang He only provided the macroscopic world with three spatial dimensions, plus the dimension of time. But this

356

doesn't mean that higher dimensions don't exist. Up to seven additional dimensions are locked within the micro scale, or, more precisely, within the quantum realm. And added to the four dimensions at the macro scale, fundamental particles exist within an eleven-dimensional space-time."

"So what?"

"I just want to point out this fact: In the universe, an important mark of a civilization's technological advancement is its ability to control and make use of micro dimensions. Making use of fundamental particles without taking advantage of the micro dimensions is something that our naked, hairy ancestors already began back when they lit bonfires within caves. Controlling chemical reactions is just manipulating micro particles without regard to the micro dimensions. Of course, this control also progressed from crude to advanced: from bonfires to steam engines, and then generators. Now, the ability for humans to manipulate micro particles at the macro level has reached a peak: We have computers and nanomaterials. But all of that is accomplished without unlocking the many micro dimensions. From the perspective of a more advanced civilization in the universe, bonfires and computers and nanomaterials are not fundamentally different. They all belong to the same level. That's also why they still think of humans as mere bugs. Unfortunately, I think they're right."

"Can you be more specific? What does all this have to do with those two protons? Ultimately, what can the two protons that have reached the Earth do? Like the interrogator said, a single cilium on a bacterium can contain several billion protons. Even if these two protons turned entirely into energy on the tip of my finger, at most it would feel like a pinprick."

"You wouldn't feel anything. Even if they turned into energy on a bacterium, the bacterium probably wouldn't feel anything."

"Then what were you trying to say?"

"Nothing. I don't know anything. What can a bug know?"

"But you're a physicist among bugs. You know more than I do. At least you aren't completely at a loss when faced with the knowledge of these protons. I beg you. Tell me. Otherwise I won't be able to sleep tonight."

"If I tell you more, you really won't be able to sleep. Forget it. What's the point of worrying? We should learn to be as philosophical as Wei Cheng and Shi Qiang. Just do the best within your responsibility. Let's go drinking and then go back to sleep like good bugs."

31

Operation Guzheng

"Don't worry," Shi Qiang said to Wang, as he sat down next to him at the meeting table. "I'm not radioactive anymore. The last couple of days they've washed me inside and outside like a flour sack. They didn't originally think you needed to attend this meeting, but I insisted. Heh. I bet the two of us are going to be important this time."

As Da Shi spoke, he picked a cigar butt out of the ashtray, lit it, and took a long drag. He nodded, and, in a slow, relaxed manner, blew the smoke into the faces of the attendees sitting on the other side of the table. One of the people sitting opposite him was the original owner of the cigar, Colonel Stanton of the U.S. Marine Corps. He gave Da Shi a contemptuous look.

Many more foreign military officers were at this meeting than the last. They were all in uniform. For the first time in human history, the armed forces of the world's nations faced the same enemy.

General Chang said, "Comrades, everyone at this meeting now has the same basic understanding of the situation. Or, as Da Shi here would put it, we have information parity. The war between alien invaders and humanity has begun. Our descendants won't face the Trisolarans for another four and a half centuries. For now, our opponents are still human. Yet, in essence, these traitors to the human race can also be seen as enemies from outside human civilization. We have never faced an enemy like this. The next war objective is very clear: We must capture the intercepted Trisolaran messages stored on *Judgment Day*. These messages may have great significance for our survival.

"We haven't yet done anything to draw the suspicion of *Judgment Day*. The ship still sails the Atlantic freely. It has already submitted plans to the Panama Canal Authority to pass through the canal in four days. This is a great opportunity for us. As the situation develops, such an opportunity may never arise again. Right now, all the Battle Command Centers around the globe are drafting up operation plans, and Central will select one within ten hours and begin implementation. The purpose of this meeting is to discuss possible plans of operation, and then report one to three of our best suggestions to Central. Time is of the essence, and we must work efficiently.

"Note that any plan must guarantee one thing: the secure capture of the Trisolaran messages. *Judgment Day* was rebuilt from an old tanker, and both the superstructure and the interior have been extensively renovated with complex structures to contain many new rooms and passageways. Supposedly even the crew relies on a map when entering unfamiliar areas. We, of course, know even less about the ship's layout. Right now, we cannot even be certain of the location of the computing center on *Judgment Day*, and we don't know whether the intercepted Trisolaran messages are stored in servers located in the computing center, or how many copies they have. The only way to achieve our objective is to completely capture and control *Judgment Day*.

"The most difficult part is preventing the enemy from erasing Trisolaran data during our attack. Destroying the data would be very easy. The enemy would not use conventional methods to erase the data during an attack, because it's easy to recover the data using known technology. But if they just emptied a cartridge clip at the server hard drive or other storage media, it would all be over, and doing so would take no more than ten seconds. So we must disable all enemies near the storage equipment within ten seconds of their detecting an attack. Since we don't know the exact location of the data storage or the number of copies, we must eliminate all enemies on *Judgment Day* within a very brief period of time, before the target has been alerted. At the same time, we can't heavily damage the facilities within, especially computer equipment. Thus, this is a very difficult task. Some think it's impossible."

A Japanese Self-Defense Forces officer said, "We believe that the only chance for success is to rely on spies on *Judgment Day*. If they're familiar with where the Trisolaran information is stored, they can control the area or move the storage equipment elsewhere right before our operation."

Someone asked, "Reconnaissance and monitoring of *Judgment Day* have always been the responsibility of NATO military intelligence and the CIA. Do we have such spies?"

"No," the NATO liaison said.

"Then we have nothing more to discuss except bullshit," said Da Shi. He was met with annoyed looks.

Colonel Stanton said, "Since the objective is eliminating all personnel within an enclosed structure without harming other equipment within, our first thought was to use a ball lightning weapon."

Ding Yi shook his head. "The existence of this kind of weapon is now public knowledge. We don't know if the ship has been equipped with magnetic walls to shield against ball lightning. Even if it hasn't, a ball lightning weapon can indeed kill all personnel within the ship, but it cannot do so simultaneously. Also, after the ball lightning enters the ship, it may hover in the air for some time before releasing its energy. This wait time can last from a dozen seconds to a minute or longer. They will have enough time to realize they've been attacked and destroy the data."

Colonel Stanton asked, "What about a neutron bomb?"

"Colonel, you should know that's not going to work." The speaker was a Russian officer. "The radiation from a neutron bomb cannot kill right away. After a neutron bomb attack, the amount of time left to the enemy would be more than enough for them to have a meeting just like this one."

"Another thought was to use nerve gas," a NATO officer said. "But releasing it and having it spread throughout the ship would take time, so it still doesn't achieve General Chang's requirements."

"Then the only choices left are concussion bombs and infrasonic waves," Colonel Stanton said. Others waited for him to finish his thought, but he said nothing more.

Da Shi said, "I use concussion bombs in police work, but they're toys. They're indeed capable of stunning people inside a building into unconsciousness, but they're only good for a room or two. Do you have any concussion bombs big enough to stun a whole oil tanker full of people?"

Stanton shook his head. "No. Even if we did, such a large explosive device would certainly damage equipment inside the ship."

"So what about infrasonic weapons?" someone asked.

"They're still experimental and cannot be used in live combat. Also, the ship is very large. At the power level available to current experimental prototypes, the most that a full assault on *Judgment Day* could do is to make the people inside feel dizzy and nauseous."

"Ha!" Da Shi extinguished the cigar butt, now as tiny as a peanut. "I told you all we have left to discuss is bullshit. We've been at it for a while now. Let's remember what the general said: 'Time is of the essence!' " He gave a sly grin to the translator, a female first lieutenant who looked unhappy with his language. "Not easy to translate, eh, comrade? Just get the approximate meaning across."

But Stanton seemed to understand what he was saying. He pointed at Shi Qiang with a fresh cigar that he had just taken out. "Who does this policeman think he is, that he can talk to us this way?"

"Who do you think *you* are?" Da Shi asked.

"Colonel Stanton is an expert in special ops," a NATO officer said. "He has been a part of every major military operation since the Vietnam War."

"Then let me tell you who I am. More than thirty years ago, my reconnaissance squad managed to sneak dozens of kilometers behind Vietnamese lines and capture a hydroelectric station under heavy guard. We prevented the Vietnamese plan to demolish the dam with explosives, which would have flooded the attack route for our army. That's who *I* am. I defeated an enemy who once defeated *you*."

"That's enough!" General Chang slammed the table. "Don't bring up irrelevant matters. If you have a plan, say what it is."

"I don't think we need to waste time on this policeman," Colonel Stanton said contemptuously, as he lit his cigar.

Without waiting for a translation, Da Shi jumped up. " '*Pao-Li-Si*'—I heard that word twice. What? You look down on the police? If you're talking about dropping some bombs and turning that ship into smithereens, yeah, you military are the experts. But if you're talking about retrieving something out of it without damage, I don't care how many stars are on your shoulder, you aren't even as good as a thief. For this kind of thing, you have to think outside the box. OUT. OF. THE. BOX! You will never be as good at it as criminals, masters of out-of-the-box thinking.

"You know how good they are? I once handled a robbery where the criminals managed to steal one car out of a moving train. They reconnected the cars before and after the one they were interested in so that the train got all the way to its destination without anyone noticing. The only tools they used were a length of wire cable and a few steel hooks. Those are the real special ops experts. And someone like me, a criminal cop who has been playing cat and mouse with them for more than a decade, has received the best education and training from them."

"Tell us your plan, then," General Chang said. "Otherwise, shut up!"

"There are so many important people here that I didn't think it was my place to speak. And I was afraid that you, General, would say I was being rude again."

"You're already the definition of rudeness. Enough! Tell me what your out-of-the-box plan is."

Da Shi picked up a pen and drew two parallel curves on the table. "That's the canal." He put the ashtray between the two lines. "This is *Judgment Day*." Then he reached across the table and pulled Colonel Stanton's just-lit cigar out of his mouth.

"I can no longer tolerate this idiot!" the colonel shouted, standing up.

"Da Shi, get out of here!" General Chang said.

"Give me one minute. I'll be done soon." Da Shi extended a hand in front of Colonel Stanton.

"What do you want?" the colonel asked, puzzled.

"Give me another one."

Stanton hesitated for a second before taking another cigar out of a beautiful wooden box and handing it to Da Shi. Da Shi took the smoking end of the first cigar and pressed it against the table so that it stood on the shore of the Panama Canal that he'd drawn on the table. He flattened the end of the other cigar and erected it on the other shore of the canal.

"We set up two pillars on the shores of the canal, and then between them we string many parallel, thin filaments, about half a meter apart. The filaments should be made from the nanomaterial called 'Flying Blade,' developed by Professor Wang. A very appropriate name, in this case."

After Shi Qiang finished speaking, he stood and waited a few seconds. Then he raised his hands, said to the stunned crowd, "That's it," turned, and left.

The air seemed frozen. Everyone present stayed still like stone statues. Even the droning from the computers all around them seemed more careful.

After a long while, someone timidly broke the silence, "Professor Wang, is 'Flying Blade' really in the form of filaments?"

Wang nodded. "Given our current molecular construction technique, the only form we can make is a filament. The thickness is about one-hundredth the thickness of human hair. . . . Officer Shi got this information from me before the meeting."

"Do you have enough material?"

"How wide is the canal? And how tall is the ship?"

"The narrowest point of the canal is one hundred fifty meters wide. *Judgment Day* is thirty-one meters tall, with a draft of eight meters or so."

Wang stared at the cigars on the table and did some mental calculations. "I think I should have enough."

Another long silence. Everyone was trying to recover from their astonishment.

"What if the equipment storing Trisolaran data, such as hard drives and optical disks, is also sliced?"

"That doesn't seem likely."

"Even if they were sliced," a computer expert said, "it's not a big deal. The filaments are extremely sharp, and the cut surfaces would be very smooth. Given that premise, whether it's hard drives, optical disks, or integrated circuit storage, we could recover the vast majority of the data."

"Anyone got a better idea?" Chang looked around the table. No one spoke. "All right. Then let's focus on this and work out the details."

Colonel Stanton, who had been silent the whole time, stood up. "I will go and ask Officer Shi to come back."

General Chang indicated that he should remain seated. Then he called out, "Da Shi!"

Da Shi returned, grinning at everyone. He picked up the cigars on the table. The one that had been lit he put into his mouth, and the other he stuffed into his pocket.

Someone asked, "When *Judgment Day* passes, can those two pillars bear the force applied against the Flying Blade filaments? Maybe the pillars would be sliced apart first."

Wang said, "That's easy to solve. We have some small amounts of Flying Blade material that are flat sheets. We can use them to protect the parts of the column where the filaments are attached."

The discussion after that was mainly between the naval officers and navigation experts.

"*Judgment Day* is at the upper limit in terms of tonnage

that can pass through the Panama Canal. It has a deep draft, so we have to consider installing filaments below the waterline."

"That will be very difficult. If there's not enough time, I don't think we should worry about it. The parts of the ship below the waterline are used for engines, fuel, and ballast, causing a lot of noise, vibration, and interference. The conditions are too poor for computing centers and other similar facilities to be located there. But for the parts above water, a tighter nanofilament net will give better results."

"Then it's best to set the trap at one of the locks along the canal. *Judgment Day* is built to Panamax specifications, just enough to fill the thirty-two-meter locks. Then we would only need to make the Flying Blade filaments thirty-two meters long. This will also make it easier to erect the pillars and string the filaments between them, especially for the underwater parts."

"No. The situation around the locks is too unpredictable. Also, a ship inside the lock must be pulled forward by four 'mules,' electric locomotives on rails. They move slowly, and the time inside the locks will also be when the crew is most alert. An attempt to slice through the ship during that time would most likely be discovered."

"What about the Bridge of the Americas, right outside the Miraflores Locks? The abutments at the two ends of the bridge can serve as the pillars for stringing the filaments."

"No. The distance between the abutments is too great. We don't have enough Flying Blade material."

"Then it's decided: The site of operation should be the narrowest point of the Gaillard Cut, a hundred and fifty meters across. Add in some slack for the pillars . . . let's call it a hundred seventy meters."

Wang said, "If that's the plan, then the smallest distance between the filaments will be fifty centimeters. I don't have enough material for a tighter net."

"In other words, we have to make sure the ship crosses during the day," Da Shi said, blowing out another mouthful of smoke.

"Why?"

"At night the crew will be sleeping, which means they'll all be lying down. Fifty centimeters between filaments leaves too much of a gap. But during the day, even if they're sitting or crouching, the distance is sufficient."

A few scattered laughs. The attendees, all under heavy stress, felt a bit of release tinged with the smell of blood.

"You're truly a demon," a female UN official said to Da Shi.

"Will innocent bystanders be hurt?" Wang asked, his voice trembling.

A naval officer replied, "When the ship goes through the locks, more than a dozen cable workers will come onboard, but they'll all get off after the ship passes. The Panama Canal pilot will have to accompany the ship the entire eighty-two kilometers, so the pilot will have to be sacrificed."

A CIA officer said, "And some of the crew aboard *Judgment Day* probably don't know the real purpose of the ship."

"Professor," General Chang said, "do not concern yourself with these thoughts. The information we need to obtain has to do with the very survival of human civilization. Someone else will make the call."

As the meeting ended, Colonel Stanton pushed the beautiful cigar box in front of Shi Qiang. "Captain, the best Havana has to offer. They're yours."

Four days later, Gaillard Cut, Panama Canal

Wang could not even tell that he was in a foreign country. He knew that to the west, not too far away, was beautiful Gatun Lake. To the east was the magnificent Bridge of the Americas and Panama City. But he had had no chance to see either of them.

Two days earlier, he had arrived by direct flight from China to Tocumen International Airport near Panama City and then rode a helicopter here. The sight before him was very common: The construction work under way to widen the canal caused the tropical forest on both slopes to be quite sparse, revealing large patches of yellow earth. The color felt familiar to Wang. The canal didn't seem very special, probably because it was so narrow here, but a hundred thousand people had dug out this part of the canal in the previous century, one hoe at a time.

Wang and Colonel Stanton sat on lounge chairs under an awning halfway up the slope. Both wore loose, colorful shirts, with their Panama hats tossed to the side, looking like two tourists.

Below, on each shore of the canal, a twenty-four-meter steel pillar lay flat against the ground, parallel to the shore. Fifty ultrastrong nanofilaments, each 160 meters long, were strung between the pillars. At the end on the eastern shore, every filament was connected to a length of regular steel wire. This was to give the filaments enough slack so that they could sink to the bottom of the canal, aided by attached weights. The setup permitted other ships safe passage. Luckily, traffic along the canal wasn't quite as busy as Wang had imagined. On average, only about forty large ships passed through each day.

The operation's code name was "Guzheng," based on the similarity between the structure and the ancient Chinese zither by that name. The slicing net of nanofilaments was thus called the "zither."

An hour earlier, *Judgment Day* had entered the Gaillard Cut from Gatun Lake.

Stanton asked Wang whether he had ever been to Panama before. Wang said no.

"I came here in 1989," the colonel said.

"Because of that war?"

"Yes, that was one of those wars that left me with no impression. I only remember being in front of the Vatican embassy as 'Nowhere to Run' by Martha and the Vandellas played for the holed-up Noriega. That was my idea, by the way."

In the canal below them, a pure white French cruise ship slowly sailed past. Several passengers in colorful clothing strolled leisurely on the green-carpeted deck.

"Second Observation Post reporting: There are no more ships in front of the target." Stanton's walkie-talkie squawked.

Stanton gave the order. "Raise the zither."

Several men wearing hard hats appeared on both shores, looking like maintenance workers. Wang stood up, but the colonel pulled him down. "Professor, don't worry. They know what to do." Wang watched as those on the eastern shore rapidly winched back the steel wires attached to the nanofilaments and secured the tightened nanofilaments to the pillar. Then, slowly, the two pillars were stood upright using their mechanical hinges. As a disguise, the pillars were decorated with some navigational markings and water depth indicators. The workers proceeded leisurely, as though they were simply carrying out their boring jobs. Wang gazed at the space between the pillars. There seemed to be nothing there, but the deadly zither was already in place.

"Target is four kilometers from the zither," the voice in the walkie-talkie said.

Stanton put the walkie-talkie down. He continued the conversation with Wang. "The second time I came to Panama was in 1999, to attend the ceremony for the handover of the canal to Panama. Oddly, by the time we got to the Authority's building, the Stars and Stripes were already gone. Supposedly the U.S. government had requested that the flag be lowered a day early to avoid the embarrassment of lowering the flag in front of a crowd. . . . Back then, I thought I was witnessing history. But now that seems so insignificant."

"Target is three kilometers from the zither."

"Yes, insignificant," Wang mumbled. He wasn't listening to Stanton at all. The rest of the world had ceased to exist for him. All of his attention was focused on the spot where *Judgment Day* would appear. By now the sun that had risen over the Atlantic was falling toward the Pacific. The canal sparkled with golden light. Close by, the deadly zither stood quietly. The two steel pillars were dark and reflected no sunlight, looking even older than the canal that flowed between them.

"Target is two kilometers from the zither."

Stanton seemed to not have heard the voice from the walkie-talkie. He continued, "After learning that the alien fleet is coming toward the Earth, I've been suffering from amnesia. It's so strange. I can't recall many things from the past. I don't remember the details of the wars I experienced. Like I just said, those wars all seem so insignificant. After learning this truth, everyone becomes a new person spiritually, and sees the world anew. I've been thinking: Suppose two thousand years ago, or even earlier, humanity learned that an alien invasion fleet would arrive a few thousand years later. What would human civilization be like now? Professor, can you imagine it?"

"Ah, no . . ." Wang answered perfunctorily, his mind elsewhere.

"Target is one point five kilometers from the zither."

"Professor, I think you will be the Gaillard of this new era. We're waiting for your new Panama Canal to be built. Indeed, the space elevator is a canal. Just as the Panama Canal connected two oceans, the space elevator will connect space with the Earth."

Wang knew that the colonel's babbling was meant to help him through this very difficult time. He was grateful, but it wasn't working.

"Target is one kilometer from the zither."

Judgment Day appeared. In the light from the setting sun coming over the hills to the side, it was a dark silhouette against the golden waves of the canal. The sixty-thousand-ton ship was much larger than Wang had imagined. Its appearance was like another peak abruptly inserted among the hills. Even though Wang knew that the canal was capable of accommodating ships as large as seventy thousand tons, witnessing such a large ship in such a narrow waterway was a strange feeling. Given its immensity, the canal below seemed to no longer exist. The ship was a mountain gliding across solid earth. After he grew used to the sunlight, Wang saw that *Judgment Day*'s hull was pitch black, and the superstructure was painted pure white. The giant antenna was gone. They heard the roar from the ship's engines, accompanied by the churning sound of waves that had been generated by the round prow slapping against the shores of the canal.

372

As the distance between *Judgment Day* and the deadly zither closed, Wang's heart began to beat faster, and his breath became short. He had a desire to run away, but he felt so weak that he could no longer control his body. All at once, he was overwhelmed by a deep hatred for Shi Qiang. *How could the bastard have come up with such an idea? Like that UN official said, he is a demon!* But the feeling passed. He thought that if Da Shi were by his side, he would probably feel better. Colonel Stanton had invited Shi Qiang to come, but General Chang refused to give permission because he said that Da Shi was needed where he was. Wang felt the colonel's hand on his back.

"Professor, all this will pass."

Judgment Day was below them now, passing through the deadly zither. When its prow first contacted the plane between the two steel pillars, the space that seemed empty, Wang's scalp tightened. But nothing happened. The immense hull of the ship continued to slowly sail past the two steel pillars. When half the ship had passed, Wang began to doubt whether the nanofilaments between the steel pillars really existed.

But a small sign soon negated his doubt. He noticed a thin antenna located at the very top of the superstructure breaking at its base, and the antenna tumbling down.

Soon, there was a second sign indicating the presence of the nanofilaments, a sign that almost made Wang break down. *Judgment Day*'s wide deck was empty save for one man standing near the stern hosing down the ship's bollards. From his vantage point, Wang saw everything clearly. The moment that that section of the ship passed between the pillars, the hose broke into two pieces not too far from the man, and water spilled out. The man's body stiffened, and the nozzle tumbled from his hand. He remained standing for a few seconds, then fell. As his body contacted the deck, it came apart in two halves. The top half crawled through the expanding pool of blood, but had to use two arms that were bloody stumps. The hands had been cleanly sliced off.

After the stern of the ship went between the two pillars, *Judgment Day* continued to sail forward at the same speed, and everything seemed normal. But then Wang heard the sound of the engine shift into a strange whine, before turning into chaotic noise. It sounded like a wrench being thrown into the rotor of a large motor—no, many, many wrenches. He knew this was the result of the rotating parts of the engine having been cut. After a piercing, tearing sound, a hole appeared in the side of the stern of *Judgment Day*, made by a large metallic piece punching through the hull. A broken component flew out of the hole and fell into the water, causing a large column of water to shoot up. As it briefly flew past, Wang recognized it as a section of the engine crankshaft.

A thick column of smoke poured out of the hole. *Judgment Day*, which had been sailing along the right shore, now began to turn, dragging this smoky tail. Soon it crossed over the canal and smashed into the left shore. As Wang looked, the giant prow deformed as it collided into the slope, slicing open the hill like water, causing waves of earth to spill in all directions. At the same time, *Judgment Day* began to separate into more than forty slices, each slice half a meter thick. The slices near the top moved faster than the slices near the bottom, and the ship spread open like a deck of cards. As the forty-some metal slices moved past each other, the piercing noise was like countless giant fingernails scratching against glass.

By the time the intolerable noise ended, *Judgment Day* was spilled on the shore like a stack of plates carried by a stumbling waiter, the plates near the top having traveled the farthest. The slices looked as soft as cloth, and rapidly deformed into complicated shapes impossible to imagine as having once belonged to a ship.

Soldiers rushed toward the shore from the slope. Wang was surprised to find so many men hidden nearby. A fleet of helicopters arrived along the canal with their engines roaring; crossed the canal surface, which was now covered by an iridescent oil slick; hovered over the wreckage of *Judgment Day*; and began to drop large quantities of fire suppression foam and powder. Shortly, the fire in the wreckage was under control, and three other helicopters began to drop searchers into the wreckage with cables.

Colonel Stanton had already left. Wang picked up the binoculars he'd left on top of his hat. Overcoming his trembling hands, he observed *Judgment Day*. By this time, the wreckage was mostly covered by fire-extinguishing foam and powder, but the edges of some of the slices were left exposed. Wang saw the cut surfaces, smooth as mirrors. They reflected the fiery red light of dusk perfectly. He also saw a deep red spot on the mirror surface. He wasn't sure if it was blood.

Three days later

INTERROGATOR: Do you understand Trisolaran civilization?

YE WENJIE: No. We received only very limited information. No one has real, detailed knowledge of Trisolaran civilization except Mike Evans and other core members of the Adventists who intercepted their messages.

INTERROGATOR: Then why do you have such hope for it, thinking that it can reform and perfect human society?

YE: If they can cross the distance between the stars to come to our world, their science must have developed to a very advanced stage. A society with such advanced science must also have more advanced moral standards.

INTERROGATOR: Do you think this conclusion you drew is scientific?

YE: . . .

INTERROGATOR: Let me presume to guess: Your father was deeply influenced by your grandfather's belief that only science could save China. And you were deeply influenced by your father.

YE: *(sighing quietly)* I don't know.

INTERROGATOR: We have already obtained all the Trisolaran messages intercepted by the Adventists.

YE: Oh . . . what happened to Evans?

INTERROGATOR: He died during the operation to capture *Judgment Day*. But the posture of his body pointed us to the computers holding copies of the Trisolaran messages. Thankfully, they were all encoded with the same self-interpreting code used by Red Coast.

YE: Was there a lot of data?

INTERROGATOR: Yes, about twenty-eight gigabytes.

YE: That's impossible. Interstellar communication is very inefficient. How can so much data have been transmitted?

INTERROGATOR: We thought so at first, too. But things were not at all as we had imagined—not even in our boldest, most fantastic imaginations. How about this? Please read this section of the preliminary analysis of the captured data, and you can see the reality of the Trisolaran civilization, compared with your beautiful fantasies.

32

Trisolaris: The Listener

The Trisolaran data contained no descriptions of the bio-logical appearance of Trisolarans. Since humans would not lay eyes on actual Trisolarans until more than four hundred years later, Ye could only envision the Trisolarans as human-oid as she read the messages. She filled in the blanks between the lines with her imagination.

Listening Post 1379 had already been in existence for more than a thousand years. There were several thousand posts like it on Trisolaris, all of them dedicating their efforts to detecting possible signs of intelligent life in the universe.

Initially, each listening post had several hundred listeners, but as technology advanced, there was only one person on duty. Being a listener was a humble career. Though they lived in listening posts that were kept at a constant temperature, with support systems that guaranteed their survival without requiring them to dehydrate during Chaotic Eras, they also had to live their lives within the narrow confines of these tiny spaces. The amount of joy they got from Stable Eras was far less than others got.

The listener at Post 1379 looked through the tiny window

at the world of Trisolaris outside. This was a Chaotic Era night. The giant moon had not yet risen, and most people remained in dehydrated hibernation. Even plants had instinctively dehydrated and turned into lifeless bundles of dry fiber lying against the ground. Under the starlight, the ground looked like a giant sheet of cold metal.

This was the loneliest time. In the deep silence of midnight, the universe revealed itself to its listeners as a vast desolation. What the listener of Post 1379 disliked the most was seeing the waves that slowly crawled across the display, a visual record of the meaningless noise the listening post picked up from space. He felt this interminable wave was an abstract view of the universe: one end connected to the endless past, the other to the endless future, and in the middle only the ups and downs of random chance—without life, without pattern, the peaks and valleys at different heights like uneven grains of sand, the whole curve like a one-dimensional desert made of all the grains of sand lined up in a row: lonely, desolate, so long that it was intolerable. You could follow it and go forward or backward as long as you liked, but you'd never find the end.

On this day, however, the listener saw something odd when he glanced at the waveform display. Even experts had a hard time telling with the naked eye whether a waveform carried information. But the listener was so familiar with the noise of the universe that he could tell that the wave that now moved in front of his eyes had something extra. The thin curve, rising and falling, seemed to possess a soul. He was certain that the radio signal before him had been modulated by intelligence.

He rushed in front of another terminal and checked the computer's rating of the signal's recognizability: a Red 10.

Before this, no radio signal received by the listening post had ever garnered a recognizability rating above a Blue 2. A Red rating meant the likelihood that the transmission contained intelligent information was greater than 90 percent. A rating of Red 10 meant the received transmission contained a self-interpreting coding system! The deciphering computer worked at full power.

Still caught up by the dizzying excitement and confusion, the listener stared at the waveform display. Information continued to stream from the universe into the antenna. Because of the self-interpreting code, the computer was able to perform real-time translation, and the message began to show up immediately.

The listener opened the resulting document, and, for the first time, a Trisolaran read a message from another world.

> With the best of intentions, we look forward to estab-lishing contact with other civilized societies in the uni-verse. We look forward to working together with you to build a better life in this vast universe.

During the next two Trisolaran hours, the listener learned of the existence of Earth, learned of the world that had only one sun and remained always in a Stable Era, learned of the human civilization that had been born in a paradise where the climate was eternally mild.

The transmission from the solar system ended. The deciphering computer now ran uselessly. The post was once again only hearing the noise of the universe.

But the listener was certain that what he had just experienced was not a dream. He knew as well that the several thousand listening posts spread across Trisolaris had also received this message, which Trisolaran civilization had awaited for eons. Two hundred cycles of civilization had been crawling through a dark tunnel, and there was finally a glimmer of light before them.

The listener read over the message from the Earth again. His thoughts drifted over the blue ocean that never froze and the green forests and fields, enjoying the warm sunlight and the caress of a cool breeze. *What a beautiful world! The paradise we imagined really exists!*

The thrill and excitement cooled, and all that remained was a sense of loss and desolation. During the long loneliness of the past, the listener had asked himself more than once: *Even if one day a message from an extra-Trisolaran civilization were to arrive, what would that have to do with me?* His own lonely and humble life would not change one iota because of it.

But I can at least possess it in my dream. . . . And the listener drifted off to sleep. In their harsh environment, the Trisolarans had evolved the ability to switch sleep on and off. A Trisolaran could put himself to sleep in seconds.

But he did not get the dream that he wanted. The blue Earth did appear in his dream, but under the bombardment of an enormous interstellar fleet, the beautiful continents of Earth were burning, the deep blue oceans were boiling and evaporating. . . .

The listener woke up from his nightmare and saw the giant moon, just risen, casting a thin ray of cold light through the small window. He looked at the frozen ground outside the window and reviewed his lonely life. By now, he had lived six hundred thousand Trisolaran hours. The life expectancy of Trisolarans ranged between seven hundred to eight hundred thousand Trisolaran hours. Most people, of course, would have lost the ability to work productively long before then.

They would have been forcibly dehydrated, and the resulting dry fibers cast to the flames. Trisolaris did not keep the idle around.

But now the listener saw another possibility. It was inaccurate to say that the receipt of the extra-Trisolaran message had no influence on his life. After confirmation, Trisolaris would surely reduce the number of listening posts. And posts like this one, behind the times, would be among the first to be cut. Then he would be unemployed. A listener's skills were very specialized, consisting only of some routine operations and maintenance. It would be very difficult to find another job. If he couldn't find another job within five thousand Trisolaran hours, he would be forcibly dehydrated and then burnt.

The only way to escape this fate was to mate with a member of the opposite sex. When that happened, the organic material making up their bodies would meld into one. Two-thirds of the material would then become fuel to power the biochemical reaction that would completely renew the cells in the remaining one-third and create a new body. Then this body would divide into three to five tiny new lives: their children. They would inherit some of the memories of their parents, continue their lives, and begin the cycle of life anew. But given the listener's low social position, lonely and enclosed workspace, and advanced age, what member of the opposite sex would be interested in him?

In the last few years, the listener had asked himself millions of times: *Is this all there is to my life?* And millions of times he had answered himself: *Yes, this is all there is. All that you have in this life is the endless loneliness in the tiny space of this listening post.*

He couldn't lose that paradise, even if it was only in a dream.

The listener knew that at the scale of the universe, due to the lack of a sufficiently long measurement baseline, it was impossible to determine the *distance* of a source of low-frequency radio transmission from space, only the direction. The source could be high-powered but far away, or low-powered but close by. In that direction were billions of stars, each shining against a sea of other stars at different distances. Without knowing how far away the source was, it was impossible to ascertain its exact coordinates.

Distance, the key was distance.

Indeed, there was an easy way to ascertain the distance of the transmission source. Just respond to the message, and if the other party replies quickly to the response, the Trisolarans could determine the distance based on the round-trip time and the speed of light. Or maybe they would take a really long time to reply and cause the Trisolarans to be unable to determine how long the message was en route.

But the question was: Would the other party reply? Since this source had actively sent out a call into the universe, it was very likely that they *would* reply after getting a response from Trisolaris. And the listener was sure that the Trisolaran government had already given the order to send a message to that distant world to lure them to respond. Maybe the message had already been sent, but maybe not. If the latter was true, then the listener had a singular chance to make his own humble life glow.

The listener dashed in front of the operations screen and composed a short, simple message on the computer. He directed the computer to translate the message into the same language as the message received from the Earth. Then, he pointed the listening post's antenna in the direction the message from Earth had come from.

The Transmit button was a red rectangle. The listener's fingers hovered above it.

The fate of Trisolaran civilization was now tied to these slender fingers.

Without hesitation, the listener pressed the button. A high-powered radio wave carried that short message, a message that could save another civilization, into the darkness of space.

Do not answer! Do not answer!! Do not answer!!!

We don't know what the official residence of the princeps of Trisolaris looked like, but we can be sure that thick walls separated him from the outside so as to protect him against the extreme weather. The pyramid from the *Three Body* game was one guess about what it could look like. That they built the residence deep underground is another.

Five Trisolaran hours earlier, the princeps received the report of the extra-Trisolaran communication. Two Trisolaran hours earlier, he received another report: Listening Post 1379 had sent out a warning message in the direction of the transmission.

The first report did not cause him to leap up in ecstasy, and the second report did not cause him to sink into depression. He wasn't even angry or resentful. All of these emotions—and other emotions, such as fear, sorrow, happiness, and appreciation of beauty—were things that the Trisolaran civilization strove to avoid and eliminate. Such emotions caused the individual and society to be weak spiritually and did not help with survival in the harsh environment of this world. The mental states that Trisolarans needed were calmness and numbness. The history of the past two hundred-some cycles of civilization proved that civilizations that relied on these two states as their spiritual core were the most capable of survival.

"Why did you do this?" the princeps asked the listener from Post 1379.

"So that my life isn't wasted," the listener answered calmly.

"The warning you sent out may have cost Trisolaran civilization the chance at survival."

"But it gave Earth civilization such a chance. Princeps, Trisolaran civilization's desire to possess living space is like the desire of a man who has been starving for a long time for food, and it is similarly boundless. We cannot share the Earth with the people of that world. We could only destroy Earth civilization and completely take over that solar system. . . . Am I right?"

"Yes. But there is another reason for destroying Earth civilization. They're also a warlike race. Very dangerous. If we try to coexist with them on the same planet, they will shortly learn our technology. Continuing in that state would allow neither civilization to thrive. Let me ask you: You wish to be the savior of the Earth, but do you not feel any sense of responsibility for your own race?"

"I am tired of Trisolaris. We have nothing in our lives and spirit except the fight for survival."

"What's wrong with that?"

"There's nothing wrong, of course. Existence is the premise for everything else. But, Princeps, please examine our lives: Everything is devoted to survival. To permit the survival of the civilization as a whole, there is almost no respect for the individual. Someone who can no longer work is put to death. Trisolaran society exists under a state of extreme authoritarianism. The law has only two outcomes: The guilty are put to death, and the not guilty are released. For me, the most intolerable aspects are the spiritual monotony and desiccation. Anything that can lead to spiritual weakness is

384

declared evil. We have no literature, no art, no pursuit of beauty and enjoyment. We cannot even speak of love. . . . Princeps, is there meaning to such a life?"

"The kind of civilization you yearn for once existed on Trisolaris, too. They had free, democratic societies, and they left behind rich cultural legacies. You know barely anything about them. Most details have been sealed away and forbidden from view. But in all the cycles of Trisolaran civilization, this type of civilization was the weakest and most short-lived. A modest Chaotic Era disaster was enough to extinguish them. Look again at the Earth civilization that you wish to save. A society born and bred in the eternal spring of a beautiful hothouse would not be able to survive even a million Trisolaran hours if it were transplanted here."

"That flower may be delicate, but it possesses peerless splendor. She enjoys freedom and beauty in the ease of paradise."

"If Trisolaran civilization ultimately possesses that world, we can also create such lives for ourselves."

"Princeps, I'm doubtful. The metallic Trisolaran spirit has infiltrated each of our cells and solidified. You really believe it can melt again? I'm an ordinary man living at the bottom of society. No one would pay any attention to me. My life is spent alone, without wealth, without status, without love, and without hope. If I can save a distant, beautiful world that I have fallen in love with, then my life has not been wasted. Of course, Princeps, this also gave me a chance to see you. If I had not done this, a man like me could only ever hope to admire you on TV. So permit me to express myself as honored."

"You're guilty beyond doubt. You're the greatest criminal in all the cycles of Trisolaran civilization. But now we make an exception in Trisolaran law: You're free to go."

"Why?"

"For you, dehydration followed by burning is not even remotely adequate as punishment. You're old, and you will not live to see the final destruction of Earth civilization. But I will at least make sure that you know that you cannot save her. I want to let you live until the day she loses all hope.

"All right. You may leave."

After the listener from Post 1379 left, the princeps called in the consul responsible for the monitoring system. The princeps also avoided being angry at him. He dealt with it as a routine matter. "How could you allow such a weak and evil man into the monitoring system?"

"Princeps, the monitoring system employs hundreds of thousands. To screen them all strictly is very difficult. After all, the man managed to perform his duties at Listening Post 1379 without error for most of his life. Of course, this most serious mistake is my responsibility."

"How many others bear some responsibility for this failure in the Trisolaran Space Monitoring System?"

"My preliminary investigation shows about six thousand, accounting for all levels."

"They're all guilty."

"Yes."

"Dehydrate all six thousand and burn them together in the square in the middle of the capital. As for you, you can be the kindling."

"Thank you, Princeps. This will at least calm our consciences a little."

"Before carrying out this punishment, let me ask you: How far can that warning message travel?"

"Listening Post 1379 is a small facility without high

transmission power. The maximum range may be twelve million light-hours, about twelve hundred light-years."

"That's far enough. Do you have any suggestions for what Trisolaran civilization should do next?"

"How about transmitting a carefully composed message to that world to lure them to respond?"

"No. That might make matters worse. At least the warning message is very short. We can only hope that they ignore it, or misunderstand its contents . . . All right. You may leave."

After the consul left, the princeps summoned the commander of the Trisolaran Fleet.

"How long would it take to complete the preparations for the first wave of the fleet?"

"Princeps, the fleet is still in the last phase of construction. At least sixty thousand more hours are needed before the ships are spaceworthy."

"I will soon present my plan for approval by the Joint Session of Consuls. After construction is complete, the fleet should set sail in that direction at once."

"Princeps, given the frequency of the transmission, even the direction of the source cannot be ascertained with great accuracy. The fleet is only capable of cruising at one-hundredth the speed of light. Also, it only has enough power in reserve to perform one deceleration, making it impossible to conduct a wide-area search in that direction. If the distance to the target is unclear, the fleet will ultimately fall into the abyss of space."

"But look at the three suns around us. At any moment, the plasma outer layer of one of them may begin to expand and swallow its last planet, our world. We have no other choice. We must make this gamble."

33

Trisolaris: Sophon

Eighty-five thousand Trisolaran hours (about 8.6 Earth years) later

The princeps had ordered an emergency meeting of all Triso-laran consuls. This was very unusual. Something important must have happened.

Twenty thousand Trisolaran hours ago, the Trisolaran Fleet had launched. The ships knew the approximate direction of their target but not its distance. It was possible that the target was millions of light-hours away, or even at the other end of the galaxy. Faced with the endless sea of stars, the expedition had little hope.

The meeting of consuls occurred under the Pendulum Monument. [As Wang Miao read about this episode, he couldn't help but recall the session at the UN Building in the *Three Body* game. In reality, the Pendulum Monument was one of the few objects in the game that really did exist on Trisolaris.]

The princeps's choice of meeting site confused most of the attendees. The Chaotic Era wasn't over yet, and a small sun had just risen over the horizon, though it could also set at any moment. The temperature was cold, and all the

388

attendees were forced to wear fully enclosed electric-heating suits. The massive metal pendulum swung magnificently, pounding the frigid air. The small sun cast a long shadow against the ground, as if a giant whose head touched the sky were striding there. Under the watchful eyes of the crowd, the princeps ascended onto the base of the pendulum and flipped a red switch.

He turned to the consuls and said, "I have just shut off power to the pendulum. It will gradually stop under the influence of air resistance."

"Princeps, why?" a consul asked.

"We all understand the historical significance of the pendulum. It's intended to hypnotize God. But now we know it's better for Trisolaran civilization to have God awake, because God is now blessing us."

Everyone was silent, pondering the meaning of the princeps's words. After three more swings from the pendulum, someone asked, "Has the Earth responded?"

The princeps nodded. "Yes. Half an hour ago I received the report. It was a response to the warning that was sent."

"So soon! Only eighty thousand hours have passed since then, which means . . . which means . . ."

"Which means that the Earth is only forty thousand light-hours from us."

"Isn't that the closest star from here?"

"Yes. That is why I said God is blessing Trisolaran civilization."

The attendees grew ecstatic, but they couldn't express the feeling, so the crowd seemed like a pent-up volcano. The princeps knew that allowing such weak emotions to explode would be dangerous. So he poured cold water on their sentiments.

"I have already ordered the Trisolaran Fleet to turn toward this star. But things are not quite as optimistic as you think. Given what we know, right now the fleet is sailing toward certain death."

The consuls calmed down.

"Does anyone understand my conclusion?"

"I do," said the science consul. "We've all studied the first messages from Earth carefully. The section most worthy of attention is their history. Let's observe the facts: Humans took more than a hundred thousand Earth years to progress from the Hunter-Gatherer Age to the Agricultural Age. To get from the Agricultural Age to the Industrial Age took a few thousand Earth years. But to go from the Industrial Age to the Atomic Age took only two hundred Earth years. Thereafter, in only a few Earth decades, they entered the Information Age. This civilization possesses the terrifying ability to accelerate their progress.

"On Trisolaris, of the more than two hundred civilizations, including our own, none has ever experienced such accelerating development. The progress of science and technology in all Trisolaran civilizations has been at a constant or decelerating pace. In our world, each technology age requires approximately the same amount of time for steady, slow development."

The princeps nodded. "The fact is that four million and five hundred thousand hours from now, when the Trisolaran Fleet has reached the Earth, that civilization's technology level will have long surpassed ours, due to their accelerating development. The journey of the Trisolaran Fleet is long and arduous, and the fleet must pass through two interstellar dust belts. It's very likely that only half of the ships will reach the Earth's solar system, while the rest perish along the way.

And then, the Trisolaran Fleet will be at the mercy of a much more powerful Earth civilization. This is not an expedition, but a funeral procession!"

"But if this is true, Princeps, then there are even more frightening consequences . . ." the military consul said.

"Yes. It's easy to imagine. The location of Trisolaris has been exposed. To eliminate future threats, an interstellar fleet from Earth will launch a counterattack against us. It's very possible that long before an expanded sun swallows this planet, Trisolaran civilization will have already been extinguished by humans."

The bright future had suddenly turned impossibly grim. The attendees fell silent.

The princeps said, "What we must do next is contain the progress of science on Earth. Luckily, as soon as we received the first messages from Earth, we began to develop plans to do so. As of now, we've discovered a favorable condition for realizing these plans: The response we just received was sent by an Earth traitor. Thus, we have reason to believe that there are many alienated forces within Earth civilization, and we must exploit such forces to the fullest."

"Princeps, that is not at all easy. We have but a thin thread of communication with the Earth. It takes more than eighty thousand hours to complete an exchange."

"But remember that, like us, the knowledge that there are extraterrestrial civilizations will shock all of Earth society and leave profound marks. We have reason to believe that the alienated forces within Earth civilization will coalesce and grow."

"What can they do? Sabotage?"

"Given a time gap of forty thousand hours, the strategic value of any traditional tactics of war or terror is insignificant, and they can recover from them. To effectively contain a civilization's development and disarm it across such a long span of time, there is only one way: kill its science."

The science consul said, "The plan focuses on emphasizing the negative environmental effects of scientific development and showing signs of supernatural power to the population of Earth. In addition to highlighting the negative effects of progress, we'll also attempt to use a series of 'miracles' to construct an illusory universe that cannot be explained by the logic of science. After these illusions have been maintained for some time, it's possible that Trisolaran civilization may become a target of religious worship there. Then, unscientific ways of thinking will dominate scientific thinking among human intellectuals, and lead to the collapse of the entire scientific system of thought."

"How do we create miracles?"

"The key to miracles is that they cannot be seen as tricks. This may require that we transfer certain technologies far above current human technology level to the alienated forces on Earth."

"That's too risky! Who knows who will ultimately control such technologies? That's playing with fire."

"Of course, which specific technologies should be transferred to produce miracles requires further study. . . ."

"Please hold on for a moment, Science Consul," said the military consul as he stood up. "Princeps, I am of the opinion that this plan will be almost useless in terms of stopping human science."

"But it's better than nothing," the science consul argued.

"Barely," the military consul said contemptuously.

"I agree with your view," the princeps said. "This plan will only interfere slightly with human scientific development.

We need a decisive act that will completely suffocate science on Earth and freeze it at its current level. Let's focus on the key here: Overall technological development depends on the advancement of basic science, and the foundation of basic science lies in the exploration of the deep structure of matter. If there's no progress in this field, there can be no major breakthrough in science and technology as a whole. Of course, this is not specific to civilization on Earth. It is applicable to all targets that Trisolaran civilization intends to conquer. We had begun work in this area even before receiving the first extra-Trisolaran communication. But we've recently stepped up the effort.

"Now, everyone, look up. What's that?"

The princeps pointed at the sky. The consuls lifted their heads to gaze in that direction. They saw a ring in space giving off a metallic glow in the sunlight.

"Is that the dock for building the second space fleet?"

"No. That's a large particle accelerator still under construction. The plans for building a second space fleet have been scrapped. All resources are now devoted to Project Sophon."

"Project Sophon?"

"Yes. We've kept this plan secret from most of you present. I now ask the science consul to give an introduction."

"I knew about this plan, but didn't know it had progressed so far." The speaker was the industry consul.

The culture and education consul said, "I knew about this plan as well, but thought it was like a fairy tale."

The science consul said, "Project Sophon, to put it simply, aims to transform a proton into a superintelligent computer."[42]

---

42 *Translator's Note:* There is a pun in Chinese between the word for a proton, *zhizi* (智子), and the word for a sophon, *zhizi* (智子).

"This is a science fantasy that most of us have heard about," the agricultural consul said. "But can it be realized? I know that physicists can already manipulate nine of the eleven dimensions of the micro-scale world, but we still can't imagine how they could stick a pair of tiny tweezers into a proton to build large-scale integrated circuits."

"Of course that's impossible. The etching of micro integrated circuits can only occur at the macro scale, and only on a macroscopic two-dimensional plane. Thus, we must unfold a proton into two dimensions."

"Unfold a nine-dimensional structure into two dimensions? How big would the area be?"

"Very big, as you will see." The science consul smiled.

Another sixty thousand Trisolaran hours went by. Twenty thousand Trisolaran hours after the completion of the huge particle accelerator in space, the unfolding of the proton into two dimensions was about to begin in a synchronous orbit around Trisolaris.

It was a beautiful and mild Stable Era day. The sky was particularly clear. Like the day when the fleet had set sail eighty thousand Trisolaran hours ago, the entire population of Trisolaris looked up into the sky, gazing at that giant ring. The princeps and all the consuls again came and stood under the Pendulum Monument. The pendulum had long stopped, and the weight hung still like a solid rock between the tall pillars. Looking at it, it was hard to believe that it had once moved.

The science consul gave the order to unfold into two dimensions. In space, three cubes drifted around the ring— the fusion generators that powered the accelerator. Their winglike heat sinks gradually began to glow with a dim reddish light. The crowd anxiously stared at the accelerator, but nothing seemed to happen.

A tenth of a Trisolaran hour later, the science consul held his earpiece to his ear and listened intently. Then he said, "Princeps, unfortunately, the unfolding failed. We reduced the dimensions by one too many, and the proton became one-dimensional."

"One-dimensional? A line?"

"Yes. An infinitely thin line. Theoretically, it should be about fifteen hundred light-hours long."

"We spent the resources intended for another space fleet," said the military consul, "just to obtain a result like this?"

"In scientific experiments, there has to be a process during which kinks are worked out. After all, this was the very first time the unfolding has been tried."

The crowd dispersed in disappointment, but the experiment wasn't over. Originally, it was thought that the one-dimensional proton would stay in synchronous orbit around Trisolaris forever, but due to friction from solar winds, pieces of the string fell back into the atmosphere. Six Trisolaran hours later, everyone outside noticed the strange lights in the air, gossamer threads that flickered in and out of existence. They soon learned from the news that this was the one-dimensional proton drifting to the ground under the influence of gravity. Even though the string was infinitely thin, it produced a field that could still reflect visible light. It was the first time people had ever seen matter not made out of atoms—the silky strands were merely small portions of a proton.

"These things are so annoying." The princeps brushed his hand against his face over and over. He and the science consul were standing on the wide steps in front of Government Center. "My face always feels itchy."

"Princeps, the feeling is purely psychological. All the strings added together have the mass of a single proton, so it's impossible for them to have any effect on the macroscopic world. They can't do any harm. It's as if they don't exist."

But the threads that fell from the sky grew more numerous and denser. Closer to ground, tiny sparkling lights filled the air. The sun and the stars all appeared inside silvery halos. The strings clung to those who went outside, and as they walked, they dragged the lights behind them. When people returned indoors, the lines glimmered under the lamps. As soon as they moved, the reflection from the strings revealed the patterns in the air currents they disturbed. Although the one-dimensional string could only be seen under light and couldn't be felt, people became upset.

The torrent of one-dimensional strings continued for more than twenty Trisolaran hours before finally ending, though not because the strings had all fallen to the ground. Although their mass was unimaginably minuscule, they still had some, and so their acceleration under gravity was the same as normal matter. However, once inside the atmosphere, they were completely dominated by the air currents and would never fall to the ground. After being unfolded into one dimension, the strong nuclear force within the proton became far more attenuated, weakening the string. Gradually, it broke into tiny pieces, and the light they reflected was no longer visible. People thought they had disappeared, but pieces of the one-dimensional string would drift in the air of Trisolaris forever.

Fifty Trisolaran hours later, the second attempt to unfold a proton into two dimensions began. Soon, the crowd on the ground saw something odd. After the heat sinks of the fusion generators began to glow red, several colossal objects appeared near the accelerator. All of them were in the form of regular geometric solids: spheres, tetrahedrons, cubes, cones, and so on. Their surfaces had complex coloration, but close examination showed that they were, in fact, colorless. The surfaces of the geometric solids were completely reflective, and what the people saw were just distorted, reflected images of the surface of Trisolaris.

"Have we succeeded?" the princeps asked. "Is that the proton unfolded into two dimensions?"

The science consul replied, "Princeps, it's still a failure. I just received the report from the accelerator control center. The unfolding left one too many dimensions in, and the proton was unfolded into three dimensions."

The giant, reflective geometric solids continued to pop into existence in great numbers, and their forms became more various. There were tori, solid crosses, and even something that looked like a Möbius strip. All the geometric solids drifted away from the location of the accelerator. About half an hour later, the solids filled more than half the sky, as though a giant child had emptied a box of building blocks in the firmament. The light reflected from the mirror surfaces doubled the brilliance of the light hitting the ground, but the intensity continuously shifted. The shadow of the giant pendulum flickered in and out, and swayed from side to side.

Then, all the geometric solids began to deform. They gradually lost their regular shapes, as though they were melting in heat. The deformation accelerated and the resulting lumps became more and more complex. Now the objects in the sky no longer reminded people of building blocks, but of a giant's dismembered limbs and disemboweled viscera. Because their shapes were no longer so regular, the light they reflected to the ground became softer, but their own surface coloration turned even more strange and unpredictable.

Out of the mess of three-dimensional objects, a few in particular drew special attention from observers on the ground. At first, it was only because the objects in question were very similar to each other. But upon closer examination, people recognized them, and a wave of terror swept Trisolaris.

They were all eyes! [Of course, we don't know what Trisolaran eyes look like, but we can be certain that any intelligent life would be very sensitive to representations of eyes.]

The princeps was one of the few who kept calm. He asked the science consul, "How complicated can the internal structure of a subatomic particle be?"

"It depends on the number of dimensions of your observation perspective. From a one-dimensional perspective, it's only a point—that's how ordinary people think of the particles. From a two- or three-dimensional perspective, the particle begins to show internal structure. From a four-dimensional perspective, a fundamental particle is an immense world."

The princeps said, "To use a word like 'immense' to describe a subatomic particle such as a proton seems incredible to me."

The science consul ignored the princeps and continued, "As we move to higher dimensions, the complexity and number of structures within a particle increase dramatically. The comparisons I'm about to make will not be precise, but should give you an idea of the scale. A particle seen from a seven-dimensional perspective has a complexity comparable to our Trisolaran stellar system in three dimensions. From an eight-dimensional perspective, a particle is a vast presence like the Milky Way. When the perspective has been raised to nine dimensions, a fundamental particle's internal structures and complexity are equal to the whole universe. As for even higher dimensions, our physicists haven't been able to explore them, so we cannot yet imagine the degree of complexity."

The princeps pointed to the giant eyes in space. "Do these show that the microcosmos contained within the unfolded proton harbors intelligent life?"

"Our definition of 'life' is probably not appropriate for the high-dimensional microcosmos. More accurately, we can only say that universe contains intelligence or wisdom. Scientists have long predicted this possibility. It would have been odd for such a complex and vast world to not have evolved something akin to intelligence."

"Why have they transformed into eyes to look at us?" The princeps looked up at the eyes in space, beautiful, life-like sculptures, all of them gazing upon the planet below strangely.

"Maybe they just want to demonstrate their presence."

"Can they fall down here?"

"Not at all. You may rest easy, Princeps. Even if they were to fall, the mass of all these huge structures added together is only that of a proton. Just like the one-dimensional string from last time, they won't have any effect on our world. People just have to get used to the strange sight."

But this time, the science consul was wrong.

People noticed the eyes moved faster than the other solids filling the sky, and they were gathering into one spot. Soon, two eyes met and merged into one bigger eye. More and more eyes joined this big eye, and its volume grew. Finally, all the eyes melded into one. It was so large that it seemed to represent the gaze of the universe upon Trisolaris. The iris was clear and bright, and at the center was the image of a sun. Over the broad surface of the eyeball, various colors cascaded in a flood. Soon, the details over the giant eye faded and gradually disappeared, until it became a pupil-less blind eye. Then it began to deform until it finally lost the shape of an eye and became a perfect circle. When the circle began to slowly rotate, people realized that it was not flat, but parabolic, like a slice cut from a giant sphere.

As the military consul stared at the slowly spinning colossal object in space, he suddenly understood and shouted, "Princeps and others, please go into the underground bunker right away." He pointed upward. "That is—"

"A parabolic mirror," the princeps said calmly. "Direct the space defense forces to destroy it. We will stay right here."

The parabolic mirror focused the sun's beams onto the surface of Trisolaris. Initially, the spot of light was very large, and the heat at the focal point wasn't yet lethal. This spot moved across the ground, searching for its target. The mirror discovered the capital, the largest city of Trisolaris, and the light spot began to move toward it. Soon, the beam was over the city.

Those standing under the Pendulum Monument only saw a great brightness in space. It overwhelmed everything else, accompanied by a wave of extreme heat. Then the light spot over the capital shrank as the parabolic mirror began to focus the light more tightly. The brightness from space grew stronger until no one could lift up his head, and those standing within the spot felt the temperature rise rapidly. Just as the heat became unbearable, the edge of the light spot swept past the Pendulum Monument and everything dimmed. It took a while before the crowd's sight readjusted to normal light.

When they looked up, the first sight that greeted them was a pillar of light between the sky and earth, shaped like an inverted cone. The mirror in space formed the base of the cone, and the tip stabbed into the heart of the capital, turning everything there incandescent at once. Waves of smoke began to rise. Tornadoes caused by the uneven heat of the light cone formed several other pillars made of dust that connected to the sky, twisting and dancing around the light cone. . . .

Several brilliant fireballs appeared in different parts of the mirror, their blue color distinct from the light reflected from the mirror. These were the exploding nuclear warheads launched by the Trisolaran space defense corps. Because the explosions were happening outside the atmosphere, there was no sound. By the time the fireballs disappeared, several large holes appeared in the mirror, and then the entire surface of the mirror began to tear and crack, until it had broken into more than a dozen pieces.

The deadly light cone disappeared and the world returned to a normal level of illumination. For a moment, the sky was as dim as a moonlit night. Those broken pieces of the mirror, now devoid of intelligence, continued to deform and soon could not be distinguished from the other geometric solids in space.

"What will happen with the next experiment?" The princeps's expression was derisive as he spoke to the science consul. "Will you unfold a proton into four dimensions?"

"Princeps, even if that were to occur, it's nothing to worry about. A proton unfolded into four dimensions will be much smaller. If the space defense corps is prepared to attack its projection in three-dimensional space, it can be destroyed just the same."

"You're deceiving the princeps!" said a furious military consul. "You have not mentioned the real danger. What if the proton is unfolded into zero dimensions?"

"Zero dimensions?" The princeps was interested. "Wouldn't that be a point with no size?"

"Yes, a singularity! Even a proton would be infinitely big compared to it. The entire mass of the proton will be contained in this singularity, and its density will be infinite. Princeps, I'm sure you can imagine what that would be."

"A black hole?"

"Yes."

"Princeps, let me explain," the science consul broke in. "The reason we picked a proton instead of a neutron to unfold into two dimensions is precisely to avoid this kind of risk. If we really were to unfold into zero dimensions, the charge of a proton would also be carried over into the unfolded black hole. We can then capture and control it using electromagnetism."

"What if you can't find it or control it?" the military consul asked. "It can then land on the ground, suck in everything it encounters, and increase its mass. Then it will sink into the core of this planet and eventually suck down all of Trisolaris."

"That will never happen. I guarantee it! Why are you always making things difficult for me? Like I said, this is a scientific experiment—"

"That's enough!" the princeps said. "What is the probability of success next time?"

"Almost one hundred percent! Princeps, please believe in me. Through these two failures, we have already mastered the principles governing unfolding subatomic structures into low-dimensional macro space."

"All right. To ensure the survival of Trisolaran civilization, we must take this risk."

"Thank you!"

"But if you fail again, you and all the scientists working on Project Sophon will be guilty."

402

"Yes, of course, all guilty." If Trisolarans could perspire, the science consul must have been soaked in cold sweat.

It was much easier to clean up the three-dimensional remnants of the unfolded proton in synchronous orbit than it was to clean up the one-dimensional string. Small spaceships were able to drag the pieces of proton matter away from Trisolaris and prevent them from entering the atmosphere. Those objects, some as large as mountains, had almost no mass. They were like immense silver illusions; even a baby could have moved them easily.

Afterwards, the princeps asked the science consul, "Did we destroy a civilization in the microcosmos in this experiment?"

"It was at least an intelligent body. Also, Princeps, we destroyed the entire microcosmos. That miniature universe is immense in higher dimensions, and it probably contained more than one intelligence or civilization that never had a chance to express themselves in macro space. Of course, in higher dimensional space at such micro scales, the form that intelligence or civilization may take is beyond our imagination. They're something else entirely. And such destruction has probably occurred many times before."

"Oh?"

"In the long history of scientific progress, how many protons have been smashed apart in accelerators by physicists? How many neutrons and electrons? Probably no fewer than a hundred million. Every collision was probably the end of the civilizations and intelligences in a microcosmos. In fact, even in nature, the destruction of universes must be happening at every second—for example, through the decay of neutrons. Also, a high-energy cosmic ray entering the atmosphere may destroy thousands of such miniature universes. . . . You're not feeling sentimental because of this, are you?"

"You amuse me. I will immediately notify the propaganda consul and direct him to repeatedly publicize this scientific fact to the world. The people of Trisolaris must understand that the destruction of civilizations is a common occurrence that happens every second of every hour."

"Why? Do you wish to encourage the people to face the possible destruction of Trisolaran civilization with equanimity?"

"No. It's to encourage them to face the destruction of Earth civilization with equanimity. You know very well that after we publicized our policy toward the Earth civilization, there was a wave of extremely dangerous pacifism. We have only now discovered that there are many like the listener of Post 1379. We must control and eliminate these weak sentiments."

"Princeps, this is mainly the result of recent messages received from the Earth. Your prediction has come true: The alienated forces on Earth really are growing. They have built a new transmission site completely under their control, and have begun to send us large amounts of information about Earth civilization. I must admit that their civilization has great appeal on Trisolaris. For our people, it sounds like sacred music from Heaven. The humanism of Earth will lead many Trisolarans onto the wrong path. Just as Trisolaran civilization has already become a religion on Earth, Earth civilization has this potential on Trisolaris."

"You've pointed out a great danger. We must strictly control the flow of information from the Earth to the populace, especially cultural information."

The third attempt to unfold a proton into two dimensions began thirty Trisolaran hours later. This time, it was at night. From the ground, it was impossible to see the ring of the accelerator in space. Only the red glow from the heat sinks of the fusion reactors around it marked its location. Shortly after the accelerator was started, the science consul announced success.

People gazed up at the night sky. Initially, there was nothing to see. But soon, they saw a miraculous sight: The heavens separated into two pieces. Between the two, the pattern of the stars did not match, as though two photographs of the sky had been stacked together, with the smaller one overlaid on top of the big one. The Milky Way broke at the border between the two. The smaller portion of the star-studded firmament was circular, and it rapidly expanded against the normal night sky.

"That constellation in there belongs to the southern hemisphere!" the culture and education consul said, pointing at the expanding, circular patch of the sky.

As people exercised their imaginations to understand how stars that could be seen only from the other side of the planet were now superimposed over the northern hemisphere's view, an even more astonishing sight appeared: At the edge of the expanding patch of the night sky from the southern hemisphere, a part of a giant globe appeared. The globe was brownish, and it was being revealed a stripe at a time, as though on a display with a very slow refresh rate. Everyone recognized the globe: On it were the clear outlines of familiar continents. By the time the entire globe came into view, it already occupied one-third of the sky. More details on the globe could be made out: the wrinkles of mountain ranges covering the brownish continents, the scattered cloud cover like patches of snow over the continents . . .

Someone finally blurted out, "That's our planet!"

Yes, another Trisolaris had appeared in the sky.

Next, the sky brightened. Next to the second Trisolaris in space, the expanding circle of the night sky from the southern hemisphere revealed another sun. This was clearly the same sun that currently was shining over the southern hemisphere, but it appeared at only half the size.

Finally, someone figured it out. "It's a mirror."

The immense mirror that appeared over Trisolaris was the proton being unfolded, a geometric plane without any meaningful depth.

By the time the unfolding was complete, the entire sky had been replaced by the reflection of the night sky of the southern hemisphere. Directly overhead, the sky was dominated by the reflection of Trisolaris and the sun. And then the sky began to deform just above the horizon all around, and the reflections of the stars stretched and twisted as though they were melting. The deformation began at the edges of the mirror, but climbed up toward the center.

"Princeps, the proton plane is being bent by our planet's gravity," the science consul said. He pointed to the numerous spots of light in the starry sky. They looked as though people were waving flashlights up at the domed vault. "Those are electromagnetic beams being sent up from the ground to adjust the curvature of the plane under gravity. The goal is to eventually wrap the unfolded proton completely around Trisolaris. Afterwards, the electromagnetic beams will continue to hold up and stabilize this enormous sphere, like so many spokes. Thus, Trisolaris will be the workbench to secure the two-dimensional proton, and the work to etch electronic circuits on the surface of the proton plane can begin."

The process of wrapping the two-dimensional proton plane around Trisolaris took a long time. By the time the deformation of the reflection reached the image of Trisolaris at the plane's zenith, the stars had all disappeared because the proton plane, now curved around the other side of the planet, blocked them completely. Some sunlight continued to leak inside the curved proton plane, and the image of Trisolaris in this fun-house mirror in space was distorted beyond recognition. But, finally, after the last ray of sunlight was blocked, everything sank into the darkest night in the history of Trisolaris. As gravity and the electromagnetic beams balanced each other, the proton plane formed a gigantic shell in synchronous orbit around Trisolaris.

Bitter cold followed. The completely reflective proton plane deflected all sunlight back into space. The temperature on Trisolaris dropped precipitously, reaching levels comparable to the appearance of three flying stars, which had ruined many cycles of civilization in the past. Most of the population of Trisolaris dehydrated and were stored. A deathly silence fell over much of the darkness-enclosed surface. In the sky, only the faint light spots from the beams that held up the proton membrane flickered. Occasionally, a few other tiny, sharp lights could be seen in synchronous orbit: the spaceships etching circuits into the gigantic membrane.

The principles governing micro-scale integrated circuits were completely different from those of conventional circuits, as the base material wasn't made of atoms, but matter from a single proton. The "p-n junctions" of the circuits were formed by twisting the strong nuclear forces locally on the surface of the proton plane, and the conducting lines were made of mesons that could transmit the nuclear force. Because the surface area for the circuit was extremely large, the circuits were also very large. The circuit lines were as thick as hairs, and an observer close enough could see them with the naked eye. Flying close to the proton membrane, it could be seen as a vast plane made of complex, elaborate integrated circuits. The total area covered by the circuits was dozens of times the area of the continents on Trisolaris.

Etching the proton circuits was a huge engineering feat, and thousands of spaceships worked for more than fifteen thousand Trisolaran hours to complete it. The software debugging process took another five thousand Trisolaran hours. But finally, it was time to test the sophon for the first time.

The big screen at the sophon control center deep underground showed the progress of the long self-test sequence. Next came the loading of the operating system. Finally, the blank blue screen showed a line of large-font text: *Micro-Intelligence 2.10 loaded. Sophon One ready to accept commands.*

The science consul said, "A sophon has been born. We have endowed a proton with wisdom. This is the smallest artificial intelligence that we can make."

"But right now, it appears as the largest artificial intelligence," said the princeps.

"As soon as we increase the dimensionality of this proton, it will become very small."

The science consul entered a query at the terminal:

> Sophon One, are the spatial dimensionality controls
  operational?
Affirmative. Sophon One is capable of initiating spatial
  dimensionality adjustments at any moment.
> Adjust dimensionality to three.

After this command was issued, the two-dimensional proton membrane that had wrapped itself around Trisolaris began to shrink rapidly, as though a giant's hand was pulling away a curtain over the world. In a moment, sunlight bathed the ground. The proton folded from two dimensions into three and became a gargantuan sphere in synchronous orbit, about the size of the giant moon. The sophon was over the dark side of the planet, but the sunlight reflected from its mirror surface turned the night into day. The surface of Trisolaris was still extremely cold, so the crowd inside the control center could only observe these changes through a screen.

> Dimensionality adjustment successful. Sophon One is
> ready to accept commands.
> > Adjust dimensionality to four.

In space, the gargantuan sphere shrank until it eventually looked to be the size of a flying star. Night again descended over this side of the planet.

"Princeps, the sphere we see now is not the complete sophon. It's only the projection of the sophon's body into three-dimensional space. It is, in fact, a giant in four-space, and our world is like a thin, three-dimensional sheet of paper. The giant stands on this sheet of paper, and we can only see the trace where its feet touch the paper."

> Dimensionality adjustment successful. Sophon One is
> ready to accept commands.
> > Adjust dimensionality to six.

The sphere in the sky disappeared.

"How big is a six-dimensional proton?" the princeps asked.

"About fifty centimeters in radius," the science consul replied.

Dimensionality adjustment successful. Sophon One is
   ready to accept commands.
> Sophon One, can you see us?
Yes. I can see the control center, everyone inside, and
   the organs inside everyone, even the organs inside
   your organs.

"What is it saying?" The princeps was stunned.

"A sophon observing three-space from six-space is akin
to us looking at a picture on a two-dimensional plane. Of
course it can see inside us."

> Sophon One, enter the control center.

"Can it go through the ground?" the princeps asked.

"It's not exactly going 'through.' Rather, it's entering from
a higher dimension. It can enter any enclosed space within
our world. This is again similar to the relationship between
us, existing in three-space, and a two-dimensional plane. We
can easily enter any circle drawn on the plane by coming in
from above. But no two-dimensional creature on the plane
can do such a thing without breaking the circle."

Just as the science consul finished, a mirror-surfaced
sphere appeared in the middle of the control center, floating in air. The princeps walked over and gazed at his own
distorted reflection. "This is a proton?" He was amazed.

"This is the six-dimensional body of the proton projected
into three-space."

The princeps extended a hand. When he saw that the science consul did not object, he touched the surface of the
sophon. A very light touch pushed the sophon a considerable
distance.

"It's very smooth. Even though it has only the mass of a proton, I could feel some resistance against my hand." The princeps was puzzled.

"That's due to air resistance against the surface of the sphere."

"Can you increase its dimensionality to eleven, and make it as small as a regular proton?"

As soon as the princeps said this, the science consul shouted to the sophon, his voice tinged with fear, "Attention! This is *not* a command!"

Sophon One understands.

"Princeps, if we increased the dimensionality to eleven, we would lose it forever. When the sophon shrinks to the size of a regular subatomic particle, the internal sensors and I/O ports will be smaller than the wavelength of any electromagnetic radiation. That means it would not be able to sense the macro world, and would not be able to receive our commands."

"But we must eventually make it shrink back to a sub-atomic particle."

"Yes, but that must await the completion of Sophon Two, Sophon Three, and Sophon Four. Multiple sophons may be able to form a system to sense the macro world through quantum effects. For example, suppose a nucleus has two protons. The two of them will interact and follow certain patterns of motion. Take spin: Maybe the direction of spin of the two protons must be opposite from each other. When these two protons are taken out of the nucleus, no matter how far apart they are, this pattern will remain in effect. When both protons are made into sophons, they will, based on this effect, create a mutual-sensing system. More sophons can then form a mutual-sensing formation. This formation's scale can be adjusted to any size, and can thus receive electromagnetic waves to sense the macro world at any frequency. Of course, the actual quantum effects necessary to create such a sophon formation are very complicated. My explanation is only an analogy."

The unfolding of the next three protons into two dimensions succeeded on the first try. The construction of each sophon also took only half as long as Sophon One. After the construction of Sophon Two, Sophon Three, and Sophon Four, the quantum sensing formation was also created successfully.

The princeps and all the consuls once again came to the Pendulum Monument. Above them hovered four sophons shrunk to six-space. In the crystalline mirrored surface of each was an image of the rising sun, recalling the three-dimensional eyes that had once appeared in space.

> Sophon formation, adjust dimensionality to eleven.

After the command was issued, the four mirrored spheres disappeared. The science consul said, "Princeps, now Sophon One and Sophon Two will be launched toward the Earth. Using the large knowledge base stored in the micro circuits, the sophons understand the nature of space. They can draw energy from the vacuum and become high-energy particles in a moment, and navigate through space at nearly the speed of light. This might appear to violate the law of conservation of energy, but in fact the sophons are only 'borrowing' energy from the structure of vacuum. However, the time for returning such energy is far in the future, when the proton decays.

By then, the end of the universe will not be far.

"After the two sophons arrive on Earth, their first mission is to locate the high-energy particle accelerators used by humans for physics research and hide within them. At the level of science development on the Earth, the basic method for exploring the deep structure of matter is to use accelerated high-energy particles to collide with target particles. After the target particles have been smashed, they analyze the results to try to find information reflecting the deep structure of matter. In actual experiments, they use the substance containing the target particles as the bull's-eye for the accelerated bullets.

"But the inside of the substance being struck is almost all vacuum. Suppose an atom is the size of a theater; the nucleus is like a walnut hovering in the center of the theater. Thus, successful collisions are very rare. Often large quantities of high-energy particles must be directed against the target substance for a sustained period of time before a collision occurs. This kind of experiment is akin to looking for a raindrop of a slightly different color in a summer thunderstorm.

"This gives the sophons an opening. A sophon can take the place of a target particle and accept the collision. Because they're highly intelligent, they can precisely determine through the quantum sensing formation the paths that the accelerated particles will follow within a very short period of time and move to the appropriate location. Thus, the likelihood that a sophon will be struck will be billions of times greater than the actual target particle. After a sophon is struck, it can deliberately give out wrong and chaotic results. Thus, even if the actual target particle is occasionally struck, Earth physicists will not be able to tell the correct result from the numerous erroneous results."

"Wouldn't this destroy the sophon as well?" asked the military consul.

"No. When a sophon is smashed into several pieces, several new sophons are born. And they continue to have secure quantum entanglements between them, just like how, if you break a magnet in half, you would get two magnets. Even though each partial sophon's capabilities will be much lower than the original, whole sophon, under the direction of the self-healing software, the pieces will move together and reassemble into the original sophon. This process only requires a microsecond and will occur after the collision in the accelerator, and after the pieces of the sophon have left the wrong results in the bubble chamber or on sensitive film."

Someone asked, "Would it be possible for Earth scientists to find a way to detect sophons and then use a strong magnetic field to imprison them? Protons have positive charge."

"That's impossible. To detect sophons requires humans to make breakthroughs in the study of the deep structure of matter. But their high-energy accelerators will all have been turned into heaps of junk. How can they make progress in such research? The hunter's eyes have already been blinded by the prey he intends to catch."

"Humans may still resort to a brute-force method," the industry consul said. "They can build a large number of accelerators, faster than the rate at which we can build sophons. Then, at least some accelerators on Earth will not be infiltrated by sophons and can yield the correct results."

"This is one of the most interesting aspects of Project Sophon!" The science consul was visibly excited by the question. "Mister Industry Consul, do not worry that creating large numbers of sophons will cause the collapse of the Trisolaran economy. We will not need to resort to that. We might build a few more, but not too many. Indeed, just these two are more than enough, because each sophon is capable of multitasking."

"Multitasking?"

"This is a bit of jargon related to ancient serial computers. Back then, a computer's central processing unit could only carry out a single instruction at a time. But, because it was so fast, and aided by interrupt scheduling, from our low-speed perspective, the computer was carrying out multiple programs at the same time. As you know, the sophons move at close to the speed of light. The surface of the Earth is a tiny space for sophons. If sophons patrol around the accelerators on Earth at this speed, then, from the perspective of humans, it is as if they simultaneously exist in all the accelerators and can almost simultaneously create erroneous results in all the accelerators.

"By our calculations, each sophon is capable of controlling more than ten thousand high-energy accelerators. It takes about four to five years for humans to build each of these accelerators, and it seems unlikely that they can be mass produced based on their economy and available resources. Of course, they can increase the distance between the accelerators, for example, by building accelerators on the different planets in their planetary system. That would indeed destroy the multitasking operation of the sophons. But in the time it would take to do that, it would not be difficult for Trisolaris to build ten or more sophons.

"More and more sophons will wander in that planetary system. Added all together, they still won't add up to the mass of even one-billionth of a bacterium. But they will cause the physicists on Earth to never be able to glimpse the secrets hidden deep in the structure of matter. Humans will never be able to access the micro dimensions, and the ability for them to manipulate matter will be limited to below five dimensions. From now on, whether it's four point five million hours or four hundred and fifty trillion hours, Earth civilization's technology will never achieve this fundamental breakthrough. They will remain forever in the primitive stage. The science of Earth has been completely locked down, and the lock is so secure that humans will never be able to escape from it by their own strength."

"That's wonderful! Please forgive my lack of respect for Project Sophon in the past." The military consul's tone was sincere.

"In fact, there are currently only three accelerators with sufficient power to produce results that can lead to possible breakthroughs. After Sophon One and Sophon Two arrive on Earth, they will have a lot of extra capacity. In order to fully utilize the sophons, we will assign them other tasks in addition to interfering with the three accelerators. For example, they will be the main means to carry out the Miracle Plan."

"Sophons can create miracles?"

"For humans, yes. Everyone knows that high-energy particles can expose film. This is one of the ways that primitive accelerators on Earth once showed individual particles. When a sophon passes through the film at high energy, it leaves behind a tiny exposed spot. If a sophon passes back and forth through the film many times, it can connect the dots to form letters or numbers or even pictures, like embroidery. The process is very fast, and far quicker than the speed at which humans expose film when taking a picture. Also, the human retina is similar to the Trisolaran one. Thus, a high-energy sophon can also use the same technique to show letters, numbers, or images on their retina. . . . And if these little miracles can confuse and terrify humans, then the next *great* miracle will be sufficient to frighten their scientists—no better than bugs—to death: Sophons can cause background cosmic radiation to flash in their eyes."

"This would be very frightening for our scientists as well. How would this be accomplished?"

"Very simple. We have already written the software to allow a sophon to unfold itself into two dimensions. After the unfolding is complete, the huge plane can wrap itself around the Earth. This software can also adjust the membrane so that it's transparent, but the degree of transparency can be tuned in the frequencies of the cosmic microwave background. . . . Of course, as sophons fold and unfold into different dimensions, they can display even more amazing 'miracles.' The software for accomplishing these is still being developed, but these 'miracles' will create a mood sufficient to divert human scientific thought onto the wrong path. This way, we can use the Miracle Plan to effectively restrain scientific endeavors outside of physics on Earth."

"One last question: Why not send all four of the completed sophons to Earth?"

"Quantum entanglement can work at a distance. Even if four sophons were placed at opposite ends of the universe, they could still sense each other instantaneously, and the quantum formation between them would still exist. Keeping Sophon Three and Sophon Four here will enable them to receive the information sent back by Sophon One and Sophon Two instantaneously. This gives us a way to monitor the Earth in real time. Also, the sophon formation allows Trisolaris to communicate in real time with the alienated forces within Earth civilization."

Unnoticed, the sun that had just risen disappeared below the horizon and turned into a sunset. Another Chaotic Era had arrived on Trisolaris.

While Ye Wenjie was reading the messages from Trisolaris, the Battle Command Center was hosting another important meeting to perform further analysis of the captured data. Before the meeting, General Chang said, "Comrades, please be aware that our meeting is probably already being monitored by sophons. From now on, there will be no more secrets."

When he said this, the surroundings were still familiar. The shadows of summer trees swayed against the drawn curtains, but in the eyes of the attendees, the world was no longer the same. They felt the gaze of omnipresent eyes. Under these eyes, there was nowhere to hide in the world. This feeling would follow them all their lives, and their descendants would not be able to escape it. It would take many, many years before humans finally made the mental adjustment to this situation.

Three seconds after General Chang finished his remark, Trisolaris communicated with humanity outside the ETO for the first time. After this, they terminated all communications with the Adventists. For the remainder of the lives of all attendees, Trisolaris never sent another message.

Everyone in the Battle Command Center saw the message in their eyes, just like Wang Miao's countdown. The message flashed into existence for only two seconds and then disappeared, but everyone got it. It was only a single sentence:

You're bugs!

34

Bugs

By the time Shi Qiang entered the door of Ding Yi's home, Wang Miao and Ding Yi were already very drunk.

The two were excited to see Shi Qiang. Wang stood up and hugged the newcomer's shoulders. "Ah, Da Shi, Officer Shi . . ."

Ding, who couldn't even stand straight, found a glass and put it on the pool table. He poured some liquor into it, and said, "Your out-of-the-box thinking was not helpful. Whether we look at those messages or not, the result four hundred years from now will be the same."

Da Shi sat down in front of the pool table, glancing at the two with a crafty gaze. "Is it really like you say? Everything's over?"

"Of course. It's all over," Ding said.

"You can't use the accelerators and can't study the structure of matter. That means it's all over?" Da Shi asked.

"Um . . . what do you think?"

"Technology is still making progress. Academician Wang and his people just created the nanomaterial—"

"Imagine an ancient kingdom, if you will. Their technology is advancing. They can invent better swords, knives, spears, et cetera. Maybe they can even invent auto-repeating crossbows that can shoot many arrows like a machine gun—"

Da Shi nodded, understanding. "But if they don't know that matter is made from molecules and atoms, they will never create missiles and satellites. They're limited by their level of science."

Ding patted Da Shi on the shoulder. "I always knew that our Officer Shi was smart. It's just that you—"

Wang took over. "The study of the deep structure of matter is the foundation of the foundations of all other sciences. If there's no progress here, everything else—I'll put it your way—is bullshit."

Ding pointed at Wang. "Academician Wang will be busy for the rest of his life, and continue to improve our swords and knives and spears. What the fuck am *I* going to do? Who the hell knows?" He threw an empty bottle onto the table and picked up a billiard ball to smash it.

"This is a good thing!" Wang lifted his glass. "We will be able to live out the rest of our lives one way or another. After this, decadence and depravity can be justified! We're bugs! Bugs that are about to go extinct! Haha . . ."

"Exactly!" Ding also lifted his glass. "They think so little of us that they don't even bother to disguise their plans for us, telling the Adventists everything. It's like how you don't need to hide the bottle of bug spray from the little critters. Let's toast the bugs! I never thought the end of the world would feel so good. Long live bugs! Long live sophons! Long live the end of the world!"

Da Shi shook his head and drained the glass. He shook his head again. "Bunch of pussies."

"What do you want?" Ding stared at Da Shi drunkenly. "You think you can cheer us up?"

420

Da Shi stood up. "Let's go."

"Where?"

"To find something to cheer you up."

"Whatever, buddy. Sit back down. Drink."

Da Shi took the two by their arms and dragged them up. "Let's go. Bring the liquor if you have to."

Downstairs, the three got into Da Shi's car. As the car started, Wang asked in slurred speech where they were going. Da Shi said, "My hometown. Not too far."

The car left the city and sped west along the Beijing-Shijiazhuang Highway. It exited the highway as soon as they were inside Hebei Province. Da Shi stopped the car and dragged his two passengers out.

As soon as Ding and Wang got out of the car, the bright afternoon sun made them squint. The wheat fields of the North China Plain spread out before them.

"What did you bring us here for?" Wang asked.

"To look at bugs." Da Shi lit one of the cigars Colonel Stanton had given him and pointed at the wheat fields with it.

Wang and Ding now noticed that the fields were covered by a layer of locusts. Every wheat stalk had a few crawling over it. On the ground, more locusts wriggled, like some thick liquid.

"They're plagued by locusts here?" Wang brushed away some locusts from a small area near the edge of the field and sat down.

"Like the dust storms, they started ten years ago. But this year is the worst."

"So what? Nothing matters now, Da Shi." Ding spoke, his voice still drunk.

"I just want to ask the two of you one question: Is the

technological gap between humans and Trisolarans greater than the one between locusts and humans?"

The question hit the two scientists like a bucket of cold water. As they stared at the clumps of locusts before them, their expressions grew solemn. They got Shi Qiang's point.

Look at them, the bugs. Humans have used everything in their power to extinguish them: every kind of poison, aerial sprays, introducing and cultivating their natural predators, searching for and destroying their eggs, using genetic modification to sterilize them, burning with fire, drowning with water. Every family has bug spray, every desk has a flyswatter under it . . . this long war has been going on for the entire history of human civilization. But the outcome is still in doubt. The bugs have not been eliminated. They still proudly live between the heavens and the earth, and their numbers have not diminished from the time before the appearance of the humans.

The Trisolarans who deemed the humans bugs seemed to have forgotten one fact: The bugs have never been truly defeated.

A small black cloud covered the sun and cast a moving shadow against the ground. This was not a common cloud, but a swarm of locusts that had just arrived. As the swarm landed in the fields nearby, the three men stood in the middle of a living shower, feeling the dignity of life on Earth. Ding Yi and Wang Miao poured the two bottles of wine they had with them on the ground beneath their feet, a toast for the bugs.

"Da Shi, thank you." Wang held out his hand.

"I thank you as well." Ding gripped Da Shi's other hand.

"Let's get back," Wang said. "There's so much to do."

35

The Ruins

No one believed that Ye Wenjie could climb Radar Peak by herself, but she did it anyway. She didn't allow anyone to help her along the way, only resting a couple of times in the abandoned sentry posts. She consumed her own vitality, the vitality that could not be renewed, without pity.

After learning the truth of Trisolaran civilization, Ye had become silent. She rarely spoke, but did make one request: She wanted to visit the ruins of Red Coast Base.

When the group of visitors ascended Radar Peak, its tip had just emerged from the cloud cover. After walking a whole day in the foggy haze, seeing the bright sun in the west and the clear blue sky was like climbing into a new world. From the top of the peak, the clouds appeared as a silver-white sea, and the rise and fall of the waves seemed like abstractions of the Greater Khingan Mountains below.

The ruins that the visitors had imagined did not exist. The base had been dismantled thoroughly, and only a patch of tall grass was left at the top. The foundations and the roads were buried below, and the whole place appeared to be a desolate wilderness. Red Coast seemed to have never happened.

But Ye soon discovered something. She walked next to a tall rock and pulled away the vines covering it, revealing the mottled, rusty surface below. Only now did the visitors understand that the rock was actually a large metallic base.

"This was the base for the antenna," Ye said. The first cry from Earth heard by an extraterrestrial world was sent from the antenna that had been here to the sun, and then, amplified, broadcast to the whole universe.

They discovered a small stone tablet next to the base, almost completely lost in the grass.

Site of Red Coast Base (1968–1987)
Chinese Academy of Sciences 1989.03.21

The tablet was so tiny. It didn't seem so much a memorial as an attempt to forget.

Ye walked to the lip of the cliff. Here, she had once ended the lives of two soldiers with her own hands. She did not look over the sea of clouds as the others were doing, but focused her gaze in one direction. Below the clouds, there was a small village called Qijiatun.

Ye's heart beat with effort, like a string on some musical instrument about to break. Black fog appeared before her eyes. She used the last bit of her strength to stay upright. Before everything sank into darkness, she wanted to see sunset at Red Coast Base one more time.

Over the western horizon, the sun that was slowly sinking into the sea of clouds seemed to melt. The ruddy sun dissolved into the clouds and spread over the sky, illuminating a large patch in magnificent, bloody red.

"My sunset," Ye whispered. "And sunset for humanity."

Author's Postscript
for the American Edition

A night from my childhood remains crisply etched in my memory: I was standing by a pond before a village somewhere in Luoshan County, Henan Province, where generations of my ancestors had lived. Next to me stood many other people, both adults and children. Together, we gazed up at the clear night sky, where a tiny star slowly glided across the dark firmament.

It was the first artificial satellite China had ever launched: *Dongfanghong I ("The East is Red I")*. The date was April 25, 1970, and I was seven.

It had been thirteen years since *Sputnik* had been launched into space, and nine years since the first cosmonaut had left the Earth. Just a week earlier, *Apollo 13* had safely returned from a perilous journey to the moon.

But I didn't know any of that. As I gazed at that tiny, gliding star, my heart was filled with indescribable curiosity and yearning. And etched in my memory just as deeply as these feelings was the sensation of hunger. At that time, the region around my village was extremely poor. Hunger was the constant companion of every child. I was relatively fortunate because I had shoes on my feet. Most of the friends standing by my side were barefoot, and some of the tiny feet still had unhealed frostbite from the previous winter. Behind me, faint light from kerosene lamps shone out of cracks in the walls of dilapidated thatched huts—the village wasn't wired for electricity until the eighties.

The adults standing nearby said that the satellite wasn't like an airplane because it flew outside of the Earth. Back then the dust and smoke of industry hadn't yet polluted the air, and the starry sky was especially clear, with the Milky Way clearly visible. In my mind, the stars that filled the heavens weren't much farther away than the tiny, gliding satellite, and so I thought it was flying among them. I even worried that it might collide with one as it passed through the dense stellar clusters.

My parents weren't with me because they were working at a coal mine more than a thousand kilometers away, in Shanxi Province. A few years earlier, when I had been even younger, the mine had been a combat zone for the factional civil wars of the Cultural Revolution. I remembered gunshots in the middle of the night, trucks passing in the street, filled with men clutching guns and wearing red armbands. . . . But I had been too young back then, and I can't be sure whether these images are real memories, or mirages constructed later. However, I know one thing for certain: Because the mine was too unsafe and my parents had been impacted by the Cultural Revolution, they had had no choice but to send me to my ancestral home village in Henan. By the time I saw *Dongfanghong I,* I had already lived there for more than three years.

A few more years passed before I understood the distance between that satellite and the stars. Back then I was reading a popular set of basic science books called *A Hundred Thousand Whys.* From the astronomy volume, I learned the concept of a light-year. Before then, I had already known that light could traverse a distance equal to seven and a half trips around the Earth in a single second, but I had not contemplated what kind of terrifying distance could be crossed by flying at such a speed for a whole year. I imagined a ray of light passing through the cold silence of space at the speed of 300,000 kilometers per second. I struggled to grasp the bone-chilling vastness and profundity with my imagination, felt the weight of an immense terror and awe, and simultaneously enjoyed a druglike euphoria.

From that moment, I realized that I had a special talent: Scales and existences that far exceeded the bounds of human sensory perception—both macro and micro—and that seemed to be only abstract numbers to others, could take on concrete forms in my mind. I could touch them and feel them, much like others could touch and feel trees and rocks. Even today, when references to the 15-billion-light-year radius of the universe and "strings" many orders of magnitude smaller than quarks have numbed most people, the concepts of a light-year or a nanometer can still produce lively, grand pictures in my mind and arouse in me an ineffable, religious feeling of awe and shock. Compared to most of the population who do not experience such sensations, I don't know if I'm lucky or unlucky. But it is certain that such feelings made me first into a science fiction fan, and later a science fiction author.

In that same year when I was first awed by the concept of a light-year, a flood (known as the Great Flood of August '75) occurred near my home village. In a single day, a record-breaking 100.5 centimeters of rain fell in the Zhumadian region of Henan. Fifty-eight dams of various sizes collapsed, one after another, and 240,000 people died in the resulting deluge. Shortly after the floodwaters had receded, I returned

427

to the village and saw a landscape filled with refugees. I thought I was looking at the end of the world.

And so, satellite, hunger, stars, kerosene lamps, the Milky Way, the Cultural Revolution's factional civil wars, a light-year, the flood . . . these seemingly unconnected things melded together and formed the early part of my life, and also molded the science fiction I write today.

As a science fiction writer who began as a fan, I do not use my fiction as a disguised way to criticize the reality of the present. I feel that the greatest appeal of science fiction is the creation of numerous imaginary worlds outside of reality. I've always felt that the greatest and most beautiful stories in the history of humanity were not sung by wandering bards or written by playwrights and novelists, but told by science. The stories of science are far more magnificent, grand, involved, profound, thrilling, strange, terrifying, mysterious, and even emotional, compared to the stories told by literature. Only, these wonderful stories are locked in cold equations that most do not know how to read.

The creation myths of the various peoples and religions of the world pale when compared to the glory of the big bang. The three-billion-year history of life's evolution from self-reproducing molecules to civilization contains twists and romances that cannot be matched by any myth or epic. There is also the poetic vision of space and time in relativity, the weird subatomic world of quantum mechanics . . . these wondrous stories of science all possess an irresistible attraction. Through the medium of science fiction, I seek only to create my own worlds using the power of imagination, and to make known the poetry of Nature in those worlds, to tell the romantic legends that have unfolded between Man and Universe.

But I cannot escape and leave behind reality, just like I cannot leave behind my shadow. Reality brands each of us with its indelible mark. Every era puts invisible shackles on those who have lived through it, and I can only dance in my chains. In science fiction, humanity is often described as a collective. In this book, a man named "humanity" confronts a disaster, and everything he demonstrates in the face of existence and annihilation undoubtedly has sources in the reality that I experienced. The wonder of science fiction is that it can, when given certain hypothetical world settings, turn what in our reality is evil and dark into what is righteous and bright, and vice versa. This book and its two sequels try to do just that, but no matter how reality is twisted by imagination, it ultimately remains there.

I've always felt that extraterrestrial intelligence will be the greatest source of uncertainty for humanity's future. Other great shifts, such as climate change and ecological disasters, have a certain progression and built-in adjustment periods, but contact between humankind and aliens can occur at any time. Perhaps in ten thousand years, the starry sky that humankind gazes upon will remain empty and silent, but perhaps tomorrow we'll wake up and find an alien spaceship the size of the moon parked in orbit. The appearance of extraterrestrial intelligence will force humanity to confront an Other. Before then, humanity as a whole will never have had an external counterpart. The appearance of this Other, or mere knowledge of its existence, will impact our civilization in unpredictable ways.

There's a strange contradiction revealed by the naïveté and kindness demonstrated by humanity when faced with the universe: On Earth, humankind can step onto another continent, and without a thought, destroy the kindred civilizations found there through warfare and disease. But when they gaze up at the stars, they turn sentimental and believe that if extraterrestrial intelligences exist, they must be civilizations bound by universal, noble, moral constraints, as if cherishing and loving different forms of life are parts of a self-evident universal code of conduct.

I think it should be precisely the opposite: Let's turn the kindness we show toward the stars to members of the human race on Earth and build up the trust and understanding between the different peoples and civilizations that make up humanity. But for the universe outside the solar system, we should be ever vigilant, and be ready to attribute the worst of intentions to any Others that might exist in space. For a fragile civilization like ours, this is without a doubt the most responsible path.

As a fan of science fiction, it has molded my life, and a considerable part of the science fiction I've read comes from America. The fact that American readers can now enjoy my book makes me both pleased and excited. Science fiction is a literature that belongs to all humankind. It portrays events of interest to all of humanity, and thus science fiction should be the literary genre most accessible to readers of different nations. Science fiction often describes a day when humanity will form a harmonious whole, and I believe the arrival of such a day need not wait for the appearance of extraterrestrials.

I express my heartfelt thanks to Ken Liu, the translator of this and the third volume, and to Joel Martinsen, the translator of the second volume. Their diligence and care created the English edition. I am grateful to China Educational

Publications Import & Export Corporation Ltd. (CEPIEC), *Science Fiction World* Publishing, and Tor Books, whose trust and faith have made this publication possible.

Liu Cixin (刘慈欣),
December 28, 2012

Translator's Postscript

When I was asked to translate *The Three-Body Problem*, I was incredibly honored, but also full of trepidation: Translating another writer's work is a heavy responsibility. It's almost like being asked to care for someone's child.

The act of translation involves breaking down one piece of work in one language and ferrying the pieces across a gulf to reconstitute them into a new work in another language. When the gulf separating the two is as wide as the Pacific Ocean that separates China from America, the task can be daunting.

The obvious difficulties, such as differences in linguistic structure and cultural references, are actually relatively easy to resolve. *The Three-Body Problem* begins with the Cultural Revolution, and there are numerous allusions to Chinese history. I've tried to keep the number of explanatory footnotes to a bare minimum by, wherever possible, filling in the necessary knowledge for non-Chinese readers by the judicious addition of a few informational phrases in the text (all approved by the author).

But there are more subtle issues involving literary devices and narrative techniques. The Chinese literary tradition shaped and was shaped by its readers, giving rise to different emphases and preferences in fiction compared to what American readers expect. In some cases, I tried to adjust the narrative techniques to ones that American readers are more familiar with. In other cases, I've left them alone, believing that it's better to retain the flavor of the original.

I've also tried, wherever possible, to avoid shading Western interpretations into those passages dealing with Chinese history and politics.

Overly literal translations, far from being faithful, actually distort meaning by obscuring sense. But translations can also pay so little attention to the integrity of the source that almost nothing of the original's flavor or voice survives. Neither of these approaches is a responsible fulfillment of the translator's duty. In a sense, translating may be harder than writing original fiction because a translator must strive to satisfy the same aesthetic demands while being subjected to much more restrictive creative constraints.

In translating, my goal is to act as a faithful interpreter, preserving as much of the original's nuances of meaning as possible without embellishment or omission. Yet a translator must also balance fidelity to the source, aptness of expression, and beauty of style. The best translations into English do not, in fact, read as if they were originally written in English. The English words are arranged in such a way that the reader sees a glimpse of another culture's patterns of thinking, hears an echo of another language's rhythms and cadences, and feels a tremor of another people's gestures and movements.

I may not have succeeded, but these were the standards I had in mind as I set about my task.

In moving from one language, culture, and reading community to another language, culture, and reading community, some aspects of the original are inevitably lost. But if the translation is done well, some things are also gained—not the least of which is a bridge between the two readerships. I hope my fellow American readers enjoy this novel.

I am indebted to the following individuals, who gave me invaluable feedback on various drafts of this translation: Eric Abrahamsen, Anatoly Belilovsky, Aliette de Bodard, David Brin, Eric Choi, John Chu, Elías F. Combarro, Hui Geng, Michael Kwan, Derwin Mak, Joel Martinsen, Erica Naone, Alex Saltman, Alex Shvartsman, Marie Staver, Igor Teper, Bingen Yang, Bingwei Yang, and E. Lily Yu. I lack words to sufficiently express my gratitude for their help in making this translation better, and I wish every translator had such wonderful beta readers.

Others also deserve thanks. Joe Monti, my former agent (and current editor of my original fiction), dispensed much useful advice. Liz Gorinsky, my editor at Tor Books, helped me improve the translation in a thousand ways large and small, and I can't imagine a better editorial experience than working with her. My wife, Lisa, provided the support and encouragement to keep me going on many late nights. More than anyone else, she made this possible.

Finally, I thank Liu Cixin, who entrusted me with his work and, in this process, became my friend.

Ken Liu,
June 20, 2014

CIXIN LIU

TRANSLATED BY JOEL MARTINSON

THE DARK FOREST

Prologue

The brown ant had already forgotten its home. To the twilight Earth and the stars that were just coming out, the span of time may have been negligible, but, for the ant, it was eons. In days now forgotten, its world had been overturned. Soil had taken flight, leaving a broad and deep chasm, and then soil had come crashing down to fill it back in. At one end of the disturbed earth stood a lone black formation. Such things happened frequently throughout this vast domain, the soil flying away and returning, chasms opening up and being filled, and rock formations appearing like visible markers of each catastrophic change. Under the setting sun, the ant and hundreds of its brethren had carried off the surviving queen to establish a new empire. Its return visit was only a chance passing while searching for food.

The ant arrived at the foot of the formation, sensing its indomitable presence with its feelers. Noting that the surface was hard and slippery, yet still climbable, up it went, with no purpose in mind but the random turbulence of its simple neural network. Turbulence was everywhere, within every blade of grass, every drop of dew on a leaf, every cloud in the sky, and every star beyond. The turbulence was purposeless, but in huge quantities of purposeless turbulence, purpose took shape.

The ant sensed vibrations in the ground and knew

from how they intensified that another giant presence was approaching from somewhere on the ground. Paying it no mind, the ant continued its climb up the formation. At the right angle where the foot of the formation met the ground, there was a spider web. This, the ant knew. It carefully detoured around the sticky hanging strands, passing by the spider lying in wait, its legs extended to feel for vibrations in the threads. Each knew of the other's presence but—as it had been for eons—there was no communication.

The vibrations crescendoed and then stopped. The giant being had reached the formation. It was far taller than the ant and blotted out most of the sky. The ant was not unfamiliar with beings of this sort. It knew that they were alive, that they frequently appeared in this region, and that their appearances were closely related to the swiftly disappearing chasms and multiplying formations.

The ant continued its climb, knowing that the beings were not a threat, with a few exceptions. Down below, the spider encountered one such exception when the being, which had evidently noticed its web reaching between the formation and the ground, whisked away the spider and web with the stems of a bundle of flowers it held in one limb, causing them to land broken in a pile of weeds. Then the being gently placed the flowers in front of the formation.

Then another vibration, weak but intensifying, told the ant that a second living being of the same sort was moving toward the formation. At the same time, the ant encountered a long trough, a depression in the surface of the formation with a rougher texture and different color: off-white. It followed the trough, for its roughness made for a far easier climb. At each end was a short, thinner trough: a horizontal base from which the main trough rose, and an upper trough that extended at an angle. By the time the ant climbed back out onto the slick black surface, it had gained an overall impression of the shape of the troughs: "1."

Then the height of the being in front of formation was cut in half, so it was roughly even with the formation. Evidently it had dropped to its knees, revealing a patch of dim blue sky where the stars had begun to come out behind it. The being's eyes gazed at the top of the formation, causing the ant to hesitate momentarily while deciding whether it ought to intrude into his line of sight. Instead, it changed direction and started crawling parallel with the ground, quickly reaching another trough and lingering in its rough depression as it savored the pleasant sensation of the crawl. The color was reminiscent of the eggs that surrounded its queen. With no hesitation, the ant followed the trough downward, and after a while, the layout become more complicated, a curve extended beneath a complete circle. It reminded the ant of the process of searching out scent information and eventually stumbling across the way home. A pattern was established in its neural network: "9."

Then the being kneeling before the formation made a sound, a series of sounds that far exceeded the ant's capacity to comprehend: "It's a wonder to be alive. If you don't understand that, how can you search for anything deeper?"

The being made a sound like a gust of wind blowing across the grass—a sigh—and then stood up.

The ant continued to crawl parallel to the ground and entered a third trough, one that was nearly vertical until it turned, like this: "7." The ant didn't like this shape. A sharp, sudden turn usually meant danger or battle.

The first being's voice had obscured the vibrations, so it was only now that the ant realized that the second being had reached the formation. Shorter and frailer, the second being had white hair that stood out against the dark blue background of the sky, bobbing silver in the wind, connected somehow to the increasing number of stars.

The first being stood up to welcome her. "Dr. Ye, is it?"

"You're . . . Xiao Luo?"[1]

"Luo Ji. I went to high school with Yang Dong. Why are you . . . here?"

"It's a nice place, and easy to get to by bus. Lately, I've been coming here to take walks fairly often."

"My condolences, Dr. Ye."

"That's all in the past. . . ."

Down on the formation, the ant wanted to turn toward the sky, but then discovered another trough ahead of it, identical to the "9"-shaped trough it had crawled through before the "7." So it continued horizontally through the "9," which it found better than both the "7" and the "1," although it could not say exactly why. Its aesthetic sense was primitive and single-celled. The indistinct pleasure it had felt upon crawling through the "9" intensified. A primitive, single-celled state of happiness. These two spiritual monocells, aesthetics and pleasure had never evolved. They had been the same a billion years ago, and would be the same a billion years hence.

"Xiao Luo, Dong Dong often spoke of you. She said you're in . . . astronomy?"

"I used to be. I teach college sociology now. At your school, actually, although you had already retired when I got there."

"Sociology? That's a pretty big leap."

"Yeah. Yang Dong always said my mind wasn't focused."

---

[1] *Translator's Note: Xiǎo* is a diminutive meaning "little" or "young" and is used before a surname when addressing children or to show affection.

"She wasn't kidding when she said you're smart."

"Just clever. Nothing like your daughter's level. I just felt astronomy was an undrillable chunk of iron. Sociology is a plank of wood, and there's bound to be someplace thin enough to punch through. It's easier to get by."

In the hope of reaching another "9," the ant continued its horizontal advance, but the next thing it encountered was a perfectly straight horizontal like the first trough, except longer than the "1" and turned on its side. And no smaller troughs at the ends. A "–" shape.

"You shouldn't put it like that. It's a normal person's life. Not everyone can be Dong Dong."

"I really don't have that kind of ambition. I drift."

"I've got a suggestion. Why don't you study cosmic sociology?"

"Cosmic sociology?"

"A name chosen at random. Suppose a vast number of civilizations are distributed throughout the universe, on the order of the number of detectable stars. Lots and lots of them. Those civilizations make up the body of a cosmic society. Cosmic sociology is the study of the nature of this supersociety."

The ant had not crawled very much farther along the formation. It had hoped, after crawling out of the "–" depression, to find a pleasurable "9," but instead it encountered a "2," with a comfortable initial curve but a sharp turn at the end that was as fearsome as that of the "7." The premonition of an uncertain future. The ant continued onward to the next trough, a closed shape: "0." The path seemed like part of a "9," but it was a trap. Life needed smoothness, but it also needed direction. One could not always be returning to the point of origin. This, the ant understood. Although there were still two more troughs up ahead, it had lost interest. It turned vertically again.

"But . . . ours is the only civilization we know of right now."

"Which is why no one's done it before. The opportunity is left to you."

"Fascinating, Dr. Ye. Please go on."

"My thinking is that this can link your two disciplines together. The mathematical structure of cosmic sociology is far clearer than that of human sociology."

"Why do you say that?"

Ye Wenjie pointed at the sky. Twilight still illuminated the west, and they could still count the stars that had come out, making it easy to remember how the firmament had looked a few moments ago: a vast expanse and a blue void, or a face without pupils, like a marble statue. Now, though the stars were few in number, the giant eyes had pupils. The void was filled. The universe had sight. The stars were tiny, just single twinkling points of silver that hinted at some unease on the part of its creator. The cosmic sculptor had felt compelled to dot pupils onto the universe, yet had a tremendous terror of granting it sight. This balance of fear and desire resulted in the tininess of the stars against the hugeness of space, a declaration of caution above all.